Cheerfulness Breaks In

ANGELA THIRKELL

Cheerfulness Breaks In

Carroll & Graf Publishers, Inc.
New York

"I have tried too in my time to be a philosopher; but, I don't know how, cheerfulness was always breaking in."
(Mr. Edwards to Dr. Johnson)

Published by arrangement with Alfred A. Knopf, Inc.

First Carroll & Graf mass market edition 1990.
First Carroll & Graf trade paper edition 1996.

Carroll & Graf Publishers, Inc.
260 Fifth Avenue
New York, NY 10001

ISBN 0-7867-0318-0

Manufactured in the United States of America

CONTENTS

1

HASTE TO THE WEDDING

To all those who had admired and disliked the lovely Rose Birkett it appeared (with the greatest respect for the Royal Navy) quite inevitable that she should marry a naval man. As the elder daughter of the Headmaster of Southbridge School she had every opportunity for trying the effect of her charms on as many as three hundred and twenty-seven members of the opposite sex, ranging from the newest comer in the junior school to Mr. Walker who dealt out the very highest mathematics to a privileged and harassed few and was popularly supposed to be coeval with the late Queen Victoria, but except for one or two junior masters to whom she simply couldn't help getting engaged, a term which appeared to her parents to mean absolutely nothing except that she would always neglect the man of her choice for any later arrival, the whole school united in a total disregard of "that Rose," as they called her on the infrequent occasions when they bothered to think about her. Young gentlemen up to eighteen, or at a pinch, and if one can't pass one's School Certificate and is really good at cricket, nineteen, rightly regard their Headmaster's daughter as beyond the pale, while the senior masters had little but dislike for the exquisite nitwit who played havoc with their juniors' hearts and work. Everard Carter, Housemaster of the largest House, had particular cause to feel annoyance with Rose, as she had three years ago so devastated his second-in-command,

Philip Winter, that he could willingly have shaken her till her lovely head fell off her perfect shoulders.

Since the fateful summer when Rose had first got engaged and then got unengaged, to use her own description, to Philip Winter, she had plighted her troth to at least six admirers and with equal fervour unplighted it. Her parents, who had not the faintest control over their wayward child, began to fear that she would live with them for ever, when Lieutenant John Fairweather, R.N., who had made her the object of his attentions for several years whenever he was on leave, came into a very nice fortune and was appointed Naval Attaché to the South American capital of Las Palombas. Immediately on the receipt of these pieces of news he proposed to Rose, was at once accepted, for such was her artless custom when wooed, and told her parents he was very sorry but he must marry her at once.

Mr. and Mrs. Birkett, who had known Lieutenant Fairweather ever since he and his brother were in the junior school, made a faint protest for form's sake and then arranged with joy to have the wedding in the school chapel two days after school broke up for the summer holidays, a date which only gave Mrs. Birkett a fortnight to get her daughter's trousseau and send out invitations. In this her husband would, she well knew, be little or no help, partly because he wouldn't in any case, partly because end of term occupied his every moment, but in the joy of getting rid of her daughter she would willingly have undertaken a far more onerous task. It was difficult to believe that in two weeks Rose would be safely married and no longer drive everyone mad by coming down late, combing her hair and making up her face all over the house, bringing young men in for drinks at all hours and being very rude to her parents, or having equally exhausting fits of remorse accompanied by loud crying and yelling, but if any effort of hers could help towards this long-desired end, Mrs. Birkett was ready to make it. In all her preparations she was loyally seconded by her younger daughter, Geraldine, who while not envying her elder sister her beauty or her admirers (for she was an intellectual), very much looked forward to having the old nursery, which Rose had in vain attempted to rechristen a sitting-room, for her sole use and to receiving there such old girls of the Barchester High School as she happened to favour.

Under normal conditions it would have been perfectly easy for Rose to get unengaged within a fortnight and even get engaged to someone else, but two things contributed to make her love burn with a steadfast glow. The first was that her mother firmly took her up to town for such an orgy of dress-buying that even Rose's delicate frame, proof against a twenty-four hour day of cinemas, driving in fast cars, dancing at nightclubs and listening to the wireless at full blast while she talked to all her friends, was slightly affected; the second that she had nearly learnt to play the ocarina and did not wish to lose any moment in which she might be perfecting herself on that uninteresting instrument.

There had been moments when Mr. and Mrs. Birkett had suffered from compunction, wondering whether they had done right in delivering an Old Boy into the hands of their lovely Rose, and Mr. Birkett had gone so far as deciding to enlighten his old pupil as to the character of his daughter. For this sacrificial act he had chosen a Sunday evening after dinner. Lieutenant Fairweather had been spending the week-end at the school and had filled his future parents-in-law with admiration by telling Rose that if she couldn't be down and dressed by ten o'clock on Sunday morning he wasn't going to wait for her, as he had promised to meet Everard Carter on the Southbridge Golf Links at half-past. Rose, sauntering down at five minutes to ten, her golden locks tied up in a scarlet fish net, her exquisite figure draped in a yellow short-sleeved shirt and grey flannel slacks, her feet with their gleaming red toenails thrust into blue beach shoes with soles two inches thick, carrying her ocarina under one arm and a large, dirty, white vanity bag under the other, found her betrothed sitting on the front doorstep of the Headmaster's house in the sun.

"You can't come like that, my girl," said Lieutenant Fairweather, looking with affectionate disgust at his Rose.

"Don't be so dispiriting, darling," said Rose.

"Four minutes and a half to put on some decent clothes," said the Lieutenant, turning his back on his beloved, going down the steps to his car and looking with great interest at the bonnet. He then took a neatly folded piece of washleather out of a pocket in the car and began to polish some chromium work. When he had finished he folded the washleather neatly up again, put it away and got into the driving seat. As he did so Rose in a becoming light woolen coat and skirt (for the day, though near the end of July, was not very hot), her hair confined by a neat bandeau, her beautiful legs and feet in silk stockings and brogues, ran down the steps and round the car and took her place beside him, remarking as she did so that he was foully dispiriting.

"Not half so dispiriting as that pumpkin of yours, my girl," said the gallant Lieutenant, and taking the ocarina from Rose he stretched out his long arm and put it in one of the stone flower-pots at the bottom of the steps.

Rose said that was *too* dispiriting and foul.

"That's all right," said Lieutenant Fairweather, starting his high-powered sports car with a jump and roar that would have shaken the teeth out of anyone less toughly made and insensitive than the exquisite Rose. "It'll do nicely in the flower pot. Grow into an ocarina tree. Isn't there a book called that by some fellow?"

Rose said it sounded a pretty dispiriting sort of book

and she daresaid it was one of those foul books Mummy got from the libery.

"Fellow called something or other," said the Lieutenant, swinging the car out of the school gates into the main road on one wheel while he lighted a cigarette. "Morn, or Morm, or something. The Torpedo Lieutenant of the *Anteater* lent it to me and I lost it."

The rest of this intellectual conversation was lost in the joys of overtaking every car on the road and the happy pair were not seen again till dinner-time. Sunday dinner, for the loathsome meal called Sunday supper Mrs. Birkett had always managed to avoid, was the usual mixture of family, three masters, and a couple of rather spotty senior boys, upon all of whom Rose lavished her charms with great impartiality and but little success, for the masters talked shop with the Headmaster as a relaxation from talking shop with him all the week, and the boys regarded her much as Hop o' My Thumb regarded the Ogre's daughter, finding her sister Geraldine a much better sort of fellow. Lieutenant Fairweather talked very happily with Mrs. Birkett about old days in the junior school and his elder brother in the Barsetshire Regiment, and when Rose sauntered out of the room no one missed her in the least.

When the guests had gone Mr. Birkett looked at his wife and in an offhand way invited Lieutenant Fairweather to come into his study and smoke a pipe. As the Headmaster and most of his guests had been smoking pipes ever since supper the invitation might have struck an unprejudiced observer as quite unnecessary, but the Lieutenant, who took everything as he found it unless he wanted to alter it, at once got up.

"Good night," said Mrs. Birkett, "I suppose I ought to call you John, but I always think of you as Fairweather Junior."

"Well, I always think of you as Old Ma Birky," said

the Lieutenant. "Jove, those were the days, Mrs. Birky. Do you remember the boxing competition when I was in the Lower Fourth?"

"Of course I do," said Mrs. Birkett. "You and Swift-Hetherington were in the under four-stone class."

"And Mrs. Watson went out of the hall till the fighting was over because she was afraid young Watson might bleed," said Lieutenant Fairweather. "He was a glutton for a fight."

"Now Bill is waiting for you," said Mrs. Birkett, always a good Headmaster's wife.

Lieutenant Fairweather knocked his pipe out against the revolting tiles of the drawing-room fireplace, put in at vast expense by the Governing Body under the influence of one of their members who had been to the Paris Exhibition of 1900, and followed his old Headmaster to the study. The long summer evening was drawing to its close and from the study window lights could be seen in the various Houses across the school quad. Mr. Birkett turned on the light at his writing-table.

"Sit down, Fairweather," he said.

"Makes me feel quite young again," said the Lieutenant, taking a chair within the little pool of light. "Those were the days, sir. One used to get the wind up like anything when you sent for us. I remember you giving me six of the best for cheeking Mr. Ferris in the Upper Dor., when I was in the Lower School."

"Did I?" said Mr. Birkett, feeling more and more how awkward it was to have to warn an Old Boy against Rose, especially an Old Boy whom he had beaten for cheeking that dreadful Ferris who had since become one of H.M. Inspectors of Secondary Schools and the right place for him too.

"I don't suppose you'd remember, sir," said the Lieutenant, warming to his memories. "Rose was yelling like anything that day because Mrs. Birky wouldn't let her bang her toy drum in the hall."

"Yes; Rose," said the Headmaster absently. "Yes. Fairweather, I feel I ought to speak to you seriously about Rose."

He paused. Much as he disliked his exquisite daughter he must be loyal to her and between this feeling and his deep loyalty to all Old Boys he must decide.

"Sounds a bit like the Chaplain's jaws before we were confirmed, sir," said Lieuenant Fairweather cheerfully. "Of course we knew all about facts of life but we used to give him his head."

He laughed cheerfully.

"It's not that," said Mr. Birkett in great discomfort. "Rose is a very good girl, but I don't think you quite understand what you're undertaking. I'm afraid my wife and I have spoilt her rather."

"Take it from me, sir, you have," said the Lieutenant. "But this is where the Navy puts its foot down. Do you mind if I smoke, sir?"

He filled his pipe again and began lighting it. From the far corner of the room where by now it was quite dark came a low sound as of a melancholy and not very musical owl hooting in syncopated time.

"Hi! Rose!" said Lieutenant Fairweather, quite unperturbed. "Come out of that."

At his loving words Rose with her ocarina came slowly and gracefully towards the table, remarking that it was quite dispiriting if one couldn't practise because people would talk so much, and she had nearly got "Hebe's got the jeebies but they're not so bad as Phoebe's" right.

"Right, my girl? You wouldn't get it right if you tried for a fortnight," said the Lieutenant. "And listen; that thing of yours is not coming on my honeymoon."

"Don't be so foul, John," said Rose. "Daddy, I think it's too dispiriting to be told one's spoilt."

Mr. Birkett, though he knew that he was in the right and his lovely daughter an intruder, an eavesdropper and a nuisance, felt more embarrassed than ever and was quite delighted when his younger daughter Geraldine came into the room with an avenging expression and went up to Rose.

"You've taken my stockings again," said she.

"I couldn't find mine, and anyway they're a foul pair," said Rose languidly.

"They aren't," said Geraldine coldly. "They are my good new pair that Mrs. Morland sent me for my birthday. Rose, you *are* a mean beast. You always take my things and you know I wanted specially to keep this pair for your wedding."

Rose played a few uninterested notes on her ocarina. Mr. Birkett's heart sank. This was a judgment on him for trying to warn Fairweather against Rose. Now he had seen Rose in this very unfavourable light he would break off the engagement and Rose would go on living at home, probably for ever. At this thought the Headmaster almost groaned aloud.

"Come, come, my girl, that's not cricket," said Lieutenant Fairweather getting up. "Give Geraldine her stockings. No, not now," he added, as Rose began pulling up her skirt and showing apparently yards of a very elegant silk-clad leg. "Go along now, and give them to Geraldine when you get upstairs."

Rose dropped her skirt again and went towards the door.

"And don't forget to say good night," said the ardent lover. "Your father first, my girl."

To her own great surprise Rose kissed her father good night, an attention to which he was little accustomed, and then put her face up for her betrothed to salute her, which he did with great affection, at the same time taking the ocarina from her, saying that she would keep everyone awake all night.

"Darling John, I *do* love you," said Rose, clinging heavily about his neck.

"Of course you do," said Lieutenant Fairweather, "you're not a bad sort when one comes to know you, Rose. Good night, Gerry. Let me know if Rose tries to put it over you about those stockings."

Geraldine, who as a rule resented any shortening of her name, kissed her future brother-in-law with almost as much affection as Rose had done and the two girls went off together, perfectly reconciled.

"You know I'm awfully fond of Rose," said Lieutenant Fairweather, sitting down again, "and you needn't be anxious about her, sir."

"No, I don't think I am," said the Headmaster.

"Nor about me, sir, if it comes to that," said the Lieutenant, looking his future father-in-law straight in the face with an immovable countenance.

Mr. Birkett came as near blushing as a middle-aged Headmaster can do and was silent for a moment.

"It's a queer world, Fairweather," he said at length. "We can't tell what's going to happen and none of us feel very safe. My wife and I rely on you implicitly."

Lieutenant Fairweather again looked steadily at the Headmaster with his sailor's concentrated gaze.

"I think I get you, sir," he said. "If there is any trouble about and I have to join my ship instead of going to South America, I shall get a special licence and marry Rose out of hand. I've known her ever since she was a little girl, and I know she's been engaged to lots of fellows, but this time she's for it, so don't worry, sir."

Mr. Birkett's first impulse on hearing that he need not fear that his lovely daughter would be left on his hands was to say, "Thank God," but as Headmasters have to keep up a pretence of being slightly more than human he merely said that he hoped things wouldn't be as bad as that and inquired after the Lieutenant's elder brother, Captain Geoffrey Fairweather, who was at the moment doing a staff course at Camberley and was going to be best man.

The last few weeks of the term sped away, the prize-giving and breaking-up took place, boys were whisked away to Devonshire, or the South of France, or walking tours in Scandinavia, or Public Schools camps at the South Pole, while masters prepared to pretend they were ordinary people for six or seven weeks. The matrons of the various Houses had left everything sheeted and tidied and gone to join their married sisters at Bournemouth or Scarborough, and an unwonted hush lay on the school quad, only broken by the occasional roar of a car as the guests who were coming for the night before the wedding arrived.

Everard Carter, the senior Housemaster, and his wife were among the few members of the staff who were still in residence. Mrs. Carter's brother, Robert Keith, had married Lieutenant Fairweather's older sister Edith, which made Mrs. Carter almost a relation, and under the Carters' roof Lieutenant Fairweather was to spend his last bachelor night. There had been talk of dining in town that evening, but London is not at its best at the end of July, most of Lieutenant Fairweather's friends were away and his brother reported that Camberley seemed a bit sticky about giving leave, so the idea was abandoned. Rose had then suggested that they should all go to a cinema at Barchester, but this her mother vetoed, with firm support from the bridegroom, who told his Rose it was simply not done and she would see quite enough of him when they were married. Rose had shed a few very becoming tears and then forgot all about it in the excitement of unpacking a large china pig with pink roses on its back, the gift of the matron of Mr. Carter's House.

The party at the Carters' was not large. Everard Carter was tired at the end of term, Lieutenant Fairweather was quite happy to smoke with his host and talk with his hostess, and there were only three other guests at dinner. One was the Senior Classical master, Philip Winter, who had been engaged to Rose for a few months of the hot summer three years before, an engagement which he had bitterly repented and from which he had only been saved by the fit of temper in which Rose had thrown him over, since which time he had almost loved her for not marrying him.

The two ladies, if one may use the expression, were Geraldine Birkett and Lydia Keith, Mrs. Carter's younger sister, who had been at the Barchester High School together and were to be bridesmaids next day.

Miss Lydia Keith at about twenty-one had toned down a little from her schoolgirl days, though not so much as her mother might have wished. Her family had thought that when she left school she might wish to train for some sort of work in which swashbuckling is a desirable quality, though they could hardly think of any form of employment, short of Parliament, that would give Lydia's powers sufficient scope. But to everyone's surprise she had preferred to stay at home, where she wrested the housekeeping reins from her mother and ran the house with a ferocious yet tolerant competency that made her mother prophesy dolefully that Lydia would never get married, though on what grounds she based this opinion, or indeed any other, no one quite knew. To all such young men as were prepared to accept her as an equal Lydia extended a crushing handshake and the privilege of listening to her views on all subjects. As for any more tender form of feeling no one had ever dared to approach the subject with her and Lydia's general idea of matrimony appeared to be that it was an amiable eccentricity suitable for parents in general who were of course born too long ago to have any sense, her sister Kate, and really silly people like Rose Birkett. In these matters her sentiments were echoed by Geraldine Birkett who had been her admiring follower ever since she used to do Lydia's maths at school and Lydia did Geraldine's Latin. In fact, except that Lydia was tall, dark-haired and good-looking while Geraldine could only be described as a girl with a rather clever face, they were twin souls and had often toyed with the idea of breeding Cocker spaniels together. But Mr. Birkett wouldn't hear of it and as Lydia's mother had developed a heart Lydia couldn't be spared. Most of Lydia's contemporaries would have regarded an invalid mother as an additional and cogent reason for leaving home and breeding dogs, but Lydia, in spite of her swashbuckling, had too good a heart and, though she would have died sooner than admit it, too firm a sense of duty to desert her mother and led on the whole a very contented life.

"Who are the other bridesmaids?" asked Philip Winter, who had not taken much interest in the wedding.

"Delia Brandon," said Lydia, "you know, the one that her mother's Mrs. Brandon at Pomfret Madrigal and one of the Dean of Barchester's girls that is called Octavia."

"And how," said Geraldine, who had a passion, her only trait in common with her sister Rose, for American gangster films.

"How?" asked Philip, amused.

Before Geraldine could reply Lydia, fully armed, leapt lightly to the breach, as she nearly always did when it was an affair of answering a question, whether addressed to her or to someone else, preferably someone else.

"Anyway," she said scornfully, "if I had a lot of daughters I wouldn't call one of them Octavia, even if she *was* the eighth. It seems invidious, if you know what

I mean," she added, glaring belligerently at the company.

Her sister Kate Carter who was so good and sweet-tempered that one would hesitate to apply the word dull to her if there were any more suitable description said that after all it showed she *was* the eighth.

"As a matter of fact she isn't," said Geraldine, seizing her chance where mathematics were in question, "because two of them were boys and one died quite young, really before he was born I think."

Kate quietly and anxiously changed the subject by saying that the delphiniums in the School Chapel looked quite lovely and a blue wedding would be so nice and bridesmaids always looked nice in blue. But her sister Lydia, who despised such palterings with stern facts, said even if the brother hadn't really been born someone must have known about him or they wouldn't have known, and it might have seemed unkind to give him a miss when they were counting up the family.

"And anyway," she continued, slightly raising her powerful voice, "being called Octavia doesn't really show. I mean Octavian, the one who was Augustus you know, Philip," she said to the Senior Classical master, "there's nothing to say that he was the eighth, whether anyone was born or not. At least if there is I haven't read it and it's not in Shakespeare," she added with the air of one making a handsome concession.

Kate with an effort wrenched the talk round to the wedding guests and the preparations for refreshments afterwards, which quite distracted Lydia and Geraldine from the problem of the Dean's daughters, and the talk became more general.

Lieutenant Fairweather, who had said nothing because his pipe was drawing well and he did not know the Dean or any of his daughters, asked Mr. Carter about various Old Boys and school notorieties.

"Did you know Harwood was dead?" said Everard Carter.

"No, sir. By Jove!" said Lieutenant Fairweather, rather weakening his interjection by adding, "Who was he?"

"Of course I forgot, you wouldn't know him. He only took the Senior boys," said Everard.

"He was the cricket coach," said Kate, coming to the Lieutenant's rescue.

"By Jove, yes," said Lieutenant Fairweather. "He had that ripping cottage in Wiple Terrace. Who lives there now?"

"People called Gissing," said Kate. "He is something in the films, I think, and she is an artist; at least she paints. And they have a son who I am sure is very nice."

"Out with it, Kate," said Philip Winter. "Your understatements are worth their weight in gold."

"Well, I dare say he is quite nice," said Kate, defending herself and modifying her statement simultaneously. "Often it is only shyness that makes people seem conceited."

"Then he must be uncommon shy," said Philip dryly. "And if shyness makes him so confoundedly rude and patronising in the Red Lion bar, I wish he would get over it."

Kate then invited anyone who liked to come and see Bobbie Carter aged nearly one in bed. Lydia and Geraldine accepted the invitation and the men were left alone.

"You were engaged to Rose, weren't you?" said Lieutenant Fairweather to the Senior Classical Master.

"Yes," said Philip, rather wondering if the bridegroom proposed to fight a duel, or keelhaul him. "But it was some years ago—not for long."

"Don't apologise," said the Lieutenant. "That girl has a genius for thinking she is in love. I thought she might get tied up before I could cut in. One doesn't get much chance with a sailor's life, you know. But that's the end of it. I hope she didn't give you much trouble."

Philip politely said none at all. Everard Carter said that his wife was not the only person with a genius for understatement and that Rose had nearly wrecked the peace of his House during her brief engagement to Philip.

"She only needs handling," said Lieutenant Fairweather. "I've got her pretty well where I want her and she knows it, and it's the best day's work I ever did in my life. The Dagoes will go quite mad about her, bless her heart."

Everard asked when he was leaving for South America.

"Day after the wedding," said the Lieutenant. "I had a sort of idea I might be recalled to my ship, but it doesn't look like a scrap now. I shan't be sorry to get a couple of years ashore. What are you and Mr. Winter doing, sir?"

Philip said he was going into camp with the Territorials after the wedding and then to Constantinople to do some work, unless of course there were a scrap and then he supposed Senior Classics would know him no longer.

"I thought you were a Communist, sir," said the Lieutenant. "Do you remember that time my brother and I came over to see Rose when her people took Northbridge Rectory, and you told us all about Communism? Geoff and I thought it was jolly interesting to meet a chap that knew such a lot, but it didn't worry us. One has enough to do in the Navy without worrying."

"I think you were right," said Philip, colouring a little. "I wasn't busy enough then. I dare say I'm still a Communist if it comes to arguing, but for all practical purposes I have quite enough to do being a schoolmaster."

"And if it came to a scrap, sir?" said Lieutenant Fairweather.

"Then I suppose I'd have enough to do being a Territorial," said Philip, after a moment's thought.

"Excuse me, sir, I didn't mean to barge in," said Lieutenant Fairweather, "but when one isn't a brainy chap it bucks one up a lot to find that the brainy chaps see it the same way the rest of us do."

At this ingenuous compliment Philip Winter coloured even more deeply to the roots of his flaming hair, feeling that to be called sir and deferred to by a naval officer, even if he was really only Fairweather Junior in disguise, made him almost older than he could bear. Everard, who was a good deal older and had even been called "sir" by the brilliant young Attorney-General of a short-lived Administration, took it all more calmly and said he expected to do nothing but go on schoolmastering.

"If anything did happen," he said, carefully choosing a form of words that would not be likely to let any Higher Powers know what he was talking about (for to such superstitions even a Housemaster may be prone) "we have our work more than cut out for us, because we are going to take in the Hosiers' Boys Foundation School."

Lieutenant Fairweather sat up.

"The Hosiers' Boys, sir. But aren't those the chaps who had a week's camp down by the river the summer I left school? I mean they were very decent chaps—"

There was a silence, so charged with agreement that Philip almost expected an immediate vengeance for snobbish feelings to fall on them all three. Then Kate came back with the girls and a very interesting conversation took place about the horribleness of the physical exercises mistress at Barchester High School. When we say conversation it is of course to be understood that Lydia did most of the talking, backed by

Geraldine, while the others listened, amused, and Lieutenant Fairweather smoked and thought of an improvement in the fourth hole at Southbridge golf course, after which Geraldine went home and they all went to bed.

2

THE BRIDESMAIDS' TALE

•

If it was inevitable that Rose Birkett should marry a naval man, it was equally inevitable that the day of her wedding should be the most perfect day of unclouded sun tempered by a breeze not powerful enough to disarrange her hair or her veil. Mrs. Birkett, going into her elder daughter's bedroom at half-past nine o'clock, found her in bed with two large, loose-jointed, depraved-looking dolls and a rather dirty plush giant panda, the wireless turned on at its loudest to an enchanting programme from Radio Luxembourg sponsored by the makers of a famous corn cure, eating an enormous breakfast off a tray balanced on her knees and blowing melancholy blasts on her ocarina between mouthfuls.

"Hullo, Mummy," said Rose, "they're doing *Lips of Desire* at the Barchester Odeon, you know, the film about the Brownings, the ones that were poets, and Glamora Tudor is Mrs. Browning and to-day's the last performance. It's too dispiriting for words."

Mrs. Birkett, wondering in an exhausted way if Rose would rather go to the cinema than be married, turned the wireless down, for the noise made it very difficult to converse.

"*Don't,* Mummy," shrieked Rose, spilling a good deal of tepid coffee into her bed as she reached towards the wireless and turned it on again. "I'd nearly got 'Hebe's got the jeebies' right on Radio Luxembourg. Mummy, the first house is at twelve o'clock. Couldn't I and John go? We'd easily get back in time for the wedding."

Mrs. Birkett, praying to keep her temper for the few hours during which Rose was yet under her wing, said, "Certainly not."

"If I rang up Noel Merton, he's staying at the Deanery, could I go with him then?" said Rose.

Mrs. Birkett said with some severity that Rose did not seem to understand that a wedding was a wedding and that until she was married she was not going to leave the house. Rose clasped the giant panda and her lovely eyes filled with tears.

There was a knock at the door and Mr. Birkett came in.

"Good morning, Rose," he said. "Everything all right? I was just looking for you, Amy."

"Oh, Daddy," said Rose, gulping. "It's too foully dispiriting. It's the last performance of *Lips of Desire* and Mummy won't let me go."

"Now, be sensible, there's a good girl," said Mr. Birkett giving his daughter's shoulder a nervous but well-meant pat. "Amy, the Dean has just rung up to say his car is out of order, and his secretary is going to drive him over."

"Then if I went to *Lips of Desire* at the 12 o'clock session the Dean could drive me back," said Rose, throwing the panda on the floor, jumping out of bed and slipping on a flowered dressing-gown in which she looked like Botticelli's Flora, except that intelligent mischief was an expression entirely beyond her powers. "Oh, Mummy! Oh, Daddy! Could I?"

Mrs. Birkett snapped at Mr. Birkett for bringing such a foolish message. If the Dean were coming in any case, she said, it was quite immaterial how, and she only hoped all the buttons would fly off his gaiters, and Rose had better go and have her bath and see about finishing her packing. Rose picked up the panda again and clutching it to her bosom began to cry. Mr. Birkett, considerably alarmed by the storm he had innocently helped to raise, was trying to get away unseen when Geraldine came in, followed by Lydia Keith.

"I thought you and Daddy wouldn't have much grip today," said Geraldine, speaking with the kind firmness of a District Visitor to the Deserving Poor, "so I brought Lydia along to help. The man from Barchester about the extra glasses and things is here, Mummy, and there's a man called a name I couldn't hear like Gristle it sounded that wants you on a trunk call, Daddy."

The distracted parents, only too glad of the excuse, left the room.

"Who can Gristle be?" said Mrs. Birkett to her husband, who replied that he hadn't the faintest idea.

Rose, left alone with her unsympathetic bridesmaids, at once became her normal self and taking a box of chocolate creams out of her stocking drawer shared the contents with Geraldine and Lydia. Geraldine, as a sister and an intellectual, objected to the number of chocolates Rose had bitten into to see if they were soft, but Lydia, who liked hard ones, said it would save her biting them herself, and Rose and Geraldine could have all the soft ones. The head housemaid, sent by Mrs. Birkett to assist with the packing, was dismissed by Lydia who having seen an elder sister into matrimony was an authority on trousseaux. What with packing, trying some of Rose's face creams, listening to the wireless, playing swing records on the gramophone, discussing the probable cast for a film about Building the Pyramids in which Rose hoped that the Marx Brothers would be Totems or whatever it was (which Geraldine was able to explain by saying Rose meant hieroglyphics and even then it wasn't sense), getting Rose by degrees bathed, partly dressed and made-up, the morning passed as swiftly as lightning. At half-past twelve Mrs. Birkett, feeling that she would rather not see Rose again for the present, sent up cold lunch on a tray and all three young ladies made a hearty meal. Over the depraved dolls and the plush panda there was a slight difference of opinion, Geraldine maintaining that they ought to be sent to the Barchester Hospital, Lydia that they would be invaluable for her mother's Jumble Sale, and Rose, who after all was their mistress, declaring that nothing would part her from them and anyway the panda zipped up the back and made a splendid bag for her ocarina.

Then Mrs. Birkett, bearing her courage in both hands, came in with the head housemaid and Rose was dressed in her bridal robes. The head housemaid said Miss Rose looked just like her name and everyone saw what she meant. To Mrs. Birkett's intense relief, not only had Rose entirely forgotten and forgiven the scene she had made earlier in the morning, but so far did her forgiveness extend that she actually kissed her mother and said it was rotten not seeing *Lips of Desire* but perhaps they'd have it at Las Palombas and she supposed there would be an Odeon or whatever people called it out there.

Geraldine and Lydia, who had brought her bridesmaid's dress over from the Carters' House in a suitcase for the occasion, suddenly thought they had better get dressed too and at a quarter to two they escorted Rose to the drawing-room where the other bridesmaids, Delia Brandon and Octavia Crawley, were waiting.

"Hullo, Rose," said Delia Brandon, "you do look gorgeous. I wish I could have a wedding dress like that."

Rose said she thought white satin was a bit dispiriting, but Mummy would have it.

"And anyway," she said with great simplicity, "if there was a war or anything and John got killed or something, I could have it dyed black."

Octavia Crawley, who did not look her best in blue, or indeed in any other colour, nice girl though she was, said if there was a war or anything she would drive an ambulance and then she needn't go to dinner parties in the Close, but she knew there would be no such luck.

Rose said it would be just like her luck to be at Las Palombas if there was a war and too foully dispiriting.

"If there did happen to be a war, not that there will," said Delia Brandon, "I shall go to Barchester General Hospital as a V.A.D. I've done all my exams. In the War they had some perfectly *ghastly* face wounds there," said Delia, her kind heart aglow with hopeful excitement. "I'd like to see Sir Abel Fillgrave operate more than anything in the world."

Rose thought it sounded a bit dispiriting.

When Mrs. Birkett got downstairs from Rose's room, she found Mr. Tozer, the representative of Messrs. Scatcherd and Tozer, Caterers, of Barchester (described by Geraldine as the man about the extra glasses and things) waiting for her in the dining-room. Already trestle tables had been set up and spread with what in fiction used to be known as fair white cloths, though rather badly ironed by the Barchester Sanitary Laundry. Two skilled underlings disguised as waiters were setting out glasses, cups, saucers and plates, and erecting the giant urns or samovars from which Messrs. Scatcherd and Tozer dispensed tea and coffee. A large cylindrical object in a corner promised ices, and the sandwiches and cakes were stacked in cardboard boxes. In the middle of the largest table graceful folds of butter muslin kept the wedding cake from contamination.

Mrs. Birkett took this all in with the well-trained eye of a Headmaster's wife, used to entertaining on a large scale. Everything appeared to be in order. Messrs. Scatcherd's representatives had often worked for her before and knew what was required, but there was a feeling of silent enmity about that froze Mrs. Birkett to the marrow.

"Mr. Birkett said you wanted to speak to me, Mr. Tozer," said Mrs. Birkett. "Is everything all right?"

Mr. Tozer coughed behind his hand and said it was always a pleasure to do the arrangements at Southbridge School. Always a pleasure, he added.

"I haven't much time," said Mrs. Birkett.

"It is like this, madam," said Mr. Tozer, who really despised anyone not in orders and had particularly strong feelings about lay Headmasters, though he spoke of Mrs. Birkett as a lady that understood how things should be done, "there is a slight hiatus about tumblers. Your order was for three hundred guests. We had fully assumed that we could meet any calls upon us, but owing to the militia camp at Plumstead having co-opted us to assist with their catering, we are short on the small tumblers."

"I suppose you can make up with large wine-glasses," said Mrs. Birkett. "They would do quite well for lemonade."

"That is precisely what I was going to suggest, madam," said Mr. Tozer. "We have plenty of large wine-glasses; not the champagne size, for they would be required for champagne, but the largest size of non-champagne if I make myself clear. Though of course lemonade should *never* be drunk except from small tumblers," said Mr. Tozer with a slight shudder.

"Well, the wine-glasses will do nicely," said Mrs. Birkett.

"We shall be lucky if we have them this time next year with the Hun creating the way he is," said Mr. Tozer, whose military vocabulary belonged to the years 1914-18 during which he had been a mess waiter on Salisbury Plain. "Some say it will all blow over, madam, but I say to talk like that is tempting Providence. Expect the worst and then it can't get you down is what I say."

As Mr. Tozer was well known for never leaving off talking, Mrs. Birkett was accustomed to drift away from him, leaving him to finish his periods to the circumambient air, but the feeling of silent enmity that had approached her at her first entrance was now just behind her right shoulder and turning slightly she saw her butler, Simnet, holding the champagne-nippers in his hand in a very threatening way.

"What is it, Simnet?" said Mrs. Birkett.

"I was merely waiting, madam, till Mr. Tozer had finished," said Simnet with icy politeness, "to inquire who is to open the champagne."

Mr. Tozer, speaking to an unseen audience, said that when he arranged the reception at the Palace for the colonial bishops, he had personally opened every bottle himself and His Lordship had said everything couldn't have gone off better.

Simnet, by saying nothing, managed to convey that he had planted, pruned and watered the vines, picked the grapes, personally trodden them in the wine press, bottled and labelled every pint of the wine, superintended its shipping to England, retailed it to Mr. Birkett and (which was indeed true) fetched it up from the cellar that morning with his own hands.

To the outer world he merely remarked in a distant way that he understood His Lordship to have allowed one bottle to every ten guests, but perhaps that was as well, being as some of them were black.

Mr. Tozer, whose feelings about people in orders included a conviction that a coloured bishop was a contradiction in terms, found his position considerably weakened. To say that a tenth of a bottle was enough for a dusky prelate would have been a betrayal of the whole Established Church; to say it was not enough would have reflected upon the Bishop of Barchester's celebrated want of hospitality. So he said nothing and the battle hung suspended in a chill silence.

But Mrs. Birkett, who though she never tried to organise the school had to order practically everything else for her husband, and was used to composing quarrels between matrons, head housemaids, parlourmaids and cooks, was, except where her daughter Rose was concerned, a woman of practical decision.

"If you are announcing the guests, you can't open the champagne, Simnet," she said. "Mr. Tozer will be good enough to open it and I dare say he has brought his own champagne nippers."

Only the genius of a born organiser could have prompted Mrs. Birkett to say this. Some sixth sense told her that the champagne nippers were to Simnet a mysterious badge of authority which he would sooner die, or at any rate be very disagreeable about, than give up.

Mr. Tozer without a word produced two pairs of champagne nippers from behind the wedding cake. Simnet said that he had put four dozen bottles on the table by the service door and if Mr. Tozer would give him the word, he had several dozen more on ice in his pantry.

As more than half an hour had been wasted Mrs. Birkett after an anxious look at her watch went to dress. She and Mr. Birkett were to have a sandwich lunch in his study and she hoped to get a few moments' peace with him and ask who Mr. Gristle was, but so late was he that the Dean of Barchester and his secretary arrived on his heels and Simnet severely removed the rest of the sandwiches as partaking of blasphemy.

The Dean took Mrs. Birkett's hand.

"As it is neither morning nor afternoon, I must say goodday," he announced. "And a good day in every sense of the word it is. Ha, Birkett," he said to the Headmaster.

"Ha, Crawley," said Mr. Birkett, who had been at Oxford with the Dean, though Dr. Crawley, being in his earlier years a young and penniless clergyman, had naturally married much sooner than Mr. Birkett and had a much larger family.

"You know my secretary, Thomas Needham," said the Dean, presenting a young clergyman with a pink cheerful face. "He has driven me over like Jehu."

"We only touched sixty once, sir," said Mr. Needham deprecatingly.

"And so Rose is going to be married," said the Dean. "Ah."

As the whole of Barchester had known this for some weeks and the Dean was about to perform the ceremony, assisted by the School chaplain, Mr. Smith, there seemed to be no real answer. Mrs. Birkett told Simnet, who was tidying away the last remains of lunch, to tell Mr. Smith that the Dean was there.

Young Mr. Needham, who had been looking round the walls, suddenly exclaimed, "By Jove, there's my uncle!"

"Where?" said the Dean.

Mr. Needham pointed to a photograph of fifteen boys in jerseys, shorts and football boots with a blurred background of school buildings.

"Your uncle?" said Mr. Birkett. "I thought I knew every name, but I don't remember a Needham."

"My mother's brother, sir," said Mr. Needham, "Oldmeadow is the name. That's him with his legs crossed, in the middle. Good old Uncle Tom."

"Tom Oldmeadow?" said Mr. Birkett. "Of course I remember Tom. He was Captain of Games in his last year. You remember Oldmeadow, Amy?"

"Of course I do," said Mrs. Birkett. "He had measles twice running in one term. Where is he now?"

"I think he's in Switzerland," said Mr. Needham, "mountaineering, but he's in the Reserve of Officers, so he might have to come back any time if there's a row. It makes me a bit sick that I didn't go into the Army now, but I might get out as a stretcher-bearer with luck."

He then went bright red with confusion and looked at his employer to see if he had given offence. The Dean said it was laid upon us to love our enemies but one might be allowed to distinguish between enemies and devils, and then in his turn wondered if he had gone too far. But the School chaplain cut short the conversation by coming in with a cordial greeting and the remark that the nuptial hour drew on apace and would the Dean like to be preparing himself. The Dean looked at his secretary, who said the doings, he begged his pardon, the robes, were in the suitcase outside and should he bring them in. Mrs. Birkett, feeling that she might be consumed with fire if she profaned these mysteries, said she would go and see about Rose. The School chaplain said this parting was well made and he would himself conduct the Dean to the School Chapel and see that Mr. Needham was suitably placed among the congregation.

"You know, Smith, that Oldmeadow is Needham's uncle," said Mr. Birkett as he too left the room.

The Chaplain, who had played for Cambridge as a young man, was so enchanted to find that the Dean's secretary was a relation of the best football player the School had ever produced that he took Mr. Needham under his wing, extracted from him that he had played for a well-known club and discussed with such ardour the chances of the Universities for the autumn that the Dean was metaphorically and almost literally elbowed into a corner and had to get on with his robing as best he could.

As it was now time for the ceremony the School Chaplain led the way by the private passage from the Headmaster's study to the little vestry or anteroom of the Chapel.

At Mr. Carter's House, Everard, Kate and Philip Winter marvelled as they watched Lieutenant Fairweather eat through fish, eggs and bacon, cold ham, scones, toast, butter and marmalade, and drink two large cups of coffee, that love could have so little effect on the human appetite. Lydia, who it is true was not going to be married, ate neck to neck with him over the whole course till they got into the straight when with no visible effort she came in first by a large piece of toast thickly spread with butter and potted ham.

"It's a pity," she said reflectively, "that bridesmaids don't still go on the honeymoon like Miss Squeers with Mr. and Mrs. Browdie. I'd love to come to Las Palombas."

"Come and visit us," said Lieutenant Fairweather, "and stay as long as you like."

"I do wish I could," said Lydia, "but Mother has a heart and I rather look after things for her, and Father seems to need me a bit. I know it sounds awfully priggish," she added apologetically.

Kate looked at her younger sister with admiring affection. Everard and Philip felt, as they often did, what an extraordinarily good fellow Lydia was.

"Well, we shall be there for two years," said Lieutenant Fairweather, "unless there's a scrap and they want me back, so come along any time."

"Thanks most awfully," said Lydia. "Old Bunce, you know, at the Northbridge Ferry, says he knows there's going to be a war this autumn because he knows the signs, but he won't say what the signs are and anyway no one believes him."

Philip said from his brief experience of Old Bunce, the summer he stayed at Northbridge with the Birketts, the signs must be several extra pints of old and bitter at the Ferryman's Arms. Lydia went over to the

Headmaster's House with her suitcase and peace reigned until eleven o'clock when Captain Geoffrey Fairweather of the Barsetshire Regiment arrived in a roaring little car to be best man to his brother. The two brothers and the two schoolmasters sat in the garden and kept an eye on Master Bobbie Carter who was imprisoned in a kind of square sheepfold on the lawn and surprised himself very much by standing up and falling down from time to time. The conversation was chiefly about the Fairweathers' days in the junior school and a great deal of news was exchanged about Old Boys and the fate of various masters.

"I don't know if you remember Johnson," said Everard. "He did quite well at Oxford in Modern Greats, though it is a falling-between-two-stools school that I personally deplore, and is coming here next term as a master in the Junior School for a bit, unless—"

He stopped, sacrificing the end of his sentence to a craven wish to propitiate any deity that might be about.

"Johnson was a bit junior to me," said Lieutenant Fairweather. "He had a bottle of hair fixative in the Junior School and we all used it. Hard luck."

What Everard and Philip felt about the hard luck, to give it no harder name, that might tear all their ex-pupils (for they could not help looking at the situation from their own schoolmastering point of view and especially from the point of view of their own school) from their various avocations and pitchfork them into the paths of glory which may lead but to the grave, was so mixed that neither of them could quite have put it into words. When you have done your best for your pupils, you hope to have fitted them in some measure for the conduct of life, but you always envisaged a life that is to go on, not a life that is very possibly to take its place in a living rampart and so be given up. You sicken at the thought of the waste, yet you cannot call it waste. You are thankful for those who can remain undisturbed, yet you cannot altogether be glad for them. There seems to be no end to the warring loyalties in your mind, except the certainty that the end is appointed.

"Yes, it's jolly hard luck on those youngsters," said Captain Fairweather from his twenty-five years and the immense tolerant kindness of the real professional for the amateurs. "Still, even if there is a scrap I dare say it'll be over before most of them get out. You can't make an army in three weeks."

"I must say I'll be sick if there is a show and I'm at Las Palombas," said Lieutenant Fairweather. "You blighters have all the luck, Geoff. What do they say at your shop?"

Captain Fairweather said the Lord alone knew, but apart from a certain stickiness about leave the Brass Hats hadn't given tongue, and as far as he was concerned his leave was due in the middle of August and he was going to Scotland to have a shot at a grouse. He then applied himself to the entertainment of Master Bobbie Carter whose language he at once understood and they enjoyed themselves very much together till Nurse came out and said Baby must thank the soldier for playing with him so nicely and come along and have his din-din.

"I suppose I am a soldier," said Captain Fairweather, straightening himself and looking vengefully after Nurse, "but she needn't rub it in. That chap of yours is very intelligent, sir," he said to Everard. "He got the hang of my moustache almost at once. By Jove, I thought he'd have it out by the roots."

If a Housemaster can simper, Everard almost simpered.

"He *is* a bit intelligent," he admitted. "You should see him in his bath. If he wants his celluloid fish and Nurse gives him his duck, he begins to howl at once."

Captain Fairweather said it was certainly *jolly* good to know a fish from a duck at that age and he'd like to see him in his bath if there was time before he went back to Sparrowhill Camp. Lieutenant Fairweather expressed sincere regrets that the fact of getting married and starting on his honeymoon would deprive him of this treat and said that talking of getting married he supposed he had better put his uniform on before lunch. So they all went in.

3

GO, LOVELY ROSE

•

The School Chapel really looked very nice, just as Kate had said it would, though nothing could disguise its complete hideousness. It had been built about seventy years previously by the same architect who had built Lord Pomfret's seat, Pomfret Towers, and though the architect, hampered by the restrictions of space, had not been able to carry out his Neo-Gothic wishes to full effect, he had managed to combine inconvenience and darkness in a manner hitherto unparalleled in any of his work. The Chapel was a very long, narrow, lofty building, richly panelled in pitch-pine. The windows which were placed near the roof were of most elaborate tracery, filled with lozenges of green and purple glass. The pews, also of pitch-pine, had specially constructed seats, not only very narrow, but with a slight forward tilt that obliged the worshipper to brace himself against the encaustic tiled floor with both feet. The stalls at the east end were so profusely ornamented with carving that they constituted a kind of Little Ease for the senior boys and masters who occupied them, and were furnished with seats which folded back on a hinge at such an angle that at least two boys were able to say that their seats had fallen down with a bang of themselves at every service. The Great East Window, presented by former pupils in memory of the Rev. J. J. Damper, Headmaster from 1850 to 1868, when he retired to an honorary canonry of Barchester which he held in a state of mild imbecility for the next ten years, was one of the finest examples of the Munich school of stained glass in the country, sustaining very favourably a comparison with the glass in St. Mungo's, Glasgow. It cast indeed, as the School Chaplain had more than once said, a dim religious light, so that the electric fittings (installed in 1902, as a memorial to Old Boys killed in the Boer War, in the finest *art nouveau* style) had to be used all through the year. As for the organ (now electrically controlled), the lectern, given in memory of an unpopular master who was killed in the Alps because he would not take his guide's advice but had a rich mother (who also put up a less expensive memorial to the guide in his village church), the tiles on each side of the altar (copied from those used in the kitchen at Pomfret Towers), they are described (with five stars) in all guide books to Barsetshire, so we will say no more.

Short of burning it all to the ground, there was not much to be done, but Mrs. Birkett had put lilies and delphiniums all over the choir and up the altar steps and, greatly daring, ordered quantities of blue carpet to cover the aisle and the handsome Kidderminster rug that lay in front of the altar and vied in richness of colour with the East window.

Soon after lunch the guests began to arrive. Mr. and Mrs. Birkett naturally had an enormous number of friends and acquaintances, nearly all of whom had sent a present to Rose because they were fond of her parents, and so had to be asked. A certain number were already abroad, or dispersed in far parts of England and Scotland, but even so there were enough acceptances to make Mrs. Birkett a little anxious about accommodation in the Chapel. However, the more people are jammed together at any social function, the more they will enjoy it, so from her place of vantage in the choir stalls she was able to survey the audience without too much discomposure.

It is well known that proper weddings in a church, as distinguished from hole and corner affairs for conscience or convenience sake in what even quite well-educated people will call registry offices, are conducted entirely for the benefit of the bride's mother and the bridesmaids. The bride, beyond a general feeling that it will be marvellous to be married, has usually been reduced by dressmakers, presents, nervous and unintelligible advice from her very ignorant mother, visits to her lover's great-aunts, and doubts about the setting of her hair, to a state of drugged imbecility in which she would as easily be led to suttee (or sati, if you prefer it, both being probably incorrect) as to the altar; while the bridegroom is merely an adjunct or bleating victim. As for the bridegroom's family and friends, everyone knows that they are only there by courtesy, being as naught, and relegated to the right or decani side of the church which for some ecclesiastical reason is the less honourable. And what is more, it is rare for the bridegroom's friends to turn up in such force as the bride's, so that the ushers are fain to hustle poor relations of the bride's, old governesses, nannies, and obvious members of the domestic staff into the bridegroom's side to fill up the pews, while the bridegroom and his best man have to hang about in new boots with no particular *locus standi* as it were.

But on the left or cantoris side, how different is the scene. All the bride's friends have come to talk to each other, all her parents' friends have turned up, majestic, distinguished, and except for an aunt or two, well dressed. Everyone says, "Where is the bride's mother? Oh, there she is. Doesn't she look well in that blue (or purple, or flowered silk or whatever it may be)?

Dear Elsie, she looks as happy as if she were going to be married herself. I suppose those are his people up in front. I don't think I've met them. Taunton, isn't it, or somewhere in Yorkshire. Look, there is Cynthia. Come into our pew, my dear, there's heaps of room and I have something I want to tell you."

So on this occasion did the Birketts' party and Rose's large body of bosom friends surge into the church and storm the pews. So did Mrs. Birkett look quite delightful in a shade of cyclamen that she had not been quite sure about and dispense welcoming smiles to anyone who caught her eye and co-opt into her pew her old friend Mrs. Morland, the well-known novelist, whose youngest boy Tony had been through Southbridge School from the bottom of the Junior School to the top of the Senior School and had just left in a cloud of glory with a Formership (corrupted from Formaship and pronounced Formayship, because scholars were supposed to apply for free tuition *in forma pauperis* at Paul's College, Oxford). Mrs. Morland's hat was too apt to lose its moorings on her head, her abundant brown hair was too apt to escape and rain hairpins on the floor, but no one could call her undistinguished, and Mrs. Birkett was very fond of her.

As for the bridegroom's parents they were both dead, which simplified everything very much, and Philip Winter, who was doing duty as usher for Lieutenant Fairweather, saw to it that the front pews were filled with the best specimens of the bridegroom's friends, including some very pretty young wives of Old Southbridgeians who had been at school with the Fairweathers, and the Dean's secretary who was well known as a football player by all the younger men and so gave lustre to the scene.

The organ pealed forth, though never except in fiction does it do this, rather blaring and bursting, or in more refined cases quavering. In every heart began to spring that exquisite hope, seldom if ever realised, that the bride will have had a fit, or eloped with someone else.

Meanwhile Mr. Birkett was approaching the drawing-room, more nervous than he had ever been since he had to explain to the Dean of his College why he had frightened the wife of the President of St. Barabbas next door by stumbling against her camp bed in the garden at three o'clock on a June morning, an action formally deprecated but privately condoned by the Dean, who did not hold with married Presidents, or indeed anyone else, and most especially not with people who slept out of doors in the summer, as he himself had slept with all his windows shut for nearly seventy years, and who also defended the members of his own College against all comers, whatever the offence, and that with such venom and gusto that only the President of St. Barabbas's fear of his wife had driven him to make the complaint. Mr. Birkett had been dismissed with an injunction not to be a young fool and the information that in his, the Dean's, young days when undergraduates *were* undergraduates, the way back into College via St. Barabbas was condemned as milk-soppery and child's play by all self-respecting men, who took the higher road by the crocketted gable end of Colney House, then but lately built for nondenominational non-collegiate students. At the present moment Mr. Birkett felt that he would rather face the Dean, or even the President of St. Barabbas's wife, than the ordeal of escorting Rose to the Chapel, but it had to be done, so he pulled himself together and went into the drawing-room, where Octavia Crawley and Delia Brandon were practising Court curtsies, much despised by Lydia and Geraldine, while Rose made up her face.

"It's time, Rose," said Mr. Birkett, finding an odd difficulty in speaking.

"Oh, Daddy, need I?" said Rose, with rather impeded

articulation as she applied a lipstick to her beautiful mouth.

"Now come along, Rose," said Mr. Birkett helplessly. But he might have appealed in vain had not Lydia Keith taken Rose's bag and lipstick away from her and put her bouquet into her hand. Rose was so surprised that she allowed her father to tuck her arm into his and lead her through the private passage to the anteroom, from which one door led to the choir, the other to the west end of the Chapel. Lydia and Geraldine arranged themselves behind the bride, Delia Brandon and Octavia Crawley followed, and the bridal procession began to move up the aisle towards the Dean. There was an audible gasp from the audience as Rose appeared on her father's arm and they all turned their heads to look. Never had her exquisite figure shown to more advantage than on what Everard Carter's House Matron described in a letter to her married sister as the Day of Days, and if her lovely face appeared to be vacant of all expression her friends were used to it. Lydia, who with Geraldine's passing acquiescence had constituted herself chief bridesmaid, was pleased by the admiration around her, and collecting Rose's bouquet prepared to stand by. To her old friend Noel Merton, who had driven Mrs. Crawley and a selection of the Deanery girls over from Barchester in his car, she had something of the air of a very competent second, bouquet in hand instead of a sponge, ready to give first aid between the rounds.

And indeed it looked at one moment as if her services would be required, for Rose, suddenly recognising her bridegroom, was about to say, "Hullo, darling, isn't this marvellous." Her lips had actually parted to say the words; her father's frown was unnoticed, and Noel Merton told Mrs. Crawley afterwards that he was certain Lydia would have garrotted Rose. But Lieutenant Fairweather, who had no illusions at all about his lovely bride, saw with his sailor's eye what was in the wind and stepping forward one pace gave his Rose a warning look that for once silenced her completely. Mr. Birkett stood back, weak with relief; the Dean and Mr. Smith did their duty; Captain Fairweather produced the ring at exactly the right moment; and with a feeling of loss and an even deeper feeling of thankfulness Mr. and Mrs. Birkett saw their daughter and her husband kneeling together, Rose's dress perfectly arranged, Lieutenant Fairweather, as seen in perspective, appearing to consist chiefly of the soles of his boots. For the brief moment of silent prayer Mrs. Birkett wondered if she had been a bad mother, and decided with her usual admirable common sense that she had made the best of a difficult job. Her mother's heart was divided, one half feeling a so natural pang at the sight of her lovely daughter setting out into a new life in a distant country, far from her parents' care, the other and by far the larger half feeling a gratitude amounting to idolatry for the son-in-law who was going to relieve her of a child that had done her best for the last five or six years to drive her parents mad.

Relations and old friends began to move towards the vestry. Lydia marshalled the bridesmaids and herded them along, stopping for a moment to exchange greetings with Noel Merton.

"Hullo, Noel," she said, "hullo, Mrs. Crawley, come along and sign the register."

Noel Merton said he would gladly accompany Mrs. Crawley, but didn't think he would sign as he hardly knew the Birketts.

"Rot," said Lydia. "You were at Northbridge with us in the summer Rose got unengaged to Philip and threw his ring into the pond. You can't call that not knowing her. Come on."

As there was no point in resisting, Noel followed with Mrs. Crawley as Lydia swept them into her wake.

In the vestry the register was lying ready. The Dean

himself conducted the bride to the table and showed her where to sign.

"Your full name," he said, "Rose Felicity Birkett."

"Not Birkett," said Rose, "Fairweather."

"For this last time," said the School Chaplain kindly, "you sign in your maiden name."

"But I can't," said Rose, looking round for sympathy. "I mean I've just got married, haven't I, and it works the minute you're married. I mean if anyone talked to me that I didn't know them, they'd say Mrs. Fairweather."

The Dean and Mr. Smith, who had never been up against this particular difficulty before, looked at each other with what in anyone but a professed Christian would have been despair, when Lieutenant Fairweather, who had waited out of respect for superior officers, saw that the moment had come for the sécular arm to assert itself.

"Don't argue, my girl," he said. "You know nothing about it. Write Rose Felicity Birkett or you won't be married at all."

Rose threw an adoring look at her husband, and murmuring that it was foully dispiriting and on one's wedding day too, did as she was told and immediately recovered her spirits. The other requisite signatures were quickly affixed and a general orgy of kissing took place.

"I'm glad it wasn't me," said Lydia to her friend Noel Merton, giving him a violent hit on the arm. Noel, who in spite of being a very distinguished barrister and about fifteen years older than Lydia was always treated by her as an equal and enjoyed it, inquired whether it was the bridegroom or the ceremony that she objected to.

"Oh, John's all right," said Lydia negligently. "I mean all this marrying business. Do you remember, Noel, a very good conversation we had about getting married the first time you stayed with us or the second and you said you didn't think you'd get married and I said I probably would if it was only not to be like the Pettinger."

"Look out, she's just behind me," said Noel, casting a warning glance in the direction of the Headmistress of the Barchester High School, who was exercising the fascination of a snake over a small bird upon the Dean's secretary, Mr. Needham.

"Well, I've changed my mind," said Lydia, taking no notice of Noel's warning, "and I think I'll not get married. Supposing one had a daughter like Rose."

"I can promise you that you won't," said Noel. "And if you do think of marrying anyone, be sure to tell me, and I'll see if he's nice enough for you and have proper settlements."

Lydia said of course she would, only if Noel wanted to marry anyone he had better not tell her till afterwards, as she was sure it would be someone ghastly that she'd absolutely loathe. This compact having been made, it was time to reform the bridal procession. The organ suddenly trumpeted like an elephant and Rose on the arm of Lieutenant Fairweather, followed by her bridesmaids, passed down the aisle, between their admiring friends, out at the little door and so by the private passage back to the drawing-room where the reception was to take place.

"Here you are," said Lydia firmly, as she handed Rose her bag. "You can stick on some more powder and lipstick if you like, but I think you've quite enough, don't you, John?"

"Don't be so dispiriting," said Rose, "and this lipstick doesn't come off anyway."

"I should think not," said her husband, "I wouldn't let you put it on if it did. That's enough, Lydia. Take it away."

"Darling John," said Rose, relinquishing the bag to Lydia.

And now Simnet in all his glory began to announce

the guests. Rose kissed everyone with fervour and said it was too marvellous of them to have given her such a marvellous present, while Lieutenant Fairweather shook everyone's hand in a very painful way and smiled, for there seemed to him no particular reason to say anything. Considering that it was the end of July Mrs. Birkett had collected a very good bag. Lord Pomfret, who had been for many years a Governor of the School, was unfortunately abroad, but had sent a silver rose bowl chased, as Philip Winter had said, within an inch of its life. Lord Stoke too was absent, enjoying himself very much at an Agricultural Congress in Denmark, and was represented by a mezzotint (framed). But there were several parents with titles, and some Old Boys who were distinguished in various walks of life, among them a young Cabinet Minister, two actors, a film star who had endeared himself to the public by always acting with his wife, whoever she might happen at the moment to be, an Admiral, and an Indian prince who had been in the School Eleven. Add to these a good sprinkling of dignitaries from Barchester Close, quantities of subalterns and young naval officers on the Fairweather side and enough pretty girls to go round, and it will be seen that Mrs. Birkett had cause for satisfaction. For half an hour she did her duty in receiving guests as they flowed steadily through the room, and then she felt free to do what she really wanted, which was to talk to as many of the Old Boys as possible. There was not a boy who had been in the Junior School when she and her husband were there, but liked and admired Ma Birky, and before long she had twenty or thirty young men about her, competing for her attention, so that Rose's friends had to content themselves with the older, more distinguished, and to their minds much duller men.

It was a long time since Mrs. Birkett had had so many of her chickens under her wing at once and questions and answers flew between them, with much laughter. All the naval men and the subalterns were eager to tell her what they planned to do on their next leave, and all said much the same thing. So long, Mrs. Birkett gathered, as there wasn't a scrap, or a blow-up, they proposed to climb, fish, tramp, bathe, shoot for every moment of daylight. If there was any sort of trouble, they said, it would be jolly hard luck on the fellows who were in India, or on the China station, or attached to Embassies, but of course nothing was likely to happen, because we had had quite enough trouble over Munich to last us for a long time and anyway Old Moore said it was going to be all right. Mrs. Birkett was sensible of a chill that she didn't stop to analyse, told herself not to be silly, and felt that a world with so many very nice healthy young men in it couldn't be so very wrong.

Mr. Birkett had also neglected his guests for various old Oxford friends, mostly in public life. As they too talked of their summer plans one or two said that it looked like trouble with the railway men again and how annoying it would be to be held up at Dover on one's way back from the Continent if there were a strike.

"Strikes are a nuisance," said the President of St. Barabbas, "but nothing to the nuisance we shall have if there did happen to be any trouble. The Government want to take over part of the College for the Divorce Court. We should have to send half our men to St. Jude's and it will upset the work greatly, besides making us a laughing stock. And Judges expect much more comfort than we can give. They expect bathrooms!" said the President with the just indignation of one who had lived on a flat tin bath ever since he first came up to Oxford.

"The only man who is going to enjoy it is Crawford at Lazarus," said Mr. Fanshawe, the Dean of Paul's.

"He was my predecessor here," said Mr. Birkett.

"I hate a crank," said Mr. Fanshawe dispassionately, "and Crawford cranks about Russia till most of us are thoroughly ashamed of him. He's got a queer lot at Lazarus now, all doing Modern Greats and thinking they understand politics. He has managed to get the promise of the Institute of Ideological Interference being billetted on Lazarus, if there is any question of its leaving London. They are going to bring a lot of typists, and his men will have to go to St. Swithin's. Do them good," said Mr. Fanshawe with gloomy pleasure. "St. Swithin's are the hardest drinking college in Oxford just now and they'll lead Crawford's flock astray all right. I don't think any of this is likely to happen, but I must say I rather hope there will be some evacuating from London, just to serve Crawford right. Never ought to have got the Mastership. Ha!"

"You should hear my butler, Simnet, on Crawford," said Mr. Birkett. "He was a Scout at Lazarus but resigned because he didn't hold with the Master's political and social views."

As he spoke Simnet suddenly materialised at his side and murmured, "Mrs. Birkett says The Cake, sir."

"You were on No. 7 staircase at Lazarus, weren't you?" said Mr. Fanshawe, whose knowledge and memory of Oxford characters were unique. "I'll have a word with you later."

The guests were then swept into the dining-room where Lieutenant Fairweather and Rose were standing by the cake. Mr. Tozer was plying the champagne nippers with demoniac fury, his satellites, reinforced by the Headmaster's staff and some of the servants from the Houses, were already speeding about the room with trays of glasses. Simnet corralling by the power of his eye the most distinguished of the guests, served them himself. A photographer from the *Barchester Chronicle* suddenly elbowed his way to the front. Lieutenant Fairweather drew his sword, and offered the hilt to Rose. The flashlight went off. Rose, her hand guided by her husband, gave a loud shriek and cut into the cake.

The photographer disappeared. Mr. Tozer then fell upon the cake with a kind of caterer's hacksaw and dismembered it with the rapidity of lightning. Healths were drunk, Simnet produced unending supplies of champagne for Mr. Tozer, and Mrs. Birkett suddenly wished it were all over.

"How are you bearing up, Amy?" said Mrs. Morland at her elbow.

Mrs. Birkett said as well as could be expected, and she must get Rose away to change soon.

A young man in rather disreputable clothes approached Mrs. Birkett with a glass of champagne.

"You ought to drink this," he said gravely, offering it to Mrs. Birkett. "It will do you good."

"Tony!" Mrs. Birkett exclaimed, suddenly recognising Mrs. Morland's youngest son.

"I thought you weren't coming," said his mother.

"I wasn't," said Tony, "because I was mending my bike, but as I got it mended I thought I'd come, but the pedal came off at the level crossing so I left it at a shop to be mended."

"Let me know if you'd like me to fetch you and the bicycle from anywhere on my way back, darling," said Mrs. Morland.

"It would be too complicated," said Tony. "If I had a car of my own, Mamma, it would save you a lot of trouble."

"And give me a lot of trouble," said Mrs. Morland with some spirit. "Well, good-bye, darling. It was so nice to see you."

Tony, divining that his mother might kiss him, sketched a salute to the two ladies and with gentle determination forced his way to the thickest of the crush where Lieutenant and Mrs. Fairweather and the bridesmaids were to be found.

"Many happy returns of the day," he said politely to

Rose. "Hullo, John. Hullo, Geoff. Hullo, Geraldine. Hullo, Lydia."

"Come and stay with us when you're out of camp," Lydia yelled above the tumult.

"Can't," said Tony. "My Mamma will take me abroad."

"There'll be a railway strike and you'll never get home," shouted Lydia. "I heard someone say so."

"It all comes of listening to the wireless," said Tony. "You ought to learn to think for yourself." And before Lydia could counter this accusation he had slipped away.

Mrs. Birkett now approached her married daughter and said it was time to change. Rose, who was vastly enjoying a flirtation with all her husband's and her brother-in-law's friends, said in rather a whining voice Need she really?

"Indeed you need, my girl," said her husband, looking at his wrist-watch. "Half an hour. At half-past four, you'll find me clean and sober at the front door, so get up steam."

"All right, angel," said Rose and followed her mother from the room.

Lieutenant Fairweather, accompanied by a large body of select friends, went to Mr. Birkett's dressing-room to change his uniform and the crowd began to disperse. Mr. Birkett, who was acting host while his wife was with Rose, stood and shook hands with his guests. He was tired and felt as if he were somehow apart from the scene, and as if for a hundred years people had shaken his hand and said they would be seeing him when term began again unless anything happened, though of course it wouldn't.

Presently only the near friends of the two families and some uninteresting relations were left and then Lieutenant Fairweather came down with his bodyguard.

Captain Fairweather put the bridegroom's suitcase into his car, which was already loaded with Rose's luggage. Simnet brought more champagne into the hall where the remains of the party were now waiting for the bride. The school clock chimed two quarters. Lieutenant Fairweather went to the bottom of the stairs and shouted "Rose!"

Even as he spoke his wife came downstairs in a ravishing silk coat and skirt, clasping the two depraved dolls in one arm and the plush panda in the other.

"Here, Geraldine," said Lieutenant Fairweather, "take those dolls."

"Oh, John—" Rose began.

"And give me that other thing," said her bridegroom, laying hands on the panda.

"John, *don't* be so dispiriting," said Rose.

"What on earth have you got inside him?" asked Lieutenant Fairweather, and without waiting for an answer he unzipped the panda's back and the ocarina fell out.

"You might take that coco-nut thing away," said Lieutenant Fairweather to Simnet, who was in deep converse with Mr. Fanshawe. Simnet was so surprised that he stooped and picked it up.

"Catch!" continued the Lieutenant, tossing the panda to Lydia. "And now say good-bye, Rose."

He then embraced his mother-in-law very kindly, kissed all the bridesmaids and shook hands with his father-in-law.

"Don't you worry," he said. "I'm going to look after Rose with all my might and all my heart. Thank you all. Bless you all. Come along, Rose."

Rose hugged her parents tempestuously, and kissed everyone in a careless way. Mrs. Birkett, who could hardly bear it now that the moment of parting had come, saw that Rose's lovely eyes were brimming.

"John," she said, laying her hand on her son-in-law's arm and looking towards Rose.

"It's absolutely all right," said he very kindly. "Anything wrong, Rose?"

"No," said Rose, bursting into tears. "It's only because of leaving Mummy and Daddy, but I do love you better than anything in the WORLD, darling."

In proof of which she flung herself sobbing into her husband's arms.

"That's absolutely all right," said he, patting her back. "And now we'd better go."

He took Rose's arm. Her tears ceased as if by magic, leaving her face unravaged. On the bottom step she suddenly turned and ran back to her mother.

"Mummy, *did* they put my little suitcase with my bathing things in the car?" she asked earnestly, "because we're going to bathe to-morrow if there's time."

Geraldine said it was all right. Rose ran down the steps again and got into the car. With a frightful noise it leapt forward and the married couple whirled away down the drive. The younger guests who had been making up parties for cinemas or dancing went off, taking Delia Brandon and Octavia Crawley with them. Mr. Fanshawe said he had much enjoyed his talk with Simnet and had got the lowdown on Crawford, and would now walk to Southbridge station and take the next train that came, which he found more restful than being driven by his wife.

"Come and sit down, Amy," said Mrs. Morland, who was staying to dinner. "You look tired."

"I am," said Mrs. Birkett. "Oh, must you go, Dr. Crawley? It *has* been so good of you to come. I think Rose will be very happy."

"I couldn't help hearing her last words to you," said the Dean. "They reminded me so curiously of a story my grandfather used to tell about the late Lady Hartletop. It was when she married Lord Dumbello, before he succeeded to the Marquisate. They are a kind of connection of ours, you know. My Aunt Grace married Major Grantly who was Lady Hartletop's brother."

"But it was a moiré antique she wanted, wasn't it," said Mrs. Morland, "not a bathing dress."

The Dean laughed and said good-bye.

Dinner was very quiet. As Geraldine had gone back with Lydia to dine with the Carters, taking with her Captain Fairweather who wanted to see Bobbie Carter in his bath before going back to camp, only the Birketts and Mrs. Morland were there to eat the crumbs of the wedding feast. Mr. Tozer had cleared away with his usual thoroughness and the dining-room was quite habitable again. Simnet with great tact had put away the unopened champagne, feeling that it would remind his employers too vividly of their loss and had, without waiting for orders, brought up a very good claret under whose soothing influence everyone relaxed. Mrs. Morland spoke of her plans for going to France with Tony unless anything happened.

"Everyone has said that to-day," said Mrs. Birkett wearily. "Oh, Henry, who was Gristle that rang you up this morning? I've been meaning to ask you all day."

"Gristle?" said the Headmaster. "Not Gristle; Bissell. He is the Headmaster of the Hosiers' Boys Foundation School. If there is any evacuating of the London schools," he continued, addressing himself to Mrs. Morland, "we are taking them in, damn them. I'm sorry; the day has been trying. But it will be a difficult job with the best will in the world. If anything did happen, not that I think it will, but one must be prepared, a good many of our younger masters will have to go automatically. So will my secretary."

Mrs. Morland did not stay late. Before she went she said to Mrs. Birkett:

"I was wanting to ask you, Amy. If there is any trouble, which I shall *not* encourage by talking about it, my publisher Adrian Coates and his wife, George Knox's daughter, you know, rather want to take my house. I don't suppose there'll be any air raids, but if there were Adrian wants Sybil and the three children to be in the country. Tony will be at Oxford, so I wondered if it would be any use to you if I came to you for a bit, as a secretary, or a P.G., or anything you like. But only if you'd like it. Think about it.

"I shan't think at all," said Mrs. Birkett, "I'd love to have you. You can P.G. if you'd feel happier and have Rose's room to write in. Bill, wouldn't it be nice if Laura came to us in the autumn if things get difficult?"

"Very nice indeed," said Mr. Birkett warmly. "And there isn't another parent, past, present, or future, that I'd say that to. Do come, Laura."

Mrs. Morland stared into vacancy and took a deep breath.

"I am *not* superstitious," she said firmly, "and though I don't believe in encouraging things by talking about them, it is silly not to face facts. If there is a war, I will come to you. There!"

"I always said you saw things clearly," said Mrs. Birkett. "You can tell the truth better than anyone I know. If there is a war, come to us."

"And now let it do its worst," said Mrs. Morland heroically but irrelevantly, and so took herself away.

"I still don't think it can happen," said Mrs. Birkett to her husband, "but I'm glad Rose will be safely away."

"I don't believe it either," said Mr. Birkett, "for to admit it would be to admit the possibility of the Hosiers' Boys coming here, which will undoubtedly be worse than death. I think John will look after her."

4

THE STORM BEGINS TO LOWER

On a September afternoon about six weeks later than the interesting events just described Mrs. Morland drove up to the Headmaster's House at Southbridge and rang the front door bell. Simnet, who was prepared for her arrival, opened the door and himself removed her suitcases from the car and took them up to what, to Geraldine's secret resentment, was still called Miss Rose's room. Mrs. Morland went straight to Mrs. Birkett's sitting-room where she found her friend writing letters.

"Well, here I am," said Mrs. Morland dramatically.

Mrs. Birkett embraced her friend and rang for tea.

"Tell me about everything," said Mrs. Morland.

"There's not much to tell," said Mrs. Birkett. "The Hosiers' Boys Foundation School has decided to extend its holidays, so they don't come here till the 25th. All the masters who were Territorials won't be coming back of course, including Philip Winter whom we shall miss very much. Bill and Everard Carter go mad together for hours every evening, trying to work out a time-table that will satisfy Mr. Gristle, though I suppose I must remember to call him Bissell."

Mrs. Morland, who knew that the present disturbed state of things made people rather unlike themselves, looked piercingly at her friend to see if she were going mad.

"Gristle?" she said.

"That was what Geraldine said his name was when he rang up on Rose's wedding day," said Mrs. Birkett, "and the name somehow stuck."

"There is a carpet-sweeper called Bissell," said Mrs. Morland thoughtfully, "and one forgets to empty the rubbish out of it and then it puts dirt on the carpet instead of taking it off. But I suppose everyone has electric ones now."

"He may or may not be a carpet-sweeper," said Mrs. Birkett, "but he is the Headmaster of the Hosiers' Boys Foundation School and very, very well meaning. He is coming here for the night to talk to Bill, so you'll see him at dinner. I have asked the Carters, so we shall be six."

"Where is Geraldine then?" said Mrs. Morland.

Mrs. Birkett sighed.

"She did First Aid last spring," she said, "and is working with Delia Brandon at the Barchester Infirmary. When I say work, they sit there all the time with nothing to do, because all the patients were turned out last week which was *most* depressing for all their families that thought they had got rid of them. And none of the doctors are allowed to take any private cases, so it is very dull for everybody. Better, I suppose, than having hundreds of wounded soldiers, yet in a way if one didn't know any of the soldiers one would be glad to think of the nurses and doctors being employed."

Mrs. Morland felt this question too difficult for her and asked after Rose. Mrs. Birkett said proudly that she had written by every mail and was loving Las Palombas and very happy, and offered to show Mrs. Morland some of her letters. Mrs. Morland with great kindness accepted the offer, but her kindness was not unduly tried, for Rose's large scrawling hand, though it covered a great deal of paper, had nothing particular to impart except that Las Palombas was marvellous which she spelt with one "l" and the language a bit dispiriting and

Mummy and Daddy must come out and see her as soon as they could and she supposed the war must be a bit dispiriting and sent tons and tons of love. Mrs. Morland said how nice the letters were and they gossiped about the wedding and so time passed and it was time to dress for dinner.

When Mrs. Morland got down to the drawing-room she found Mr. Birkett talking to a stranger whom she rightly guessed to be Mr. Gristle or more correctly Bissell. The Headmaster of the Hosiers' Boys Foundation School, erroneously described by its well-wishers as one of our Lesser Public Schools, was a lean middle-sized man of about thirty-five. He wore a neat blue suit and looked as if he wasn't sure if he ought to attack his hosts, or be on the defensive.

Mr. Birkett introduced Mrs. Morland and Mr. Bissell, who shook hands and said he was pleased to meet her, and was sorry the wife wasn't with him as she was a great reader. Mrs. Morland, who in spite of some fifteen years of ceaseless and successful novel writing had no opinion of her own works at all, thanked Mr. Bissell warmly for his kind words and asked which of her books Mrs. Bissell liked best.

"Not but what they are all the same," she added, "because my publisher says that pays better and I have to go on earning money for the present, because although the three elder boys have been supporting themselves for some time except of course for Christmas and birthday presents which I always make as large as I can, I still have my youngest boy at Paul's and you know what Oxford is."

Mr. Bissell said not being a Capittleist he didn't.

"But aren't there heaps of scholarships and things?" said Mrs. Morland. "I thought everyone had a Field-Marshal's bâton in his knapsack now, only that isn't exactly what I mean."

Mr. Bissell said Conscription was one of Cap-

Robert Philip, after Mr. Winter, whom I really ought to call Captain Winter now, but it all seems so unreal. How many children have you, Mr. Bissell?"

Mr. Bissell, thawed by Kate's obvious sincerity and interest, said it was a great grief to Mrs. Bissell and he that they had no chicks. Kate saw in Geraldine's eye a professional nursing wish to ask him why, and knowing that no sentiment of what was suitable would keep her from her purpose, plunged into an interesting account of Bobbie's first birthday and how he had been sick with excitement at the sight of his birthday cake, a plain sponge cake with one candle on it, but had subsequently recovered. During her soothing monologue Mr. Bissell began to feel at home and although he could not reconcile dinner jackets with his principles he enjoyed the good food and wine without knowing it and softened towards the representatives of Capittleism and an effete educational system more than he would have thought possible.

It was not till Mrs. Morland unfortunately spoke of a book she had been reading about the Russian ballet that Mrs. Birkett had any cause for anxiety about her dinner party. Even as Philip Winter a few years ago had bristled at the name of Russia, so did Mr. Bissell now look defiantly about him, anxiously watching for his chance to become a martyr. Nor did he have long to wait, for Philip put forward the opinion that it was just as well we hadn't had a trade pact with the Russians, as they would have turned round and bitten us. This was not to be borne.

"Have you ever been to Russia?" said Mr. Bissell, not quite sure if he ought to say Captain, but deciding against it as of a militarist tendency.

"No," said Philip, and he and Everard began to laugh.

Mrs. Birkett asked what the joke was.

"It was when I was staying with you that summer at

Northbridge," Philip answered her, "and the Oxbridge Press accepted my little book on Horace. I was going to Russia, but Everard said if the proofs were sent to me there they might be confiscated, so I went to Hungary with him and Noel Merton instead."

"You missed a most valuable opportunity," said Mr. Bissell. "It is practically unknown for letters to go astray in Russia."

Philip, balking the main issue in a very cowardly way, said he hadn't got the proofs till November, so it wouldn't really have mattered.

"Mark me," said Mr. Bissell.

Everyone looked at him with interest.

"Mark me," he said, "Russia is a Power to be reckoned with. Look what she has done for civilisation."

A confused hubbub rose about him in which the words Tchekov, Ballet, Rimsky, Diaghilev, Tchaikovsky, Flying over the Pole were heard. Mr. Bissell, who meant something quite different, found it impossible to make himself heard.

"It is more like Flying over the Poles now," said Mrs. Morland in her tragedy voice. "I never quite know how large Poland really is, because it seems to get bigger or smaller in history till one is quite giddy, but to have Russians there must be quite dreadful. Cossacks, only I don't think they fly, and why the French are always allies of Poland I cannot think."

Mr. Bissell seizing upon a second's silence said no one could begin to understand the World Problems of today who did not reckon with Stalin.

"That's what you used to say, Philip," said Geraldine accusingly.

Philip said he used to say Lenin, but the principle was the same, only he found himself too busy ever to think of either of them when he was in camp.

"Anyway," said Mrs. Morland, pushing her hair back, "they got it all from us."

"Got what, Laura?" said Mr. Birkett.

"You know perfectly well that you know what I am talking about and that I can never explain what I mean," said Mrs. Morland severely. "The Italians getting sympathy from us for the Risorgimento and look at them now, all Fascist and Abyssinian. And reading books in the British Museum, which is *free*, for weeks and months at our expense like Karl Marx. And the Russian ballet at Covent Garden charging the most frightful prices for everything, that *we* have to pay, though I must say it's worth it, because when one goes to an English ballet one has to say how wonderful it is considering what a short time it has been going on."

Mr. Bissell felt himself reeling. Capable of close, sustained argument, with facts of all kinds at his finger tips, he was as baffled by Mrs. Morland's mental flights as one of his own junior boys would have been by the differential calculus. How the Franco-Polish friendship, the Risorgimento, Karl Marx, and English ballet had sprung from Stalin he could not conceive. Either he was mad, or Mrs. Morland was mad, and a Public School Headmaster with his Senior Housemaster and his Senior Classical Master, now a Captain in the Army, not to speak of wives and daughters, were taking her irrelevant and illogical ramblings seriously, and therefore must be mad too. Exactly how much he longed for the bracing atmosphere of a debate at the Isle of Dogs Left Wing Athenaeum no one but himself knew, but Mr. Birkett, Everard and Philip had a fairly good guess, and much as the Birketts loved Mrs. Morland even they found her swallow flights of thought a little confusing at times. Mrs. Birkett looked at her husband and rose with her ladies. As they left the room Geraldine who had been silent, or as she preferred to imagine thinking things out, stopped near Mr. Bissell.

"If you want to nationalise the hospitals I'm your man," she said, rather threateningly. "Of course the

Government ought to pay for them and not us. We pay a jolly sight too much for things like hospitals and education that no one really wants. I've thought it all out and I'll tell you what you ought to do—"

But Philip, who saw Mr. Bissell going mad before his eyes and was on very old friendly terms with Geraldine, pushed her kindly out of the room and shut the door.

"Have some port, Bissell," said Mr. Birkett. "No? I'm afraid Geraldine is a little overpowering. She can't think of more than one thing at a time and just now it is hospitals. She is entirely uneducated and you must forgive her. She was never good at anything but mathematics. I got Carter here to-night so that we could have a good talk about the fitting in of our time-tables and I am glad Winter has turned up, as he will be a great help. If you really don't want any port, suppose we all adjourn to my study. And then tomorrow we'll go over the school and I will show you exactly what we propose to do and you will doubtless have some suggestions to make."

Accordingly the four men went to the study where Simnet brought them coffee. Philip spoke of his month in camp and his chances of staying in England and being sent abroad, and posted himself up in school matters. While the three Southbridge masters talked Mr. Bissell reflected upon the extraordinary people among whom this war was going to force him to live. As far as he could see, though they were all very kind and obliging, not one of them had any clear idea about anything. Mr. Birkett and Mr. Carter, whom he must remember to call Birkett and Carter, were what was called educated men who had been to Oxford (though here he was wrong, for Everard was a Cambridge man) and Captain Winter, whom it would perhaps be all right to call Winter, had learnt Classics, a degree that one knew to be really difficult, though pure waste of time and getting you nowhere. Yet these men could sit and listen to conversation that the Isle of Dogs would not for a moment tolerate. When he and Mrs. Bissell went to tea with Mr. and Mrs. Lefroy of the Technical School, and Mr. Jobson from the Chemical Works and Mrs. Jobson, and Mr. Pecker from the Free Library and his unmarried daughter who taught music and folk dancing at the L.C.C. evening classes were there, then there *was* conversation. Mrs. Bissell, Mrs. Lefroy, Mrs. Jobson and Miss Pecker were in a woman's proper place. At tea the talk would be general; Mr. Jobson would tell Mrs. Bissell about the indigo trade, Mr. Lefroy would tell Mrs. Jobson about the new wood-carving class and what Miss Makins of the art weaving class had said, Mr. Pecker would give Mrs. Lefroy information about the Borough Council's stinginess in the matter of gum for the labels, while he himself would explain to Miss Pecker the latest developments in his feud with the officials responsible for University grants, after which the men would retire to Mr. Lefroy's den, so-called apparently because it was the back room in the basement and had bars at the window, though to keep burglars out rather than Mr. Lefroy and his friends in, and discuss the coming Social Revolution and Russia's part in it, with well chosen reasoning (mostly chosen from sixpenny books of a Red and tendentious nature) and almost complete unanimity of view. After this they would go early on account of Monday morning, spiritually much refreshed.

How Mrs. Morland, who wrote books that Mr. Pecker often handed out at the Free Library and therefore must be intellectual, could be allowed to talk as she did, with no visible chain of thought and a total want of depth and earnestness, he could not imagine. And Miss Birkett, though she might be good at mathematics, seemed to have no knowledge of economics whatever. Mrs. Birkett and Mrs. Carter were certainly nice, but in any revolution they would obviously be the first to go. Still, he had made up his mind when this war began in which Russia, betrayed by England, had so far forgotten herself as to make a pact with the Ryke, that though he could not conscientiously approve of anything here or elsewhere, his duty to his profession was to meet everything as coolly as he could, carry out orders, look after his boys and masters, keep Mrs. Bissell's spirits up and never grumble at anything. So he put the disquieting behaviour of his hostess and her friends away in his mind for future reflection and prepared himself for discussion.

Mr. Birkett and Everard, when the subject of sending London schools to the country had first been raised, had secretly hoped to get one of the London public schools, but pressure had been put on them to take in the Hosiers' Boys Foundation School, and thinking with their guest that their obvious duty was to do what came to their hand, had during the preceding spring a good deal of correspondence with Mr. Bissell, so that they knew pretty well the numbers and requirements of the school, luckily not a very large one. As a larger number of boys were leaving than usual they were able to clear one of the boarding-houses for a number of the Hosiers' Boys. The rest were to be put in a large empty house owned by the Governors which had been fitted up as a boarding house, largely by Kate's energy and common sense in all domestic matters. The Hosiers' Boys would have their classes partly in the School itself, partly in some wooden huts that Mr. Birkett's foresight had collected before the rush began. It might be possible to pool some of the junior classes, but the whole arrangement still needed a good deal of consideration. However two hours' solid work did a great deal and then Mr. Birkett said they would all go to bed.

"By the way, Bissell," he said as they went into the hall, "what about you and your wife? Will you live with your staff in the boarding-house? We haven't considered that."

"I hadn't thought of it either," said Mr. Bissell. "Mrs. Bissell would be quite agreeable I'm sure. She isn't one for thinking of herself. Of course she isn't used to sharing, but we talked it over, her and I, and I'm sure she feels like I do."

Mr. Bissell looked so tired as he made this noble but not very helpful statement that Everard felt sorry for him. To have to move a hundred boys or so into new surroundings, to make yourself responsible for them as boarders when most of them were day boys, to have to share school accommodation with unknown and possibly hostile strangers, to leave your own home, it was all quite difficult enough, without having to eat and live with your staff and forty boys. On an impulse he said:

"I don't know how the idea would suit you, Bissell, but if you and your wife cared to come to us for a bit and see how you like it, we would be delighted. Ask her and let me know"

Mr. Bissell said he daresaid Mrs. Bissell wouldn't mind, and Everard understood him. Simnet came forward with the news that Mrs. Carter had gone home some time ago, so Everard and Philip said good night and walked across the School Quad, in silence. Kate was still up when they came in and while they had drinks she asked how everything had gone. Everard said very well, and next morning they were to go over the boarding-house reserved for the Hosiers' Boys and settle about some of the classrooms.

"I asked Bissell and his wife to come to us for a bit, Kate," said Everard. "It doesn't seem quite fair for them to have to live with their masters and boys. They couldn't even have a sitting-room of their own. Is that all right?"

"Quite right," said Kate, her eyes assuming the

faraway expression which always meant very sensible thoughts about practical things and which Everard still thought the most enchanting sight in the world. For had not she looked with just such eyes at a loose button on his waistcoat when he had first met her. "Quite right. If I give them the spare room I could turn the dressing-room into a sitting-room and let them use the other bathroom. The only thing is that Philip would have to share the bathroom with them when he comes back on leave, or else use the prefects' bathroom. Would you mind, Philip?"

Philip said of course he wouldn't and Everard and Kate were angels and personally he would far rather be in a draught-ridden hut on Sparrowhill than shut up with Mr. Bissell and the unknown Mrs. Bissell.

"Well it won't be for ever," said the practical Kate, "and I was so sorry for Mr. Bissell when he said they hadn't got any children. Would you like to see Bobbie asleep before you go to bed, Philip?"

Mr. Birkett and Mr. Bissell looked into the drawing-room to say good night. Much to Mr. Bissell's relief Geraldine had gone to bed and as the two other ladies were very sleepy good nights were said at once.

"Did you have a good evening?" said Mrs. Birkett when she and her husband were alone together.

"Quite good. We got a lot of work done and can finish the practical details to-morrow. Laura was very Lauraish to-night."

"She was tired," said Mrs. Birkett. "She didn't enjoy having to rush home from France with Tony when things began to look bad, and the elder boys will probably be in the army, except John who is the sailor, and she doesn't know if anyone will be buying books now. I'm very glad we've got her here."

"Bissell doesn't realise the intelligence of what he must look on as uneducated women," said Mr. Birkett, "and I thought he would go mad at the dinner table. I suppose Geraldine simply must bore people about the hospital. Well, thank goodness Rose is out of it."

So they went to bed. And Mr. Bissell in the second-best spare room wondered at the peculiar surroundings in which his lot had been cast and saw but little hope for the future if the so-called educated classes were so hopelessly ignorant and shallow. Birkett, it is true, would be a good man to work with and Mrs. Carter was very sympathetic, and after all the boys were the chief thing to be considered. So, with less distrust than he had felt on his arrival and great thankfulness that Miss Birkett would mostly be at the Hospital, he too went to sleep.

5

A ROOM WITH A PICTURE

•

Next day, much to Mr. Bissell's relief, he had breakfast alone with his host, after which they walked across the School Quad to the Carters' house. Here they collected Everard and Philip and with them made an extensive tour of the proposed new quarters of the Hosiers' Boys. By midday everything was settled and Mr. Bissell was able to feel that his school would not be badly housed.

"By the way," said Everard, "have you thought about coming to us with Mrs. Bissell? No hurry, but my wife would like to know in time to get things ready for you."

Mr. Bissell had forgotten all about it. But even as he heard Everard speaking he realised that to share a house with other people, however sympathetic their wives, was the one thing he and his wife could not do. Their house they would leave dust-sheeted and empty, their books and furniture and picture (a coloured reproduction of the Van Gogh sunflowers) they would abandon, but if they were to keep their balance in this new and peculiar world where no one knew what dialectic meant, they must somehow be alone in their spare time. The thought of evenings spent with the Carters was more than he could face. Even at the risk of giving offence he must strike out for freedom. In halting words he began to explain that to stay at the Carters' house would give very great pleasure to Mrs. Bissell and he, but his misery was so apparent that Philip Winter on an impulse came to his rescue.

"Before Mr. Bissell decides," said Philip to Everard, "what about taking him to see that cottage in Wiple Terrace? I know it's empty because Jessie's brother delivers the milk there and he says it is to be let furnished. Jessie is the head housemaid at Carter's," he added to Mr. Bissell, "and her brother does the milk round for Abner Brown who grazes one of the school fields and carts coal."

Everard's relief at this suggestion was not less than Mr. Bissell's. He liked Mr. Bissell and felt that they could pull together, but the thought of housing indefinitely a fellow worker who regarded the School as a product of Capittleism was not bliss, the more so as he knew his own code would not let him point out to Mr. Bissell that the Hosiers' Boys was supported by one of the richest of the City Companies on money obtained partly from their appropriation of several very rich abbeys under Henry VIII, partly from the investment of funds obtained by rather piratical trading with the East in the seventeenth century, and that its original purpose was to educate the sons of Hosiers and enable them to enter the church through one of the Universities. So he said that he thought it a good idea, but Mr. Bissell must feel perfectly free to come to them or not.

"My wife will be delighted if you do come," he said truthfully, knowing that his Kate enjoyed any guests, even Mr. Holinshed, a parent who had disgraced his family by suddenly taking orders at an unusually advanced age and having family prayers, which he insisted on conducting wherever he stayed, regardless of the embarrassment he caused his hosts before their servants, "but of course if you and Mrs. Bissell prefer to be on your own we shall quite understand."

He then wondered if he would ever dare to call Mrs. Bissell "your wife" to Mr. Bissell; put away from him as harsh the thought that "the wife" might be tolerated, vaguely wondered again if that lady's Christian name would ever be made known to him and thought probably not. Philip said he would take Mr. Bissell down to the village and he could have a look at the cottage, and they might drop in at the Red Lion and talk to Mr. Brown, Abner Brown's uncle, who was a useful man to know. Mr. Bissell unexpectedly said he could do with a pint and the doctor had put Mrs. Bissell on stout last winter which had done her a lot of good; so they went off across the playing-fields, by the footbridge over the river, across the allotments, and so by the lane that led into the backyard of the Red Lion.

During the eighteenth and early nineteenth century the Red Lion had been, as its capacious stables showed, a coaching inn on a fairly large scale, and its handsome red brick front on Southbridge High Street was to be seen in more than one engraving, copies of which can still be picked up in antiquarian shops in Barchester. Now its stables were used as garages except for one wing where a young woman kept a few hunters and hacks on hire, and through the great archway under one side of the hotel came nothing more exciting than a flock of sheep or a drove of cows once a month on market day. Philip led Mr. Bissell into the public bar.

"There is a Saloon, why so called I can't imagine," he said, "but it despises one and the drinks cost more. Besides here we get Eileen. Look at her."

The most dazzling blonde Mr. Bissell had ever seen, dressed in skin-tight black, was behind the bar, passing the time of day with two commercial travellers and a farmer. Catching sight of Philip she bent her swanlike bust forward over the counter and asked if he would have the usual. Philip said yes and would Mr. Bissell like the same, namely Old and Mild.

"I'll have Old and Bitter if it's all the same to you," said Mr. Bissell to the vision, only just stopping himself saying "Miss."

The vision drew two pints and as a mark of special favour did not put them on the counter, but saying to the commercial travellers and the farmer, "Well, ta-ta boys, I must be looking after my guests," brought them herself on a tin tray to Philip's table.

"Thanks, Eileen," said Philip paying. "This gentleman is the Headmaster of a school in London and he is coming down here with all his boys."

"Well, I'm sure!" said Eileen. "More of them evacuees, poor things, and really, Mr. Winter, what they have on their heads or in their heads as you might say makes you want to give Hitler a kick in the pants as the saying is. Three my married sister has, and the number of those nasty creatures they brought with them, well as I said to her, Gladys, I said, if there's a word I do not like it is lousy, but I wouldn't be doing those poor kids justice if I didn't say it. So she does them three times a week and I give her a hand and a nicer set of kids I must say you couldn't find. Greta, Gary and Gable their names are, not triplets as you might think, but hardly ten months between them and their mother, she's at the Vicarage, expecting again, poor thing, but always look on the sunny side I said to her and now your husband's at sea brighter days may be in store."

Philip saw that Mr. Bissell would shortly burst at Eileen's misconception of his young charges and hastened to inform her that Mr. Bissell's boys were not evacuees, but a school like Southbridge, only in London. The look of relief on Mr. Bissell's face on hearing this noble lie was so great that Philip could almost see the Recording Angel drop his expunging tear upon it.

"Come along then, Bissell," he said, "and we'll find Mr. Brown. Where is he, Eileen?"

Eileen said he was out in front talking to the beer, so

the two schoolmasters went out into the High Street, and there was Mr. Brown talking to the driver of a fine dray full of casks and bottles, the property of Messrs. Pilward and Sons Entire.

"Morning, gents," said Mr. Brown. "Beer's up a penny."

"That's bad," said Philip. "This gentleman is looking for a small cottage, Mr. Brown. Do you know if Maria Cottage is still to let?"

Mr. Brown said that rightly speaking it was and the key was at Adelina Cottage and he knew Miss Hampton was in because Bill had just taken the usual over, six gin, two French, two Italian, two whisky and a half-dozen syphons that was, as regular as clockwork once a week, besides what Miss Hampton bought extra and what she drank when she came in, and he'd been in the street himself ever since and would have seen Miss Hampton go out.

"Thank you," said Philip. "This is Mr. Bissell. He is the Headmaster of a London school and they are all coming down to us in case of air raids."

"I was at a London school myself," said Mr. Brown, looking at Mr. Bissell with interest. "My Grandfather, Grandfather Smith that was, had a tied house in Camden Town and when my mother, his daughter that was, married my father and came down here to manage because Grandfather Brown was beginning to fail, she used to send me up to keep him company for a bit when I was a nipper. And I went to the Old Sewerworks Road Board School. Elementary they call them now," he added explanatorily to Mr. Bissell, "but boys are boys call them what you like. Hope we'll see more of you, sir."

As this was clearly in the nature of a royal congé Philip moved on with Mr. Bissell, hoping that his colleague would not have resented the comparison of the Hosiers' Boys with a London Board School in the 'eighties. Could he have seen into Mr. Bissell's mind he would have found no resentment, only an intense bewilderment at a world where every value seemed to be wrong and an increasing wish to find a roof under which he and his wife could be safe from the turmoil and misunderstanding of this new life.

"Just across the road," said Philip encouragingly.

Mr. Bissell looked and saw a little Terrace of four two-storied cottages in mellow red brick, with a wide strip of grass lying between them and the road. They were surmounted by a stucco pediment on which the words "Wiple Terrace" 1820 were visible. Mr. Wiple, whose monument is to be seen in Southbridge Church, though rather the worse for wear and in parts illegible owing to the lettering being painted and not incised, was a small master builder of the village who had erected the terrace as a monument to his four daughters, Maria, Adelina, Louisa and Editha, calling each cottage after one of them. The property now belonged to Paul's College, who also owned the Vicarage and the living, but was always run in a very friendly way, the tenant of longest standing having a shadowy claim to pre-eminence. It was on this account that Miss Hampton, a spinster lady residing at Adelina Cottage with her friend Miss Bent, was in possession of the key of Maria Cottage which the Vicar's aunt, who had gone to join her husband at Gibraltar, wished to let furnished. Of the other two cottages, Louisa Cottage, residence of the late cricket coach at Southbridge School, was tenanted by the Gissings of whom mention has already been made, and Editha Cottage by the Vicar's other aunt who was a widow and would have Nottingham lace curtains, but otherwise will not I think, come into this story at all. Each cottage had a very narrow flower bed at the foot of its wall, divided from the footpath by low white posts with chains. Maria Cottage had a red door, Adelina a green, Louisa a yellow and Editha, owing to the insistence of the Vicar's other aunt, imitation oak grained with so many twiddles and such a liberal coat of varnish that all highbrow tourists stopped to exclaim at it and the Nottingham lace curtains as Perfect Period.

"That's the empty one," said Philip pointing out Maria. "We'll go and ask Miss Hampton for the key."

Mr. Bissell said it was quite Old-World.

At Adelina Cottage Philip rang the bell. The door was opened by a rather handsome woman with short, neatly curled grey hair, not young, in an extremely well-cut black coat and skirt, a gentlemanly white silk shirt with collar and tie, and neat legs in silk stockings and brogues, holding a cigarette in a very long black holder.

"Come in and have a drink," said Miss Hampton.

"Certainly," said Philip. "This is Mr. Bissell, the Headmaster of the Hosiers' Boys Foundation School, who is bringing his staff and boys down here and wants to find a cottage. Brown says you have Maria's key."

"French or Italian?" said Miss Hampton, who had already three-quarters filled four very large cocktail glasses, or indeed goblets, with gin. "Bent has just taken Smigly-Rydz out, so I might as well mix hers too. She won't be a moment."

"Is Smigly-Rydz a new dog?" said Philip. "It was Benes last winter."

"Gallant little Czecho-Slovakia!" said Miss Hampton in a perfunctory way. "But it's gallant little Poland now, so we've changed Schuschnigg's name; Benes's I mean, but one gets a bit mixed, everyone being gallant."

"And wasn't he Zog at Easter?" said Philip.

"So he was. Gallant little Albania," said Miss Hampton. "We bought him after Selassie died. We buried Selassie in the garden. Put it down, Philip, and you too, Mr. Bissell. That's the name, isn't it? I never forget names. So you keep a boy's school; and in London; interesting; much vice?"

Mr. Bissell spilt a good deal of his cocktail and remained tongue-bound.

"Come, come," said Miss Hampton filling his glass up to the brim again. "We're all men here and I'm doing a novel on a boys' school, so I might as well know something about it. I'm thinking of calling it 'Temptation at St. Anthony's'; good name, don't you think?"

"Excellent," said Philip.

Mr. Bissell was pretty strong on psychology and had for years been accustomed to explain certain facts to his pupils, drawing his examples first from botany, then from nature study, and later from outspoken serious talks, from which most of his boys had emerged with a very low opinion of their Headmaster's intellect, who could think them such chumps as he evidently did. He had also had many an interesting and intellectual exchange of views with other authorities at conferences, but his soul was extremely innocent and when he thought of exposing Mrs. Bissell to such a woman as Miss Hampton he heartily wished the war had never been invented. But he lacked the social courage to flee, and the strong cocktail was reacting unfavourably on his legs, so he looked at her, fascinated, and said nothing.

"Well, here's fun," said Miss Hampton, taking a deep drink of what Mr. Bissell saw with terror to be her second cocktail. "I study vice. Interesting. It's a thing you schoolmasters ought to know about. Prove all things, you know, and stick to what's good. Here comes Bent. She'll tell you about vice."

The door of the little sitting-room burst open and a black dog came in dragging Miss Bent after him. The dog, presumably Smigly-Rydz-Zog-Benes-Schuschnigg, was one of those very stout little dogs with a black shaggy coat, short in the leg, with a head as large as an elephant's and mournful eyes. Miss Bent, whom he had just taken round the village, was a rather flabby edition of Miss Hampton. Her coat and skirt of an indefinite tartan had obviously been made locally, her figure bulged in a very uncontrollable way, her short hair of a mousy colour looked as if she trimmed it with her nail-scissors, her stockings were cotton and rather wrinkled, her shoes could only be called serviceable, and she wore several necklaces.

"Come along, Bent," said Miss Hampton, handing the fourth cocktail to her friend. "Put it down. Here's Mr. Winter come for Maria's key. Mr. Bissell has a boys' school and I'm going to pick his brains for my new novel."

"Hampton sold one hundred and fifty thousand of her last novel in America," said Miss Bent, looking very hard at Mr. Bissell. "That was the one that was the Banned Book of the Month here. But of course one can't hope for that luck again. After all, other people must have their turn. I have a friend on the Banned Book Society Council and he says Esmé Bellenden's *Men of Harlech* will probably be the next choice. Have you read it?"

Mr. Bissell, helpless with confusion and cocktails, said he hadn't, and was Esmé Bellenden a man or a woman.

"I couldn't possibly say," said Miss Bent, "and what is more I don't suppose anyone could."

Miss Hampton who had been staring at Philip for some time said,

"Do my eyes deceive me, or are you in khaki?"

"Indeed I am," said Philip, "and only on twenty-four hours' leave, so if we can have Maria's key we will look at her now. I have to get back to camp and Mr. Bissell to London, and incidentally we both have to get back for lunch."

"Will you fight?" said Miss Bent in a deep voice.

"I haven't the faintest idea," said Philip. "It all depends where they send me. Probably I'll get stuck on Ilkley Moor, with or without a hat, till the war is over, doing gunnery courses."

"It is only a mockery to fight now," said Miss Bent, giving herself another cocktail. "You should have fought Italy, four years ago."

Philip, who was used to Miss Bent's ferocity, only smiled, but Mr. Bissell, in whose pacifist soul gin and French were doing their appointed work, took the wind out of Miss Bent's sails by saying:

"If we had fought Franco three years ago, all this wouldn't have happened."

"That," said Miss Bent, "is where you are entirely wrong. Civil war is quite, quite different. Besides Franco is a Churchman, or what corresponds to a Churchman in Spain, though under the Bishop of Rome who has *no* jurisdiction in England, so we should try to understand him. Have you ever been in Spain?"

Mr. Bissell had to admit that he hadn't.

"No more have I," said Miss Bent, "so it is absolutely no good arguing with you. We'll go and look at Maria."

Accordingly she took a large key off the mantelpiece, but Miss Hampton said before they went they must just look over Adelina, so the whole party inspected the rest of the cottage, which consisted of a kitchen behind the sitting-room, a narrow breakneck staircase, a bedroom overlooking the street almost entirely filled by a very large square flat divan which made Mr. Bissell back out of the room in terror, a little bedroom behind called the guest room, and a tiled bathroom, all spotlessly clean.

"Mrs. Dingle comes three times a week to clean," said Miss Hampton. "You can have her the three other days. She's a treasure. You can trust her with any amount of drink."

"She is Eileen's sister and a very nice woman," said Philip.

Then they all went next door and Miss Bent put the

key in the lock and opened Maria. The moment Mr. Bissell saw Maria he knew that in spite of the terrifying (and yet rather attractive) proximity of Miss Hampton and Miss Bent, this was where he and Mrs. Bissell could be happy. If the Vicar's aunt had been his own aunt and a nice aunt at that, she could not have made a house more after his heart's desire. He could almost have fancied himself back at 27 Condiment Road, E.48, except that no trams clanged down the road and there was a long garden instead of a little back yard. In the hall was the fumed oak umbrella stand with hooks above it. The sitting-room, carpeted up to the walls, had a sofa (or couch as Mr. Bissell preferred to call it) and two arm-chairs that made both ingress and egress impossible, the dining-room-kitchen had the same red-tiled linoleum as his own. Upstairs the bathroom he was pleased to see had a geyser of the same type as that at No. 27, so he knew it would not blow him up, or if it did, exactly when and how. The guest room had two narrow divan beds and a fumed oak chest-of-drawers. In the front bedroom, also carpeted up to the walls, were twin beds (not divan) and a fixed basin, a luxury he had always secretly coveted, and facing him, above the fireplace, was a coloured reproduction of the Van Gogh sunflowers. There was no doubt that the house must be his if he could afford it. So kind was Fate that Mr. Hammer, the estate agent, had just not gone out for his dinner, the rent was most reasonable, and within twenty minutes everything was settled, with the enthusiastic assistance of the ladies from Adelina Cottage.

Miss Hampton and Miss Bent were delighted with their new neighbour, the one hoping to pick his brains, the other to improve his political outlook, and offered to negotiate with Mrs. Dingle, to which end they kept Maria's key.

"Good-bye," said Miss Hampton, as they all left the

agent's office. "Bring your wife in for a drink any time. She doesn't wear trousers, does she?"

"Trousers?" said Mr. Bissell, who could hardly believe his ears.

"That's all right," said Miss Hampton. "Can't abide those women who go about in slacks trying to look like men."

"I suppose you mean Mrs. and Miss Phelps," said Philip.

"I do," said Miss Hampton, "and how Admiral Phelps can stand it I don't know. Women don't need trousers to drive motor ambulances, and the Southbridge ambulance is only the baker's van, 1936 Ford. Drove an ambulance all over the North of France myself in the War and never once thought of trousers. Good-bye. I must take Bent home. We'll hardly have time for a drink before lunch."

So saying she took a firm grasp of Smigly-Rydz's lead and walked away with Miss Bent. Philip, seeing the grocer's motor van passing, hailed it, asked if it was going up to the school, and within three minutes had landed himself and Mr. Bissell at Mr. Birkett's back door.

"We had given you up, Mr. Bissell," said Mrs. Birkett placidly, "but luckily it's a Monday-ish sort of lunch. You'll stay, Philip, won't you?"

"Many thanks," said Philip, "but I must get back to the Carters, so I'll say good-bye. Good-bye, Bissell, and good luck with Maria Cottage."

Mr. Birkett took him to the front door.

"You'll be seeing me here on and off when I get leave," said Philip. "My love to Geraldine, though I know it's wasted. If I turned up as a casualty with one leg and half my head blown away she would take far more interest."

"Do you remember Featherstonhaugh?" said Mr. Birkett irrelevantly.

"The Captain of Rowing in '37?" said Philip. "He went into the Nigerian Police, didn't he?"

"Yes. And he was coming home on leave and was in the *Lancashire* when she was torpedoed. He wasn't among the rescued. That's the beginning, Philip. Good-bye."

Mr. Birkett went back to lunch and Philip ran across to the Carters, who had also given him up for lost and welcomed him with rejoicing. Everard's joy that Mr. Bissell was not to live with him was unfeigned, and though Kate visibly regretted the housewifely turmoil that their coming would have meant, she was so fond of her husband that she bore it very well. The talk all through lunch was of school shop, in which the two men were still deeply engaged when the front door bell rang.

"That must be young Holinshed," said Everard.

"I remember giving young Holinshed C minus in his General Knowledge paper three years ago," said Philip, "and never did boy more deserve it. What does he want?"

"I don't know," said Everard. "He wrote to ask if he could come and see me as he was in trouble, which might mean anything. He's pretty sure of a mathematical scholarship in December if he sticks to it, and he may be worrying. If you aren't in a hurry, Philip, come and see him."

The two masters left the dining-room and went to Everard's study where young Holinshed was waiting. He shook hands with his housemaster and seeing a stranger in khaki said, "How do you do, sir."

"I'll give you C minus again, Holinshed, if you cut me," said Philip.

"Good lord, it's Mr. Winter," said young Holinshed. "I *am* sorry, sir. I didn't know you were in the army."

"Captain Winter, to be accurate," said Everard. "Anything wrong, Holinshed?"

Young Holinshed went bright red and looked so

wretched that Everard and Philip wondered again which of the usual scrapes a boy of seventeen had got into and how long it would take to explain to him that whatever he had done did not mean death and damnation.

"Would you rather talk to me alone?" said Everard, and Philip made as if to get up and go.

"It's nothing of that sort, sir," said Holinshed desperately. "It's this war, sir. I simply *can't* get into it."

At this unexpected confession the two masters' surprise and relief were so great that they could almost have laughed.

"Tell us about it," said Everard, "and I dare say Captain Winter can help a bit. Have you had any lunch?"

Young Holinshed admitted that he hadn't. Everard, leaving him with Philip, found Kate and put the situation before her. Kate was enchanted to do a little fussing about food, and in an incredibly short time a tray of lunch was brought into the study. Holinshed was told to get on with his lunch and talk at the same time if he could, as Mr. Winter had to get back to Sparrowhill.

"It's like this, sir," said Holinshed, pitching into his food with an appetite undimmed by mental agony and addressing himself to Everard. "I didn't tell you I tried to get into the navy in Munich week last year and I was awfully sick that they wouldn't have me, but they made it pretty clear that no outsiders were wanted. Of course I was only a kid then."

"Sixteen," said Everard to Philip, aside.

"Well, when they started the same racket over again, I felt I must do something or burst. And I've tried *everything*, sir, and no one will look at me. I've got terrific biceps," said Holinshed doubling his arm, "and I won the Half-mile in the sports and I've got my Certificate A in the O.T.C., but I might as well be a humpback for all the notice they take. All I get is 'Go away and play,' or 'Wait till you're wanted.' I simply *can't* go on being at school, sir. I tried to tell my pater about it, but he said something about my duty to stay on at school, and if anyone says duty to me again I'll go mad. Both the Fairweathers are serving, and you are in the army, Mr. Winter, and heaps of fellows I know are doing something and if I can't join in I'll go mad, sir, I really will. Couldn't you or Mr. Winter do something for me? I could easily say I was older than I am. I wouldn't mind being a private a bit."

As he finished his apologia Holinshed looked so wretched that Philip's mind suddenly went back to the summer when a boy called Hacker, now at Lazarus, and a certainty for the Craven and the Hertford, had offered him his much-loved chameleon as thanks for coaching before a scholarship exam. Before Philip kindly refused it he had seen in Hacker's face what he now saw in Holinshed's, and if he had had a Fairy Godmother's wand he would have given Holinshed a Colonel's commission in the Guards at once, sooner than see his misery. But that couldn't be, and now that his official connection with the School was so slight, perhaps not to be renewed for a long time, perhaps never again, Everard must handle the job. And he had to admit that Everard did it well, for after an hour's talk, during which young Holinshed had been allowed to interrupt, storm, rage and rebel as much as he liked, he gradually began to see a faint glimmering of reason on the following points:

(*a*) that the Navy had no use for untrained amateurs;

(*b*) that he was only seventeen;

(*c*) that the Army didn't at present want anyone till he was twenty;

(*d*) that if he got his scholarship in December, finished his school year, went on to the University and started his engineering course, or even, if circumstances were favourable, finished it, he would be every day and in every way better fitted to kill a great many enemies than he was at present.

"Thanks most awfully, sir," said Holinshed. "It's most awfully good of you to have bothered and I know I've been rather an ass. The only thing is, do you think there'll still be a war by then?"

Everard said he would do his very best to see that a bit was kept back for him and he had better come and see Mrs. Carter and have some tea. Kate was delighted to see a boy in the holidays as the house seemed so empty when they were all away, and young Holinshed, undeterred by a large lunch at two-thirty, ate an enormous tea at four o'clock and much fortified physically and mentally went off again.

"We'll have more trouble of that sort," said Everard. "About twenty of the senior boarders here and in the other Houses went quite mad last year in Munich week. Some of them went mad at home, which was very trying for their parents, and some did their going mad here, which was fairly trying for me. However they all simmered down in time and we heard no more about it."

Mr. Bissell was then announced. He had come to say good-bye to Mrs. Carter and thank her for her kind offer of hospitality. Kind Kate assured him that if by any chance Maria Cottage didn't suit him, or was uncomfortable for the first few days, he and his wife must use the House for meals, baths, or anything they liked. Mr. Bissell, while not quite liking the use of the word "bath" as applied to Mrs. Bissell, was none the less grateful.

"If you're going to the station, I'll run you into Barchester in my car," said Philip. "It will save you a change, and it's a pretty drive."

Mr. Bissell said he didn't mind. This being rightly

interpreted as an expression of great gratitude by the company, good-byes were said, and Mr. Bissell and Philip went to the front door, accompanied by Everard.

"It's been a pleasure to meet you, Carter," said Mr. Bissell, remembering his manners. "I'm sure we shall pull together. The world has deteriorated of late, and it's up to we schoolmasters to make it a better place for the boys."

Everard's eye met Philip's with extreme gravity as he said good-bye. With a sudden inspiration he told Mr. Bissell that he reciprocated his sentiments and then went indoors.

"I am so sorry," said Kate when he came back, "that the poor Bissells have no children. I wonder why?"

"I didn't ask, darling," said Everard, "but I'm sure you'll have it out of Mrs. Bissell an hour after you have made her acquaintance."

6

THE WORKING PARTY

•

In due course the Hosiers' Boys Foundation School came down to Southbridge, partly in motor coaches, partly in its parents' cars. Masters and boys were duly installed in their new quarters and got into their routine pretty quickly. By great good luck very few of the masters were married and those that had wives were able to find lodgings for them in the village, or in Barchester. Mr. and Mrs. Bissell took up their residence in Maria Cottage, with the enthusiastic help of Miss Hampton and Miss Bent. Miss Bent it was who showed them the crack in the scullery sink, but it was Miss Hampton who bearded the agent in his office and got it repaired at once, quite out of its turn. Mrs. Birkett helped her husband and the staff with her usual quiet efficiency and in a very short time the two schools had arrived at a working arrangement about the hours for games, the use of the masters' common room and other vital interests. The masters on both sides were on the whole heroic in concealing their feelings about the things they disliked in each other and it was only when goaded beyond bearing by Mr. Hopkins, the science master of the Hosiers' Boys who loudly proclaimed himself a Conscientious Objector although he was forty-five and limped, that Everard said to Mr. Birkett he had never quite known what common room meant before.

Everything being in tolerably good order, Mrs. Birkett and Mrs. Morland decided to go over one afternoon to Northbridge and call on the Keiths. They had heard, through Kate, that Mrs. Keith was not quite so well, and felt sorry for Lydia whose ardent spirit would, they knew, have liked to fling itself into uniform or some kind of war job.

Nothing could have been more lovely and more peaceful than the drive to Northbridge, in those early autumn days. The road skirted the river for a few miles, water meadows on one side and the downs on the other. On their lower slopes the stubble was pale gold, while from their grassy heights came the melancholy yet pleasing dissonance of sheep bells. Then, avoiding Barchester and a great loop of the river, the road mounted the downs, ran for a mile between wide stretches of thyme-grown turf where juniper bushes deployed their crooked armies of fantastic men and animals, with an infinitely wide, hazy distance encircling the world, and dropped again to the river. The short lime avenue that led to Northbridge Manor was beginning to turn yellow, and Michaelmas daisies shone in every amethystine colour below it. It seemed quite useless to speak of this peaceful beauty, which needs must make one think of other autumn fields where the earth was red, the trees broken, the harvest ravaged, so neither lady said anything about it.

Mrs. Morland, who was driving her own car, had to park it at some distance from the house, as the little circular sweep before the front door was already occupied by half a dozen cars.

"Oh, dear," said Mrs. Birkett, "it must be the Sewing Party to-day. I had forgotten that Mrs. Keith has it on Tuesdays. Well, it can't be helped. We'll go straight in."

As is so often the pleasant custom in the country the outer door of the house was kept open through the warmer months, and all friends were accustomed to turn the handle of the inner glass door and walk straight in. A wide passage ran through the house from front to back; and glass doors open at the further end showed a vista of a wide gravel walk between grass plots and a magnificent cedar, while on one side creepers were reddening on a brick wall. A sound of confused gabbling on the left showed that the Sewing Party was in full progress. Mrs. Birkett opened the drawing-room door and went in, followed by Mrs. Morland. A dozen ladies or thereabouts were sitting among billows of rather unpleasant-looking flannelette and art woollens, with Mrs. Keith in nominal command, but Mrs. Birkett was uncomfortably struck by the change in her friend since they had last met before Rose's wedding. There was no doubt that Mrs. Keith was far from well and Mrs. Birkett didn't like it.

"I'm afraid we've come on the wrong day," she said, "but this is the first free afternoon I've had since term began. You know Laura Morland. She is staying with me for the present."

Mrs. Keith said she remembered Mrs. Morland's nice boy that she had brought to tea once so well and how was he.

"He is very well, thank you," said Mrs. Morland, who had also noted Mrs. Keith's altered appearance and was impelled by nervous sympathy to talk far more than was necessary. "At least I suppose he is, but he is staying with hunting friends and doesn't write. Of course the hunting season has been over for some time, but they may be cubbing, though whether they cub as early as this, I don't know. It is extraordinary how little one knows about hunting when one doesn't have hunting friends or take much interest in it and has never ridden."

She looked rather wildly round her for corroboration.

"Can you sew?" said Lydia, suddenly surging up from a group of workers and speaking in a threatening way to Mrs. Morland, while she carelessly snapped a large pair of scissors.

Mrs. Morland said she could.

"Here's a pyjama leg, then," said Lydia. "I'm not much good at sewing myself, but I can cut out, which is more than most people have the sense to do," she added with a withering glance at the workers. "And if you want a needle and cotton, or pins, or anything, you'll find one in the basket on the table, unless Mrs. Gissing has taken them all."

With which words of help Lydia returned to her cutting out.

Mrs. Morland, after greeting several ladies who were known to her, made her way to the basket on the table. The basket was quite full of an empty needle-book, a large pincushion with no pins in it, and two or three dozen reels of cotton of different colours, all with long ends trailing from them and all of these trails hopelessly entangled. There were also half a dozen thimbles, some made for giants with large hands, others for undersized dwarfs. Mrs. Morland, always diffident, stood hovering over the basket, the pyjama leg dangling from her hand.

"Mrs. Morland, isn't it," said a lady who was sitting in a very comfortable arm-chair sewing, though owing to the size and fatness of the arms of her chair she was pinioned as it were and could only sew by holding her work high in the air.

Mrs. Morland said it was.

"I am Gloria Gissing," said the lady, a dark, ravaged, intense creature. "You wouldn't remember me."

"No, I wouldn't quite," said Mrs. Morland, always truthful. "Was it somewhere we met?"

Mrs. Gissing laughed in a profound way.

"Do you remember," she said, "a cocktail party at Johns and Fairfield?"

Mrs. Morland cast her mind back to several cocktail parties at the house of the well-known publishers with whom, despite their blandishments and her refusal to listen to them, she had always been on excellent terms, and asked if Mrs. Gissing meant the one where everyone was so drunk.

"You were talking," said Mrs. Gissing, ignoring this question, "to a man."

She said the word man in such a way that all conversation ceased and every worker looked up from her sewing.

"I expect I was," said Mrs. Morland, "unless it happened to be a woman. Were you there?"

She put this question with such anxious if idiotic interest that Mrs. Gissing, while finding her almost half-witted, could not suspect any malice.

"Yes, I was there, with my husband," she said. "I expect you know him. We live in Wiple Terrace."

Mrs. Moreland said she didn't *quite* know Wiple Terrace and was it S.W. 7.

"No, no," said Mrs. Gissing, laughing even more profoundly, "in Southbridge. Oscar is in Dante-Technifilms. They have moved down here from London. I knew I had seen you somewhere. My boy Fritz is down here too. He is on the production side of course. You must come in and have a drink and bring your husband."

"Well, I can't exactly *bring* him," said Mrs. Morland with the air of one making a concession, "because he is dead, and I am not living in my own house at present, but if I could find any pins or a needle I could start on this leg. Lydia thought you might have some."

Mrs. Gissing, saying with her contralto laugh that she had a fatal attraction for pins, rummaged about in her chair and produced a small pincushion quite well stocked which she handed to Mrs. Morland, who thanked her, sat down as far away as possible, and began industriously to pin the seam of the leg together.

"Here's a needle," said Lydia, who managed to keep a firm eye on all the party. "You'll need one. And Miss

Hampton will give you some of her cotton. This is Mrs. Morland, Miss Hampton."

The rest of the party, mostly nice local people who might just as well have been anyone else, were again silent. Every one of them had read at least one of Mrs. Morland's and one of Miss Hampton's books, in most cases one that was in a sixpenny edition, and they all hoped to hear a clash of intellects and really literary conversaton.

"Glad to meet you," said Miss Hampton. "Been wanting to meet you for some time. You and I do the same sort of job, so I gather from Mrs. Birkett."

"Well, I've never been a Banned Book of the Month, I'm afraid," said Mrs. Morland, "and I never could be. My publisher wouldn't like it, and I'm afraid I'm not up to it."

"Bah!" said Miss Hampton vigorously. "Banned Books! Why do you think I write them?"

Mrs. Morland said she had always wondered.

"Four nephews to support," said Miss Hampton. "And you have four sons, Mrs. Birkett tells me. They take a bit of supporting. They are all off my hands now, two in the Army, one in the Navy and one in the Consular Service, but it took a bit of doing."

Upon this the two celebrated authoresses fell into a heart to heart conversation about boys which lasted without a break till Miss Hampton wanted a pair of scissors. Although Mrs. Keith provided several pairs for the working party they always became absorbed during the afternoon, and by tea-time there was usually a single pair which was passed from hand to hand like the eye of the Graiae. On the present occasion the scissors were run to earth in the folds of the hostess's work, which was not considered quite fair, and Miss Hampton continued the story of her fourth nephew, the one in the Consular Service in Spain, while Mrs. Morland, an excellent listener in spite of her own sons and their doings, sewed industriously away, running and felling.

"I say," said Lydia, coming round on a tour of inspection, "you must be ready for that other pyjama leg. Here it is."

Mrs. Morland took it and compared it in a puzzled way with the leg on which she had been working.

"You've sewed your leg up all the way round, Mrs. Morland," said Lydia pityingly. "Give it to Miss Hampton and come and talk to Mother."

Mrs. Morland obediently went across to her hostess and listened with real kindness and interest to what she had to say about her married son Robert and his three children, her daughter Kate Carter and her younger son Colin. As Mrs. Morland saw the Carters nearly every day she was able to give Mrs. Keith the latest news of Master Bobbie Carter. That phenomenal child had just cut another tooth and his grandmother enjoyed herself very much telling Mrs. Morland the approximate dates of every tooth of all her children and her other grandchildren. While this entrancing conversation was going on, tea had been brought in on a trolley by Palmer the parlourmaid whose expression clearly showed what she thought of sewing parties in her drawing-room. Mrs. Keith called Palmer to her side.

"Oh, Palmer," she said, "Mr. Keith tells me that there was a bright light in one of the maids' windows when he came in last night from the garage. I don't know whose it was, but you must be careful, or we shall have the police down on us."

Palmer stiffened all over.

"I'm sure it wasn't me, madam," she said, with a good servant's immediate reaction to any criticism of the staff, namely to take the criticism as directed especially and venomously to herself and angrily rebut it. "And it couldn't have been cook nor the girls madam, as they was in bed quite early and cook passed the remark to me, only this morning while we were drinking a cup of tea, that Mr. Keith was very late home last night and banged the garridge door so loud she thought it was the air raids."

Having thus established the good servant's second reaction, namely the solidarity, surpassing that of any trade union, which makes her shelter any other member of the staff with lies, if necessary, of the most unblushing incredibility, Palmer became even more rigid and stood over her mistress in a very unpleasant way. Mrs. Keith suddenly looked very grey and tired.

Lydia, who appeared to be like Niobe all ears (as Mrs. Morland subsequently said when relating the incident to Mrs. Birkett who had been at the other end of the room talking to the Vicar's wife and had not heard this encounter, or, said Mrs. Morland, was it Argus she meant) suddenly materialised at her mother's elbow.

"It doesn't matter whose window it was, it mustn't happen again," said Lydia, still brandishing her cutting-out scissors as a kind of wand of office. "I did all the black-out myself and I know it's all right, so if anyone shows a light, it's their own fault."

"Well, I'm sure Miss Lydia," said Palmer, retiring to her third line of whining self-justification, "no one could be more careful than I am. When I go to bed I turn on the light and first thing I do is to go straight to the window and draw the curtains the way you said, and there's not a chink of light showing, because I asked cook to oblige me by going out and having a look and she said if there had been a corpse in the room it couldn't have been darker."

Lydia, entirely unmoved by cook's remarkable appreciation of a good black-out, said she had told Palmer that the black-out must be done every night before lighting-up time and if it wasn't she would put blue bulbs into the maids' bedrooms.

Palmer, with a face that foreboded at least twenty-four hours' sulks, said the girls had quite enough to do as it was and their bedrooms were all at the back of the house, so no one could see. With which piece of reasoning she scornfully collected the tea-things and took the trolley away.

"I don't know why it is," said Mrs. Morland, "that so many people think air raids can only come in at the front windows. One ought to be just as careful at the back, and after all a lot of people's houses point the wrong way. I mean if the back of your house is east you ought to be particularly careful because one never knows."

The Vicar's wife said the danger of unscreened lights was that they could be seen by enemy aircraft above, a statement so eminently reasonable as to paralyse all further conversation on the subject.

"I wanted to ask you about our next week's work, Mrs. Keith," she said. "The billetting officer tells me that the evacuees have all got nightgowns now, but a lot of them will be needing frocks and knickers. I thought we might be getting on with some, if Lydia has a pattern."

"We've got plenty of green stuff and of blue too," said Mrs. Keith. "Lydia, where are those two frocks we made?"

Lydia went over to some neatly stocked shelves and produced two frocks, one the colour of dead spinach, the other a dull peacock blue, saying they were a bit Liberty but Mrs. Foster, the head of the Personal Service parties, had sent the material over from Pomfret Towers so they might as well use it.

The Vicar's wife examined and approved the frocks which she found very satisfactory except that the necks, she said, wanted arting up a bit, as the frocks were so very plain in cut. To this end she advised a little embroidery, something like a few flowers or leaves done in floss silk. She had at home, she said, some transfers that she could iron off on to the necks of the frocks when Lydia had cut them out. To this Mrs. Keith and Lydia agreed and the party began to break up.

"Stay a minute," said Mrs. Keith to Mrs. Birkett and Mrs. Morland. "I haven't seen you at all."

Miss Hampton shook hands warmly with Mrs. Morland and pressed her to visit Adelina Cottage. Any one of her nephews, or all of them, might turn up at any moment on leave, she said, but there was always a spot of drink somewhere. Mrs. Gissing, coming up to Mrs. Keith, said she felt too frightfully *de drop,* but her husband was coming to fetch her on his way back from the Studios, so might she wait. Mrs. Keith looked very faint and said of course and would Lydia ring for some sherry. Lydia did as she was asked and then accompanied Miss Hampton to the front door. Mrs. Birkett, who knew her well, saw that she was boiling up with rage against Mrs. Gissing who would undoubtedly tire and exhaust her mother, but was controlling her feelings in a way that she would have been incapable of six months earlier. Palmer with deep displeasure brought in the sherry which Mrs. Gissing quaffed, for no other word can express her sweeping manner of handling a glass, with abandon.

"And now I want to know all about your wonderful boy, Mrs. Keith," she said.

"He is very well. He has cut a new tooth," said Mrs. Keith.

"A wisdom tooth, I suppose," said Mrs. Gissing, "at his age."

"If you mean his father, he cut all his wisdom teeth years ago," said Mrs. Keith, "and then had to have them all out, so wasteful, but Nature doesn't seem to have got used to teeth yet. You would think that after so many thousand or is it million years of evolution she would know that we don't need wisdom teeth, but nothing seems to teach her."

"But I didn't know he was married," said Mrs. Gissing. "Such a *nice* boy."

It had become evident to Mrs. Birkett that her hostess and Mrs. Gissing were at cross purposes, so she intervened.

"I think, Helen," she said to Mrs. Keith, "that Mrs. Gissing is talking about Colin."

"I really forget if he cut his wisdom teeth or not," said Mrs. Keith in a very tired voice.

"It is Mrs. Keith's little grandson who has cut a tooth," said Mrs. Birkett to Mrs. Gissing. "Her daughter's little boy. Colin is somewhere in England with his gunners."

"What a pity—that *nice* boy," said Mrs. Gissing.

"I don't think it a pity at all," said Mrs. Keith, almost sharply. "He has been in the Territorials for a long time and I must say he looks wonderfully well, better than he has for months, for the life in London didn't really suit him. And there are a lot of other lawyers in his regiment, so they get on very well."

"But the WASTE," said Mrs. Gissing.

No one answered.

"You must be thankful that your boy isn't old enough to be conscripted, Mrs. Morland," said Mrs. Gissing, with a hiss on the "s" of conscripted that caused her hearers to shudder.

Mrs. Morland, who was very truthful, said she supposed she was, and paused.

Mrs. Gissing, helping herself to another glass of sherry, said if only all young men refused to fight and we gave back all our colonies to their rightful owners, the world would be a different place. With this sentiment all her hearers agreed, though not quite in the sense she intended. Mrs. Keith felt so unwell that she could not argue the point. Mrs. Birkett, who had no sons, kept silence, feeling that a woman with no sons to lose could not sit in judgment upon a woman who had a son, however disagreeable he might be. Mrs. Morland realised that the defence of anything that she and her friends cared about was in her hands. Heartily did she wish that Lydia were there to do reckless battle, but Lydia did not reappear. Mrs. Morland knew herself to be at her worst in a crisis. To be flustered, as she always was by people she didn't like, made her talk wildly and at far too great length, and she knew it. Looking madly about her she collected her wits for a reply: It was true that of her four sons the eldest was on an exploration expedition in Central South America and was in any case well over the present military age, the second was with his regiment in Burma, and the third a professional sailor, while Tony, her youngest, was a good eighteen months under military age, but even because of that she felt that it would seem like boasting to speak of what they were doing, or not yet able to do.

"Well," she said apologetically, "I don't see how one can stop them. And of course if one is in the Navy there one is, and it's much the same with the Army, or exploring where you get no news for six months, and Tony really likes the O.T.C. At least he didn't much like it the first time, but after that he met a sergeant-major in the regular army who swore more dreadfully than anyone he had ever heard which made him feel a real interest. I'm sure your boy must feel the same."

As she spoke she heard herself getting sillier and sillier, but was quite unable to do anything about it. Mrs. Birkett and Mrs. Keith exchanged glances of surreptitious amusement at their friend's flounderings.

"Luckily my boy Fritz is in a reserved occupation," said Mrs. Gissing, making up her lips again after the sherry.

"Is he a dentist?" said Mrs. Morland in a final outburst of trying to be intelligent and do her best.

"Films," said Mrs. Gissing in a voice that implied, "my good woman."

To this there was no answer. A glacial silence, to which Mrs. Gissing appeared quite insensible, descended upon the room, while the three other ladies cudgelled their brains in vain for anything to say. To their great relief and surprise Lydia then came back, bringing Miss Hampton with her.

"I say, Mrs. Gissing," said Lydia in what her mother distinguished as a peculiar voice, "your husband rang up to say he was stuck on a film or something, so Miss Hampton is going to take you back."

"Must get back at once," said Miss Hampton. "Red Lion opens at six and it's that now. Can't keep Bent waiting."

With which stalwart words she hustled Mrs. Gissing out of the room and into her car before that lady knew what was happening.

"Lydia!" said Mrs. Keith accusingly, but in a very affectionate way.

"Well, I had to do something, Mother," said Lydia. "I couldn't have that ghastly spy boring you to death till her awful husband came and wanted a drink. So I told Miss Hampton and we rang up the film studio and told Mr. Gissing that his wife had gone home."

"But you'll be found out!" said Mrs. Morland dramatically. "They will compare notes and discover that you told a lie!"

"I must say," said the unregenerate Lydia, "that it was rather fun telling that one. I didn't know I had it in me. Mother, do you think you ought to rest before dinner?"

But Mrs. Keith, who had recovered a little since her horrid visitor had left, said she thought not, but she would lie down on the sofa if no one minded. So she did, and Lydia produced a hot-water bottle almost at once and put a light shawl over her mother, while Mrs. Morland thought how nice Lydia was and Mrs. Birkett, who had known her intimately for several years, thought how admirably she was teaching herself to be kind and thoughtful in a gentle way; for a hearty indiscriminate good nature there had never been any lack.

The four ladies talked very peacefully for half an hour about families and friends. Mrs. Keith asked Mrs. Morland if she was writing a new book. At first Mrs. Morland drew in her horns and retreated into her shell, for as we well know she had no opinion of her own work at all. After much pressure, applied with genuine interest, she said she was trying to work on a new story, centreing as usual round the dressmaking establishment of Madame Koska, but her great difficulty was to know what nationality to make her distressed heroine. The head villain, who had taken a job as commissionaire at Madame Koska's shop in Mayfair the better to spy upon the English aristocracy, was of course a member of the Gestapo, but the heroine, a countess of exquisite form, face and breeding, had to be a refugee and the trouble was, said Mrs. Morland, that refugees were as bad as chameleons and kept on being someone else. On being pressed for an explanation she said she had begun by having a Czecho-Slovakian, but had been obliged to change her for an Albanian and was at the moment turning her into a Pole, which, she added, was extremely difficult because their names were all alike except Paderewski and in any case she would probably be out of date before the book was published and one couldn't turn her into a Belgian, or a Swiss, or whatever the next refugees were going to be, when the proofs had been passed. And, she added, with deep meaning, and in a slow emphatic voice, she knew Whose fault it was.

"Whose fault, Mrs. Morland?" said Lydia eagerly.

"Do you know that pair of stockings with black marks on them that I sometimes wear?" said Mrs. Morland to Mrs. Birkett.

Mrs. Birkett said she was afraid she didn't.

"You must, Amy," said Mrs. Morland, "because you noticed them. All speckled down the front."

"Do you mean those stockings you had on the evening the Crawleys came to dinner and I thought you must have put them on by mistake?" said Mrs. Birkett.

"And what evening was that?" said Mrs. Morland, so portentously that all her hearers and especially Lydia felt that they would burst with so much mystery.

Mrs. Birkett said with a tinge of impatience that it was the evening the Crawleys came.

"And the day the *Royal Oak* was sunk," said Mrs. Morland.

She then looked round her as if confident that everyone must now understand everything. But Mrs. Keith, who was never very good at understanding things and had the dogged character of the rather stupid, said One thing at a time and what Lydia had asked was Whose fault it was, though what the fault was about she could not now remember.

"It all hangs together," said Mrs. Morland, "and I was just explaining to Lydia about my stockings. You see, Tony and I were in France when all this trouble began and most luckily I read in someone else's old *Times* that there was going to be a railway strike in England, so I said really if there were going to be a strike we had better be at home. So we came back in great discomfort and crossness and of course when we got back the strike was off. Then Tony and I went down to High Rising and did the black-out which was very difficult because my cook Stoker doesn't approve of it and then the last straw came."

She stopped and looked vengefully into the distance.

"Yes, Laura," said Mrs. Birkett encouragingly.

Mrs. Morland started, tucked a strand of hair behind one ear and began in a very noble narrative style.

"I had blacked out everything," she said, "except the kitchen and scullery, because Stoker said if Mr. Reid at the shop was the Air Raid Warden we were all right. It was a fine evening and I hadn't drawn the curtains yet and I waited to take a sixpenny bottle of ink and some manuscript from my bedroom where they really had no business down to the drawing-room. I began carrying them downstairs, but the landing was rather dark. I was just going to turn the light on when I suddenly remembered that the curtains weren't drawn. So I determined to go on, very carefully. But I stumbled a little, just where that bit of carpet is always getting loose at the corner and the ink bottle fell on to the floor, and the cork came out, and a shower of ink spirted over the floor and over my stockings."

She paused and glared at her audience with the expression of the Delphic Sybil.

"I can forgive a great deal," said Mrs. Morland. "Air raids are air raids and there they are, and Stoker got the ink off the floor, but there is one thing I shall never forgive and that is that pair of stockings. It isn't as if I had a pair on with darns in the heels. They happened to be new, and that is what I cannot forgive. And when I think who it is that deliberately made me spill ink on my stockings and makes it impossible to know who will be a refugee at any given moment, you will understand my feelings."

By this time Mrs. Morland had, by her remorseless logic, left all her friends in various degrees of bewilderment. Mrs. Keith had long ago given up any attempt to follow the argument and was thinking about the sheet that had come home from the laundry with a corner torn. Mrs. Birkett was thinking that they really must be going soon. But Lydia, scenting high romance, could hardly contain her interest.

"Do you mean, Mrs. Morland, that you are always going to wear those stockings when anything awful happens like London being blown up, or Peace?" she asked.

But her question was never answered. The drawing-room door was opened, a kind of vision of men in khaki struggling with Palmer was seen, and two uniformed figures appeared, one of whom came quickly forward.

"Colin!" Lydia shrieked at the top of her voice, and flung herself into the arms of her brother.

Colin gave her a hearty hug and putting her firmly aside went to his mother on the sofa. Mrs. Keith, suddenly looking much younger, sat up and greeted her son with joy. Mrs. Birkett was also delighted to see him, for he had been a junior master at Southbridge School for a term a few years ago. Mrs. Morland was added to the party and a happy confusion reigned.

Meanwhile the second arrival stood by the drawing-room door, smiling in an amused way at the family hubbub. Colin was explaining to his mother that he had wanted to arrive unannounced, but Palmer had not seen eye to eye with him, which accounted for the fracas at the drawing-room door.

"If I hadn't had Noel with me," he said, "I think she'd have won. Where is Noel? Has he gone to help Palmer in the pantry and soothe her ruffled spirits?"

"Indeed I haven't," said Noel Merton indignantly, "but I felt that the homeless wanderer should not intrude on the family circle in this moment of reunion. How are you, Mrs. Keith?"

He came over to the sofa and kissed Mrs. Keith's hand, a gesture which filled his friend Lydia with mingled admiration and contempt.

"Hullo, Noel," she said. "*I* know what's wrong with you. You're an officer. Why didn't you tell me? I thought you were much too old to be in the army."

"So I was," said Noel Merton, "but a friend of mine

said that my quick mind and trained intelligence, not to speak of my distinguished bearing, would benefit any army. So he got me a second lieutenant's uniform and here I am."

Everyone knew that Noel was doing himself less than justice, but judged it more tactful to let him tell his story in his own way. After a few moments' talk Mrs. Birkett collected Mrs. Morland and took her away. Mrs. Keith evidently wanted to have a motherly talk with Colin, so Noel, disregarding Colin's piteous signs of distress, carried Lydia off to the library.

"First of all," said Lydia, stopping and looking at him with a housekeeper's eye, "do you want to stay the night?"

Noel said he would like it of all things if not inconvenient.

"Don't be silly," said Lydia severely. "You know it'd always be convenient. I will just go and tell them about a room for you—you can have Robert's that we keep for him—and dinner. I shan't be a second."

She strode resolutely towards the kitchen. Noel Merton, left alone, stood by the fire in amused and faintly melancholy meditation. A few years ago, when he first became acquainted with the Keith family, he had mapped out his career very neatly for himself. He was doing very well at the bar and intended to do better. He had a large circle of friends among whom he was much in request for dinners, dances, week-ends, shooting, yachting, and the hundred agreeable activities that life offers to a rising young man with pleasant manners. Marriage, he had decided, was not in his line, and he infinitely preferred to amuse himself with charming married women who could keep the shuttlecock of heart-whole flirtation briskly flying. There had been a moment when his heart was gently attracted by Lydia's sister Kate, but the attraction had been so slight that it died in the bud at the moment when he found that

Everard Carter was in love with her, and now, in spite of his admiration for Kate's sterling qualities and sweet temper, he was very thankful that he had stopped when he did, for to be bored was no part of his scheme. At that time Lydia had been an extremely bouncing and irrepressible schoolgirl, and why these two so very different creatures had become great friends nobody could understand. Mrs. Keith, seeing her younger daughter, still in her revolting school uniform, carry off the much-sought-after barrister as captive of her bow and spear, had been considerably flustered and prophesied woe. But as she really minded nothing very much except novelty, her apprehensions soon wore off, the more so as her younger son Colin who was reading law in Noel Merton's rooms liked him very much and often brought him down to Northbridge Manor.

Here it had become Noel's custom to pass a good deal of his time with Lydia with whom he walked, played tennis, and had endless discussions about life and literature. Lydia, for whom life had very few fine shades and literature meant the books she happened to like, began to apprehend through Noel that there were other worlds where her violent and downright methods might not pass muster, where there were values of which she was ignorant. Like many wilful natures she could be very docile where she was conscious of meeting her match, and had a natural quickness of wit that told her what to copy. Noel had never deliberately tried to alter or improve his young friend, liking her very well indeed as she was, but from time to time he was amused and a little touched to see Lydia modifying her uncompromising manner of speech and judgment by something he had said, or repeating as an original and striking thought something he had told her.

As for being in uniform he was nearly as surprised as Lydia. Nothing had been further from his thoughts when he last stayed with the Keiths in August. Looking at his age and his entire want of military qualifications he saw nothing for it but to go on as he was and make the best of it. Various applications for employment in the fighting services had led nowhere and he was reduced to frank envy of Colin who, like Philip Winter a Territorial, had gone into camp about Bank Holiday and had remained in the army ever since, enjoying himself on the whole and putting on a stone and three inches round the chest. Then suddenly a highly placed friend had sent for Noel and in a short mysterious interview had asked him if he would feel like doing some Intelligence Work. Noel said he would like it very much and within three days he found himself a Second Lieutenant. Upon this he ordered a very good British warm from his tailor and went off to a place whose name was never mentioned (though quantities of people knew where it was) to do a very severe intensive course with twenty or thirty other temporary subalterns many of whom turned out to be personal friends in various walks of life. From this course he had just emerged with a week's leave, and meeting Colin Keith in town, also on leave, had accepted his invitation to come down to Northbridge for a night.

Although Northbridge Manor was outwardly unchanged he was conscious of a difference. His welcome was as warm as ever, the garden lay steeped in sunset autumn peace, Lydia was arranging for his comfort but he was not altogether part of it. He had a journey before him, whither and for what purpose he did not yet know, whether to some place overseas or to an office in Whitehall or elsewhere, whether a voyage for the body or for the mind. But as soon as the traveller knows he must be gone, he has already left the place that has been his home, and though Noel was in his own country and among old friends, he felt that a thin sheet of glass was between him and them. There would be much in his new life that he could not share with them and a part of him would from now onwards have reticences where he had been used to speak very much at his ease. Then he told himself that he was being fanciful, but he knew that he wasn't, and was very glad when Lydia crashed back into the room.

"I *am* glad you and Colin have come," said Lydia. "Mother hasn't been very well and it will cheer her up like anything. It seems frightfully funny you being a Second Lieutenant and Colin a Captain though."

Noel said he had every hope of turning into a Captain before long, as he was going to meet all sorts of people who simply couldn't speak to anything as low as a subaltern.

"Will you vanish into the unknown like Richard Hannay and then turn up at Constantinople or somewhere?" said Lydia. "I'll write to you all the time. Where are you going?"

Noel explained that he didn't know and even if he did he wouldn't be allowed to say, but if Lydia would write to his chambers her letters would all be faithfully passed on.

Lydia was silent for a moment and then asked how he thought her mother was looking.

"Not so well as I'd like," said Noel without hesitation, knowing that Lydia required facts.

"Nor as I'd like either," said Lydia. "Dr. Ford says she must be very careful. We had a ghastly time with evacuee children for a month. Six children and two teachers. I think they really made Mother so ill, because they worried her so."

"Poor Lydia," said Noel.

"Poor Mother, you mean," said Lydia. "But a most fortunate thing happened which was that all the children were so revolting, and the teachers, who were called Miss Drake and Miss Potter but they called each other Draky and Pots, did nothing but walk about the garden with their arms round each other's waists, that Dr. Ford went and bullied the Billeting Officer like anything and they were all moved to Southbridge. Oh Noel, I *am* pleased to see you."

"So I am," said Noel, "as pleased as anything. And I hope you won't get any more evacuees."

Lydia said not, because her father had offered to take troops if Barchester was too full and had said he would rather have a hundred of the Barsetshire Light Infantry camping in the grounds, with the run of the squash court, tennis court, and billiard room, than one child or one teacher.

"It took three coats of whitewash and two coats of paint to make the rooms where the children were not smell of child," said Lydia, "not to speak of the teachers being so horrid to Palmer that she nearly gave notice."

"I expect Palmer was pretty horrid to them too," said Noel.

"She was," said Lydia, "I am glad to say. But it made Mother have a bad heart attack, because Miss Drake and Miss Potter came and were very red in the drawing-room."

"Red?" said Noel.

"Red, Communist, you know what I mean," said Lydia. "Being very rude and arguing about Russia. I was over at the Vicarage helping them to make marrow jam or it wouldn't ever have happened. Would you like a drink before dinner?"

Noel said it was his heart's desire. Lydia mixed cocktails very professionally and handed one to Noel.

"I believe I ought to say 'All the best' or something in that line as I'm an officer," said Noel, "but it goes against the grain. Here is to your health."

"And to yours," said Lydia. But instead of drinking she paused and set her glass down again. "Noel," she said very earnestly, "could you tell me something?"

"Short of betraying my country's secrets I'll tell you anything," said Noel.

"Do you think Mother is going to die?" said Lydia.

Used as Noel was to his dear Lydia's straightforward ways, he was taken aback by her question. He had no particular experience of people with hearts, but seeing Mrs. Keith after an interval he had been struck and indeed horrified by the change in her appearance. His first thought was to tell a thumping lie and say he had never seen her look better; his second thought was that Lydia believed in him so much that he could not dare to wreck that belief by a lie which she would undoubtedly detect; and between the two he hesitated for a fraction of a second too long.

"Don't say anything," said Lydia. "Anyway it's a good thing I'm here to take care of her. And I've made her let me do the house accounts and Father lets me do the estate accounts and go round the place with him, and Robert tells me about the family finance, so I can be a bit of help. I did think it would be fun to go as a V.A.D. to the Barchester Hospital with Delia Brandon and Geraldine, but one can't expect to have fun all the time, can one? You'd better go and get washed for dinner now."

Noel did as he was told, as indeed most people did when Lydia took their interests in hand. While he was washing his hands and hunting for the clean handkerchief which, together with his other scanty effects, Palmer had unpacked and hidden with as much virtuosity as if he had brought two cabin trunks, he reflected again upon Lydia. That Lydia, the domineering, the devil-may-care, the rebel from domesticity, should have turned into a housekeeper, a thoughtful guardian of her mother's frail health, a useful companion to her father, was a change for which, in spite of his fondness for her, he was not at all prepared. He could only suppose that seeing her again after an interval in which so much had happened had made him notice what had been slowly going on for some time.

Although he could think a few things more revolting than to be a V.A.D. with that dull Geraldine Birkett at the Barchester Hospital, he quite realised that Lydia had made a considerable sacrifice in giving up her plans. The more he thought of her general conduct the more admirable it appeared to him. He stood in a trance, the damp towel in his hands, considering the change from the Lydia who had so ungracefully taken possession of him a few years ago to the Lydia who appeared to be thinking sensibly and affectionately of the needs of others, and not of new and romantic friends, but of her parents, a creature which few of his younger friends considered as human in any way. And yet the same violent, confiding Lydia. The gong sounded and he went downstairs.

Mr. Keith had got back by this time and was quietly delighted to see Colin and had a friendly greeting for Noel. He had meant to give up the solicitor's office in Barchester altogether that summer, leaving it in Robert's capable hands, and retire to the management of his little estate, but the turmoil of the world had made it impossible. Robert who had been taking on various important unpaid jobs in the town and the county found himself needed for many more, and could not give the necessary time to the office. One of the younger men had, like Colin, gone into camp with the Territorials in August and remained there, another had been called up for the Air Force, so Mr. Keith had gone back to his work and made himself useful in every department. At the same time his bailiff, a retired naval man, had vanished at the call of the Admiralty, and he found himself with more work than he ever thought at his age to be doing. When Lydia said she helped with the accounts she was understating. The bailiff had been a great friend of hers, and with him she had learnt in the last two years all that he could teach her about the farm and the men, so when he left she informed her father that she would look after everything, which with the help of the head cowman, to whom the bailiff had bequeathed her as a valuable legacy, she did. Mr. Keith was at first nervous about the experiment, but finding that Lydia was perfectly pleased to discuss things with him, he allowed her to go her own way, though whether he could have stopped her is another question.

To Noel's amusement the earlier part of dinner was devoted to a discussion of cows and winter kale, upon which subject Lydia imparted her views with great freedom. After that the conversation ran upon books, a concert or two that Lydia had heard in town, a little legal business on which Mr. Keith asked his younger son's views with pleasant pride, and the continued horribleness of Miss Pettinger, who was now housing the Hosiers' Girls Foundation School and being as overbearing to their very nice Headmistress as she could possibly be.

No one wanted to hear the nine o'clock news, for as Mrs. Keith truly said one could read all the disgusting things that had happened in *The Times* next day, and it was better to be depressed in the morning than at night.

"And," she said, "you *read* the paper, instead of hearing those ladylike young men talking from Bangor or wherever they are."

Lydia said she expected if *The Times* could speak it would have a voice like that but luckily it couldn't.

Colin said he had taken to the *Daily Express* and found it wonderfully soothing because he now knew exactly what to think and needn't ever be broadminded again.

"Quite right too," said Lydia. "No one ought to be broadminded now. I'm not."

No one contradicted her.

Mr. Keith said he could bear anything, even the Income Tax, if only *The Times* would stop fiddling about with the Crossword Puzzle and put it in its proper place, down in the right-hand corner of page three or possibly page five. And as for putting it in that small print, he would take in the *Daily Telegraph* if it went on. One must have something to cling to in this world of shifting values, he said, and the Crossword appeared to him to be essential. In this he was heartily supported by the company, with the exception of Mrs. Keith who had never yet succeeded in grasping the principle of the crossword.

At about ten o'clock Lydia said she was going to bed if no one minded, as she had to go round the farm next morning before she went to Barchester to a Red Cross Meeting and then on to lunch with Mrs. Brandon at Pomfret Madrigal about a sewing party. Noel escorted her to the drawing-room door.

"I just wanted to ask you," said Lydia, "if you've got everything you want. I've got some spare toothbrushes if you didn't bring one. I don't suppose I'll see you again if you are going up with Colin as I shall have my breakfast early."

"I have got a toothbrush, though Palmer thinks poorly of it," said Noel, "and has hidden it behind my sponge instead of planting it bravely in the toothbrush vase, or whatever it is called. But thank you all the same. You are as good as Kate at making people comfortable."

"I *couldn't* be," said Lydia, genuinely surprised.

"Well you are," said Noel, but did not add and a great deal more amusing, because he knew that Lydia's loyalty to Kate would resent such a remark. "And I'll come down to your early breakfast if you'll tell me when."

"No, honestly don't," said Lydia. "I never know how early I'll be and you ought to sleep. Let us know next time you get leave."

Noel promised that he would and furthermore pledged his word not to leave England without coming in person to say good-bye. Lydia hesitated and then said:

"Would you mind if I asked you one more thing, Noel?"

"Not a bit," said Noel.

"When you said about sending letters to your chambers to be forwarded, you didn't mean because you thought I'd tell anyone where you were if it's a secret, or be a Traitor, did you?" said Lydia earnestly.

"If I am allowed to tell my address to one single person you shall be the one," said Noel. "Even my clerk doesn't know. He only sends them on to a mystic address at the War Office."

Lydia wrung his hands violently and went upstairs.

"And Lydia," Noel called after her, "do give Mrs. Brandon messages from me. That woman is the joy of my heart."

"All right," shouted Lydia and continued her journey upstairs. In the intervals of having her bath and getting into bed she thought with some pride of the compliment Noel had paid her. That it was untrue she well knew, for no one could make a home as really comfortable as Kate did, and Lydia was only too conscious of how far she fell short of that ideal, but that Noel should even pretend that she was as good as Kate made her heart feel comfortably warm. The thought of a heart suddenly roused some slightly unpleasant echo. She got into bed and opened *Wuthering Heights* in which she was at present indulging, but the echo teased her so much that she shut her book and turned out the light.

To-morrow she must get round the farm by ten o'clock. She would take her car and go straight on to Barchester getting there before eleven and then take Pomfret Madrigal on the way home. The echo sounded again. A heart. The joy of a heart. She knew that Noel and Mrs. Brandon, who were both quite grown-up, talked in a way that she did not quite understand though she looked with tolerance upon their childishness. But suddenly because of a word Noel had said, a light word she knew, spoken with his customary exaggeration, she felt far more like a child herself than was pleasant. She liked Mrs. Brandon very much and admired her looks and ways without the slightest wish to imitate them, and to envy her had never for a moment crossed her mind. So she decided not to envy her. After all Noel had promised to tell her and her alone what his address was, if he was allowed to tell, and on this comforting thought she fell asleep.

7

MRS. BRANDON AGAIN

•

Lydia, after a good night's sleep, had her breakfast early, went round the farm, spoke severely about a cow and a hedge, and pursued her way to Barchester. The Red Cross meeting was at the Deanery, so she drove into the Close and parked her car. In the drawing-room she found Mrs. Crawley sorting a number of papers in a very efficient way.

"Good morning, Lydia," said Mrs. Crawley. "You are the first. Octavia is so sorry she won't see you. She is on night duty at present and has just come off and had her breakfast and gone to bed."

"Can I go up and see her?" asked Lydia.

Mrs. Crawley rather unwillingly gave permission, and Lydia went upstairs. The Deanery, a fine early Georgian house, was as inconvenient as it was beautiful. The low rooms on the ground floor made excellent libraries and offices for the Dean's work, and the lofty white panelled rooms on the first floor with their tall sash windows overlooking the Close were perfect for entertaining, but after that the house split up into so many staircases and corridors and small bedrooms carved out of large bedrooms, and bathrooms carved out of nowhere, that many of the inferior clergy who hadn't a sense of direction and were afraid to ask the servants had wretched memories of a night under the Dean's hospitable roof, unable to find a bathroom and late for dinner. Until the middle of the nineteenth century the

Deanery had been little changed. The Arabins it is true had put in a bathroom about the year 1876, but this was a massive affair in a heavy mahogany surround with a battery of taps called Sitz, Douche, Plunge and other ominous names, hitting the unwary visitor full in the tenderer parts of his (for no lady visitor ever used it) anatomy with jets of water sometimes scalding, sometimes ice cold. It was set up in a large dressing-room (for there were then no small ones) thus making it impossible to put a married couple into the West Room and wasting a very good brass double bedstead with a good feather mattress on single members of the Church of England, though not on professed celibates for such Dean Arabin did not tolerate, broadminded as he was in other ways.

This state of things continued till the beginning of the twentieth century when a bachelor Dean, ex-Master of an Oxford college, angrily had the bath removed on the ground that a flat tin bath was good enough for him and hence for anyone else. After his death the new Dean, who had married a grand-daughter of old Mr. Frank Gresham, who used to be Member for East Barsetshire, with a fine fortune, had modernised the house as above described and after a running fight with the Ecclesiastical Commissioners, conducted with great spirit on both sides, had got his own way at his own expense, and so cut the bedrooms up that four bathrooms and a servants' bathroom had been extracted from the existing rooms.

The present Dean and Mrs. Crawley, who were comfortably off for their station, left things much as they were and loved the house so much, though it was expensive to keep up, that they never repined. Indeed they often had cause to bless their predecessor for making something of a rabbit warren, as otherwise their eight children would have had to sleep several in a bed. All these children were grown-up and most of them married, and Octavia, the only one left at home, was able to have the biggish room on the second floor looking into the garden and down the river for her own, with easy access to the third best bathroom.

Here Lydia found her fellow bridesmaid in dressing-gown and pyjamas, looking out of the window with a pair of opera glasses.

"Hullo," said Lydia. "Your mother said you were in bed."

Octavia turned round and explained that she was looking across the river at the Hospital.

"I should have thought you saw enough of it," said Lydia. "Have you any patients?"

"Three," said Octavia proudly, "and two of them are in my ward. They were on anti-aircraft and fell over a pig in the dark and one got a broken wrist and one had shock; shell-shock it would be if the pig had been a shell."

Lydia said that was better than nothing, or even than one patient.

"Yes, but the snag is," said Octavia, "that Matron who is the Limit, is putting one of my patients into D. Ward and Geraldine will get him. Sister is furious and so is Delia. I can't see the sense in a war if there aren't any casualties. I wish my people had let me drive an ambulance. Ambulances quite often run over people in the black-out."

Lydia looked admiringly at her single-hearted friend, though she could not feel her enthusiasm, and asked what Octavia wanted to look through opera glasses for.

"Delia promised she'd wave a swab out of the window at eleven o'clock if Matron really takes our patient away," she said, "and I was waiting. Have a look. It's the fourth window from the left on the top floor."

Lydia adjusted the glasses and looked earnestly at the Hospital. The cathedral bell boomed eleven times.

"There's something waving," she said, handing the glasses to Octavia, "but it's bigger than a swab."

"It's probably a draw-sheet then," said Octavia without interest, and drawing the curtain she got into bed. "I wish I could get a first-aid job in a munitions factory. People get blown up or caught in the machinery there."

"Well I must go to the meeting," said Lydia, and went down again.

In the drawing-room she found nine or ten ladies already seated in a kind of semi-circle in front of Mrs. Crawley's writing-table at which Mrs. Crawley, the convener of the meeting, was sitting. Among the audience Lydia recognised young Mrs. Roddy Wicklow whose husband was Mrs. Foster's brother, the Archdeacon's daughter from Plumstead, and some friends of her mother's of great worthiness and dullness. At the far end of the semi-circle were Mrs. Birkett and Mrs. Morland, and to them Lydia betook herself.

"Are we all here?" said Mrs. Crawley.

Everyone looked at everyone else.

"Well, I am not really here," said Mrs. Morland, "but as I am staying at Southbridge, Mrs. Birkett thought it would be all right."

Mrs. Birkett explained that her friend Mrs. Morland was staying with her for the present and was helping her with the Red Cross in Southbridge, so she was sure Mrs. Morland would be a welcome addition to the committee.

Mrs. Roddy Wicklow turned her large dark timid eyes upon Mrs. Morland and asked in a whisper if it was THE Mrs. Morland.

One of the dull worthy ladies said with a laugh that none of them would dare to read Mrs. Morland's next book as she was sure Mrs. Morland would have a scene about a Red Cross Committee. Mrs. Morland, who detested being recognised in her professional capacity more than anything, tried to smile. Another dull worthy lady said she had been asking for Mrs. Morland's new book at Gaiter's Library ever since the beginning of September but it was always out and she felt sure Mrs. Morland would be pleased to know how popular her books were. Mrs. Morland again tried to smile, though nothing is more annoying than to be told that people can't get your book because Messrs. Gaiters or P.B. Baker & Son, Ltd. will not buy a few more copies. The second dull lady, leaning across the Archdeacon's daughter, said to the first dull lady, Whom *do* you think she had seen in the Close as she came along but Canon Banister, at which the first dull lady laughed and the Archdeacon's daughter said Well now they would be hearing what really *did* happen at the funeral. All the Barchester ladies then talked at once till Mrs. Crawley, who had finished writing some notes, said that they were delighted to welcome Mrs. Morland and all remarks must be addressed to the chair.

During the brief silence that followed, the minutes of the last meeting were taken as read.

"And now," said Mrs. Crawley, "I have to put before you a special appeal for books from the Barchester Hospital."

A lady got up and said she was so very sorry she must be going, but she had a teacher billeted on her who had to have lunch at twelve and she must get home as she couldn't manage separate lunches. Another lady said she was afraid she must go too, as her three evacuees also had to have lunch at twelve to attend afternoon school and she didn't like to leave it to her one maid. Two more hostesses had to leave at the same time, one to take her evacuee boy to the doctor because she felt sure it was impetigo whatever anyone might say and *such* a nice bright little fellow, the other to receive an angry father and mother from Dalston who threatened to remove their girl because the mother was expecting to have another baby and wanted Janice to look after the house as she wouldn't leave her husband and *such* a nice bright little girl it seemed really a pity, but what can you do. The first dull lady said that time alone would show whether evacuation had been a wise move. The second dull lady said that whatever the wisdom of the scheme there would be no two opinions as to the importance of removing young children and more particularly expectant mothers from danger areas. It was well known, she said, that many people were now a mass of nerves because they had been born during the last War after the air raids had begun.

"I must say," said Mrs. Morland, following as usual a personal line of thought, "that I have a very poor opinion of prenatal influence. Two of my boys were born in London during the War and are not nervous in the least, though I was, at least of the noise our own anti-aircraft guns made in Hyde Park, far far more frightening than any bombs exploding though I never heard one. But, on the other hand," she added impressively in her deepest voice, "a friend of mine who was perfectly sane and so was her husband had a baby which was born in 1913 and turned out a hopeless idiot, and is still alive, but of course in a home, where it will probably live for ever at great expense like people that are left annuities."

Mrs. Roddy Wicklow, who was very kind, said it seemed dreadful about idiots but what was one to do, and as it was now twelve o'clock the meeting broke up and Mrs. Crawley said she would see about the books herself.

"Do come and see us soon, Lydia," said Mrs. Birkett as she and Mrs. Morland took their leave.

"I'd love to," said Lydia, "but I don't know how the petrol ration will work out. I've put in for extra on account of Red Cross and working parties, but I mayn't get it. Anyway Saunders, our chauffeur, has a huge secret hoard somewhere."

As Lydia went through the hall Mr. Needham the Dean's secretary came out of the small study, so obviously waylaying her that she stopped.

"I'm awfully sorry, Miss Keith," he said, "I don't suppose you remember me at Miss Birkett's wedding, but Mrs. Crawley mentioned at breakfast that you were going on to Mrs. Brandon's, so I wondered if you would mind taking me, as the Dean has gone to Courcy Castle in the car and my motor bicycle is being repaired where I ran into the market cross at High Rising in the black-out. Mrs. Brandon, whom I don't know, has very kindly asked me to lunch to meet the Vicar, Mr. Miller, who is an old friend of my father's, and his wife, and I can get a train back but there isn't any train before lunch except the 11.12."

Lydia said of course.

"You know Miss Pettinger, don't you, Miss Keith?" said Mr. Needham.

Lydia said if you called a person being one's Headmistress knowing them, she supposed she did.

"She will ask me to come in to social evenings after dinner," said Mr. Needham plaintively, "to meet Miss Sparling, the Headmistress of the Hosiers' Girls Foundation School, who is an extraordinarily nice person, and then she is rude to her and I feel so uncomfortable. I suppose one oughtn't to say one's hostess is rude, but she really is."

"She's always been like that," said Lydia, "and I expect if I kept a High School I would be too. But why do you go? Can't you say the Dean wants you?"

"I would, even if it wasn't true," said Mr. Needham, "but she finds out from Octavia, who seems to like her, what evenings the Dean is out."

"Of course Octavia was potty about Miss Pettinger at school," said Lydia scornfully, "and I must say she isn't much better now, only it's the Hospital."

"I think the way Octavia has taken her war work is

magnificent," said Mr. Needham firmly. "Sitting in the Hospital day after day with nothing to do. I almost find myself praying for a few casualties for her on Sunday."

Lydia felt privately that Mr. Needham was much nicer when he didn't have a clergy-voice and that anyone who thought Octavia magnificent was potty too, but where a few years ago she would have expounded those views with the utmost frankness, she now merely accelerated and took the hill at Little Misfit at quite an alarming pace.

Stories, Mrs. Brandon's charming Georgian house, was looking its best in the peaceful late September sunshine. When Lydia stopped the car there was no sound. At least no natural sound, for something like the voices of children came from the house, and as Mrs. Brandon's son and daughter were unmarried there seemed to be no particular reason for it. Lydia, who was at home with Stories, opened the front door and was going into the drawing-room when Rose the parlourmaid appeared and taking up a Catherine Barlass attitude before the door said Mrs. Brandon was in her sitting-room. The babble of children was quite clear behind the door. Lydia, followed by Mr. Needham, went into the sitting-room. Here Mrs. Brandon was established on a sofa with a great bag of embroidery silks beside her. At the sight of her visitors she took off her large spectacles and got up, dropping her work all over the floor.

"Lydia!" she said, folding her guest in a warm, scented, unemotional embrace, "I am so glad to see you. And Mr. Needham? You were going to bring him with you. At least Mrs. Crawley rang up just now to say that you were."

"He's on the floor," said Lydia.

Mr. Needham, who had chivalrously been picking up the profusion of scissors, needlecases, thimbles and material that his hostess had let fall, got up and shook hands.

"It is such a pleasure to have any friend of Mr. Miller's here," said Mrs. Brandon, gazing into Mr. Needham's eyes.

Mr. Needham said he didn't exactly know Mr. Miller because he had never seen him, but his father had known him at college and he hoped Mrs. Brandon didn't mind. It was quite evident to Lydia that Mrs. Brandon was having her usual unconscious but quite inevitable effect upon Mr. Needham and she wished Delia were there, so that she could share the pleasure.

Mrs. Brandon said vaguely that old friends were such a help and she didn't know what one would do without them. She then looked so piercingly at Mr. Needham's neck that he began to wonder if his collar was dirty.

"Of corse," she said. "Mr. Miller said you had been ordained lately, and now I see what he meant. I thought he said *it* was ordained, and I didn't know what. Of course you are a kind of relation of his now."

Mr. Needham, unable to remove his eyes from Mrs. Brandon, said not a relation. It was only, he said, that his father had been at Mr. Miller's college. He didn't mean, he added stutteringly, that Mr. Miller had a college, but that Mr. Miller had been at his father's old college. He then felt that he might have expressed it all better and became dumb.

"I only meant a spiritual relation," said Mrs. Brandon, looking, so Mr. Needham thought, exactly like a Murillo Virgin, for that was where his tastes lay. "But Mr. and Mrs. Miller will be here soon and will explain everything. You will like Mrs. Miller so much. She was companion to my husband's old aunt and has been a perfect blessing in the parish. And her father was a clergyman too, but an odious one. I suppose I oughtn't to say that to *you*," she added, suddenly stricken by conscience, "but he was extremely Low Church, so I daresay you won't mind."

"Mrs. Brandon," said Lydia, who felt that her hostess had had a long enough innings, "who are the children? Are you having evacuees?"

"Not exactly," said Mrs. Brandon. "I mean they aren't dirty or difficult, so I suppose they really have no right to the name."

By severe cross-questioning Lydia managed to get from Mrs. Brandon a fairly reliable account of her guests, but it will save everyone's time and temper to explain in an omniscient way what had really happened.

When the question of receiving children from danger zones was first discussed, Mrs. Miller, who had taken on the ungrateful job of Billeting Officer, had been inspired to put all the children—luckily not a very large number, for Pomfret Madrigal was a small village with a very small Church School—into cottagers' houses. Here the eight shillings and sixpence a week provided for the evacuees by a grateful if bewildered country were extremely welcome and the London children, apart from their natural nostalgia for playing in dirty streets till midnight and living on fish and chips, settled down almost at once into the conditions of licence, dirt, overcrowding and margarine to which they were accustomed. The special Paradise, much envied by such children as were billeted elsewhere, was Grumper's End, the congested district of Pomfret Madrigal, and in that Paradise the most longed-for house was the Thatchers'. Here Mr. and Mrs. Thatcher, with eight children of their own, found no difficulty in housing four more, and to their hospitable kitchen, where cups of strong tea and bits of tinned salmon were almost always to be had for the asking or the taking, most of Pomfret Madrigal's twenty evacuated children gravitated. As they only went to school in the morning, the afternoon being kept for the village children, they had played, screamed, fought, made mud pies, or fallen into a little pond covered with green slime for four blissful weeks and all called Mr. and Mrs. Thatcher Daddy and Mummy. As for Percy and Gladys Thatcher, the children of shame of the two eldest Thatcher girls, they had never enjoyed themselves so much in their very young lives. Pulled about in an old soap box on to which Ernie Thatcher their young uncle by shame had fixed wheels, stuffed with the sweets which all the evacuee children bought with postal orders sent every week by their parents, carefully instructed in all the latest bad words fashionable in the select locality round King's Cross Station from which St. Gingolph's (C. of E.) School had been evacuated, they became so overbearing that Mr. Thatcher said more than once that he'd have to take the stick to them, while Mrs. Thatcher, feeling that with so many children about everything was all right, went out charing from morning to night, so that what with the money she earned and the money that Edna and Doris, the mothers of the children of shame, were earning as daily helps at the Cow and Sickle, which was doing very well owing to officers' wives who wanted to be within reach of Sparrowhill Camp, Mr. Thatcher was able to lose more on the dogs than ever and was later to lose in the Football Pools an amount of money that earned him the deep respect of everyone in the Cow and Sickle Tap.

As for the really difficult children, Mr. and Mrs. Miller, who were as good as gold, had taken them into the Vicarage and though Mrs. Miller had not the faintest hope of reforming them (for she was a very sensible and practical woman) she managed to keep her eye on them to that extent that they found it less trouble on the whole to do what The Lady said. All the jobs she found for them in house or garden were cunningly chosen to include dirt or destruction in some shape, and after a

Saturday on which they had helped Cook (of whom they were in as much awe as their natures permitted) to clean out the flues of the kitchen stove, had helped the gardener to fetch a load of pig manure from a neighbouring farm, and to empty the septic tank near his cottage, they all burst into tears at the sight of their parents who came down on Sunday for the day to see them, hit at their mothers, used language to their fathers which surpassed anything that St. Gingolph's had yet produced, and said they would never go home.

At the beginning of all this trouble Mrs. Brandon had opened her purse with her customary generosity and said she would do her very best with any children that Mrs. Miller liked to send. But Mrs. Miller, who was as we have said extremely sensible, saw on the faces of Rose the parlourmaid and Nurse, Mrs. Brandon's faithful and tyrannical ex-nannie, exactly what opposition such a plan would meet. So with great cunning she discovered a little private nursery school which was anxious to get its young pupils out of danger, and taking advantage of a Saturday morning, which was the moment when Mrs. Brandon with Nurse's help did the fresh flowers for the church, cornered them both up against the chancel rails and describing the school, said she was at her wits' end where to billet it. In Nurse's eye she at once saw, as she had hoped, the lust for power over babies, ever near the surface with all good Nannies, quickly rise. With Nurse's zeal and Mrs. Brandon's kind toleration, all difficulties were smoothed away, and within a few days ten very young children with two teachers were installed. The Green Room and the Pink Room were turned into dormitories for the children. The teachers were perfectly nice about sleeping one in each dormitory, and were given the Green Dressing-room as a sitting-room for themselves, while the large drawing-room was turned into a school and play-room, with a dining-room curtained off at one end. Mrs. Brandon and

Nurse vastly enjoyed the fuss of having the best drawing-room furniture and the carpets stacked away in the spare garage, and furnishing the dormitories and schoolroom. Mrs. Brandon went so far as to say to her son Francis that the teachers had restored her faith in human nature.

"That is impossible, darling," said Francis, "because in the first place you don't understand human nature in the least and in the second you can't restore what you never lost. All I say is, don't put a refugee into my bedroom when I am waving a sword on the field of glory, or I shan't be able to come back a handsome though mutilated cripple to drag out my last days in my ancestral home."

"You know well, Francis, that the Army won't have you till you are young enough to register," said Mrs. Brandon.

"I know what you think you mean, darling," said Francis, "which comes to much the same thing. What you are trying to say is that I am an aged dodderer, well above military age; damn it," he added.

Any display of temper by Francis was so unusual that his mother was almost perturbed.

"It isn't that I want to hide you when the recruiting officer comes," said Mrs. Brandon, her eyes brimming with unexpected tears—as unexpected to her as they were to her son. "But in a wicked kind of way I can't help being glad that you are still a little over age."

"You aren't wicked, bless you," said Francis, hugging his mother with one arm, for he had his attaché-case in the other and was just leaving for the office where he worked in Barchester.

"I couldn't be anything as definite as that, I suppose," said Mrs. Brandon, with one of her rare flashes of insight. "And I wouldn't let a refugee have your room if he were *starving*."

"You mustn't say things like that, mamma," said

Francis, much shocked, "though I must say I'd rather think of an enemy alien in my bed than some of those Mixo-Lydian refugees over at Southbridge. They show a degree of determined ingratitude and unpleasantness that confirms me in my never-wavering belief that Mixo-Lydia will once again be a free and revolting nation. Bless you, darling. I must fly."

After this explanation, or digression, it will be easy to see how what Mrs. Brandon nearly always managed to stop herself calling My War Work, was little or no trouble. Nurse, after looking at the teachers with the eye and nostril of a suspicious rocking-horse, and holding aloof in awful politeness for two days, was entirely melted on the third by being begged by Miss Driver, the senior teacher, to come and look at Baby Collis who wasn't quite the thing. After this she took Miss Driver and Miss Fielding, the second in command, under her wing, superintended much of the children's toilet and meals, and became so absorbed in what she would to Delia's indignation call "Our Babies" that she quite forgot to keep up her enmity with Rose, and even allowed the head housemaid to mend Delia's stockings.

Rose now announced Mr. and Mrs. Miller. As all their friends knew, the Vicar of Pomfret Madrigal and his wife, then Miss Morris, had cared for each other when they were young, had been separated by the very intransigent attitude of Miss Morris's father, the Rev. Justin Morris, about young Mr. Miller's High Church tendencies, and had not met for many years. After several years of being companion to old ladies Miss Morris had gone to old Miss Brandon at Brandon Abbey, and on her employer's death had been manoeuvred by Mrs. Brandon into the Vicar's company. The middle-aged lovers had made up their minds almost at once and had been married under the eye of Mrs. Brandon who had personally superintended Miss Morris's wedding outfit (which was a very neatly-cut coat and skirt, a felt hat, crocodile shoes and bag) and insisted on paying for it herself with such real kindness that Miss Morris could not refuse. Mrs. Brandon had also wished to give her an unassuming fox fur, but here Miss Morris was adamant. Not only did the expense seem to her almost wicked, but she had convictions about wearing fur, feeling very strongly that all fur-bearing animals were skinned alive and left to perish in slow agony while their hapless children starved. In vain did Francis Brandon point out to her that no fur hunter would be so wasteful and that practically all silver foxes were now bred on a commercial scale and well-treated, nay pampered, till the day of their unexpected and painless death. Miss Morris remembered reading something somewhere about ospreys, and went pink whenever the word silver fox was mentioned. So the idea of a fur was abandoned, but Mrs. Brandon got even with the new Mrs. Miller by putting a modern stove and a separate furnace for the hot water into the Vicarage while the Millers were on their honeymoon, which was Oxford, and Stratford-on-Avon, where they saw *As you Like It*. When the Vicar and his wife got back, Mrs. Miller could only thank Mrs. Brandon with her usual composure but in a tremulous voice, while the Vicar said Indeed, indeed a hot bath every day would be a luxury he had never expected and how truly kind Mrs. Brandon was. He then wondered privately whether the Ecclesiastical Commissioners would mind and hoped they wouldn't.

"So you are my old friend Needham's son," said the Vicar, very kindly, as he shook the young man by the hand.

Mr. Needham, eyeing anxiously the cassock which he knew his present employer would strongly disapprove, said Yes in a mumbling sort of way.

"My dear," said the Vicar, turning to his wife, "that is Needham's boy. My wife."

His pride, even after more than a year of marriage, in those two words, was so great that Mrs. Brandon felt her soul swelling inside her, but wisely said nothing about it.

Mrs. Miller, who had heard a great deal about Mr. Needham since her husband had discovered that he was secretary to the Dean of Barchester, and was quite prepared to see a young man in a clerical collar, bore up very well and shaking hands said, also in a very pleasant way, that she had heard a great deal about him and was so glad to meet him. Everyone then fell silent, while Lydia looked at the two clergymen with dispassionate interest, rather hoping that they might argue about the Thirty-Nine Articles; for she had been giving her attention to that admirable composition of late and was burning to air her views, but didn't see how to begin. Mrs. Brandon went on with her embroidery placidly, for she was one of those lucky beings to whom silences are never awkward.

"Ha!" said Mr. Miller at lengh. "Yes; Needham. He rowed seven in the Lazarus Boat. 'Mangle' Needham, we used to call him, but I can't remember why."

Mr. Needham felt himself going crimson from the feet upwards and was dumb.

"How *is* your father?" said Mrs. Miller, who as the daughter and wife of the clergy was well used to keeping a mild conversational ball rolling.

"Oh, *Father*. He's awfully well, thank you," said Mr. Needham. "And so's Mother and both my sisters and Father said to give his love to Goggers Miller. At least that's what he said, sir, I hope you don't mind."

He stopped, paralysed by his own fluency. Mrs. Miller was sorry for anyone who so recklessly spent the whole of his small change of conversation in one breath. Mrs. Brandon chose some blue silk and threaded her needle.

" 'Goggers,' " said Mr. Miller, laughing. "Indeed,

indeed it is many a day since anyone called me by that nickname. I must tell you, my dear," he added, turning to his wife, to whom it was his habit, partly from shyness, partly from affection, to address most of his remarks, "the story of that name. It was just after the Summer Term of 1911, or possibly 1912. Needham and I and a man called Holroyd-Skinner, he was killed, poor fellow, in the early days of the war and I see his mother from time to time, but owing to her health she lives on the Riviera so it is only on her, alas, too rare visits to England that we meet, rowed down from Oxford to Kingston, spending the night at riverside inns, and on the second day we were discussing St. Thomas Aquinas, and somehow that name stuck to me."

It was just as well that Rose announced lunch at that moment, or Mr. Needham, who was not accustomed to Mr. Miller's manner of speech, might have gone mad. Mrs. Brandon got up, dropping all her embroidery again, which the gentlemen precipitated themselves to pick up.

"What are you working at now, Mrs. Brandon?" said Mr. Miller.

"Well, I can't really call it work," said Mrs. Brandon as they went into the dining-room, "but Nurse made a lot of aprons for our babies of coloured linen, green and blue and yellow, and I thought it would look so pretty if I embroidered them, so I am embroidering them. Mr. Miller, you will sit by Lydia, won't you; and Mr. Needham, come between me and Mrs. Miller. I am sorry we are five, which is an odd number, but after all there is the Pentateuch, or do I mean Pentagon, isn't there, Mr. Miller?"

With which sop to the Church she smiled dazzlingly at her Vicar.

The excellent food and the excellent light wine soon restored animation and Mr. Miller and Mr. Needham talked happily across the little round table about

Oxford. Mr. Miller had not heard that brick boat houses were beginning to supplement and were eventually to replace the barges, and nearly burst with sorrow at the news. The number of ways of getting illegally into Lazarus College was discussed and the Vicar was much interested to hear of a seventh way, unknown in his time and only made possible by the instalment in the Master's Lodgings of a second bathroom, which provided a drainpipe of very solid construction, a boon to Alpinists. Mrs. Miller and Lydia wisely ignoring their hostess, discussed the possibility of a working party once a week for such Northbridge and Pomfret Madrigal men as were in the Royal Navy or the Royal Merchant Service, but owing to petrol rationing were not quite sure if it could be arranged. Mrs. Miller said she knew at least five workers who bicycled and Lydia undertook to rally some from Southbridge, and as Mrs. Brandon had offered her dining-room for the working party, there would be the added attraction of a very good tea. After that Mrs. Miller and Mrs. Brandon had a very interesting conversation about the Vicarage stove, during which Mrs. Brandon showed great intelligence, while Lydia listened attentively, conceiving kitchen stoves to be part of her self-appointed work.

Just as they were finishing lunch, Rose came in and said Could Sir Edmund Pridham see Mrs. Brandon.

"Well, he could if he came in," said Mrs. Brandon, who was always pleased to see her old friend and trustee, now busier than ever, if that were possible, over committees of all sorts and every job that called for a great deal of work and no pay. "Come in and have coffee, Sir Edmund. Here are the Millers, and you know Lydia Keith. And this is Mr. Needham who came over with Lydia."

"Another of your young men, eh, Miss Lydia?" said Sir Edmund, who stuck to this charming if demoded address for young unmarried ladies.

"Of course not, Sir Edmund," said Mrs. Brandon severely. "Mr. Needham is a *clergyman*, as you would see if you looked at him."

"Afternoon, Mr. Needham," said Sir Edmund, sitting down heavily between Mrs. Brandon and Mr. Miller. "No; no coffee, Lavinia. Makes me bilious after lunch. I won't say no to a glass of port. Nothing to be ashamed of if you were. Parsons often carry off the prettiest girls, eh, Miller?" said Sir Edmund, poking his Vicar in the waistcoat, or about where the waistcoat, under a cassock, would be.

Mr. Miller felt, as he often did, that if his valued and excellent Churchwarden could not control himself, he would have to give notice. But Sir Edmund's poke was, he knew, intended to imply that he, Mr. Miller, had carried off one of the prettiest girls, and as in his eyes his middle-aged wife was still the girl whose wind-blown hair he had gently put aside on the day of the Church Lads' Brigade tea, more than a quarter of a century ago, he could not find it in his heart to chide Sir Edmund, and certainly had not the courage to do so.

"He's the Dean's secretary, Sir Edmund," said Lydia.

"Which bedroom have they given you?" asked Sir Edmund, turning on Mr. Needham. "The last Dean's secretary had a room I wouldn't put a dog in."

Mr. Needham said, rather stiffly, that he had a very comfortable room on the second floor looking out over the Close.

"Busman's holiday, eh?" said Sir Edmund. "Anyone heard the one o'clock news?"

"Well, everyone here was here at one o'clock and we didn't have it on, so I don't suppose they have," said Mrs. Brandon, with an air of great lucidity.

"Upon my word, Lavinia, you get sillier every day," said Sir Edmund. "Well, I haven't heard it either. Was over at Little Misfit at the British Legion. So we needn't talk about it. I won't have the wireless in my house.

Never had one in the last war and won't have one in this war. Read my *Times* in the morning and that's that. Tell you what's wrong with this war though," he added, looking round in a challenging way, "it's not like the last one. Barsetshire Yeomanry in camp ever since the trouble began. Last time we had 'em out in France in three days and cut to pieces, by Jove, in the Retreat."

Everyone knew that Sir Edmund, after commanding the Barsetshire Yeomanry with distinction for two years and taking more than a father's interest in his men, had been invalided out of the army with a permanently crippled leg, and they respected his annoyance.

"We had men like Kitchener then," Sir Edmund continued, "and Beatty and Joffre. Not got them now."

"Well, you couldn't," said Lydia. "They're all dead."

"Good thing if I was too," said Sir Edmund. "Useless old man. I'd have a smack at the Boche now if I could. So'd you, young man," he added, suddenly rounding on Mr. Needham.

Mr. Needham thought wildly of looking at his own collar in an appealing way, to show Sir Edmund his position, but the physical difficulties were too great.

"My dear Sir Edmund," the Vicar protested.

"Don't talk to me about his cloth," said Sir Edmund angrily, although the Vicar hadn't. "What's the Church Militant for, eh? Eh, young man?"

Mr. Needham was heard to mumble something about military chaplains and the Bishop.

"Bishop of Barchester's an old woman and we all know that," said Sir Edmund. "Never you mind him, young man."

Mr. Miller felt that as an unworthy son of the Church he could not listen to such subversive remarks, so although he disliked the Bishop as much as he had ever disliked anyone, he thought he ought to change the subject and reminded Sir Edmund that the following Sunday was the Day of National Prayer and he supposed the British Legion in Pomfret Madrigal would attend in full force.

"Bad thing when it comes to having a Day of National Prayer," said Sir Edmund gloomily. "It's all this Government. Wouldn't have had one if Churchill had been Prime Minister. Or Lloyd George. Mind you I never liked the man, never trusted him, in fact I'd have had him shot, but I'm a fair-minded man and I say it shows things are in a bad way. It's no good. I'm an old man and I don't understand these new ways, I suppose, but it's all beyond me."

The Vicar, who was really devoted to Sir Edmund and knew his ceaseless care for and interest in every corner of the parish and every family that lived there besides all the work he did in the county, felt deeply sorry for his old friend. That a good deal of his grumbling was habit he was fully aware, but he was equally aware that Sir Edmund was cruelly troubled by the changing times and could not understand that 1940 was not 1914.

"Indeed, indeed, the times are troubled, Sir Edmund," he said, "but we must remember that we are all in God's hands."

"I know we are," said Mrs. Brandon earnestly, laying her hand on the Vicar's sleeve, "and that is just what is so perfectly *dreadful*."

This appalling truth drove everyone into a frenzy of unnecessary conversation which lasted until Sir Edmund went. The party then broke up, the Millers going back to the Vicarage for a Mothers' Meeting and Lydia taking Mr. Needham back to Barchester. Just as she was leaving she remembered Noel Merton's message and being a thoroughly conscientious girl gave it to Mrs. Brandon.

"How nice of Mr. Merton," said Mrs. Brandon. "If he is in Intelligence perhaps he could find a job for Francis. And there is our cousin Hilary Grant, who is due to be called up about the same time and speaks Italian so well, which would be very useful if they wanted anyone who can speak Italian. Will you ask him, Lydia?"

Lydia promised she would, took Mr. Needham aboard and set off for Barchester. Mr. Needham spoke at some length of the charm and virtues of Mrs. Brandon who, he said, was more like his idea of a saint than anyone he had ever met. Lydia listened kindly. She had given Noel's message to Mrs. Brandon, and Mrs. Brandon had at once suggested that Noel should find jobs for her son and her cousin, and this, she didn't quite know why, had been very soothing. Her liking for Mrs. Brandon remained undimmed, but her opinion of Mr. Needham fell slightly.

"I say, Mr. Needham," she remarked, as they entered the Close.

"I wish you wouldn't say Mr. Needham," said that cleric. "Everyone calls me Tommy."

"All right, Tommy then if you like, only of course you must say Lydia," said Miss Keith. "I suppose Octavia will be getting up soon."

Mr. Needham said he thought about 6 o'clock.

"Then you'll be able to see her when you've done your work or whatever it is you do for Dr. Crawley," said Lydia, determined that her friend should not suffer from Mrs. Brandon's fatal charm.

Mr. Needham said he sometimes went for a walk with his employer's daughter before she had dinner and went off to her night shift. Lydia nodded approvingly, wrenched Mr. Needham's hand in a way that reminded him of the time his wrist was broken in a Rugby match in Wales, and careered away towards Northbridge and her responsibilities.

8

THE BISSELLS AT HOME

•

In spite of Sir Edmund's gloomy views the Day of National Prayer passed off without incident. At Southbridge School Mr. Smith the chaplain preached to a large congregation of his own boys and the Hosiers' Boys, doing his best to say in one and the same breath that they must go on with their work as if nothing had happened, prepare themselves earnestly for what was before them, remember that the youth of all countries held the future of the world in their hands, and certainly not forget that the youth of certain countries had been so misled by what it was now the fashion to call totalitarian methods, though he was himself old-fashioned enough to believe in the Powers of Darkness, that the world's future must never be allowed to rest in its hands. But as everyone was used to him, no one minded.

At the Headmaster's House Mrs. Morland, who when she concentrated was far from unintelligent, especially about other people's affairs, did a good deal of secretarial work for Mr. Birkett, worked away industriously at her new novel and made a good many friends in the school. To her great surprise, for she was an unassuming creature, she found that a number of the masters and the older boys were among her constant readers. This she attributed largely, and possibly with some justice, to the fact that several of her books were now in a well-known sixpenny series, but it all cheered her up. Her youngest son Tony appeared to be very happy at Oxford, her invaluable cook Stoker sent her good accounts of her house at High Rising where her publisher's wife and children were now staying, so apart from a general feeling that she was of no use at all, she was happy enough.

For some time she and Mrs. Birkett had been in consultation about calling on Mrs. Bissell. It was publicly known that Mr. Bissell had taken Maria Cottage and there installed his wife, but no one had seen her, and Mr. Bissell had not been communicative. More than once Mrs. Birkett had said to Mr. Bissell that she would like so much to call on his wife. To each suggestion Mr. Bissell had replied that Mrs. Bissell was settling the things in. What the things were Mrs. Birkett and Mrs. Morland could not exactly understand, for Maria was fully furnished and news had reached them via the carrier, who was also the coals, that the Bissells' luggage had consisted of three suitcases. But they felt that something was wrong and wished they had a book of etiquette that would tell them about calling on the wives of Headmasters of evacuated schools.

"In Simla," said Mrs. Morland, who had never been there, or indeed in any part of India, but had read a great many novels about Anglo-Indian life, "you have a letter-box, at least whatever you do have in India, on the front gate and when new people come they put their cards in your box."

Mrs. Birkett wondered how they knew which boxes to put them in.

"I suppose an A.D.C. or someone tells them," said Mrs. Morland. "But Amy, though it seems snobbish to say so, perhaps Mrs. Bissell doesn't have cards."

Mrs. Birkett thought this quite probable, which led to a discussion as to whether people who didn't have cards would think it an offensive act of Capittleism if people who had cards left them on them. As their premises were based on entire ignorance the argument was very inconclusive. The only people who were known to have made Mrs. Bissell's acquaintance were Miss Hampton and Miss Bent, but as Mrs. Birkett didn't know them very well this did not help matters. Philip Winter, whose friendship with those ladies, begun in the Red Lion bar and ripened at Adelina Cottage, would have been a link, was at a place known officially as "somewhere within fifty miles of Bath," but known in the Masters' Common Room, the School Debating and Literary Societies, the Red Lion, and practically the whole of Southbridge as Tiptor Camp, Nr. Bumblecombe, Somerset, and could not help.

The solution to this social impasse was at last provided by Mr. Bissell himself, who under cover of returning a book on the Antiquities of Barchester that Mr. Birkett had lent him, told Mrs. Birkett that Mrs. Bissell had got things a bit settled and would be very pleased if Mrs. Birkett would come to tea with her. Mrs. Birkett, who knew that tea and Tea were different things, warily inquired what time Mrs. Bissell was expecting them and was told four o'clock which was a relief, for though she would willingly have gone to Tea at six or even six-thirty, and eaten heartily for the sake of the School, she knew that she could not eat another hearty meal at eight o'clock; and that would fidget her husband.

"And do you think," said Mrs. Birkett, "that Mrs. Bissell would allow me to bring Mrs. Morland?"

Mr. Bissell said that Mrs. Bissell had hardly liked to ask Mrs. Morland but would be very pleased, and on this double-edged statement took his leave.

Accordingly Mrs. Birkett and Mrs. Morland walked

down to Southbridge and knocked at the door of Maria Cottage (for the Vicar's aunt had a brass Lincoln Imp for a knocker and refused to have a bell). The door was opened by a small, plumpish woman with very neat hair and a singularly sweet and placid expression.

"I said to myself," said Mrs. Bissell as she ushered her guests into the drawing-room, "as I saw you cross the green, 'That must be Mrs. Birkett and Mrs. Morland.' This is a great pleasure and I'm sure I'd have asked you before, but it does take time to settle things."

Mrs. Birkett, who had known Maria Cottage when the Vicar's aunt lived there, looked round. Every piece of furniture that could be moved had been placed cornerways instead of square. A tea-table was standing askew in front of the fire with a lace cloth laid diamond-wise upon it and five plates each with a small folded napkin lace-edged. There were two plates of sandwiches reposing on lace doyleys and a large cake on a doyley with fringes. In the corner of the room a little girl was playing with some coloured blocks.

"Come and say how do you do, Edna," said Mrs. Bissell.

"I?" said the little girl.

"Now we know we mustn't say 'eh,'" said Mrs. Bissell.

"Wot sy?" said the little girl.

"No, Edna, we don't say 'What did you say,'" said Mrs. Bissell. "What is it we *do* say?"

"Pardon," said the little girl, who looked remarkably like an idiot.

"That's right," said Mrs. Bissell cheerfully. "And now come and say How do you do."

"I?" said the little girl.

"I think we'll leave her for the present," said Mrs. Bissell composedly. "She is a dear little thing, a niece of Mr. Bissell's niece by marriage, but both her parents were mentally defective. She was to be evacuated with the M.D. school, but she is liable to fits. In fact it has been quite a business deciding if she ought to be at an M.D. or a P.D. school—mentally defective and physically defective I should explain perhaps—so I said I would take her. She is really improving I think since we came down here with this beautiful air and we are getting on quite nicely with our lessons. She goes to the village school and is quite good, and if she looks like having a fit the mistress just phones me up and I come and fetch her."

While she was speaking Mrs. Bissell had poured out tea, handed sandwiches, cut the cake, all with a placid efficiency that deeply impressed her visitors. Conversation then flowed pleasantly and genteelly on the weather and the school. Mrs. Birkett said, with great truth, what a pleasure it had been to her husband to work with Mr. Bissell. As she afterwards confessed to Mrs. Morland, she had perhaps given this praise rather in the manner of a Lady Bountiful and was justly rewarded for her pride, for Mrs. Bissell appeared to take all the praise as a matter of course and with perfect simplicity let her understand that Mr. Bissell had been quite relieved to find vestiges of civilization in a Public School.

"Of course," said Mrs. Bissell, "the day of the Public School is over. After this war we shall have nothing but State-supported schools. The same with Oxford and Cambridge of course. There won't be any place for young men to waste their time and their parents' money and be turned out useless burdens on the country. Mr. Bissell has supported himself with scholarships and grants ever since he was fifteen."

There was something about Mrs. Bissell that made it quite impossible to resent her calm statements. Even Mrs. Morland, who always meant to be modest about her children and always failed, didn't like to mention that her sailor son had supported himself from an even earlier age than Mr. Bissell, though, owing to being much younger, not for so long; or that her two eldest boys had not for some years had any money from her except the voluntary (she would have refrained from saying handsome) presents she gave them for Christmas and birthdays; or indeed that Tony had contributed largely to his education from the day he took a Scholarship to the Senior School up till the present moment. For she felt certain that Mrs. Bissell would regard all such self-help as proof of the advantages accruing to the sons of Capittleists; though why the fact of her husband having died many years ago leaving her to earn the money to clothe, feed and educate four boys should make her be a Capittleist she could not see, but an inner instinct told her that Mrs. Bissell would see it in that light.

A shadow passed the window.

"I dare say you wondered," said Mrs. Bissell, "who that extra plate was for. That's for Daddy. He always gets home for a cup of tea. Pardon me, but he likes me to let him in."

Accordingly she went to the front door and returned with Mr. Bissell. Mrs. Morland and Mrs. Birkett on comparing notes afterwards found they had both expected Mrs. Bissell to admit an aged and decrepit father also living in Maria Cottage, so Mr. Bissell's appearance was a relief.

"Good afternoon, ladies," said Mr. Bissell, who on crossing the threshold had shed the schoolmaster and become the domestic host. "Has Mother been looking after you?"

"Is your mother here too, then?" said Mrs. Morland.

Mr. Bissell explained that though he and Mrs. Bissell had the misfortune to have no chicks, they had always used those sweet old names and little Edna thought they were her real Mother and Daddy. The guests felt that little Edna was incapable of such a flight of reasoning but said nothing.

"And how do you like our little home?" said Mr. Bissell to Mrs. Birkett, who was loud in her commendation of its charms and with great tact said she liked the way Mrs. Bissell had arranged the furniture.

"Of course it's only our peedatair," said Mr. Bissell, "but Mrs. Bissell has quite the art of making a home."

Mrs. Morland, feeling that as a woman of letters something was expected of her, said Mrs. Bissell had given the cottage a really homey atmosphere and she hoped the *pied-à-terre* (which she tried not to pronounce in too affected a way) would be their home for a long time.

Mr. Bissell said that Mother was quite a country girl having lived at Sevenoaks so it was quite like old times for her to be in the country again and little Edna looked quite different.

"And it must be so nice for you to have the school and the masters here," said Mrs. Morland, nobly sacrificing herself in the cause of making conversation.

Mrs. Bissell was very noticeably silent.

"Of course I wouldn't say this officially," said Mr. Bissell, wiping his mouth on the lace-edged napkin and pushing his cup away, "but as we are all among friends and not speaking ex-cathedral, I must in honesty confess that some of my colleagues, though a splendid, loyal, conscientious, hard-working set of men," said Mr. Bissell, obviously crushing down his lower self, "are not exactly what I would call quite."

His guests may have imagined that the sentence was not finished, but it evidently was.

"I know what you mean," said Mrs. Morland, nervously pushing a stray hairpin into her skull. "They haven't got that kind of broadness."

"There you have hit the nail on the head, Mrs. Morland," said Mr. Bissell, shifting himself and his chair along the floor nearer to her. "Mr. Hopkins for instance, a fine scientific man with a very good degree from Aberystwyth, and excellent at keeping discipline, isn't exactly the type the Hosiers' Boys want. 'Russia was all very well, Hopkins,' I said to him no later than last Tuesday, 'when she *was* Russia, but when—and we will let alone,' I said, 'any question of whether we should or should not have made a Trade Pact with her, for that is foreign to the trend of the present discussion—when,' I said, 'Russia deliberately plays into the hands of the Ryke, all I say is she has let the N.U.T. down, and that will go very heavily against her. And don't answer me, Hopkins,' I said, 'for I know exactly what you are going to say, and you can say it at the N.U.T. Congress and see how they take it.' "

"Is Mr. Hopkins a Trade Unionist then?" said Mrs. Morland.

"National Union of Teachers," said Mrs. Birkett hastily, hoping to retrieve the honour of the bourgeoisie, though without much hope.

"Of *course*," said Mrs. Morland untruthfully. "But everything's initials now and it is so difficult to remember. And then we call Russia, at least some people do but I don't, U.S.S.R. and the French, who are supposed to be so very logical, call it U.R.S.S. which being our allies seems quite unreasonable. But nothing will stop me saying St. Petersburg," she added defiantly and looked round for support.

Mr. Bissell had gone mad once already under Mrs. Morland's divagations and it was clear that he was rapidly going mad again. He cast a frenzied glance at his wife who was taking it all very well, realising that people like Mrs. Morland who wrote books must obviously be quite uneducated and were probably doomed. But it was a relief to everyone when Miss Hampton and Miss Bent were suddenly dragged into the room by Smigly-Rydz.

"Knew I'd find you here," said Miss Hampton to Mrs. Birkett. "Elaine told me you were coming and I saw you go in. Bent and I are going to the Phelps's.

You'd better come too. The Admiral shakes a good cocktail. Well, Elaine, how's little Edna?"

"I never told you," said Mr. Bissell proudly to Mrs. Birkett, "that Mother's name was Elaine. Her father was a great reader of Tennyson and knew the *Idles of the King* by heart."

"It's a lovely name," said Mrs. Birkett, "and very suitable," and then she hoped she had said the right thing.

"You're right there," said Mr. Bissell, casting a look of adoration at his wife that quite melted Mrs. Birkett. "She'd have had all the Sir Galahads after her in the Olden Times."

Mrs. Morland, who complained afterwards that she always coloured too quickly from her surroundings, said she was sure Mrs. Bissell didn't need a Sir Galahad with Mr. Bissell there, and was thoroughly ashamed of herself. But Mr. Bissell's lean tired face shone with gratitude.

Mrs. Bissell said Edna was a good girl and getting on nicely at school.

"Why don't you teach her yourself?" said Miss Hampton.

"I'd love to," said Mrs. Bissell, "but though I am no longer a member I fear it would be disloyal to the N.U.T."

"My wife was a teacher before I married her," said Mr. Bissell proudly. "She did Psychology and understands all the complexes. She and Miss Hampton took to each other like ducks to water and many an interesting chat have we had, Mrs. Bissell on the theoretical side, Miss Hampton on the practical. Mrs. Bissell was offered the post of Headmistress in a very good Secondary School."

"I thought married teachers weren't allowed," said Miss Bent. "It takes a single woman to explain life to girls. Married women are one-sided in their views."

"I did think of keeping on my job," said Mrs. Bissell, "and I discussed it very carefully with Mr. Bissell, but the Income Tax stood in the way. I should have been taxed on his income as well as mine, which made it hardly worth while. It is really much more economical to live in sin if it can be done without attracting attention. We discussed that alternative quite frankly and decided that it wouldn't suit us as we are both home birds. Come along now, Edna, it's time to go to bed."

"I?" said Edna.

"Put the blocks away, dear," said Mrs. Bissell. "Another way is to live with a woman. It is far more economical for Miss Hampton and Miss Bent to live together as they do than if they were married. Now put the lid on nicely."

"Wot sy?" said Edna.

"We say 'pardon,' not 'what did you say,' " said Mrs. Bissell. "You must excuse her, she's a wee bit tired. I must say I cannot quite agree with you, Miss Bent, I admit that one learns much at Teachers' Training Colleges, but it is all bricks without straw. I would advocate married teachers in every case, with a suitable amount of leave on half-pay with every child. But the Income Tax laws would have to be revised first. Say good night, Edna."

"I?" said Edna.

"She's tired, poor little thing," said Mrs. Bissell and picking up her adopted child she held it tenderly in her arms, smiling at it. Mrs. Morland afterwards maintained that Edna had smiled back at her, but Mrs. Birkett, who was more prosaic, said the child had shown no change of expression at all. Mrs. Bissell went upstairs with Edna. Mrs. Birkett said they must go and thanked Mrs. Bissell warmly for a delightful tea-party.

"Now you have once found the way you must come again," said Mr. Bissell, and escorted the ladies to the door, which was tight work with five people in a very narrow passage. Smigly-Rydz pulled Miss Bent violently out of the drawing-room and fawned heavily on Mr. Bissell.

"No biscuits to-day, old fellow," said Mr. Bissell, patting the dog's enormous head.

"Mustn't spoil him," said Miss Hampton, getting out of the front door. "He expects biscuits every time he comes."

"He has a hopeful disposition," said Mr. Bissell, by now entirely at his ease. "I think Panderer must have been his sponsor."

With this classical allusion he shook hands warmly with all his guests and went back into the house to wash up the tea-things.

"What *good* people," said Mrs. Morland earnestly, as soon as they were out of earshot. "They make me feel ashamed. When I saw them so fond of each other and so good to that dreadful idiot child, I felt I ought to go to Poland, or become a munition worker, though I don't suppose I could do either."

"Saints, both of them," said Miss Hampton. "Drive you mad to live with, but saints all the same. She got a good one in on you and me, eh, Bent?"

And Miss Hampton laughed loudly.

"I don't agree with her at all," said Miss Bent. "I am perfectly prepared to pay Income Tax for the sake of my principles. What is the good of all the women like Rory Freemantle who have worn themselves out to make the world a safe place for us if we are not allowed to shoulder our part of the burden. If I had to pay Income Tax on Hampton's income to-morrow I would be proud."

"Nothing to prevent you sending conscience-money to the Chancellor of the Exchequer to-morrow," said Miss Hampton, "but you won't. Coming into the Phelps's, Mrs. Birkett?"

At any other time Mrs. Birkett would have refused,

but so weak did she feel after the unexpected developments of her tea-party that she said After all she did owe Mrs. Phelps a call and might as well pay it now. So as they were now opposite the Admiral's house, they rang the bell.

Rear-Admiral Phelps was a retired naval man who had chosen Southbridge for his retirement, bringing with him his wife and a grown-up daughter. He was a small dry-faced man, quiet and meek in the home, quiet and industrious in all forms of Social Service. There was hardly a Committee, an Institute, a Good Work of any kind in Southbridge on which he was not an active worker, besides being Secretary of the British Legion, the Boy Scouts, and the District Nursing Association, and one of the churchwardens, keeping the Vicar rigorously in order. His wife, a great, bouncing, masterful woman was so exactly what one kind of Admiral's wife is supposed to be that it was almost like a miracle. She also took an immense and overpowering interest in village life, treating everyone as if she were on the quarter-deck; the Vicar as ship's chaplain, his wife as nonexistent, such gentry as there were in Southbridge, a very small village, as captains and commanders, the higher-class tradesmen like Mr. Brown of the Red Lion as lieutenants and midshipmen, the lower class as warrant officers, and everyone else as ratings. For some time she had been unable to fit Miss Hampton and Miss Bent into her scheme, but appeared finally to have placed them as a kind of marines of an amphibious nature, as indeed they were. The Birketts, who did not live in the village, had given her some difficulty, until she decided that Mr. Birkett being in charge of some four hundred men and boys might hold brevet rank as a captain, and to Mrs. Birkett as the captain's wife she extended her friendship.

Mrs. Phelps was one of those happy women for whom wars are made and ever since September the 3rd had not been seen in a skirt except at church. She had become head of the local A.R.P. almost before it was thought of, and managed to combine these duties with running the Red Cross in the village, besides laying down a number of hens, rabbits and goats to save tonnage.

Her daughter Margot, who was as bouncing and masterful as her mother, though not yet so fat, seconded her ably in all her doings, and knitted at incredible speed a vast number of comforts for the Royal Navy. Her ill-wishers said she knitted during the sermon, but this was not true, and choir practice is quite different.

Jutland Cottage, as the admiral had re-christened The Hollies when he took it on his retirement, was not only a centre for every village activity, but a port of call for any naval officer who had ever served with or under the Admiral. There was indeed a legend among the younger men that Mrs. Phelps had accompanied the Admiral on some of his cruises, bringing with her a cow and some poultry for personal use, but this would hardly be possible in the twentieth century, so we need not believe it.

Only a few intimate friends knew that the Admiral was often in pain from a wound received at the battle from which his house took its name, and even fewer knew how badly off the Phelpses were and with what courage they faced not only the rest of their own lives, but their daughter's future, for Miss Phelps was nearly thirty and so used to being regarded as a brother by the navy that nothing else had ever come into her head.

The Admiral himself opened the door. His guests walked in and were immediately enveloped in heavy black folds of some material and, as the Admiral shut the door, in complete darkness.

"To the left," said the Admiral in his quiet precise voice. "This is my light-lock for the black-out. A good invention, don't you think? You come in: no light can get out of the house through the curtain: you shut the door: then you turn left and come through into the sitting-room."

Guided more by the sound of his voice than by his directions the ladies extricated themselves from the folds, turned to the left and passing under a curtain held aside for them by the Admiral, emerged into the little sitting-room which was also hall, dining-room, smoking-room, and often a bedroom for visiting officers. Here Mrs. Phelps in blue serge trousers of a very nautical cut, her abundant bosom but imperfectly restrained by a blue serge zip-up lumber jacket, and a spotted handkerchief round her reddish-grey hair, was entertaining two young men in naval uniform whom she introduced as Tubby and Bill, and the Vicar. She warmly welcomed the newcomers and addressing the Admiral as "Irons" told him to mix the drinks.

Mrs. Birkett begged to present her friend Mrs. Morland.

"Now, wait a minute," said Mrs. Phelps. "There's a Lieutenant Morland in the *Flatiron*. She's on the China station now."

Mrs. Morland said she expected that was her third son Dick, as he was in the *Flatiron* on the China station.

"Dick, that's it," said Mrs. Phelps. "My husband had a destroyer in the Iron class and we take a great interest in them. He was Commander of the *Scrapiron* and Captain of the *Andiron* and was with the *Gridiron* on her trials. All his friends call him 'Irons.' I saw your boy at Malta two years ago, just before the Admiral retired. Tubby, you knew Dick Morland, didn't you?"

Tubby, whose other name is unknown to history, said Rather, and with very little encouragement told Mrs. Morland all about himself. Mrs. Morland, who on seeing so many naval men had suddenly thought that the heroine of her present novel might be rescued from the fangs of the Gestapo agent by an officer on leave listened with great attention, for though she did not exactly know what she wanted to ask, she knew that the strangely working mind that writes books for one would choose and remember a few points that would be useful, so she smiled on Tubby and drank her cocktail and let it all gently soak in.

Miss Hampton and Miss Bent, to whom one cocktail was as naught, tossed theirs off, but refused any more.

"Now, you must have another," said the Admiral. "Drinks are the last economy we are going to make. Must give our friends a drink when they come aboard."

But Miss Hampton refused for herself and her friend, saying she had promised Joe Brown to be in the bar of the Red Lion at opening time and must keep a steady head. Mrs. Birkett had a shrewd guess that both ladies had a steadier head than most men and were really considering the Admiral's purse, and liked them none the less for it.

"These boys were torpedoed a month ago," said Mrs. Phelps, "and they are joining their ship to-morrow."

Tubby tore himself from his conversation with Mrs. Morland to say it had been bad luck to be so long ashore and Bill broke a cheerful silence for the first time to say he wished he hadn't lost his ocarina with his kit, because he had never had a better one. Mrs. Birkett was just going to speak when Miss Phelps, dressed like her mother, but very muddy about the legs of her trousers, came in from the back of the house and said it had taken her half an hour to catch the goats and they weren't milked yet.

"And what's more," she said, "that Mrs. Gissing and her husband came by in their great whacking car and stopped and looked over the hedge and never even offered to help and then they had the cheek to say they were coming round to have a drink. Give me a strong one, Tubby, before they get at the bottle."

"We can't refuse them drinks," said Mrs. Phelps, to whom the laws of hospitality were sacred, "but I'm sure they are spies. Mrs. Gissing has a refugee maid."

"So have I," said Miss Hampton. "Loathe Mrs. Gissing like the devil, but must be fair."

"Is that your Czecho-Slovakian?" said the Vicar, who had been talking quietly to Mrs. Birkett about the Restoration Fund.

"It was," said Miss Hampton. "But she would tell me how much better everything was in Czecho-Slovakia than in England, and I couldn't stand it. Got her a very good job in Barchester. No, it's a Pole now. Must support the Empire."

"Oh, well, a Pole," said Mrs. Phelps. "After all that doesn't count. But Mrs. Gissing has an Austrian refugee and we all know what that means."

Several people said Vienna was such an enchanting place before the last war, and how gay and courageous the Viennese were.

"Mrs. Gissing's maid *may* be gay and courageous," said Mrs. Phelps, "but I think she looks very suspicious, and I have told the Admiral repeatedly that he ought to do something about it. And the Gissings only changed their name from von Giesing just before the last war, when they got naturalised. He was something to do with films in Munich. The Admiral ought to get them interned. Especially their boy."

Miss Hampton said he was a nasty piece of work and far too often in the Red Lion bar.

"Always there when Bent and I go in," she said, "cadging drinks and listening to what people say. To be quite fair, I don't know what he could find out there except the price of potatoes and what fat stock fetched last market day, but he isn't up to any good. When our men begin coming home on leave I shall keep my eye on him."

"I have only met Mrs. Gissing once," said Mrs.

Birkett, "at Mrs. Keith's at Northbridge Manor, and Mrs. Keith told me afterwards that she hardly knew her and she had literally pushed her way into the working party. Poor Mrs. Keith."

Various other members of the party were about to express their dislike or their dark suspicion of the Gissings when the door-bell rang. The Admiral went to the door, visitors were heard making muffled sounds from among the folds of the curtains, and the Gissings came in. Mrs. Gissing we have already met. Of Mr. Gissing we need only say that looking at the shape of his head and more especially the back of it, it seemed surprising that his naturalisation papers should ever have got through.

"How sweet of the Admiral to let us in himself," said Mrs. Gissing.

Mr. Gissing said "Good evening, all," and began ploughing his way towards the drinks.

"Our maid goes home at six, because of the black-out," said Mrs. Phelps. "She lives at Elmtree Corner and her mother likes her to get home in plenty of time."

"You ought to have an Austrian like mine," said Mrs. Gissing. "She works from morning to night and loves it. She has no friends nearer than London so she never goes out. She often says to me, 'I feel quite English, gnädige Frau.' She and your Polish girl ought to meet, Miss Hampton."

"Don't see how they'd meet if yours never gets a holiday," said Miss Hampton.

"Now," said Mrs. Gissing archly, "you mustn't put that in a book. With you and Mrs. Morland here we shall all find ourselves in print. You must be picking up a lot of character in this quaint nook, Mrs. Morland."

"People always seem to think that," said Mrs. Morland plaintively, "but as a matter of fact I seem to spin things out of my inside like a spider. People have to be much funnier than usual before they penetrate into me as it were, and even then they come out quite different."

"You don't know how funny Oscar and I can be," said Mrs. Gissing laughing recklessly. "You must come to one of our Bohemian evenings."

"That is right," said Mr. Gissing suddenly. "You will all come, yes?"

This was the last thing anyone present wanted to do and there was a moment's uncomfortable silence, which the Admiral despairingly broke by asking the Vicar what they were going to do about God Save the King in church, as they ought to have it settled before the Church Council met. The Vicar, who was very shy and had been longing to get away for some time, said it was a question whether our National Anthem should be treated as a prayer, in which case it should be sung kneeling, or as an act of National Expression, outside the scope of the regular service if he made himself understood, and so sung standing. In his own opinion, he said, it would be more reverent to kneel. He said this with some trepidation, for his church-warden, having been used for many years to read the service himself, looked upon his vicar as a kind of chaplain under his orders and was apt to treat him as such.

The Admiral said there was of course only one way of looking at it, and the whole of the naval contingent supported him.

"Kneeling? Nonsense, Vicar," said Miss Hampton. "If my father were alive he would write to the *Times* about it tomorrow."

Miss Bent said in a congregation composed chiefly of women, she did not include, she said, Hampton and herself in this statement, there was a natural tendency to kneel, which could be explained psychologically in Catholic countries as a Mother Complex, but in Protestant countries was less easy to analyse, as the female element in the act of worship was less pronounced. The Vicar who was terrified of Miss Bent and Miss Hampton, though deeply grateful for their generosity and kindness in the parish, got up and said his wife would be expecting him.

"I cannot see that it is of vital importance," said Mrs. Gissing, "but then Oscar and I are not Church of England."

"Are you Catholic?" said Mrs. Morland with deep interest. "I have quite a lot of friends who are Catholics and they are really very nice and we never mention anything unpleasant and get on very well."

"Oh, dear no," said Mrs. Gissing, showing no interest in Mrs. Morland's apologia for the Catholic faith, "Oscar and I go much deeper. We simply believe in the Good and Beautiful."

If any of the eight other people now present, all of whom disliked the Gissings more and more, had tried to express politely what they thought of them, they could not have hit upon a less suitable description. Tubby choked into his drink and tried to pretend he was only drinking. Mrs. Birkett said it was very late and they must be going as she had forgotten to bring a torch and there was no moon. Bill at once offered his torch, which Mrs. Birkett gratefully accepted, saying that she would send it back that evening by the odd man when he went home.

"By the way," she added, "you were talking about an ocarina. I have one if you'd care to have it. It belongs to my daughter who is in Las Palombas with her husband and I know she won't want it."

"I say, that's awfully jolly of you," said Bill. "Funny thing, I know a chap in Las Palombas called Fairweather. I wonder if your daughter knows him. His wife is a peach. I saw her at the Barchester Palais de Danse with Fairweather last time I was on leave."

Mrs. Birkett's intense pleasure at hearing Rose so described may be imagined, as may the joy of Bill (whose name and rank are for ever unknown) on hearing that Mrs. Birkett who had been sent from heaven to give him an ocarina was also the mother of the peach. All the guests then left in a lump, much hampered by the Admiral's light-lock.

"We have our car," said Mrs. Gissing, flashing a very large torch full on to a kind of super Daimler-Rolls about ten yards long, and describing circles of light in the air all round it to show off its magnificence.

"Put out that torch, Mrs. Gissing," said the Admiral in his precise voice.

"I am really not so conceited," said Mrs. Gissing, extinguishing the light however, "as to think that hostile aircraft is looking for little me. Does anyone want a lift? Oscar has heaps of petrol. He has been storing it ever since Munich, but not a word to the police."

There was a dead silence, for everyone present would have walked home with bare and bleeding feet, or on stilts, sooner than accept Mrs. Gissing's offer. So Mr. Gissing got into the driver's seat, lit his cigar with a petrol lighter that illuminated half the village, and drove fatly away.

"High time Bent and I were at the Red Lion," said Miss Hampton. "Let me come and see you some day, Mrs. Birkett."

Mrs. Birkett said she would love it and Miss Hampton walked off with Miss Bent into the darkness.

Mrs. Morland and Mrs. Birkett walked home in silence, turning on the torch as little as possible because of not using up the batteries, though as Mrs. Morland very truly said batteries seemed to run down just as much when you didn't use them as when you did use them, to which Mrs. Birkett replied that the mysterious thing about electric irons was that they went on getting hotter after you had turned them off.

Dinner was rather quiet except for Geraldine, who

was now on day duty at Barchester Hospital and so able to entertain her parents and their guest in the evening by telling them what Matron said and drawing very trenchant comparisons between that lady and Miss Pettinger. While she talked the grown-ups were able to enjoy the good food and try not to listen. Mr. Birkett was deep in his report for the School Governors which had to be presented next week and the ladies were still ruminating on the events of the afternoon. Mrs. Birkett and Mrs. Morland were still partially stunned by all they had gone through since tea-time, and it was not till Geraldine was brought to a stop by a very good coffee pudding that they began to revive. Mrs. Morland, as a successful author, was experiencing the hopeless feeling which besets writers when life gets the better of them with one hand tied behind its back. She felt that she might have invented the Admiral and Mrs. Phelps, who were the novelist's dream of what retired Admirals and their wives should be, and might even have managed the Gissings, though the Good and Beautiful was, she freely admitted, quite beyond her. But at Maria Cottage she had been shaken from her bearings in a way she would have thought impossible. Mr. Bissell she had met, liked and could more or less deal with, but Mrs. Bissell had left her perfectly addled. If Mrs. Bissell had been as she described herself, a mere home bird, or on the other hand an ordinary sample of a teacher, she could have coped with it. But she burst out in such unexpected places. Her obvious though unspoken devotion to Mr. Bissell, her firm yet tender treatment of the dreadful Edna, her terrifying and businesslike grasp of Income Tax, Psychology, the question of the married teacher, the case of Miss Hampton and Miss Bent; all these filled Mrs. Morland's humble mind with slightly envious admiration. She felt perfectly certain that as soon as the door of Maria Cottage had closed behind them Mrs. Bissell had first tabulated them all neatly in her own mind and then forgotten all about them till next time. That Mrs. Bissell thought poorly of her she had no doubt and did not in the least resent it, for before real goodness, and that absolutely shone from Mrs. Bissell, she was silent and abashed. Then, thinking of little Edna, the happy thought swept over her that she had four sons, and thus was infinitely superior to anyone who had no children, not to speak of those that had only daughters. For this feeling she occasionally blamed herself, but it was rooted somewhere in her very deeply. People might know psychology till they were black in the face, thought Mrs. Morland, and be able to take in a business-like spirit all the sinister implications of Adelina Cottage which would never have occurred to her at all. But although such people existed they had not got four sons. And Mrs. Morland's mind began to sketch out a scene for her next story in which Madame Koska should engage two ladies like Miss Hampton and Miss Bent to be mannequins for her tailored costumes and dinner-jacket suits (with skirt), how the Gestapo agent should try his wiles on one of them while planning to abduct the heroine, and the whole should be brought to confusion by a customer, no longer young, not remarkably good-looking yet distinguished, who could only afford one good costume a year, but who had a woman's intuition and the heart of a lion, all because she had four sons.

"What is it, Laura?" said Mr. Birkett, looking up from his savoury as he heard a slight noise.

"I was only thinking about a book," said Mrs. Morland gulping, for the thought of the middle-aged customer (herself in fact) had been too much for her. "Do you think, Bill," she added with one of her snipe-flights, "that I ought to be doing propaganda?"

"Certainly not," said Mr. Birkett. "You haven't the faintest qualifications, my dear Laura. Go on amusing us for God's sake with your books, and saving my life by being my secretary."

"Fritz Gissing is bringing out a book with the Anti-Imperial Book Club," said Geraldine, who was now at a loose end owing to not liking cheese canapés. "It's called *The Lion Turns Tail.* It's all about how rotten the Government are."

Her parents said nothing, knowing well that their approval or disapproval of this remark would meet with equal disfavour from their daughter.

"I told him I thought it was an awfully silly name," said Geraldine dispassionately, "and he's going to take me over the Film Studios."

"But where did you meet him?" said Mrs. Birkett, breaking the most sacred rule of a parent's conduct, which is never to ask anything about anything where her children are concerned.

But Geraldine was in a favourable mood, so instead of glaring at her mother, or losing her temper, she said "Oh, places; I must go and telephone," and left the room.

"And I know what will happen," said Mrs. Birkett despairingly to Mrs. Morland as the door slammed; not we must say in justice to Geraldine with the slam of passion, but the slam of finding it less trouble to slam a door than to shut it quietly, "Geraldine will want to ask all the Gissings here."

"Well, I must go and get on with that report," said Mr. Birkett. "Why can't Geraldine shut the door without slamming it? Everard is coming over to go through it with me. We shall be late, so don't sit up."

"Oh, Bill, one thing before you go," said Mrs. Morland. "Who was it that had a casket with nothing but hope at the bottom of it? Not Prometheus, but you know whom I mean."

"I suppose you mean Pandora," said Mr. Birkett. "Why?"

"I only wanted to be sure," said Mrs. Morland meekly.

9

SHERRY AT THE BIRKETTS'

•

The most beautiful autumn that anyone could remember now spread its mantle over Barsetshire and the rest of England. The evacuated children, who were by now all dressed by the hand of charity in coloured woollen frocks arted up at the neck, and coloured woollen coats of no particular shape or cut, not to speak of nightgowns and dressing-gowns and underclothes, looked fatter and pinker every day. Owing to the vigorous efforts of volunteer workers there was now not a lice-infested head among them, except when one of them was taken back to London by its parents for a week, cried all the time, and was returned to start the whole thing all over again. The primitive Wessex speech of the country children was being rapidly overlaid with a fine veneer of Cockney. As far as bad words went neither side had the advantage and the grosser names of Barsetshire were bartered against the more up-to-date obscenities of the evacuated areas. In writing, however, the London children had a distinct advantage. Maturing more early than the children of the soil, quicker if shallower witted, more bad language was written on the walls of Southbridge owing to their efforts in ten weeks than had been seen since Roman soldiers inscribed facetiae on the clay tiles of the Roman villa whose foundations had lately been evacuated near Northbridge.

Various voluntary committees had by now got well into their stride. Mrs. and Miss Phelps had collected money for a cottage hospital for the London children, forced a very rich friend to let them use an empty house, furnished it by borrowing from all their not so rich friends and bullied all the girls in the neighbourhood into nursing and cooking in shifts under a professional matron; while the Admiral, who never knew when he was beaten, had so badgered the Ministry concerned both by letter and through every influential friend he possessed that the necessary permits were obtained in less than a month. Upon this all the working parties had fallen to again with zeal and provided a supply of pyjamas guaranteed not to fit any age of child, red monkey jackets, and knitted coverlets that would have kept Florence Nightingale quiet for months.

Another committee, also headed by Mrs. and Miss Phelps, had descended upon the Women's Institute and commandeered its hall as a canteen for London parents when they came down on Sundays to see their offspring. Some of the committee had wished to supply free cups of tea, but Mrs. Phelps was adamant, and Miss Hampton, who was a liberal subscriber to all Mrs. Phelps's activities, came to the meeting in her fiercest tailor-made and putting a monocle into her right eye had looked them all up and down, saying that as the parents, as far as she could see, need never spend another penny on their children's clothes and general welfare as long as they left them in the country, they could afford to pay for cups of tea and buns.

"I do think," said Mrs. Gissing, who had somehow got on to the Committee, "that the State ought to do everything for those poor women. In Germany, the State has a far better conception of its duties where children are concerned."

To which Miss Hampton had replied that if it came to that Russia had a better conception still and they were both wrong. And Mrs. Phelps had said: Were they all agreed then that the canteen was to be self-supporting, would all those in favour signify it in the usual way by holding up their hands, thank you, yes; so quickly that Mrs. Gissing put up her hand without meaning to and was so flurried that she gave half a crown towards the initial expenses before she knew where she was.

Admiral Phelps carried a gas-mask everywhere as an example and worked himself to the bone collecting volunteer casualties for his A.R.P. practice. In the evenings, now beginning far too early, he would patrol the village for illegal lights and twice had the pleasure of knocking up the Gissings and making them turn out the light in their garage.

Miss Hampton and Miss Bent who were very strong and did not know what it was to be tired, took an allotment and dug for victory in a way that compelled the admiration of the sexton, who as an amateur of spadework spent hours of his time watching them and was nearly late with old Mrs. Trouncer's grave, which he had to finish at six in the morning owing to Miss Hampton's kind offer to give him a hand with it. They also collaborated with Miss Phelps in looking after the goats, hens and rabbits who lived in the field behind Jutland Cottage. The hens were no particular trouble except that they had to be fed, watered and put to bed at such various inconvenient hours that Margot Phelps had almost to give up social life. The rabbits were more especially Miss Bent's care, as she had a loom on which she was occasionally moved to weave pieces of gaily striped material that sagged violently at the knees and elbows if made up into coats and skirts, and had visions of spinning the rabbits' fur and weaving it into even looser and more sagging material. The goats therefore fell into the hands of Miss Hampton, who, adding a pair of very well made leggings to her tweed costume, so harassed those odious animals that their spirits were quite broken. Her strength was such that the strongest

Billy was outmatched if he tried to pull in the wrong direction. Every time a Nanny trod on her feet while being milked, she gave her a resounding whack with a stick. Mrs. Phelps was at first inclined to question the humanity of these methods, but when Miss Hampton explained that goats had an unfair advantage owing to their hoofs being so small and precipitous that you couldn't tread back, she saw the point.

The real difficulty about the goats was what to do with their milk. The Phelpses, who had become acclimatised to goats at Malta, didn't mind the taste and in any case didn't take milk with their tea, but everyone else expressed their just abhorrence of it in no measured terms, till there seemed to be nothing for it but to throw the milk away, thus, as Mrs. Phelps said almost in tears, playing directly into the enemy's hands. But very luckily an immensely rich family who had taken a house outside Southbridge for the duration believed that goat's milk was Life for their six young children, so Mrs. Phelps was able to sell it at a good price, and Miss Phelps delivered it once a day on her bicycle. It seemed probable to everyone that the milk would arrive churned to death, but the children throve on it just as if it were nice cows' milk, so all was well.

Southbridge School, with the Hoisers' Boys, did not take a large part in the village life. It had always been a self-contained establishment and under present conditions everyone was too busy to look aside. Geraldine, as her father had predicted, made herself such a trouble to her parents over the Gissings, that they almost wished they had Rose back again. Mr. Birkett said to his wife, for he dared not say it to his daughter, it was difficult enough to keep the school going at present, and make the older boys stick to their scholarship work, and arbitrate on the question of whether the window in the squash court had been broken by his boys or Bissell's, and bear with that man Hopkins's Communism, and take the Classical Sixth himself till he could get a really first-class man to replace Philip Winter, without having impossible outsiders in his house. Mrs. Birkett said to her husband, for she also did not like to say it to Geraldine, that she had never seen anyone she disliked so much as the Gissings and she was sure that the son was even worse, but if Geraldine could not ask her friends to her parents' house where could she ask them?

Geraldine, relying on a war of attrition, merely went on bothering her parents whenever she was not at the Hospital till they gave in, which they might just as well have done in the first place. The only stipulation Mrs. Birkett made was that the Gissings should be asked to sherry. She had for some time wished to have a party for the pleasure of seeing people, for what with the petrol rationing, and everyone being busy, and the black-out, she had rather lost touch with her friends of late. In a gathering of this kind she hoped the Gissings might be if not drowned at least so watered down as to be fairly harmless. Accordingly, choosing a day when there would be some moonlight after darkness had set in, though with the firm conviction that there would also be clouds and heavy rain, she sent out her invitations. In case Heaven should disapprove of people enjoying themselves during a period of mingled unhappiness, anxiety and boredom which, as far as she could see, it had done nothing whatsoever to prevent, she threw it a sop in the shape of some very hideous embroidery done by the Mixo-Lydian refugees who were housed about two miles from Southbridge. These embroideries she decided to put in the dining-room, so that people needn't look at them unless they really wanted to.

On the morning of the party the two head refugees, M. and Mme Brownscu, appeared in person, carrying the embroideries in a basket. Their real titles, which might be the equivalent of Count and Countess or Mr.

and Mrs., but no one liked to ask, were Prodshk and Prodshka, but the local Committee for Mixo-Lydia, recognizing that such names must fill any self-respecting foreigner with shame, had given them brevet rank as Monsieur and Madame, so that a great many people thought they were Poles; though they would have been hard put to it to explain the mode of reasoning that led them to this conclusion. There were even unbelievers who said that Brownscu was not a Mixo-Lydian name, nor indeed a name at all, but Miss Phelps, who happened to have recently added that particular committee to her collection, said everyone knew there was somebody called Jonescu in Romania or somewhere, so why not Brownscu in Mixo-Lydia; by which remark she was considered to have scored pretty heavily.

How the Mixo-Lydians lived, no one, not even their committee, knew. While they had all fled from their country at an hour's notice leaving the dinner cooking in the oven and the beds unmade, they all lived in considerable if unhygienic comfort and even luxury, and some of them went up to town every day by the 8:10 returning to dinner. No English servant would stay, partly because of not liking foreigners and partly because they didn't hold with mucking up the food like that, so three or four inferior Mixo-Lydians were imported somehow from France, where a good many of them had got stuck. And, as Mrs. Phelps bitterly remarked, if *she* had wanted a foreign servant it would have taken her six months to get a permit and then she wouldn't have got it.

M. and Mme Brownscu, being if possible even more disagreeable, selfish and ungrateful than any of their compatriots, had assumed a kind of royal dignity at what the village called Mixerlydian House, and undertook all embassies between it and the outer world. Mme Brownscu was a small wiry woman with a mop of frizzled dark hair and a leopardskin coat, and by the hideous shape of her legs it was generally thought that she had been a dancer. M. Brownscu, yellow faced and melancholy, wore a skin-tight béret which he never removed, and was permanently huddled in a sheepskin coat.

Mrs. Birkett received them in the dining room where the exhibition was to be.

"It is not very big, your room," said Mme Brownscu by way of greeting. "The Pagnaskaya in Lydianopolis as you call it, though its true name is Lvdpov, is very much larger. That is where we have our Expositions d'Arts Néo-paysans, what you would call new peasants arts. Have you no bigger room?"

"The drawing-room is bigger," said Mrs. Birkett, "but that is where I am having my friends. I think your embroideries will look very nice here."

"They will ollways look nice," said Mme Brownscu, "but the ambiance is not paysanne at all. God wills it so. On this table I shall put them, yes? I shall arrange them for you."

"Well, I'm afraid we are going to have lunch on this table first," said Mrs. Birkett. "But if you will leave them here, I will myself put them out after lunch as attractively as possible."

Even as she spoke Mrs. Birkett found herself insensibly slipping into her visitor's style of English and wondered why it was so difficult to talk naturally to foreigners who had an idiomatic command of English.

"I shall myself come back and arrange them and change your furniture a little which is not right," said Mme Brownscu. "You would not understand. At six o'clock your party, yes? Then I shall come at five o'clock and arrange everything and put the prices very plainly. They will be rich, your friends, yes?"

Mrs. Birkett said she was afraid not.

"Then we shall chaffer," said Mme Brownscu.

"There is a market in Lvdpov every Tuesday and there I chaffer with the peasants and hit them down. Nothing will I buy till I have well examined it."

Mrs. Birkett didn't think her friends would be much good at chaffering, but held her peace.

"And Gradko shall bring his poems and read to you," Mme Brownscu continued. "Nov pvarno orlskjok chjlèm zy chokra?" she added to her husband.

M. Brownscu huddled even more into his sheepskin coat and said, "Czy provka, provka, provka."

"He says, 'No, never, never, never,' " said Mme Brownscu, and to Mrs. Birkett's great relief did not press the matter any further. In fact she was just going when, much to Mrs. Birkett's annoyance, Mrs. Morland appeared at the door.

"Oh, I thought you were here," said Mrs. Morland to her friend.

There was nothing for it but to introduce Mrs. Morland. Mrs. Birkett very meanly revenged herself by telling the Brownscus that Mrs. Morland was a celebrated writer.

"Ah-ha!" said Mme Brownscu. "Then my husband must tell you his poem. It is a great poem, epopic, about our great national hero, Gradko, for which my husband is baptized."

"Is he a Catholic then?" said Mrs. Morland, who had been writing all the morning and as usual was only just coming out of her bardic frenzy and more than usually vague, and thought the Brownscus might be something to do with the Gissings.

"Czy, provka, provka, provka," said M. Brownscu energetically.

"He expresses, 'No, never, never, never,' " said his wife. "The word Catholic, to us it is like a red rug to a bull. We are Orthodox," and she crossed herself violently in what Mrs. Morland afterwards described as a very upside-down and un-Christian kind of way. "But

I shall tell you," she continued. "Gradko is a son of a peasant girl which has been violée, you would say raped, by a nobleman, so his mother is pleased and lays three grains of millet on his cradle."

"Why?" said Mrs. Morland.

"It is a custom," said Mme Brownscu. "So Gradko grows up and becomes a famous warrior. One day he hears a shriek. He approaches. He sees a lovely maiden being séduite, seducted you say, by a Turk. Mixo-Lydia hates Turks, therefore he kills him. The maiden has run away in terror. He pursues her till night. He hears a shriek and redoubles his pace. The maiden is being forcée, taken in English, by a Bulgar. All Bulgars are enemies of Mixo-Lydia, therefore he kills him. The maiden has again run away in terror. At dawn he hears a shriek. It is the maiden who is being éventré, eventuated you would say, by a Russian. Russian and Mixo-Lydia are enemies, so he kills the Russian. Thus the prophecy is fulfilled and he is crowned King."

"And what happened to the maiden?" said Mrs. Morland, wishing she could think of as many incidents, though not quite of that kind, for her new book.

"Par suite de ses rélations avec Gradko elle devient mère et accouche de quatre fils," said Mme Brownscu, getting tired of English. "Le premier s'appelle Achmet, parcequ'il est Turc, le second Boris parcequ'il est Bulgare, le troisième, qui est Russe, Ivan, et le quatrième qui est le plus beau de tous et fait assassiner son père, sa mère et ses trois frères aînés s'appelle Gradko, comme son père. Every child in Mixo-Lydia knows that story."

Before her hearers could think of the obvious retort that they were not Mixo-Lydian children, Mme Brownscu had taken her husband away, promising again to return at five o'clock with her embroideries.

The next few hours were spent, as usually happens with a sherry party, in people who had accepted ringing up to say they were so sorry they couldn't come because the petrol had given out, or Betty or Tommy was suddenly home on leave and wanted to go to the Barchester Odeon, and people who had refused ringing up to say might they come after all as Captain King who was staying with them had gallons of petrol from the War Office if Mrs. Birkett didn't mind them bringing him too. With all of these Simnet and Mrs. Birkett dealt. The last to ring up was Mrs. Crawley who asked if she might bring Captain Merton who was staying with them, to which Mrs. Birkett said please do, though the name at the moment meant nothing to her.

At five o'clock the Brownscus arrived with the embroideries, but Mrs. Birkett basely pretended she was lying down and left Simnet to deal with them and give them some tea. That perfect butler, who had been in France from 1915 to 1917, stood no nonsense from Mme Brownscu, and by taking up a position in front of any piece of furniture that she wanted to move and saying "No bon, madam," made her confine her activities to laying out her wares on the dining-room table, after which he gave her a very good tea of which she and her husband greedily partook.

By a quarter past six the drawing-room was already seething with people, all delighted to have a treat and talk to each other about the future rationing of butter. Mrs. Birkett was informed in a quarter of an hour by four different friends who all happened to *know* they were speaking the truth that (a) the Government had immense reserves of butter at Leamington and rationing would only be for form's sake, (b) there were only three days' supplies of butter in the country, (c) that there was plenty of butter but it all had to go to Egypt, and (d) that margarine had all the vitamins of butter and you couldn't tell the difference. None of these statements did Mrs. Birkett particularly believe, and the last she knew to be a downright lie.

"People are so prejudiced," said Mrs. Gissing, who

was the last speaker. "Now that all margarine has vitamins P and Q, there is no difference at all."

"Only the filthy taste," said Miss Phelps who had just come from an A.R.P. practice in a very belligerent frame of mind.

"I always give it to my Austrian maid, and she says nothing at all," said Mrs. Gissing.

"Well, if I were Mitzi I'd say a mouthful," said Miss Phelps aloud to herself.

"But what I think so dreadful," said Mrs. Gissing, persuading herself that she had not heard Miss Phelps, "is that the price of butter is so high. Oscar and Fritz have to eat it, because they are delicate, so I eat a little myself, or they would be wretched. But even our little bill for butter is appalling and how the *real* poor live I cannot think. The Government ought to take over all the butter and let the poor have it. When I think of all the homes in England that can't afford butter now I am almost a Communist. All these poor wretched evacuee children should be having pounds of butter."

"But, Mrs. Gissing," said Kate Carter, whose housewifely mind could not keep away from a conversation in which butter took a part, "the cottage people in Southbridge really prefer margarine and so do the evacuees. It is just the same at Northbridge where my parents live. People are *so* kind about saying they would be better nourished if they ate nettles and dandelions and butter, but what they really want is meat and margarine."

Mrs. Birkett said the servants were the difficulty with margarine in the last war, because they thought it was nothing but their employers being mean.

"In the last war," said Mr. Gissing who had been listening attentively, "we bought butter and margarine and exchanged the wrappers. Then my wife said to the servants, 'You can have the butter and Mr. Gissing and I shall eat margarine.' So they were pleased to have the butter as they thought, and stayed on with us till they were interned."

"Why were they interned?" asked Miss Phelps.

"They were enemy aliens,' said Mr. Gissing simply. "So then Gloria and I moved into a service flat where we were very comfortable till we had to come down here with my business. Comfort is my motto."

No one quite knew what to say and Mrs. Birkett was glad of the excuse to greet some newcomers. At the same moment there was a slight commotion near the door and she saw her daughter Geraldine, who had managed to get the afternoon off, leading a young man by the hand, just as her sister Rose had artlessly been wont to lead her many adoring swains. The young man was of middle height, slim and fair, not to say blond, and undulated in an alarming way from the waist. Every man in the room wondered who that little bounder was. Most of the women were interested against their better selves, and the Vicar's wife, who had just been reading one of the perennial re-hashes of Byron's life (*The Truth about Byron* by Lilian Tuckwell, author of the *Truth about Shelley, Keats, The Brownings,* and many other popular works) said to her next door neighbour who happened to be Mrs. Phelps, "Mad, bad and dangerous to know."

"Who?" said Mrs. Phelps, following the direction of the Vicar's wife's eyes. "Fritz Gissing? He's a rank outsider, but that's all. No danger there. I'd let Margot go anywhere with him if she wanted to, but she doesn't. He ought to be in the Army. I told the Admiral he ought to be interned."

The Vicar's wife, with admirable good sense, said that he couldn't very well be both and she knew for a fact, because Mrs. Gissing had told her, that the boy was twenty-four.

Mrs. Phelps said Oh, was that all, in a way that expressed her poor opinion of people that were still too old to be called up, but comforted herself with the reflection that young Gissing would soon be drawn into the jaws of the Army.

Meanwhile Geraldine had dragged her prey up to her mother saying, "Mummy, here's Fritz. He has simply dashed in for a moment and has to go back to the studio almost at once so I'll get him a drink."

Young Mr. Gissing said he could do with one, but on being offered a glass of sherry said God, wasn't there any gin?

"Hi, Kate," said Geraldine to Mrs. Everard Carter, "this is Fritz. Hang on to him while I get him a drink."

Kate, who had no clue as to who Fritz might be, but was always kind, thought from his name and appearance that he must be a refugee, probably one of the Mixo-Lydians who were showing their distressed work in the dining-room, so she asked him if he did embroidery.

"Of course I do," said young Mr. Gissing. "when I'm not working. How can a man do anything else? I always have my embroidery in the studio with me and work away at it."

Kate said she supposed he had some with him to-day and she looked forward to seeing it so much, upon which young Mr. Gissing obligingly opened a soft leather portfolio that he was carrying under his arm and took out a piece of *petit point*. Kate's admiration was unfeigned and they were deep in talk about stitches and shading when Geraldine came back.

"I say," said Geraldine, "Daddy won't let me have the gin. Something about war-time. I'm frightfully sorry, Fritz."

"Gin's a filthy drink anyway," said young Mr. Gissing. "What about some sherry?"

Geraldine obediently went to get some and Kate thought how nice it was that Geraldine, usually so off-hand to everyone, should take such trouble for a refugee and was pleased to see this change of spirit. When the sherry came young Mr. Gissing drank it and said to Kate that he must be going.

"But you've only just come, Fritz," said Geraldine.

"Well, come and see the studio one day," said her young friend. "Ring up my secretary," and without any further formality he wormed his way towards the door.

"Do you suppose his embroidery is very expensive?" asked Kate, which led to an explanation that young Mr. Gissing was not a refugee but on very important work in the fiim world.

"You couldn't possibly take him for a refugee," said Geraldine indignantly. "You only have to look at him."

As this was precisely what Kate had done, she was not convinced, but she felt rather anxious about Geraldine whose manly heart was evidently touched by young Mr. Gissing. Kate could not see him as a son-in-law to the Birketts, but neither had she seen him show much interest in Geraldine and she wished that Geraldine had chosen better.

And now Miss Hampton and Miss Bent hove down upon Kate. Miss Hampton, looking incredibly smart in a black coat and skirt, a black tricorne and a white shirt with onyx links, was carrying the elephant-faced dog in her arms. She explained to Kate that he didn't like being on the floor at parties, owing to being sensitive about his height.

"Poor old Smigly-Rydz," said Kate, patting his head.

"That's just the trouble," said Miss Hampton, taking a glass of sherry from a tray that came by. "Must have a sherry. Bent and I had one before we started, but we haven't been to the Red Lion yet. Go there on the way back. Where's Mrs. Morland?"

Kate pointed her out, doing her best with the doctor's wife.

"Get her, Bent," said Miss Hampton. "She'll know. Rydz, you'll have to go down, you're too heavy."

She put him on the floor where he sat, apparently

quite free from any form of inferiority complex about his height, gently slapping the floor with his stumpy tail.

Miss Bent now returned with Mrs. Morland and at the same moment Mrs. and Miss Phelps, who had the greatest admiration for authors and belonged to practically every Book Club or Society, regardless of race or creed, joined the circle to hear the two writers talk.

The literary symposium was begun by both ladies giving an elaborate account the one of her four sons, the other of her four nephews, all of whom, we are glad to say, were at the moment well, though Mrs. Morland had reservations in favour of her eldest boy, for, as she truly said, if one is in Central America and expects to be out of touch with civilisation for six months, really anything might happen, except that natives had wonderful ways of knowing things before they could possibly know, but of course that was no use unless they could get into touch with someone and it would be so difficult to know which dialect it was.

Kate said she was sure Rose Fairweather would do something about it if she knew, but no one shared her optimism as to Rose's power of getting news about an exploring party a thousand miles from her neighbourhood, and those who knew her best felt that even if people were exploring in her garden she wouldn't take any interest in them unless they invited her to a night club or a cinema.

"But that's not the point," said Miss Hampton. "Point is, what am I to do about Rydz?"

Mrs. Morland asked if he were ill.

"Ill?" said Miss Hampton. "Never better. Bent gave him a couple of worm powders last week and he's as fit as a fiddle. News isn't at all good. Looks as if we'd have to change his name."

"Won't he answer to it?" said Miss Phelps. "Perhaps he's getting deaf."

"Not a bit deaf," said Miss Hampton. "But if Finland is invaded, and it looks like it, what can we call him? Must call him something. Gallant little Finland."

Mrs. Morland said that without being superstitious it seemed unlucky to call people gallant, because the moment they were gallent they got conquered by somebody.

Miss Bent, making one of her rare incursions into the conversation, said what about Estonia and Latvia and Lithuania. Nobody had called them gallant, not for a single moment, but there they were.

"But aren't they the same?" said Mrs. Morland. "I mean isn't Latvia how the Lithuanians pronounce Lithuania, like the Italians pronouncing Florence Firenze?"

"It was no good thinking of a name for Rydz in them," said Miss Hampton, "because there is simply nobody there."

Kate thought there must be somebody.

"No one with a name," said Miss Bent. "We studied the question, but there was no one."

"Same trouble with Finland," said Miss Hampton. "Must do our best for them. But who is there in Finland, I mean with a name?"

There was a short silence, broken by Kate, who said hadn't somebody once got a Nobel prize or was she thinking of someone else.

"There is Sibelius," said Mrs. Morland with the air of one making a concession.

"Bent thought of that," said Miss Hampton, "but it wouldn't do. If England were in trouble it wouldn't do any good to call a dog Elgar. Isn't there anyone else?"

Miss Phelps said she once went to a concert at Queen's Hall where there was a piece called the Return of Somebody. She wasn't musical, she added, but there was something in the piece that got her though she couldn't explain why.

"The awful thing is," said Mrs. Morland, in her tragedy voice, "that I am even worse off than you are, Miss Hampton. You know my heroine that I told you about; and now she may have to be Finnish. I couldn't make her an Esthonian or a Latvian, because they haven't enough appeal. My publisher wants to have my typescript by the end of January at the very latest. Are there any women's names in Finland? And then it will probably be Jugo-Slavia after all."

But before these important questions could be threshed out, Geraldine, looking very sulky, said Mother said would they go and look at the embroideries in the dining-room, because if no one went Mme Brownscu would be so disappointed. Miss Hampton, stopping Simnet and his tray, said they must all have another sherry and then they'd go.

"Well, here's fun," said Miss Phelps. "And don't forget that you are going to help us to move the Billy to the other end of the field to-morrow, Miss Hampton. He's too strong for Mother and me."

"That's because you wear those ridiculous trousers," said Miss Hampton, who was in high good humour about the billy goat and had long been meaning to speak her mind about the trousers.

"I can't think why you don't wear them," said Miss Phelps. "They're a wonderful economy. Two pairs last me a year, except for the few weeks of summer."

"Well, I know exactly what I'd look like," said Miss Hampton, "neither a man nor a woman."

And she stuck her monocle into one eye defiantly.

"Well, that's exactly what you look like now," said Mrs. Phelps, pot-valiant with sherry.

Everyone held her breath expecting a first-class row, but Miss Hampton, taking her remark in very good part, laughed uproariously and told Miss Bent that Mrs. Phelps had put one over on them this time. Kate, who in the absence of Rose, and the thundercloud presence of

Geraldine, had constituted herself a temporary daughter to Mrs. Birkett, then gently and firmly shepherded a section of the party across into the dining-room. Here a number of pieces of rather dirty embroidery on very inferior material were disposed on the dining-room table. They were all of unusual shapes and no one quite knew what they were meant for, or if they were meant to be something else. M. Brownscu was installed behind a table near the door with a pile of small change spread out before him, evidently ready to receive customers, while his wife, smoking cigarettes whose stubs Kate's eye at once detected all over the carpet and furniture, stood ready to chaffer. Mrs. Phelps, who had decided to spend five shillings, picked up something that might have been a rather hideous collar and looked at it. On the collar was pinned a piece of paper bearing the inscription £15,000. She thought this must be a mistake, so she showed it to her daughter who was equally puzzled.

"I say, Miss Hampton," said Miss Phelps, "do look at this. Mme Whoeveritis must be mad."

"That's all right," said Miss Hampton, examining the paper. "Fifteen thousand Lydions—that's the currency in Mixo-Lydia. About five shillings. But you'd better offer four."

Mrs. Phelps, who had bargained in every port where the British Navy is known, took the collar over to Mme Brownscu and said firmly, "Three and sixpence."

"You wish us to starve then?" said Mme Brownscu throwing her cigarette on to the polished sideboard from which the anxious Kate rescued it. "It is not for amusing themselves that my compatriots work, it is for their bread. Fifteen thousand Lydions, that is to say five shillings sixpence or nearabouts."

"Three and ninepence," said Mrs. Phelps.

Mme Brownscu, at last in her element, launched an attack on English hospitality which would so abuse penniless exiles as to make them sacrifice a piece of work, the fruit of months of patient toil, for five shillings and threepence. But Mrs. Phelps was as keen an amateur of chaffering as Mme Brownscu herself and for several minutes the battle hung suspended. Miss Hampton, who was prepared to buy with her usual generosity, came over to the chafferers, carrying a traycloth which looked a little less hideous and amateur than the other articles. Both buyer and seller had stuck for the moment, the one at four and threepence, the other at four and ninepence.

"Time you settled a price," said Miss Hampton. "I drove a Red Cross Ambulance all over Mixo-Lydia in 1918. Know them all well. Give me the embroidery."

Mrs. Phelps, hypnotised, handed the collar to Miss Hampton, who slapping it down on the table said a few words in Mixo-Lydian. Mme Brownscu answered volubly in her native language and thrust the collar into Miss Hampton's hands, adding to it a small square piece of embroidery in a primitive cross-stitch.

"There you are," said Miss Hampton, handing the goods to Mrs. Phelps. "Four and sixpence and she is giving you the other bit for luck because you are the first purchaser. Czjrejok it is called."

Further incursions of guests now came into the room and under the influence of Mr. Birkett's good sherry the horrid embroideries were snapped up at sums varying from 5,000 to 25,000 Lydions. Mme Brownscu kept a suspicious eye on purchasers and from time to time went to see that her husband was giving the right change. Miss Hampton, who had been back to the drawing-room and collected some more sherry, approached M. Brownscu and said a few jovial words in Mixo-Lydian.

"Czy, provka, provka, provka," said M. Brownscu, huddling his sheepskin coat more tightly round him and looking at Miss Hampton with terror.

"He expresses, 'No, never, never, never,' " said his

wife, kindly satisfying the curiosity of those present. "I shall tell you he was having frost-bitten feet in the Red Cross Ambulance and these English ladies were so good to him and give him a bath, mais ce n'est pas l'habitude du pays et cela lui a porté sur le foie. Il a une santé qu'il faut ménager et dupuis lors il a pris les infirmières anglaises en horreur. C'est un tic, mais que voulez vous? C'est comme ça chez nous. We ate what we do not like."

"Was anything wrong with the tea?" asked kind Kate, anxiously.

"HATE!" said Mme Brownscu, so vehemently that Kate wished Everard were there to look after her.

But Everard, who had come on later, was safely in the drawing-room, having a refreshing talk with Mr. Birkett and Mr. Bissell about the School Certificate examination, during which he and Mr. Birkett honestly tried to see why it was more important than birth, death, or marriage, while Mr. Bissell on his side did his very best to make allowance for the Capittleist point of view that if you had been at a private school (by which name he thought of what his fellow-talkers called Public Schools) exams mysteriously didn't matter, whereas every right-thinking person knew they were the whole end of education. But they got on very well and none of them were pleased when Mr. Hopkins, the Hosiers' Boys Science Master, joined their party.

"Have some sherry, Hopkins," said Mr. Birkett.

Mr. Hopkins said sherry was for those who could afford it.

"Well, I can afford it," said Mr. Birkett, "so have a glass. It's quite dry."

Mr. Hopkins accepted a glass and drank it venomously.

The Dean of Barchester, who had just arrived, came up to speak to Mr. Birkett, and Mr. Hopkins gave his gaiters a look of class hatred that should have burst all their buttons.

"News looks bad, I'm afraid," said the Dean. "We can but hope in these dark days."

Mr. Birkett offered him some sherry.

"Hope and trust," said the Dean, accepting it. "Finland is a small nation, but she will not lightly give up a freedom won at such cost from her powerful neighbour. I had forgotten how good your sherry is, Birkett. Yes; these are dark days and will be darker yet."

Everyone felt that this remark, though doubtless true, was not of a nature suited to a sherry party, for hope and trust, though admirable in themselves, are damping to the spirit. When we say everyone, we are only thinking of people we like, for Mr. Hopkins, the Adam's apple in his skinny throat working violently with hatred of nearly everything, said hope and trust were all very well, but we should have made a pact with Moscow two years ago. He hoped, he said, to see the Red Army at Helsingfors within a week and the Hammer and Sickle floating over the whole of Finland.

Everard Carter with deplorable levity said what a very good name the Hammer and Sickle would be for a pub.

Mr. Needham who had driven the Dean and family over said, looking very hard at Mr. Hopkins, that if he saw a pub called the Hammer and Sickle he would give it a wide berth as the beer would probably be poisoned. He then blushed bright scarlet up to the roots of his fair hair and wondered if the Dean would be offended.

"My dear Needham!" said the Dean with a deprecating but on the whole not disapproving smile, "speaking as one who—"

The doctor's wife said she thought the Russians drank vodka.

"That, we are given to understand, is so," said the Dean, thus imparting a kind of benediction and at the same time showing the doctor's wife that she had spoken out of place. "Speaking, as I was about to say, as one who knows well that beautiful country of forest and lakes," the Dean continued, "and has taken a deep interest in its language and culture, I feel we should all use the time-honoured if to our ears less euphonious name of Helsinki, in which I am sure Mr.—?"

He paused. His secretary, who was admirable at getting to know who everyone was, murmured, "Mr. Hopkins, science master of the Hosiers' Boys Foundation School."

"Quite, quite," said the Dean. "I am sure that Mr. Hopkins, I think I have the name rightly, learned as he is in the exact sciences," and into these words the Dean rather unkindly managed to throw the whole contempt of a classical man for a subject that even Cambridge must be slightly ashamed of encouraging, "would agree with me that where philology leads, we must follow. I had myself the privilege of attending a Conference in Finland last summer and it was a privilege indeed. Our arrival at Helsinki, as I think," he added with a smile, "we have agreed to call it, on a fine June morning was an experience I shall never forget. Neither, though here I may be accused of very materialistic views, shall I forget the first meal we had on landing. When I tell you, Birkett—"

It was by now evident that what the Dean really wanted to do was to describe his six days in Finland. As respect for his cloth made it difficult to interrupt him, he was able to carry his hearers, by train and steamer, over the southern part of the country, and those who had not heard it before felt that it was so dull that they would almost prefer to hear yet once again how he went to Portugal the summer before.

As for Mr. Hopkins, his rage cannot be expressed. Just when he had seen a chance of telling a group of influential, though of course absolutely uneducated and wrong-thinking men what they ought to think about

Russia, a man who was no better than a Roman (for Mr. Hopkins was a loyal son of the brand of Undenominationalism peculiar to his birthplace in Glamorganshire) was allowed to get away with the whole of the talk, simply because he wore gaiters. What was worse, he himself had been publicly convicted of using the bourgeois word Helsingfors, when heaven knew he had been saying Helsinki to himself for a considerable time. And Mr. Hopkins, on whom Mr. Birkett's sherry had had an inflaming effect, expressed upon his features a scorn that should have withered everyone present. He would have gnashed his teeth with rage, but that his uppers were a bit loose and he didn't like to spend any more money on the dentist. So he went into the hall where Simnet, who despised him, helped him into his coat with a deference that made Mr. Hopkins wish more than ever that England had made a Trade Pact with Russia, in which case (so he fondly thought) the Hosiers' Boys would never have had to be evacuated to Southbridge and he would not have been thrown into a world where people read *The Times* as a matter of course and were bigoted, ignorant and stuck-up. He was about to shake any dust that Mrs. Birkett's excellent head-housemaid had not taken up with the Hoover that morning from his feet when Miss Phelps, zealous as always in any case that presented itself to her, saw him go past the dining-room door and advancing upon him in trousered majesty took him in tow and hauled him into the dining-room where we shall at present leave him.

It must be stated with regret that no one in the drawing-room noticed his absence. The Dean, having got his audience back to Helsinki and on board the S.S. *Porphyria*, moved away and came face to face with Lydia Keith, who had only just arrived.

"Hullo, Dr. Crawley," said Lydia, giving him one of her friendly and painful handshakes. "Let's go and talk to Admiral Phelps and the Vicar. It's about God Save the King and I know they'll get it all wrong."

The Dean, who was very fond of Lydia and often felt as if she were one of his own daughters, though not so dull as some of them, was quite willing to do as she asked and following her stalwart lead came down like a shepherd on the fold upon the corner where the Vicar and his churchwarden were discussing for the third or fourth time the question of whether God Save the King was to be sung standing or kneeling. The Vicar would willingly have discussed subjects of more general or less doctrinal interest, but the Admiral was determined to win his pastor over to his way of thinking before the Church Council met, in which case he knew he could manage the rest of the members.

If Lydia had hoped—and she probably had—that the Dean would suddenly burst in with bell, book and candle and settle the whole matter, she was not to be gratified. Dr. Crawley had no illusions as to the power of a Dean and while willing to listen to the arguments on both sides was not going to commit himself. But Lydia herself had no such scruples.

"If you want to sing God Save the King, you want to *sing* it," she announced, "and if you kneel down your diaphragm is all squashed together and that's where your voice comes from, at least your breath control does. And I think it's disloyal not to stand up, don't you, Admiral Phelps? If anyone didn't stand up to sing God Save the King I'd think they were a Traitor," said Lydia defiantly.

The Vicar, who did not know Lydia well and was rather terrified by her, said he was certain that nothing was further from any thought of disloyalty than the attitude of those who felt it incumbent upon them to kneel, but he must in all such matters by guided by his own conscience and the ruling of those set in authority over him.

"If you mean the Bishop, you might as well say so," said Admiral Phelps. "We all know *his* views."

"I wasn't thinking of the Bishop at all," said Lydia indignantly. "If you had read the Thirty-Nine Articles you would know that the Supreme Governor of the Church of England is the King, because it says so. At any rate it says so in the Preface. And it says it again near the end, doesn't it, Mr. Danby?"

The Vicar, thus appealed to, had to admit that Lydia's premises were correct.

"Very well then. The King says people ought to stand up to sing God Save the King," said Lydia, "at least they always do stand up, so it comes to the same thing. I wouldn't feel I was singing God Save the King at all if I knelt down."

"The Bishop of Barchester, while feeling that everyone should act according to his conscience, prefers it to be sung kneeling," said the Dean. "In the Cathedral we stand," he added in an unimportant voice.

The Admiral, who knew, as did the Dean, that the Vicar of Southbridge hated his Bishop's views on nearly every point (though not half so much as did his fellow-Vicar at Pomfret Madrigal), felt that everything was shaping as he would wish it and said no more. A voice behind Lydia said, "I didn't know you knew the Thirty-Nine Articles, Lydia."

Lydia turned and saw her friend Noel Merton.

"Where on earth did you come from, Noel?" she asked.

"In general," said Noel, "from I mayn't say where, but in particular from the Deanery. I would have come to Northbridge," he added hastily, seeing a faint cloud of disappointment on Lydia's face, "but I only knew late last night that I would be getting leave and I thought it might upset your mother. How is she?"

Lydia said she was pretty well.

"You wouldn't care to have me for lunch to-morrow, would you?" Noel asked.

Lydia lifted troubled eyes to him.

"Of course I'd care," she said, "but to-morrow's my day at the evacuated children's Communal Kitchen, and if one once begins changing—"

"I know," said Noel. "What time is your Kitchen cver?"

Lydia said one o'clock for the children, but the helpers usually hadn't finished washing up till after half past.

"Very well," said Noel. "At a quarter of two I shall fetch you with some illegal petrol and take you for a drive. Would that do?"

Lydia nodded violently.

"The Communal Kitchen is in Northbridge High Street in that empty house next to The Hollies," she said. "You'll know it by the smell of rabbit and onions to-morrow."

Mrs. Crawley then descended upon Noel to take him to look at the delightful Mixo-Lydian embroidery in the dining-room, so after exchanging a handshake with Lydia which stopped all his circulation for thirty seconds he followed his hostess. Lydia, feeling a little lost, went in search of other company and found Geraldine with Octavia Crawley and Mr. Needham, all eating potato crisps.

"Hullo, Lydia," said Geraldine. "Isn't it a shame Fritz Gissing couldn't stay? He's going to take me round the studio one day, though."

Octavia Crawley, her utterance rather impeded by a mouthful of potato crisps that crackled like fireworks, said they had a man in from the film studios last week with the most ghastly burns on his arms, but that beast Matron had put him in D ward. Delia Brandon, she added, said they were the most splendid burns she'd ever seen. Tommy, she continued, a little more distinctly, had been in to read to him and thought he'd probably die soon.

"We've never had a funeral from the Hospital since I was there," said Geraldine. "It would be rather fun, but I wish it was a military one. Fritz could film it."

Geraldine and Octavia then continued their artless talk, each on the subject that most interested her virgin heart, while Lydia gravely listened. On any other occasion she would have given her own views in no uncertain manner, but this evening, or more correctly since the last few minutes, she was conscious of an unusual want of interest in her young friends' conversation. Mr. Needham, who had felt a certain awe of her on the day she drove him to lunch with Mrs. Brandon, suddenly had a peculiar sensation of being sorry for her, he couldn't tell why. Her quiet manner seemed to him rather touching after the overbearing ways he had previously witnessed, and he could not help contrasting her with Geraldine and Octavia, who were still eating potato crisps and enlarging in a rather boring way upon films and funerals. Lydia's handsome face in pensive repose suddenly seemed to him much more pleasing than Octavia's plain though animated countenance; even Mrs. Brandon's more mature charms were forgotten; and it must be confessed that Mr. Needham fell in love for the third time since the beginning of September, which was pretty good going.

The party was now thinning rapidly and Mrs. Birkett begged such guests as were still in the drawing-room to come across and look at the embroideries before they went. Accordingly Lydia and her friends who were still eating potato crisps and accompanied by Mr. Needham, followed the rest of the party into the dining-room from which Mr. Hopkins had been trying for at least half an hour to escape without success, till at last, to his horror, he found himself almost in the arms of Mme Brownscu, who was determined to get rid of the remains of her merchandise.

"You will buy this," said Mme Brownscu. "I will abandon it to you for three thousand Lydions, that is one shilling and you will tell all your friends to buy more. You will bring them to see me and I shall sell them much better embroideries which also cost more dear. One shilling, yes."

But Mr. Hopkins, who was very avaricious, had no wish to part with a shilling. Indeed he had more than once thought of resigning his membership of the B.S.R.S.C.S. or Brotherly (and) Scientific Relations (with our) Soviet Comrades' Society, because of the yearly subscription which with the poundage on a postal order and the postage amounted to nearly five shillings and sixpence. So he tried to slip past Mme Brownscu, but was brought up short in the doorway by Mrs. Bissell.

"Good evening, Mr. Hopkins," said his Headmaster's wife with her usual calm. "Here you see me a latecomer. Poor little Edna had one of her fits, so I said to Mr. Bissell not to wait for me. But the poor little thing got off to sleep nicely and Mrs. Dingle is sitting with her and here I am. Now you must show me the exhibits. What a pretty piece of work that is."

"One shilling," said Mme Brownscu. "That is as much as giving him a present of it. I shall lose on this bargain but God wills it so. If you have no change it does not matter. It will benefit my compatriots."

"No thanks, no thanks," said Mr. Hopkins, angry and afraid. "Very nice. Quite like the Russian work, but I don't want it to-day."

He could not have made a more unfortunate remark. Mme Brownscu's eyes flashed, she stubbed her half-smoked cigarette out among the small change on the table with the action of one ridding the world of a loathsome viper.

"Russian, you said?" she inquired. "You were in Russia, hein?"

Mr. Hopkins, wishing more and more that he had never accepted Capittleist sherry, said he had been in Moscow and must be getting back.

"Ha! Getting back to Moscow, doubtless!" said Mme Brownscu. "Tu entends, mon ami," she continued to her husband, "ce type est ami de Moscou, de ces sales Russes."

Poor M. Brownscu pulled his sheepskin coat so far up round his face that only his large miserable eyes were visible between the collar and his béret and shrinking away from Mr. Hopkins said in an agonised voice, "Czy, provka, provka, provka."

By this time all such guests as were left had gathered round in pleasurable excitement and those that were just going came back and looked over each other's shoulders in the dining-room door. Mrs. Birkett, who did not at all want her party to finish with a row, came up and begged Mme Brownscu to allow her to buy that delightful piece of embroidery which she had so much admired. But Mme Brownscu paid no attention to her at all.

"You do not know what that means," she said, addressing Mr. Hopkins but gathering the whole assembly in her eye. "He says, 'No, never, never, never. Non, jamais, jamais, jamais.' Et savez-vous pourquoi il dit cela? It is because of the Russians, c'està cause des Russes, pouah! quels sales types, which have destroyed his piano and his gramophone, lui qui est musicien par-dessus tout, and driven away, enlevé, all his stallions and mares, lui qui est cavalier accompli, et qui d'ailleurs on violé sa mère, ses quatres soeurs, sa cuisinière, lui qui adore la bonne chére, et sa femme. And when he sees this dirty type of which I do not know the name which says 'Moscou,' cela lui tourne les sangs. N'est ce pas, mon petit Gogo, ça te porte sur le foie?

Take your embroidery, Mr. Russian, et allez vous en a Moscou. C'est un shilling que vous me devez."

So saying she thrust the embroidery into Mr. Hopkins's hands.

That unfortunate gentleman who had little or no acquaintance with French had not understood what Mme Brownscu was saying, but most of those present had been delightfully shocked and horrified. Among the exceptions was Mrs. Bissell who told Miss Hampton afterwards that she had given up French as a girl, but she saw that Mr. Hopkins, whom she had never liked, was interfering with the amenities of that nice Mrs. Birkett's party.

"Give the Russian lady her shilling, Mr. Hopkins," she said in her gentle, authoritative voice.

Mr. Hopkins, against his better self, pulled out of his trousers pocket one of those leather purses of rather horseshoe shape, tilted some loose coins into the cover and held out a shilling. Mme Brownscu took it, threw it contemptuously into the plate of small change and then with a sudden effort snatched the embroidery from its purchaser, tore it in two and threw it on the floor. She then lighted another cigarette and hummed a national air very loudly. Mrs. Bissell, with the same impertubable serenity, took Mr. Hopkins by the arm, led him into the hall, said Good-night to him and returned to the dining-room where Mme Brownscu was putting the money she had collected into a bag and preparing to go home. Everyone was longing to question her about her appalling experiences at the hands of the Russians, but felt a certain delicacy in beginning. Just as despair was seizing upon all hearts Octavia Crawley, whose interest in anything to do with hospitals we already know, earned the everlasting gratitude of her mother's friends by asking Mme Brownscu if the cook had got over it.

"Over which?" asked Mme Brownscu.

"The Russians. I mean what you said about the way they treated her," said Octavia, suddenly finding it more difficult to talk about the facts of life in her mother's dining-room than she did with her V.A.D. friends.

"Oh, celle-la. Elle n'était pas mécontente. C'était d'ailleurs son amant, ce Russe," said Mme Brownscu carelessly. "Viens, Gogo; tu es prêt?"

But Octavia was of the breed of Bruce's spider and did not know the word defeat.

"And were you all right?" she asked.

"Yes, I am oll right," said Mme Brownscu.

"But I mean then; the Russians," said Octavia.

"Octavia!" said Mrs. Crawley, much to everyone's annoyance.

"Les Russes? I am not in Lydpov then. C'est la femme de Gogo qu'ils ont violée; mais enfin c'était le colonel russe, qui était son amant. God wills it so."

She then swept up the wretched M. Brownscu and took her leave, urging those present to send all their rich friends to buy embroideries. Mrs. Bissell thanked Mrs. Birkett for a most pleasant social gathering and saying how sorry she was for the poor Russian lady having to do all that embroidery went away with her husband, to release Mrs. Dingle from watching over little Edna.

The Dean then said one must not judge uncharitably of anyone, especially of those who were dependent for their bread on the charity of strangers. With this to encourage them the Birketts and Mrs. Morland together with the Deanery party and Lydia skirted with delicacy round the interesting question: If M. Brownscu's wife was not Mme Brownscu, who was Mme Brownscu? And to this question they regretfully saw no chance of ever getting an answer.

"Well, we must be getting home," said Mrs. Crawley, who had decided not to speak to Octavia about her behaviour, though chiefly, it is to be feared, because she did not dare to. "Josiah, are you ready?"

The Dean, who often wished that with all due respect to the Bible he had not been called after his grandfather, rallied to his wife and good-byes were said. Noel repeated his promise to Lydia to come and fetch her from her Communal Kitchen on the following day. Geraldine who was on night duty was to go back with the Crawleys. Mr. Needham, who was driving them, was suddenly struck with the thought of Lydia, alone, driving herself home through the black-out, and asked her earnestly if she would be all right. Lydia, seeing nothing not to be all right about, said of course she would.

"I have to be over at Northbridge to-morrow about a football match between the Boy Scouts there and our Choir School," said Mr. Needham. "I was thinking I might perhaps come and see you about tea-time if you are in and your mother is well enough, unless perhaps you are going to be busy or anything. I thought you might perhaps be kind enough to help me about something, if it wouldn't be a bother."

Lydia said of course. As she drove home she faintly wished that Mr. Needham, whom she did not in her mind call Tommy, as she had never thought of him since the day they lunched with Mrs. Brandon, weren't coming on the same afternoon as Noel Merton; but if Mr. Needham needed helping about something, that was not the way for her to think so she didn't; or if she did, she tucked it away into the back of her mind, and gave her parents an amusing account of the sherry party.

Mrs. Birkett and Mrs. Morland agreed at dinner that the party had on the whole been a great success.

"Why did you ask those pestilent Gissings, Amy?" said Mr. Birkett. "If I had any time to dislike people, which heaven knows I haven't just now with chicken pox bursting out in all the Houses, I would dislike those people as much as I have ever disliked anyone. And as for the boy—"

"After all," said Mrs. Birkett, "Geraldine has nowhere else to see her friends."

"Friends!" said Mr. Birkett angrily. "Rose's friends were bad enough, but Geraldine's are insupportable. I really wish Rose were back sometimes."

He looked very tired. Chicken pox and a sherry party and the Gissings. Mrs. Morland could not decide whether his remark was less in favour of Rose or of Geraldine, so for once she held her tongue.

10

THE PATH OF DUTY

•

On the following day Lydia Keith, after a single-handed fight with Palmer about tea-cloths in which she scored heavily, went off on foot to Northbridge village with a large flowered overall in a bag. As most of the neighbourhood was Cathedral property, and the firm of Keith and Keith had for many years done much of their legal business, Mr. Keith had been able to put gentle spokes in the way of building development, and even bully the Barsetshire County Council into building quite presentable houses for the working classes well away from the delightful village street, of which no fewer than fourteen different views, including the church, the brick and stone houses of the gentry and the remaining plaster and thatch houses of the cottages can be got at any picture postcard shop in Barchester. Next to The Hollies, a pleasant Georgian house standing back behind its shrubbery, was a plain-faced stone house that had been vacant for some time owing to a death and an entangled will. As soon as the threat of evacuee children had become a near menace, the Women's Institute, headed by Mrs. Turner, who lived at The Hollies and her two nieces who lived with her, had given an entertainment followed by a whist drive and dance by which they earned enough money to start a Communal Kitchen. The trustees had consented to the use of the large kitchen quarters of the empty house, the money from the entertainment had been used to install a new gas cooker and buy a quantity of cheap tables and forms, some very cheap cutlery and various cleaning materials. Volunteers had supplied cooking utensils, dish cloths, crockery, and other necessities. The possessors of vegetable gardens and hens had promised weekly supplies according to their means. Mrs. Turner from her own purse bought a part share in a pig whose owner was on the dole and had no intention of coming off it, and supplied a pig bucket, on the understanding that the pig's owner would fetch the bucket daily and make over certain portions of the pig to the Women's Institute when it was killed.

With a great burst of gladness and relief nearly all the hostesses of the evacuated boys and girls sent them up to the Kitchen, paying threepence a head for an excellent and substantial meal. It is true that almost in the same breath they said threepence was too much, but Mrs. Turner took no notice at all. Under her truculent despotism a number of ladies undertook to do the cooking, the serving, and the washing-up in rotation, and it must be said to the credit of Northbridge that very few had defaulted. What with her mother and the house and the Red Cross and the estate and working parties, Lydia had not much time to spare, but she helped to serve the lunches one day a week and, as we have seen, did not allow anything to interfere with it.

The church clock was striking twelve as Lydia went into the house by the side door and down a long stone-flagged passage to what were called by the estate agent the commodious offices. Here Mrs. Turner was hard at work superintending the preparation of great saucepans of rabbit stew and potatoes. She had been at the Kitchen since ten o'clock that morning and would be there till the last helper had gone, and this she did every day except Saturdays and Sundays. By her instructions the gas cooker had been installed in the scullery, so that the washing-up could go on under her eye. The kitchen itself with its wasteful range and huge dresser was not used, and the servants' hall had been turned into a dining-room. In it Mrs. Turner's nieces were laying a knife and fork and a spoon and fork and a china cup fifty times over on the bare deal tables. Lydia put on her overall and seizing two large tin loaves cut them up into small hunks, two plates of which she put on each table. She then filled a large jug with water and poured some into each cup, repeating these actions till all the cups were half-full; for if they were any fuller the children always slopped them at once.

"That's right," said Mrs. Turner, as she prodded a large saucepan of potatoes to see if they were done. "How is your mother, Lydia?"

"Pretty all right," said Lydia. "What's the pudding?"

"Stewed pears and synthetic custard, and plain cake baked in meat pans," said Mrs. Turner. "Where's my colander, Betty?"

"Ackcherly," said Betty, who was Mrs. Turner's elder niece, "it's on the hook. I'll get it."

Mrs. Turner took the colander and began turning out her potatoes, of which a dozen large dishes were put on a long table near the door of the servants' hall, together with piles of plates. At the same moment the younger niece opened the door into the stable yard and fifty children, rushing clumping into their dining-room, formed up in a rough, pushing, gabbling queue. The well-known smell of children and stew filled the air and Lydia wished for a moment everyone were dead. The other helpers, who though extremely good and conscientious are too dull to mention, lifted great fish kettles of stew from the stove on to the serving-table and the ritual began.

"Who's doing the veg?" asked Lydia, getting behind the table.

"Well ackcherly it's me," said Betty, "but you can if you like. I'll do the rabbit. I hope they didn't leave any eyes in."

Betty stationed herself behind a kettle of rabbit and with an iron ladle half filled a plate with a luscious stew. To this Lydia added potatoes and handed the plate to the child at the head of the queue. The other helpers served in the same way and each child carried its plate to its own seat. No sooner were they all served than a dozen or more came back, carrying their plates, with expressions of fastidiousness and insolence that Lydia tried hard not to see.

"Miss, I don't like rabbit."

"Miss, there's something nasty on my plate. Dorrie says it's kidneys."

"Miss, the lady didn't give me any gravy."

"Miss, Grace's got a bigger bit than me."

"Miss, mother wrote to me not to touch rabbit."

"Miss, can't I have some more rabbit? I don't like potatoes."

"Miss, Jimmy Barker took three bits of bread and I ain't got none."

"Miss, I don't like rabbit. I want fish and chips."

Gradually the plaints subsided. Lydia went round the dining-room with the jug of water replenishing mugs. Already the tables were slopped with water, gravy, rabbit bones and splashings of potato. The smell of children and stew became thicker. The children themselves looked remarkably healthy and were well and warmly dressed. Lydia recognised some of the arted-up frocks from her working party and a couple of boys' jerseys that had belonged to her brother Robert's little boy Henry. The children filed back with their plates which the helpers rapidly emptied into the pig bucket. What with those who didn't like rabbit and those who didn't like potatoes and those who didn't like gravy and those who had taken three pieces of bread and only messed it about, and those who had eaten so many sweets already, bought with postal orders sent to them by their starving parents, that they could not eat at all, the bucket did very well.

The helpers now stationed themselves behind the serving table and dealt out stewed pears and custard, with a strip of cake to each. A number of children raised plaintive cries for or against these different articles of food, but the plaints, owing to fullness, were less violent. As soon as they had finished they rushed shrieking into the stable yard and so out into the street, and quiet fell.

Mrs. Turner and her aides took off the stove the kettles and saucepans of water that had been boiling and did the wash-up. The lay helpers, by which we mean the dull and nameless ones, then said they were sorry they must go home, as their husbands didn't like it if they were late. Mrs. Turner, Lydia, Betty and the other niece washed the tables, swept the floor and washed out all the drying cloths, which the other niece hung up in the yard to dry, after which they sat down and made their own lunch off some stew and potatoes that Mrs. Turner had kept back.

"I wish it was summer and we were having a picnic at the Wishing Well," said Betty suddenly. "Ackcherly we couldn't because they've got an anti-aircraft post up there, but I wish we could."

"If those kind of things really happened like what people write about, about everything really happening at the same time only nobody knows exactly what it is," said the younger niece, "we could, but I think that's all rot."

A pensive silence fell, while the four helpers thought of Time.

"I wonder," said Mrs. Turner, "how long it will take to get this place clean again when we stop, if we ever do."

"It took us days at home," said Lydia, "and that was only six children. And *coats* of whitewash."

"Why they all smell so much I can't think," said Mrs.

Turner. "They all get one bath a week and most of them get two, and we've dressed them from the top to toe and from the inside to the outside. Peculiar. I suppose the whole of the Middle Ages smelt like that. Come along, girls, we'll just wash up our own dishes and then we've done."

"Ackcherly," said Betty, "we ought to be at the A.R.P. practice now."

Lydia said they had better go and she would wash up with Mrs. Turner. She was just hanging up the saucepan lid on its nail when Noel Merton walked in, announcing that he had tracked her by the smell of rabbit stew from as far off as the Post Office.

"It's filthy," said Mrs. Turner, with great frankness, "but the children smell much worse, bless them. I believe the whole of England will smell of children and stew before we've done. Good-bye. I've got a Polish Relief working party at two."

She turned the gas off at the meter and went away.

Lydia sat down on a wooden chair, while she folded her overall. For a moment her hands lay slack on the flowered bundle and she looked down. Then she raised her head and looked at Noel.

"You've done it again, Noel," she said. "I knew there was something wrong with you the minute you came into the kitchen."

"It wasn't my fault," said Noel apologetically. "Being of a crabbed and studious disposition I did rather well in my exams and they made me a captain. I now have blood lust and would like to be a major. One crown is an agreeable badge."

"I suppose promotion means going abroad somewhere," said Lydia.

"Not yet, so far as I know," said Noel, "but you shall be the very first person to know if I do. Oath of a captain."

Lydia got up and shook herself with her usual vigour.

"I feel if I'd never get this rabbit-evacuee smell off me," she said vehemently. "Come on."

She led the way down the flagged passage to where Noel's car was standing by the kerb and got in. Noel went round and got in on the other side.

"Look here, my girl," he said, "do you know what you did just now? You sat still with your hands in front of you. I've never seen you do that before. Is your mother worse?"

"Not really," said Lydia. "Only up and down. Luckily we've got loads of coal, because she can't stand the cold. I'm thinking of shutting up the drawing-room and using the library. Father and I do the estate work there, but that won't worry Mother. Sometimes, Noel, one gets a bit down, if you know the feeling."

Noel said he did, and in his experience it always came right again, and where would Lydia like to go for a drive, as he had vast stores of petrol.

"Do you know it's a most extraordinary thing," said Lydia, "but I actually—oh bother that word, I didn't mean to say it but Mrs. Turner's niece says it all the time so I suppose I caught it from her—I mean as a matter of fact I don't feel much like driving. You wouldn't care to come for a walk down the water meadows, would you?"

Noel said it was what he would like of all things and turned his car towards Northbridge Manor. When they got there Lydia said she would just hurl her overall into the house and wash some of the rabbit off her if Noel would wait, so he went out on to the little flagged terrace behind the house and sat on a white seat.

Against this southern wall one could still bask in a mild way. The trees were dripping their golden autumn coats on to the grass and everything breathed an undisturbed peace. Noel thought of how many pleasant visits he had paid to the hospitable Keiths, beginning with the night he had to spend there unexpectedly, four or five years ago when Mr. Keith had made him miss a train. He smiled as he remembered the large, awkward, violent, good-humoured untidy schoolgirl that Lydia was then. Looking back on their early acquaintance he came to the conclusion that if he had not stood up to Lydia at once she would have knocked him down and trampled on him morally in her stride. By the greatest good fortune he had stood up to her bludgeoning and so earned her favour, and a highly unsentimental comradeship had sprung up between them. While Noel became more and more successful at the bar and was increasingly in demand among hostesses, he could always rely on Lydia to look piercingly through him with her alarmingly honest eyes and take him down a peg whenever she felt it necessary. In his mind he compared the Lydia he had first known and the Lydia he knew to-day and found very little change except for the good. True she did not appear at river picnics any longer in a shapeless garment with her bright red face, neck, arms and legs sticking out of it, but her mind still moved with a good deal of the brusqueness of those days and she was almost as ready to lay down the law as when she had preached about Horace and Shakespeare and Browning at sixteen.

Now for the first time he was conscious that his ridiculous Lydia was in earnest. Only by chance references had he gathered from her all she was doing, but her father had spoken about her, and so had the Crawleys, and his admiration for her had grown. With her sister Kate away at Southbridge busy with her own children and the duties of a housemaster's wife, and her special brother Colin in the army, Lydia had constituted herself the guardian of her father and her ailing mother, a lonely life when all her friends were enjoying themselves with hospitals and ambulances. Noel reflected upon his own job, an uprooting it is true, but in interesting places and among interesting people, and wondered idly if he could have done what Lydia was doing: a question that he didn't like to press too far.

And now also he was conscious for the first time that his vital, tireless Lydia could feel fatigue or strain. When he came down the long flagged passage into the Communal Kitchen and saw her hanging up a saucepan lid, he had seen her as he always saw her, doing something. But when she sat so still for a moment, her hands idle on the folded overall in her lap, he had seen what he had never seen before, a Lydia putting down her burden before she shouldered it again. The remembrance pierced him. Then Lydia came out, announcing that if they were going down the water meadows they might as well tidy the boat-house, a fact which she evidently considered sufficient explanation for the very shapeless grey flannel skirt and untidy short-sleeved jumper she was wearing. Noel suddenly saw his old Lydia again and got up to accompany her.

They walked down the lawn and through the little gate into the meadows, which had already been flooded once and gleamed greyly where the waters had remained standing. The winding course of the river was marked by a fringe of alders, willows, and mountain ashes, now almost leafless, while above it rose the line of the downs with the beech clump showing its tracery against the sky.

"I do like all this," said Lydia, making a vigorous sweep with her right arm that Noel with difficulty avoided.

She said no more till they got to the boat-house.

Here she made Noel take off his tunic, though the old Lydia would not have stood over him while he folded it neatly and hung it over a fence, and for nearly an hour they worked hard. The boat and the canoe had to be emptied of the leaves that had blown in from the river bank, the oars were put into their winter quarters on the wall, the cushions and mats were heaped on a bench outside for one of the gardeners to bring up to the house. Lydia, with some solemnity, closed and locked the river doors. Then after taking a last look at the green gloom behind her she locked the outer door.

"End of the boating season," she announced. "Colin usually does the Grand Closing with me, but last time he wrote he said he didn't know when he'd be getting leave, so I'd better do it."

Noel put his tunic on again and they walked up to the house. There was a great deal that he wanted to say to her, but he couldn't find the words or the occasion. To praise her would probably only earn her good-humoured scorn; to tell her that he was anxious for her with all her burdens might annoy her; to try to explain what had pierced him in her momentary lassitude might trouble her mind. So he left everything unsaid and discussed the question of buying more pigs for the farm, or rather listened to Lydia's monologue on the subject.

In the drawing-room they found Mrs. Keith, who was pleased to see Noel.

"A friend of yours is coming to tea," she said, "Lavinia Brandon. She rang up after you had gone to the Kitchen, Lydia, and said she had a bit of petrol to spare and would like to come."

Lydia was glad her mother was to have so charming a visitor but her own heart unaccountably sank a little. She blamed herself inwardly for this feeling which she put down to the rabbit stew and the evacuees.

"Oh, and Tommy said he wanted to come to tea, Mother," she said. "He's doing something about a football match over here."

"These young people," said Mrs. Keith to Noel Merton, in what he felt to be an unnecessarily grown-up to grown-up kind of voice, "will not use surnames. Which Tommy is it, Lydia? Tommy Gresham, or that girl over at Little Misfit that has the bull terrier?"

Lydia explained that it was the Dean's secretary.

"I can't think," said Mrs. Keith with great dignity, "why the Bishop should have a chaplain and the Dean only a secretary. Considering how very Low Church the Bishop is I should have thought a secretary would be quite good enough for him. Whenever I hear of anyone having a chaplain I always think of the *Ingoldsby Legends*."

Neither her guest nor her daughter felt equal to coping with this particular thought. Noel vaguely wished that this Tommy were not coming and Lydia, who was not as a rule given to such delicacies, suddenly felt that Noel was dissatisfied, which increased her depression and made her concentrate on the rabbit stew as the cause of all evil.

While Mrs. Keith was telling Noel about her elder son Robert's children, Palmer announced Mrs. Brandon.

"You had better do the black-out in the drawing-room now, Palmer," said Mrs. Keith.

Palmer said she was sure she was sorry, but she had thought it was a pity to shut the light out so soon.

Noel could see in Mrs. Keith's eye that she was going to risk a domiciliary visit from the A.R.P. sooner than offend Palmer, but Lydia said, "Now please, Palmer," and Palmer grudgingly closed the shutters and drew the curtains.

"How nice and cosy it is. Just like old days," said Mrs. Brandon, looking round at the room with its shaded lamps and its bright fire.

It occurred to all three hearers that in the old days it had been pleasant to have the room lighted at tea-time on a late autumn afternoon, leave the curtains undrawn and watch the fading light across the water meadows: but this did not seem worth saying. Lydia poured out the tea with a combination of the ruthlessness of a Sunday School Treat and the kindness of a very good nurse on the invalid's first day up. Mrs. Keith was able to begin the saga of Robert's children all over again, to which Mrs. Brandon listened with not quite her usual deceptive appearance of attention. She was looking as charming as ever, but there was something new about her that the others could not quite place. She was dressed in black, with touches of some filmy purple at her neck and had an air of gently sad abstraction from this world and of mourning for beauty vanished which were most becoming, but rather perplexing. News travels fast in the country and Mrs. Keith read the Social columns of her *Times* very carefully every day, but from neither had she gathered that any loss had befallen the Brandon family. A question about Francis Brandon brought the assurance that he was very well and waiting with ardour for his class to be called up; if anything had been wrong with Delia it would have reached them from the hospital via the Crawleys or the Birketts. Even Noel, who did not take his charming friend too seriously, wondered if she was in black for a purpose and bravely hiding a wounded heart. At last Mrs. Keith could bear it no longer.

"One gets so anxious in these sad times," she said, "and I can't help being a little worried about you, Lavinia."

Mrs. Brandon very beautifully said that no one must worry about her.

"Your black," said Mrs. Keith, touching Mrs. Brandon's dress. "It isn't for anyone, is it?"

Mrs. Brandon with an exquisite air of discomposure said No, no; no one she knew was dead. No actual person at least.

"Is it an animal?" said Lydia. "I wore a black hat ribbon for a dormouse once when I was little."

Mrs. Brandon said she felt animals were so happy that one need not mourn for them. "At least," she added reflectively, "English animals. That very wearing woman, my cousin Hilary Grant's mother, tells me that animals are still dreadfully treated in Italy, but then she is that kind of woman who would find them being badly treated anywhere. In fact she will not be happy in heaven unless she can find a horse with ribs sticking out or a pig having its ears punched. Do you think, Mr. Merton, that heaven can really please everybody? Their tastes are all so different. And though we are told we shall see our friends again, there are several that I would so much rather not see, if it weren't too difficult to manage."

Noel said the law didn't make provision for that particular case, but the Dean's secretary was coming and they might ask him. Upon which Mr. Needham very conveniently arrived, and finding himself in the same room with the most saint-like woman and the most delightful and touching girl he had lately met, became a prey to silence.

"I know you can tell us, Mr. Needham," said Mrs. Brandon, looking devoutly at the Dean's secretary. "Does one *have* to know people in heaven or not?"

"Mrs. Brandon is a little exercised," Noel kindly explained, seeing Mr. Needham's embarrassment, "because she is so kind to such of her friends as are a little dull and boring, and wonders if she is likely to see much of them in heaven. The Inner Temple is not a good preparation for that kind of special knowledge, so we appeal to you."

Mr. Needham, after some embarrassing stutters, said he was sure no one could ever be dull with Mrs. Brandon.

"You've got it all wrong," said Lydia. "You couldn't be dull with her, but she could be dull with you."

"Oh, but I could," said Mrs. Brandon plaintively, "I could be dull with anyone."

"What Tommy meant," said Lydia, "was that no one could be dull with you. I mean there are two sorts of being dull with a person. One is when you are so dull that *they* feel dull, and the other when they are so dull that *you* feel dull; like Miss Pettinger," she added reflectively, "though with her it is really a kind of active horribleness as well."

Mrs. Brandon said she knew she was very stupid and gave a fleeting glance at her own black dress in a way that wrung Mr. Needham's withers.

"I hope—" he stuttered again, looking at the black clothes which Mrs. Brandon was wearing like weeds.

"It has been rather upsetting," said Mrs. Brandon, who had now got all her audience well in hand. "You see I saw that a steamer had been sunk and it was the same name as mine and though one doesn't believe that things like that mean anything, it is a kind of shock."

"If I may say so," said Noel, "you take shocks more becomingly than anyone I have ever known."

Mrs. Brandon caught his eye, knew that he saw through her completely and couldn't help laughing in a very pleasant way, for her illusions about herself were not really deep and it amused her when Noel pricked them. Mr. Needham, who did not know her well, thought that a woman who could laugh, almost in the face of death, was more like a saint than ever.

Mrs. Brandon, having made her effect, suddenly became very businesslike with Mrs. Keith about some clothes that she was having made for her nursery school and borrowed some patterns of frocks and coats, promising in return to send Lydia a roll of material for Mrs. Keith's working party.

"I really do feel quite wicked sometimes," she said earnestly to Mrs. Keith, "at not overworking myself and having a breakdown, but somehow I cannot, and if I broke down the babies would have to go. I am having ten more next week. I have had the old stables made into dormitories and put in fixed basins and a bath and central heating, and Sir Edmund says he can get me enough coal if I don't ask how. But it all seems so wretchedly little when I see Delia at the Hospital and Mr. Merton in uniform and the Vicar and Mrs. Miller with those *dreadful* evacuee children."

"At least, Lavinia, you are helping all those children," said Mrs. Keith. "And all I have done is to be so unwell that my husband had to get rid of our evacuees, and take up all Lydia's time, when she would like to be nursing. She is being more comfort than I can tell you."

Noel Merton now began to get up.

"I shall see you again whenever I can," he said to Lydia. "And let me tell you that when I see all that you do and what a good girl you are being to stick to this place and do the dull jobs, you make me and my uniform feel like three pennyworth of ha'pence."

Lydia looked at him.

"Well, what else could I do?" she said. "I'm sorry about not going for a drive to-day, but it was great fun to clean out the boat-house with you. If only Colin had been here too— I'll see you out. It's a bit dark on the front door step. Tommy wants to tell me something or other that he wants; more committees I suppose. Anyway I'd better get it over."

Noel said good-bye to his hostess and Mrs. Brandon and shook hands with Mr. Needham. Lydia took him to the front door with a torch, to light him into his car.

"You are a good, *good* girl," he said when he had buttoned himself into his British Warm. And he put an arm across Lydia's shoulders for a moment as they stood in the darkness. Lydia turned her torch on. Noel got into the car and drove away, rather wishing that young Needham didn't want Lydia's help about anything. She gave far too much to everyone and though he admitted that she gave very freely to himself, he suddenly had a feeling that she oughtn't to be so kind to young men of nearer her own age. "Middle-aged fool," he remarked aloud to himself and then had to give his mind to avoiding a car with far too powerful lights—the Gissing's had he known it—which was crashing along with its wheels well over the white line, causing him to change his note to "Blasted fools." But the thought of young Mr. Needham remained too near the surface for his pleasure.

Lydia snapped her torch off and stood in the cold for a moment. She told herself stoutly that Noel must have lots of friends nearer his own age, grown-up in a way that she could never hope to be. There was a freemasonry of age and associations between him and Mrs. Brandon that she could never hope to share. She was too humble to resent it and indeed liked Mrs. Brandon as much as ever, but she wished quite desperately that she were over fifty and a woman of the world. She always thought of Noel as about her own age, but every now and then it was borne in upon her that he must find her rather a green girl. She gave herself one of her impatient shakes. Tommy wanted something and must be attended to. And perhaps she would be able to prop up his feelings for Octavia, which seemed to be melting again under Mrs. Brandon's unconscious influence. Mrs. Brandon then appeared, kissed Lydia very affectionately and was in her turn driven away. Lydia went back to the drawing-room where Mr. Needham still lingered.

"It does make one feel a worm," said Mr. Needham, "to see men of Mr. Merton's age in uniform. I mean I know I am doing my duty in a kind of way, but it doesn't seem enough."

Mrs. Keith looked so tired that Lydia said she had better go up and rest before dinner.

"I expect I'm rather a nuisance," said Mr. Needham, "but if you had a few moments to spare—"

"All right," said Lydia. "Have a cigarette and I'll ring for some sherry and I'll come back when I've settled Mother."

Mr. Needham was then left to face Palmer who brought in the drinks with a manner implying that every drop of sherry consumed in the house was directly taken from her and cook's wages and that this was the kind of thing that led to a general uprising of the workers. He very basely pretended to be looking at some books in a far corner till he could feel in his back that she had gone, after which he was overcome with a sense of his own selfishness and was just going to slink away when Lydia came back.

"Are you going?" said Lydia. "I thought you wanted to talk to me."

"Well, I did," said Mr. Needham, "but I expect you'd rather I didn't."

"Don't be an ass," said Lydia good-humouredly, "it's no good coming all the way here and going away again. Only hurry up, because Father will be back and I've got to see him about some business."

Thus hurried and adjured poor Mr. Needham began to stutter again till Lydia's patience nearly gave way.

"It's often easier for people who stammer to sing than to talk," said Lydia. "You couldn't say what you want all on one note, could you? I mean like intoning, only that goes up and down. Is it about the Dean or anything?"

Mr. Needham was heard to mutter the words "Mr. Merton" and "uniform."

"Well, I simply cannot understand you if you don't say something," said Lydia, very reasonably. "Just try."

Thus exhorted Mr. Needham began again, and managed to explain that he had been much exercised in his mind as to his duty in the present series of crises. If only, he said, he could do something really horrible he would feel much better. Being a secretary was like funking everything. If he could be a curate in a very poor, atheistic, East End slum and never see a blade of green grass and be hooted in the streets and work for twenty-four hours on end and have the church open for down-and-outs all night and be in charge of a plague-stricken district and fast a great deal; or if they would send him to convert cannibals, or preach to lepers, or have his hands and feet frozen off in the Hudson Bay country, he would feel much better. As it was he thought he would go mad. Or to be a chaplain in France, though that was asking far too much. It was the older men who got all those jobs and there didn't seem to be any place for a young man at all. His speech then petered miserably out and he said he supposed he had better get back to the Deanery.

"Look here," said Lydia. "It's perfectly foul for *anyone* to be themselves just now, but it's about all one can be. I expect the Dean feels frightfully rotten too and would much rather be killed like St. Thomas à Becket, but he can't, so he has to do without. I feel pretty sick myself at doing nothing when Delia and Octavia are on night duty for weeks at a time and Mrs. Brandon is having a houseful of children and Noel doing something secret in uniform and Colin, that's my brother, training artillery in camp like anything—oh and *everyone* doing something. You really aren't the only one, Tommy. Anyway the Dean must have a secretary. And it's an awful help for Octavia to have you about. Buck up."

"Do you think it really is a help to Octavia?" said Mr. Needham.

"Of course it is," said Lydia. "If you didn't take her for a walk when she comes off duty or before she goes on, she'd never go out at all, she's so lazy, and then she'd get fat and bloated and not be able to nurse anyone. Of course you're a lot of use."

Mr. Needham, who having unloaded all his troubles on to someone else felt quite light-hearted, said he was frightfully ashamed and she was most frightfully decent to have helped him so much and he supposed he'd better go. On his way out he crossed Mr. Keith, who had just returned from Barchester, said how do you do and good-bye to him in a breath and went back to the Deanery, his mind in a confused jumble of adorations: of Mrs. Brandon because she had that effect on nearly everyone, of Lydia because she was a girl one could tell anything to without upsetting her in the least and perhaps the nicest girl he had ever met, of Octavia because it is wonderful to feel that you are really being a help to someone and almost consoles you for not being murdered by East-Enders, cannibals, or lepers. But he determined to speak to his employer again about the chance of getting to the front.

"Tiring day at the office," said Mr. Keith, sitting down heavily in the drawing-room. "You know, Lydia, it's no fun being old and out of things. It isn't only the young clerks who have been called up, but I find myself actually envying Robert, because he is in the thick of everything. He is helping with every important county activity and I must say doing it all admirably, and so is Edith. And all I can do is what any junior clerk could do, routine work at the office and my usual committees, hospital and so on. It takes the whole heart out of one. There isn't any place for the old men now."

"Rot, Father," said Lydia, kissing the top of his head. "If you didn't keep the office going, Robert would have to stop being useful in the county, and then there's the place, and Mother. And I wanted to talk to you about the third sluice in the water meadows. Something's got to be done about it."

So they talked about the sluice. And then Lydia went up to dress for dinner. As she pulled her stocking on to her right leg, there was a faint sensation on her knee and she felt the well-known feeling of a ladder rushing head-downwards from knee to toe-tip. It was not a very favourite pair of stockings, and one heel had a small darn, but suddenly it was more than Lydia could bear. She hurled herself on to her bed and there cried uncontrollably, as she had hardly done since she was a child. She would have given anything to cry herself to sleep and forget everything, but it was impossible, so with the last spasm of sobbing she got up, blew her nose several times, washed her face violently and determined to be starting a stye in her eye if anyone asked questions.

"If only Noel were here," she said aloud to her reflection. But at these words her reflection showed such unequivocal signs of beginning to cry again that she went quickly downstairs, where her father and mother would at least give her every reason for keeping up her courage.

11

THE CHRISTMAS TREAT

•

As term drew to a close, the agitating question of Christmas holidays began to press upon everyone. The Hosiers' Boys were almost without exception to go home, as their parents thought it would be nice to have them back for the holidays. The few boys that for one reason or another their parents could not have were billeted on the Carters, where Matron most nobly gave up her usual visit to her married sister, whose boy in the wireless in the Merchant Service had been torpedoed twice and was about to join his third ship with undiminished spirits, and was rewarded by one broken leg and a mastoid who had to be taken off to Barchester Hospital at half an hour's notice. The married masters relapsed into obscurity with their wives; some of the unmarried ones went back to wherever they lived and others were invited by friends they had made in the neighbourhood to spend Christmas with them. Mr. and Mrs. Bissell with little Edna remained at Maria Cottage and their friendship with Miss Hampton and Miss Bent grew and flourished. Mr. Hopkins, you will be glad to hear, got a very good job at Monmouth and left at the end of the term, unregretted by a single soul.

As for the evacuee children all over the county, their loving and starving parents, having had nearly four happy months of freedom, and seeing no reason why their children shouldn't be lodged, fed, clothed, educated and amused at other people's expense for ever, saw no reason to do anything more about them and hoped that the same fate would overtake the new baby whom most of them had had or were expecting. So all the hostesses buckled to afresh. Mrs. Birkett offered the school gymnasium for a great Christmas party with a tree, the sewing parties vied in running up party frocks for the girls, a levy on jerseys and cardigans for the boys was made in the neighbourhood. A house-to-house collection of small sums of money was made and Mrs. Phelps went to London on the cheap day return and came back with three dozen pairs of very cheap soiled white satin slippers which she and Miss Phelps dyed pink and blue and green, and two pounds' worth of toys, paper tablecloths and napkins, silver ribbons, and sparkling glass ornaments from Woolworth's. Cakes were promised by all the hostesses and their friends, fish paste, tin loaves and margarine were bought wholesale, lemondade was laid in by the gallon. In fact every possible preparation that good-will could suggest was made for an afternoon of noise, mess, over-excitement, tears and sickness.

The actual preparations were put in the hands of Kate Carter, whose gentle soul revelled in the prospect of a total upsetting of her life for a week or more and the subsequent clearing up. Under her benign and unruffled sway the Hosiers' Boys who were staying at Everard's House cleared away the gymnastic apparatus, swept the floor, brought in from under the pavilion the trestle tables that were stored for the school sports and big cricket matches, helped to unload with only three breakages the chairs that came like bony sardines in a van from Barchester, rushed down to the village for drawing-pins and string, borrowed the Scouts' trek-cart and collected all the cups and plates that were being lent, carried up the two big tea-urns from the British Legion, and brought in coke for the big stove that more or less heated the building. It was really a crowning mercy that Mason, the School drill sergeant who had come up with Mrs. Birkett from the Lower School, was in Manchester with his mother, or he would have infallibly gone mad at the desecration of his temple and the sight of the parallel bars shivering in the cold in the bicycle shed.

The question of invitations was not an easy one. It had gradually dawned upon the promoters of the party that it would be impossible to invite all the evacuated children in the neighbourhood. Mrs. Bissell, who was invaluable throughout the proceedings, suggested that the head teacher of each school represented in or near Southbridge should be given twenty-five invitations, with a request to distribute them among those of his or her scholars who were the least likely to let down the general tone. These schools were St. Bathos (C. of E.), Pocklington Road School (rigidly Baptist), St. Quantock (Catholic) and the Hiram Road School (aggressively non-sectarian not to speak of pink). The invitations were issued three weeks before the party so that the children might be chosen with care and deliberation. At first all went well; indeed too well, for on hearing of the ordeal by behaviour, every child behaved so unnaturally well that their teachers considered drawing lots. As time went on, however, the old Adam, and in a great many cases the old Eve, triumphed over virtuous resolves, and by the end of a week it seemed doubtful whether a single child would be eligible. The tickets were then distributed in a despairing kind of way and when they had all been given out it appeared that every child had several brothers and sisters who were crying all the time because they couldn't go to the Ladies' Party. It then became evident that to control a nominal twenty-five children at least one teacher per head would be needed, and failing this at least four teachers to each party. Sister Mary Joseph, who presided like a devout white pouter pigeon over St.

Quantock, sent in a petition that all her teaching nuns might come, as a party would be such a treat for them, a request that could not well be refused to anyone so charming and so used to getting her own way. Urged by professional jealousy Mr. Simon of the Pocklington Road (Baptist) School asked to be allowed to bring his whole staff, saying darkly that he was responsible for his children, by which he was understood to mean that he must guard them against the Scarlet Woman in the shape of Sister Mary Joseph, who had quite enough to do and never thought of his children at all. Mr. Simon's application was rapidly followed by one from Miss Carmichael of St. Bathos (C. of E.) School who wished to bring her entire staff on no grounds at all and was insanely jealous because she was not on the Committee. The rear was brought up by Mr. Hedgebottom of the Hiram Road School, who had at first decided to refuse to allow his children to attend a Capittleist function, but after wrestling with his conscience forced it to tell him that they ought to see how the so-called Upper Classes lived, that their teeth might be sharpened for the Class War in joyful hopes of which he lived.

By adding to these a number of evacuated mothers who wished their children under school age to participate in any over-excitement and over-eating that might be going on, Kate Carter and Mrs. Bissell, who sat as a kind of permanent Committee of Public Safety, found that they might easily have from a hundred and fifty to two hundred guests, but pinning their faith on the number of colds that were about they prepared for a maximum of a hundred and fifty.

To Kate's great pleasure Philip Winter came back at about this time on ten days' leave, asking if he might bring Captain Geoffrey Fairweather who happened to be quartered near him. Not only was Kate delighted to have two extra in the house, but in her kindly way she thought it would be nice for Mrs. Birkett to see her son-in-law's brother who might have news from Las Palombas. This was quite a mistake, for the Fairweathers, though devoted brothers, never wrote to each other, relying on chance or their various clubs to bring them into touch from time to time.

The only real blot on the entertainment was that Mrs. Gissing had invited herself and her son, choosing a moment when she could not very well be publicly refused. On hearing this Geraldine managed to get leave from Matron for twenty-four hours, as the only casualty under her care was an A.R.P. warden who had stumbled over some sandbags belonging to a rival section in the black-out and sprained his ankle, also having his nose broken by two zealous A.R.P. helpers who hearing the noise had rushed to his assistance, collided in the dark, and fallen heavily across his face. Although Geraldine had rung up young Mr. Gissing's secretary several times, she had not yet seen the film studios and her mother hoped she had got over her ill-judged affection for him, but such appeared to be far from the case. It was distinctly annoying for Mrs. Birkett to think of Geraldine wearing her heart on her sleeve for young Mr. Gissing to peck at, and she could only hope, though without much confidence, that among the crowd her virginal pursuit would not attract much attention.

By ten o'clock on the morning of the Treat the Committee were actively engaged. The Hosiers' Boys had stoked the stove till it was almost red hot and gave out such alarming cracklings that Edward the invaluable odd-man had to be sent for at full speed from the school allotments where he was repairing some fencing, to deal with the dampers which none but he had ever understood. Kate, to whose mind conflagrations from one cause or another were always an imminent danger, expressed her fear that the iron chimney of the stove might cause some adjacent woodwork to begin smouldering with slow combustion, which, growing to a head at about five o'clock, would suddenly burst into flame, lick up the Christmas Tree and the trestle tables, cause the roof, which was supported by strong steel girders resting on brick walls, to fall in with a crash in five minutes and the whole party, who would have fled shrieking in wild disorder towards the three large exits whose doors opened outwards, to be incinerated in the horrid mass which the firemen from Barchester (for of the Southbridge Fire Brigade she had no opinion at all owing to knowing most of the members personally when off duty) would not be able to approach for three days, if indeed they had not themselves been overwhelmed to a man by avalanches of red-hot masonry and jets of white flame twenty feet long. Just as she was trying to decide whether she had better share the fate of the children, nuns, teachers, mothers, children under school age and other members of the School staff, or make her escape for her children's sake, to be despised by mankind for ever more, Edward, answering her spoken question which had merely been, "Oh, Edward, don't you think the stove is rather hot?" had suggested that it should be allowed to rage unchecked until lunch time and then be allowed to die down, after which the accumulated heat plus the heat from far too many people crowded together in one room would make a delightful atmosphere. Kate felt much happier, and though at intervals her imagination still toyed with the idea of the slowly smouldering beam, we are happy to inform our readers that owing to the chimney having no beam anywhere near it, nothing of the sort happened.

The great question of the stove being settled, Kate was able to give her full attention to the arrangement of the room. The Hosiers' Boys, with a great deal of pleasurable and unnecessary shouting and shoving were getting the trestle tables up and placing the chairs. On the tables the Vicar's wife, the doctor's wife and Mrs.

Birkett were fastening large gay paper tablecloths with drawing-pins and putting a cup and plate to each chair. Paper table napkins with borders of bright red and green holly were also provided, though with but little hope of their being used. By each cup were two straws, and this was a stroke of genius on the part of the Vicar's wife who had noticed from many years' experience that tea for children meant fuss, mess and a great expense of sugar, whereas lemonade needed no adjuncts of sugar or milk, did not stain their clothes so badly, and if drunk through a straw became a Treat of the highest order. It was therefore decided that the tea urns should be used only for the grown-ups, who would refresh themselves after the children had been served.

On a spare table, in front of the urns, Eileen from the Red Lion (co-opted to the Committee as a compliment to Mr. Brown who had lent a quantity of cups and spoons), Miss Hampton and Miss Bent were cutting the loaves into slices and covering them with liberal applications of margarine and fish paste. All three ladies smoked incessantly and kept up a conversation about local affairs to which only the initiates of the Red Lion bar had any clue.

Mrs. Morland, who was not much good with her hands, had given herself the job of tidying, by which means she was able to infuriate all the helpers in turn, sometimes by folding up and putting away in a corner the paper and boxes that they particularly wanted, sometimes by sweeping dust and breadcrumbs into little heaps which were trodden upon or scattered before she could come back with a dustpan.

A large Christmas tree, sent by Lord Pomfret through his agent Roddy Wicklow, had already been planted in a tub of earth, the tub being lent by Mr. Brown and the earth by McBean, the head gardener of Southbridge School, who grudged it bitterly but could not resist Kate Carter's gentle insistence. Boxes and bags of toys and ornaments lay about ready for decorating its branches. This important part of the work was under the supervision of Mrs. Phelps who had decorated Christmas Trees in every part of the globe since her early married days, and usually in those parts of our Empire or other people's empires where Christmas comes in the middle of the summer. Under her were Miss Phelps as Flag Lieutenant and Mrs. Birkett and Kate as warrant officers.

"The tub looks a bit bare," said Mrs. Phelps, who looked very majestic with a brightly flowered overall over her zip lumber jacket and blue serge trousers. "Do you remember, Margot, the year Irons was at Flinders and we had that gumtree in a huge block of ice for the wives and children of the *Gridiron* and the *Andiron*?"

Kate wanted to know if it didn't melt very quickly as in Australia it was summer time in winter.

"Ice doesn't melt if you have enough of it," said Mrs. Phelps, who was unpacking the toys with great dispatch. "Irons got a shallow tank from the Naval Barracks and we stood the ice in it with some freezing salt. It looked very well. Margot put paper Union Jacks all over it. We ought to have something to drape round the tub. Do you remember, Margot, the year we were at Trincomalee and that nice Khanasamah draped the box our tree stood in with yards of coloured muslin. Now, what could we use? You haven't a few flags, have you, anyone?"

But at this moment Matron, who had given herself a roving commission to help in all fields of service, suddenly appeared in her white overall, followed by the biggest Hosiers' Boy who was carrying a large bulky parcel.

"What a busy hive!" said Matron, looking admiringly at the scene. "And what do you think, Mrs. Carter? I was just giving Jessie a hand to turn out that cupboard in the maids' sitting-room, because, I said, Jessie, it is just as well to see exactly what we have in the cupboard while we are about it, for you know the way things get put away and you cannot lay your hand on them just when you most want them, when lo! and behold what did Jessie find on the top shelf which I had absolutely forgotten about? So I asked Manners to carry it down like a good lad, saying to myself, 'Now that is exactly the thing.' "

Upon which simple explanation Matron proudly undid the parcel and revealed a huge roll of green baize.

"There!" said Matron with some pride. "The very piece of green baize, Mrs. Carter, that Mr. Carter bought for the doors between the House and the servants' quarters on the first and second floors, but owing to a slight misunderstanding the Governors had them re-done with red baize, so there it has been all this time. Of course you wouldn't have known about it," said Matron, who though she was devoted to Kate, liked to remind herself that she had known Mr. Carter before his marriage. "And I said to Jessie, Well, Jessie, I said, that will be exactly the thing, so Manners carried it down and quite a weight, wasn't it, Manners?"

Manners, who was one of the Hosiers' most brilliant Boys and had just been elected to an open scholarship at Cambridge, was quite used to being treated as a bright imbecile by Matron whose class feeling was very strong, and smiled engagingly, saying that he'd often carried heavier parcels for Dad on his rounds. As everyone knew that Manners's father was a greengrocer and furniture remover in those districts beyond the East End from which the Hosiers' Boys Foundation School drew most of its pupils, they all liked him the more for this statement and Kate suggested that he should go and help Mrs. Brown of the Red Lion to cut up the great slabs of currant and cherry cake and eat all the bits that fell off, which he most willingly did.

Mrs. Phelps exclaimed aloud with pleasure over the

green baize which she said would give just the Touch of Old England that she wanted. She and Miss Phelps then draped it in folds and billows round the tub and when Kate had sprinkled a shilling's worth of artificial frost over it, the effect was pronounced quite fairy-like. Then Miss Phelps, mounting a step-ladder, hung festoons of silver tinsel among the boughs and began to fasten the gold, silver, red and blue glass ornaments on to the higher branches.

"What shall I put on the top, Mother?" said Miss Phelps. "One of the silver stars?"

Matron, who had had a mysterious air of one biding her time, suddenly produced a cardboard box and said she couldn't resist bringing a little contribution. The contribution was a china-faced doll with a yellow wig, dressed by Matron's skilful hands in cloth of silver, with short full skirts, a silver star on the top of her head and a silver wand in her right hand. Mrs. Phelps said it reminded her of the doll their Number One Boy had dressed for the tree at Hong Kong, Miss Phelps tied it firmly by the waist to the topmost twig, and Matron was enchanted.

"Well, that's about enough," said Miss Hampton, strolling over from the sandwich table. "Eileen must get back to the Red Lion at twelve. Bent and I must show up too. Doesn't do to let people down. Where's Mannerheim?"

"Do you mean Manners?" said Kate. "He's helping Mrs. Brown with the cake."

"Manners?" said Miss Hampton, casting a monocled glance in the direction of the cake table. "Don't know the lad. No, no, Mannerheim. Oh, Bent has got him."

Miss Bent came up, leading the elephant-faced dog.

"He knows his name, you see," said Miss Hampton proudly. "Changed it last week. Must do something for gallant little Finland. Thought of Kalevala but no one knew how to pronounce it. Sounds Indian too. Fine fellows the Indians, but can't call them gallant. Not yet at least."

Kate said she thought our Indian troops were very, very brave.

"Brave as tigers," said Miss Hampton. "Lithe as panthers, too. But can't call people gallant till they have their backs to the wall. Hope India will never have her back to the wall."

"Come along, Hampton," said Miss Bent. "I can't hold Mannerheim much longer. He knows it's twelve o'clock as well as I do. Ready, Eileen?"

Eileen, who had just had a new platinum bleach and looked more beautiful than ever, said it had been quite a treat to cut up the sandwiches for the kiddies, but she must say ta-ta now as the lads would be waiting, and so departed with Miss Hampton and Miss Bent, the ci-devant Smigly-Rydz in tow.

They had only been gone a few moments when Philip Winter and Captain Fairweather came in, having, as they explained with a wealth of apology, just had breakfast. Kate and Matron, who liked nothing better than to see men overeat and oversleep themselves, beamed approval, and as the work was now finished they all went back to lunch, leaving Edward the odd-man, to put the final touches by winding yards of electric flex with coloured lights strung on it about the tree.

In the middle of lunch Geraldine arrived, having previously said that she wouldn't be home till two-thirty. Three people rang up for Mrs. Birkett, wouldn't give their names when Simnet asked them, and took offence. Mrs. Gissing rang up Mrs. Birkett, saying that it was urgent. Mr. Birkett growled, but Mrs. Birkett said she supposed she had better go in case it was about the party.

"Well, what did *she* want?" said Mr. Birkett when his wife came back.

"What to wear," said Mrs. Birkett. "She seems to think it is a fancy-dress party and wanted to know if she is to come as a Red Cross nurse or as a visiting royalty."

On hearing the name Gissing, Geraldine became aloof and ill-tempered, which her parents rightly diagnosed as the effects of love. Mrs. Morland, who was dramatising the stirring nature of the day by taking even less trouble than usual about her hair, dropped two tortoiseshell hairpins on the floor during pudding and as her host bent rather stiffly to pick them up, he felt that for twopence he would go to bed till after Christmas and stay there.

The party was to begin at four and end at six. By three o'clock the helpers were in their places, and just as well, for at three-fifteen precisely Sister Mary Joseph and her flying squadron of white-robed nuns arrived with thirty-six children spotlessly clean though unprepossessing, saying that the children had all been ready since two o'clock and it was eating their hearts out they were and sure we could be young but once. Her lambs, who having eaten their hearts out now had a hearty appetite, began to storm the tables and had to be kept at bay by a strong cordon of nuns and Hosiers' Boys, until the Hiram Road School poured in, when the two schools had so much to do in eyeing each other suspiciously and giggling that the cordon was able to relax. They were quickly followed by St. Bathos and the Pocklington Road School and a crowd of mothers and children, so that by the hour at which the party was supposed to begin the gymnasium was quite full of humanity.

"I think," said Mrs. Bissell to Kate, "that they had

better have tea at once. When they see food they get restive."

"Don't they have enough to eat then?" asked Kate, in some distress.

"Quite enough," said Mrs. Bissell, "but they are greedy and selfish and have no manners."

"Oh, Mrs. Bissell; the *poor* little things!" said Kate.

"You see, Mrs. Carter," said Mrs. Bissell, calmly, "I know them. I taught until my marriage. Come here, Janice, and let Mrs. Bissell put your ribbon straight. You can't really love them, Mrs. Carter, but you can do your duty by them. If I hadn't married Mr. Bissell I'd be teaching still. That's right, Janice, run along now. The worst of our profession, Mrs. Carter, is that you cannot really like your colleagues or your pupils, but it is a privilege to be able to devote oneself to the children and Mr. Bissell and I, being all in all to each other, do not see much of our colleagues except during working hours, which is I can assure you a great relief. I think tea immediately, Mrs. Carter. Sister Mary Joseph is losing control and if she does, all the others will."

Acting on this advice, Kate told the four principals that tea was now ready. Sister Mary Joseph with the utmost dexterity at once whisked her flock into their places while the rest of the schools played a kind of musical chairs at the end of which some twenty children remained standing. By the united efforts of the Hosiers' Boys and the helpers a few extra forms were brought in, some supplementary teas were spread, and in a few moments the air was thick with the bolting of paste sandwiches, chocolate biscuits and slabs of cake, while cup after cup of lemonade was upset straw and all as the young scholars grabbed for more food. With the rapidity of a flock of locusts they stripped every plate of its contents, looking at each other with suspicious eyes as they crammed their flushed and shining faces with food. The helpers rushed backwards and forwards replenishing plates till the last crumb of their reserves had been used. Meanwhile the crackers which had been provided were torn open, for a large number of children did not know about pulling them and the even larger number who did, both despised and feared the method, preferring to disembowel the crackers without delay. Mrs. Phelps had ordered nothing but caps and musical instruments. The clamour became deafening. All the children got up and banged into each other deliberately, while they puffed and blew crumbs into the whistles, mouth organs and other wind instruments provided for them. The Hosiers' Boys, who were really invaluable, cleared away the crockery and took down the tables thus giving the evacuees plenty of room to fight, as well as bang and bump and puff. Mrs. Morland, looking on from the door of the gymnasium changing-room, where she was helping to wash up, thought she had never seen a more revolting sight than so many hot children, the girls with their party frocks already crumpled and stained, the boys smeared with food from ear to ear, their unprepossessing faces full of the almost bestial look of satiety that cake and lemonade can produce even in the most gently nurtured young; so she went back to the washing up.

The helpers now got the tea-urns into action and fed the mothers and teachers, who were to have a slightly more refined tea of paste sandwiches and mixed biscuits. By the time this second tea was over a great many of the children were in tears with excitement and it was evident to any motherly eye that a number of them would probably be sick before bedtime. But such is pleasure. Kate asked Mrs. Bissell, who was entirely unperturbed by the scene, to say that the presents would now be given from the Christmas Tree.

"Now, children," said Mrs. Bissell; and a hush fell on the room. "Come up quietly, each school together, and no pushing. Anyone who pushes will go to the back."

The schools were rapidly organised. Mr. Hedgebottom managed to get the Hiram Road School into the front of the queue, hoping that his un-priestridden charges would get the pick of the presents, though in this he was disappointed for Mrs. and Miss Phelps who were responsible for the gifts were the soul of impartiality and Miss Hampton and Miss Bent who actually presented them, with Mrs. Bissell and Kate as a bodyguard, did not know one child or one present from another. When every boy had received something considered suitable for a boy, and every girl something considered suitable for a girl, they all tried to take each other's presents away, and the noise was worse than ever. In the middle of it, Geraldine, who had really been working very hard all day and was feeling tired, for there had actually been six cases in her ward on the previous day and Matron had let her go on real night duty for a treat, suddenly saw young Mr. Gissing, accompanied by his mother, who was roped with silver foxes and pearls.

"Hullo, Fritz," she said; and her heart would let her say no more.

Young Mr. Gissing, who really has very little to do with this story except to show how easy it is for anyone to fall in love with a totally unworthy object, said God, what a smell and was there a drink anywhere. Geraldine, who had secretly been exercised about this all day, and would have brought some gin with her but that (*a*) her father had not opened the new bottle and might ask questions and (*b*) she felt that she had no genius for smuggling at all, exhausted herself in apologies.

"Your *lovely* furs!" said Kate to Mrs. Gissing, with a woman's real admiration for silver foxes. "You really oughtn't to have brought them. Do be careful not to get anything on them. I'm afraid everything is very sticky."

Mrs. Gissing, smiling a queenly smile, said to Sister Mary Joseph who was standing near that she thought one should always wear one's prettiest things when one went among poor children; it was, she said, a kind of duty to give pleasure.

To these beautiful words Sister Mary Joseph's answer was that the children had had a very pleasant afternoon, accompanied by a calm look which conveyed to Mrs. Gissing that she, Sister Mary Joseph, could give pleasure to anyone at any moment by simply existing and that, being always dressed in an extremely becoming uniform, she never needed to think of what effect she was making. She then gently moved a step aside and replaced a pink bow in one of her children's hair. Mrs. Gissing, for whom one may be a little sorry, then tried to talk to Mrs. Bissell and to Miss Carmichael of St. Bathos School, but finding it somehow impossible to condescend to either of them gave it up as a bad job and floated graciously towards her son and Geraldine. Geraldine, hoping to propitiate her soul's idol, said how lovely it would be if he could make a film of the entertainment to which young Mr. Gissing crushingly replied that there was enough junk on the market as it was.

As if the Gissings were not bad enough, Mme Brownscu chose this moment to force her way through the crowd, carrying a large wooden box. As she had not been invited no one was surprised or pleased to see her, but Kate, who simply could not help being kind, received her beside the Christmas Tree and said what a pity she hadn't come before to see the children at tea.

"I do not come because I am bringing something for you," said Mme Brownscu. "You English do not understand Christmas, which is a strongly religious festival. In Mixo-Lydia our peasants each slaughter a goose which is eaten by all, and then they go to church."

Kate said in England we usually went to church in the morning and had a goose, or more often a turkey, for lunch, so it was very nice to think that the Mixo-Lydians did the same sort of thing.

"But I shall show you what it is to make a real

Christmas," said Mme Brownscu, ignoring Kate. And thereupon she opened the box and placed it on a chair. It contained a small crèche with brightly painted paper figures of the Virgin and Child, Joseph, kings, shepherds and angels. On each side of it was a fat candle stump. These Mme Brownscu lighted.

Even the cheapest crèche at Christmas time sends a prickle up and down one's spine and into one's throat. Kate and her helpers found themselves almost gulping at the sight of the two flames illuminating the pretty, touching toy.

"So. Now is the devil driven away," said Mme Brownscu with great complacency.

Such of the children as were near crowded round to look.

"Oh, Mrs. Bissell," said Kate. "The doll on the top of the Christmas Tree."

Mrs. Bissell, again calming the tumult by her extraordinary power, announced that the youngest girl present was to have the doll, which Miss Phelps got down from the tree. To avoid complications Mrs. Bissell had made previous inquiries in all four schools and ascertained that Patricia O'Rourke of St. Quantock's was the youngest girl at the party. Sister Mary Joseph, who had been primed by Mrs. Bissell, drew forward a little girl in a stiff pink organdie frock with an enchanting face, guiltless of all expression except greed and bewilderment, and a mop of fair curls. Miss Phelps put the doll into her arms and Sister Mary Joseph said thank you for her, as she was too shy to speak. The little girl stood by the crèche hugging her silver-clothed doll with its uninteresting china face and its crown and star.

"What is it, Patricia?" said Sister Mary Joseph, who saw her rather than heard her say something. She stooped and listened.

"She wants to know if it is the Holy Virgin," said Sister Mary Joseph, smiling kindly down at her charge.

Mr. Hedgebottom, who was not looking at the crèche,

as he afterwards explained to one of his assistant masters, but just happened to be there, heard the remark and looked at Sister Mary Joseph with all the gall of which his communist face was capable, and could barely control himself before such a hideous example of Mariolatry. At that moment one of his young scholars, a promising lad of nine or ten, pointed a very dirty sticky finger at the crèche and said in a loud voice, "What's that?"

Sister Mary Joseph was human, but she behaved very well. She merely cast on the questioner a look of such compassion that Mr. Hedgebottom nearly burst. For the first time in his painstaking and unpleasant life he saw that entire ignorance of what he called fetishism had publicly humiliated him in the person of one of his most promising scholars and he clashed his uppers and unders together with rage, resolving to put his whole school through a course of religious teaching, of course from a purely economic and anti-Christian point of view, so that they should not let him down again in public. To add to his humiliation, Mr. Simon of the Pocklington Road School and Miss Carmichael of St. Bathos had been close by and witnessed his discomfiture the one from a Baptist, the other from a C. of E. point of view, and though Mr. Hedgebottom bitterly despised them both, he would have liked them to be somewhere else.

Mrs. Gissing, who was just about to go as no one paid any attention to her, saw two officers come into the gymnasium and postponed her departure, not knowing that they were nothing more romantic than Philip Winter and Captain Fairweather who had basely gone for a long walk instead of helping with the treat and were now making a belated appearance hoping to acquire merit. Geraldine, who was desperately trying to entertain young Mr. Gissing, and had almost given up any hope of having a few kind words from him, pounced on her old friends and offered them up to her idol.

"Oh, Fritz," she said, "this is Philip Winter and Geoff Fairweather. Fritz makes the most marvellous films."

"I suppose I ought to salute your friends," said Mr. Gissing in a horrid way.

Philip and Captain Fairweather said in a general way what a ripping show it was.

"Stinking, if you ask me, and in every sense of the word," said young Mr. Gissing, laughing at his own wit.

Philip, who had learnt a great deal about controlling his temper since the days when he was Junior Classics Master and rather a nuisance to his colleagues, said to Geraldine that all the children seemed very happy.

"Happy!" said young Mr. Gissing. "The whole thing is revolting. A lot of women working themselves up and playing at being Lady Bountifuls. Come and have a drink whatever your names are."

"No thanks," said Philip.

"Have it your own way," said young Mr. Gissing. "Are you coming to see the studio, Geraldine, or won't Matron let you?"

Poor Geraldine, with the earth rocking under her feet, said she'd love to come, but every time she rang up he was out or busy.

"Ring again next week," said Mr. Gissing. "I should say I was busy. Some of you girls have an easy time running about the hospitals. My God, this is a rotten war. I'm getting a permit to go to America and I'll have something to say about England when I get there."

Anyone less silly than Geraldine would have realized that young Mr. Gissing must have had a drink or two before he came, which was at once apparent to Philip and Captain Fairweather. Geraldine went very pale and her eyes filled with tears, because she suddenly saw young Mr. Gissing exactly as he was and wished she could die at that very moment and be buried anonymously. Captain Fairweather, who had known her for a long time, in fact since he was in the Junior School, did not understand all her feelings, but her face and Mr. Gissing's revolting manners were enough for him. He had always been a good boxer and nothing would have given him more pleasure than to land Mr. Gissing one on the chin, but a Christmas Treat for children, nuns, mothers, teachers and children below school age did not seem the right place to do it. He gripped Mr. Gissing powerfully by the arm and led him in ominous silence towards the exit.

"Don't do that," said young Mr. Gissing shrilly.

"Don't open your filthy little mouth again," said Captain Fairweather. "Show me your car."

"Mother!" said Mr. Gissing.

"I'll find your mother," said Philip Winter, who was acting as escort on the other side. "Put him in the car, Geoff, and keep him there and I'll tell Mrs. Gissing he's sick. It's all right, Geraldine," he added, seeing her expression of misery and fright. "Geoff won't hurt him."

He then made his way to where Mrs. Gissing was boring Mrs. Birkett and Mrs. Morland dreadfully and told her that her son did not feel very well and was waiting for her in the car.

"You will forgive me then if I fly," said Mrs. Gissing. "And it may be a kind of good-bye. I believe we are off to America almost at once. Oscar and Fritz are so sensitive and really England is *no* place to live in now. But you must come and have a drink before we go. Come on Friday, just a few old friends."

Mrs. Birkett said she was afraid she and her husband were engaged.

"Then you must come, Mrs. Morland," said Mrs. Gissing graciously. "There are some men coming that it would be useful for you to meet. Klaus Klawhammer is one of New York's brightest literary agents and he would do quite a lot for you if you got on well with him."

Mrs. Morland had no pride at all, but she had a violent prejudice against agents, whom she had once described as being paid to make bad blood between authors and publishers, a point of view that had enchanted her own publisher Adrian Coates. Also she disliked Mrs. Gissing very much, and had indeed already cast her in her mind as the she-villain for one of her short stories that people liked so much. And all these feelings combined made her go very pink and talk with more vagueness than ever as she said,

"Thank you so much, but I am *really* engaged that day, because of Mrs. Keith's working party. And of course one can't help being English and I do think England is nicer, even when it is awful, than anywhere else. And as a matter of fact I deal directly with my American publisher who seems very nice, so thank you so much but I must say no thank you."

She then pushed some hairpins madly into her head and retired again to the washing up.

Mrs. Gissing, quite unabashed, gathered up her furs and her pearls and floated languidly after Philip to the exit. Here her escort produced a small torch and lighted her to the enormous car, in one corner of which young Mr. Gissing was sitting very cross and rather afraid, while Captain Fairweather and the chauffeur, who turned out to be an ex-corporal in the Barsetshires, talked about the difficulty of getting to America in safety, not without reference to the chauffeur's young master who could have been going visibly greener if there had been any light to see him by.

"Is it one of your heads again, my poor lamb?" said Mrs. Gissing to the corner in which her son was huddled. "How nice of you boys to look after him. Come along and have a drink and then I'll run you home. There's always enough petrol for little me."

Young Mr. Gissing could have killed his mother for this, but Captain Fairweather, answering rather untruthfully for himself and Philip, said they had to get back to camp.

"You poor boys," said Mrs. Gissing, from the depth of the car and a fur rug. "What a pity you didn't go to America before all this trouble, or get into a reserved occupation like Fritz. Are you sure you won't come and have a short one?"

But both officers declined her offer. Under cover of the darkness Captain Fairweather slipped half a crown into the chauffeur's hand, who speaking out of the side of his mouth expressed his opinion of what was inside the car and hoped the Captain would get a good smack at Jerry, adding that he was going into munitions himself that day fortnight and hoped the new chauffeur would drive all the family into a ditch. Upon which hope he drove away and Philip and Captain Fairweather returned to the gymnasium.

Here the party was rapidly thinning. Sister Mary Joseph with her flock had already gone, after thanking all the hostesses in a way that made them feel that they had on the whole been kindly and impartially weighed and found wanting. Mr. Hedgebottom and Mr. Simon were shepherding the last of their boys away from the Christmas Tree. Miss Carmichael, though tired, remembered that C. of E. gives one social status and was slightly outstaying her welcome.

"Did you hear that poor little lad from the Hiram Road School?" she said to Mme Brownscu, who was packing up the crèche. "Fancy not knowing what a crèche was. It does seem shocking to bring up all those lads like little heathen. It hardly seems feasible in a Christian country."

"To us," said Mme Brownscu, hitching her leopard-skin coat round her preparatory to her departure, "England is not Christian. Mixo-Lydia which is a strongly dévot—devoted country you would say—says

Pouf of this religion which is all wrong. As well might you all be Yews. Grzány provk hadjda."

Her last words were all the more terrifying as neither Miss Carmichael nor any of the helpers who were near had the faintest idea what they meant, nor indeed have we ourselves. Mrs. Bissell, who having once placed Mme Brownscu in her mind could not be troubled to reconsider her, said good-bye and hoped that all the poor Russians were well, at which and by Mrs. Bissell's attitude of calm certitude, Mme Brownscu was so flabbergasted that she was for once deprived of the power of speech and went back to Mixo-Lydian house where she picked a frightful quarrel with the unhappy M. Brownscu that raged far into the night, with enthusiastic support on both sides from all her compatriots.

Miss Carmichael, who was not very quick in the uptake, suddenly realised that Mme Brownscu had compared the C. of E. with the Jewish faith and hurriedly collecting her scholars and teachers went off in a huff.

The helpers all looked at each other.

"I think, Mrs. Carter," said Mrs. Bissell, "that we had better clear up at once. The longer you put anything off the longer it takes, and I must be back by half-past seven as Mrs. Dingle has to go and get her husband's supper."

Accordingly the whole band, including Philip Winter, Captain Fairweather and the Hosiers' Boys, set to and by ten minutes past seven the débris had all been removed, the decorations taken down, the chairs stacked ready for removal, the Christmas Tree undressed and the floor swept clean. Mrs. and Miss Phelps took the tea-urns back to the British Legion in their little car. Miss Hampton and Miss Bent with Mannerheim escorted Mrs. Bissell to Maria Cottage, stopping on the way at the Red Lion for a short one, of which Mrs. Bissell with inalterable placidity also partook.

By previous arrangement the Carters and their guests were to come up to the Headmaster's House for dinner, leaving Everard's House free for a gigantic feast with which Matron proposed to regale the Hosiers' Boys as a tribute of gratitude for their help. Mrs. Birkett had said no one must think of dressing, so they all walked up to the School together.

12

NEWS OF THE FLEET

•

At first everyone was rather tired, but under the influence of Mrs. Birkett's good food and Mr. Birkett's good drink they began to recover and by half-past nine, when they were comfortably in the drawing-room, they had all forgotten the major horrors of war as exemplified in the afternoon's Treat. All but Geraldine. First love is an astounding experience and if the object happens to be totally unworthy and the love not really love at all, it makes little difference to the intensity or the pain. Geraldine, owing to seeing so much of her sister Rose, had long despised the tender passion. Her thoughts had been more of things of the intellect, such as being fairly good at maths and the horribleness of Miss Pettinger and the odiousness of Matron, and how one's parents would ask questions and expect answers. Then suddenly young Mr. Gissing had come into her life, with his cheap assurance and his flashy good looks, and all was up with her. It must in fairness be said that young Mr. Gissing had given her no encouragement at all beyond being rather rude and offhand, but passion is self-nourished. Geraldine was not so silly as her sister, but far less dashing. Where Rose would have forced her way, quite unconscious that anyone could be busy, into the film studios and made Mr. Gissing take her out to dinner and dancing, and then forgotten him after a week for a newer swain, Geraldine was too timid in her love to assert herself at all. And as Mr. Gissing was not in the least interested in her it is not surprising that she got no further. She might have gone on like this for months, making a dejected doormat of herself before the man of her choice and blighting her home by moods of gloom, but for the events of the afternoon. She had seen young Mr. Gissing beside Philip and Geoff, who were such old friends that she never thought about them, and suddenly she had seen that he was rude and no gentleman. At the sight her whole upbringing asserted itself and with violent revulsion she hated first him, and then far, far more bitterly, herself. How deeply did she wish that Matron had not given her twenty-four hours' leave and that she could rush back to the hospital and there busy herself in swabs and bandages, but her parents expected her to stay the night and if she tried to alter her plans they would Ask Questions. And with these bitter thoughts it was all she could do to keep from crying. Her mother did notice her dejection and would dearly have liked to comfort her, but she knew her position too well and had to content herself with an occasional anxious glance in her daughter's direction which made that unhappy creature wish that Mummy had never been born or that she herself were dead. The only piece of luck in the whole evening was that she sat at dinner between Philip and Captain Fairweather, who both had a fair idea of what had been happening and kept up a conversation under cover of which Geraldine could gulp almost unnoticed.

As was but natural Mrs. Birkett talked a good deal about Rose and her letters. As was also but natural, Captain Fairweather had heard nothing from his brother since the wedding, had every confidence in his well-being, and was pleased to hear that he and Rose were enjoying Las Palombas.

"We had a letter from Rose," said Mrs. Birkett, "all about the naval battle. Would you like to see it, Geoff?"

Captain Fairweather said old John must have been

pretty sick not to be in it and he'd love to hear. Mr. Birkett looked as if he did not particularly want to hear it, but said nothing. Mrs. Birkett went to her writing-table and brought back a letter in Rose's well-known dashing handwriting, twenty-five words of which filled the largest sheet of paper.

"If I read it aloud, everyone could hear it," she said, already a little nervous about its effect and perhaps feeling that her elder daughter's idiosyncrasies of spelling would be less noticeable if orally transmitted. Captain Fairweather said that would be splendid.

> " 'Darling,' " Mrs. Birkett read. " 'I hope you and Daddy are frightfully well. It is marvelous here and Juan Robinson the one I said about is going to take me to Asturias Point to bathe. There is a marvelous hairdresser in Las Palombas and I am having my hair done in quite a new way. I went to have it set this morning and Pedro which is the one that does it wasn't there so I had to wait and when he did come he was so late that I couldn't stay. He said he had been looking at the ships which John says was too marvelous but I must say it was fouly dispiriting and I am going again to-morrow. John says he knows two officers on the Acilles and a lot of other ones so I hope they will come ashore. There is lovely dancing at a club called Mickey Mouse which seems to be the same word here. Give my love to Geraldine and Phillip and Geff and anyone else except the Pettinger.
>
> " 'With heaps of love from
>
> " 'Rose.' "

We must say, in justice to Mrs. Birkett, that although she thought her daughter's letter slightly foolish when she read it to herself, she had quite underestimated its effect when read aloud and only her great courage bore her up to the end.

"It isn't very much," she said nervously, and no one had ever heard her speak nervously before, "but it does seem so interesting to know that Rose was at Las Palombas when that marvellous battle was going on and really might have seen it."

Her brief apology had given her guests time to recover themselves and they were all loud in their gratitude for this stirring account of one of England's most heroic sea fights. Captain Fairweather said John must have been absolutely sick not to be in it and if it weren't for the Barsetshires he wished he had gone into the Navy himself. Kate said it was dreadful to think of the mothers and families of the men that had been killed, because even if people were one's enemies it was dreadful to think how unhappy they must be and she knew exactly what she would feel like if it was Bobbie. Everard blanched visibly at this vision of his son aged fifteen months gloriously killed in action. Captain Fairweather said By Jove, yes, Bobbie, and fell respectfully silent, so that Mrs. Morland, who had been rapidly visualising her explorer son transported by magic from a thousand miles in the interior of South America to the scene of the naval battle and there dying a hero's death, her naval son who was on the China Station circling half the globe in a few days only to perish among shot and flame, her third son having unknown to her become a Secret Service Agent and arrived at Las Palombas in time to foil an enemy plot at the expense of his life, not to speak of Tony, now well known to be with friends in Gloucestershire for part of the Christmas Vacation, having got into the Trans-Atlantic Air Services and so to Las Palombas and a heroic if unspecified end, surprised herself and made everyone else very uncomfortable by beginning to blow her nose violently.

"I'm so sorry," she said weakly, as her eyes dimmed

with tears she groped on the floor for a hairpin, "but it's all the glory and the misery mixed up together on the top of the Treat. I think I'd better go to bed."

At that moment Simnet came in to say that Miss Geraldine was to report at the Hospital as soon as possible because a number of German measles had come in. The message, he added, had just come on the phone. He then waited to ride the whirlwind if necessary, but Mr. Birkett said, "Thanks, Simnet," so he had to retire, balked.

"Oh, Mummy, there isn't a train to-night," said Geraldine. "Could I have the car?"

"You'll have to ask Daddy," said Mrs. Birkett. "I know we're rather low on petrol till the end of the month. I wish Matron had let you know sooner and you could have got the 9.43."

"You *could* have the car," said Mr. Birkett doubtfully, "but there'll have to be someone to bring it back. I might send down to Mason—no, he is away till Monday."

"I'll run Geraldine over, sir," said Captain Fairweather. "I've got all the petrol in the Army. I'll have her at the door in a moment, Geraldine, if you get your whatnots together. Coming too, Philip?"

Philip said he would and in a few minutes the three went off. Everard and Kate left almost at once, as the thought of a naval battle fought thousands of miles away and nearly a fortnight ago had filled them both with vague fears, which neither of them would have acknowledged to the other, as to the safety of Bobbie Carter, now asleep like a rose-petal jelly in his warm cot. Mrs. Morland retired to sublimate her feelings in her novel before she went to bed and the Birketts were able to sit and read in peace, a luxury in which they rarely indulged.

"Look here, Geraldine," said Captain Fairweather as they were nearing Barchester, Geraldine beside him and Philip in the back seat, "don't worry about things."

Geraldine sniffled loudly and gratefully.

"That's all right," said Captain Fairweather, apparently quite satisfied with her response. "And if you need anyone, I mean someone that isn't your own family, to do anything for you, I can always wangle some leave as long as I'm in England."

Geraldine made a kind of mumbling noise, choked with her handkerchief.

"After all," continued Captain Fairweather, conversationally, "damn that fellow, the police ought to arrest him with headlights like that, we've known each other quite a long time and John being married to Rose makes me your next of kin, or as near as. So if anyone bothers you, just write to me and I'll turn up and lay him out. Do I go by Foregate or by Challoner Street?"

"Challoner Street and then round by the Plough," said Geraldine, "and it's *angelic* of you, Geoff, and I have been so *miserable*."

"Of course you have," said Captain Fairweather. "That's why I mentioned it. Here we are. Get out, Philip."

Philip got out and strolled round to inspect the rear light of the car.

"Listen," said Captain Fairweather. "Do you care for anyone? I don't mean that little sweep—that was only a mistake. I mean anyone real?"

Geraldine shook her head violently.

"That's all right," said Captain Fairweather. "Then you'd better get used to liking me. You are too silly to go about alone. Not even as much sense as Rose," he added as an afterthought.

"It's *angelic* of you, Geoff," said Geraldine.

"That's all right," said Captain Fairweather, giving her a hearty hug with his left arm. "We'll probably get married, come the peace; or before that if it doesn't. Now you go on nursing and let me know anything you want. Is that fixed?"

"Thank you a million times," said Geraldine earnestly, as she got out of the car. "And I will try to be good."

"You'll be good all right," said Captain Fairweather very kindly.

Geraldine ran up the steps to the nurses' entrance and was engulfed by the hospital. Philip came back and took his seat beside Captain Fairweather, who drove back at excessive speed, singing a cheerful song and vouchsafing no explanation to Philip, who did not need any. When they got to the Carters' house Captain Fairweather told Philip that he was going over to the Birketts for a few moments and vanished into the darkness.

The Birketts were surprised by the return of Geraldine's escort and at once jumped to the conclusion that there had been an accident and Geraldine was dead and Captain Fairweather had come, singularly calm and unscathed, to tell them so.

"Sorry to barge in, sir," said Captain Fairweather, "but I thought you'd like to know I landed Geraldine at the Hospital all right. She's got my address and if she wants me I'll manage to get over at almost any time."

"That's very good of you, Geoff," said Mrs. Birkett, wondering.

"Being almost one of the family, with John and Rose married," said Captain Fairweather, "I don't think it would be a bad plan if Geraldine and I got married. I just thought I'd break it to you."

As his future parents-in-law appeared to be struck all of a heap, he continued, standing over them with a pleasant impression of self-reliance and kindness.

"She needs someone to look after her. That little blighter Gissing won't bother her again. I'm not as well off as John, because Aunt Emma didn't leave me anything, but I'll have a bit when Uncle Henry dies and the doctors have been saying for four years that it wouldn't be long. So if you don't want to turn me down, we might take that as settled."

The Birketts were so taken aback by this totally unexpected development that they were bereft of speech, till Mrs. Birkett recovered herself enough to ask weakly if Geraldine knew.

"She knows all right," said Captain Fairweather. "I gave her the idea and it'll soak in all right. She can get married whenever she likes. I should say before I get sent abroad would be better than after, because one never knows if one will come back."

By this time his shock tactics had reduced Mr. and Mrs. Birkett to such a state of imbecility that they would have agreed equally to marriage by special licence on the following morning or an engagement lasting ten years. When they compared notes afterwards they found that nothing better than tags from Victorian novels had floated into their minds, Mr. Birkett having with difficulty subdued his inclination to say, "Bless you, my boy; and may she make you happpy," and Mrs. Birkett having an almost irresistible impulse to say that she felt she was not losing a daughter, but gaining a son. Both were a little ashamed to discover that cliché can be the best expression of emotion and both secretly regretted that they had not had the fun of giving vent to it.

Mrs. Birkett was the first to pull herself together.

"It seems so sudden, Geoff," she said, reflecting even as the words left her mouth that it was rather the affianced than the affianced's mother who ought to use those time-consecrated words, "but I'm sure Geraldine will be very happy with you and I can really think of nothing nicer."

"Well, it surprised me as much as it surprised you," said Captain Fairweather with great candour, "but when I saw that little swine frightening Geraldine I thought the Barsetshires ought to do something about it. Anyway I've known her since I was a kid—and she was a pretty ghastly kid herself," said the gallant Captain meditatively, "so we ought to make a do of it. John will be pleased. He likes Geraldine."

"Oh!" said Mrs. Birkett, determined to offer all she had to give, "there is something in Rose's letter that you'd like to hear, Geoff, but I didn't read it aloud. Wait a minute."

She went to her writing-table, found Rose's letter and handed it to Captain Fairweather, pointing to the last paragraph. Captain Fairweather read the following words.

> P.S. I don't remember if I said in my last letter, but I'm going to have a baby in August. It seemed a bit dispiriting at first but now I think it's absolutely marvelous and he is to be William after Daddy Geffrey after Geff or if it's twins Amy after you Kate because of Kate. The Dr. which is Juan Robinson's father I said about says be sensible but have a good time isn't it marvelous. With heaps of love from Rose.

Captain Fairweather grinned from ear to ear and handed the letter back to Mrs. Birkett.

"Jolly good," he remarked, "I didn't quite get it all the first time, but I see what she means. We'll call ours Rose, or if he's a boy John. Well, I must be getting along. Thanks most awfully for the Christmas Treat and dinner and everything, Mrs. Birkett. Good night, sir."

He departed, leaving the Birketts shattered, but on the whole content. Though neither of them would have said it for words, the prospect of their younger daughter being married filled them with a sense of relief, only comparable to that which they had felt when Rose was safely off their hands. They were good parents and would rather have gone on putting up with Geraldine than see her married to the Gissing of her choice, though they knew that if she had wanted it they were powerless to prevent her. But to think of her in the reliable keeping of Fairweather Senior, who (and though one should not think of such things they are of the utmost importance) would not be badly off, was as good as having a hot bath and a large tea after a long walk in the rain. As for the possibilities, the probabilities, of some quick tragedy cutting across Geoff and Geraldine's life, on these it was worse than useless to brood and from them they resolutely turned their minds.

On his return to Mrs. Carter's house, Captain Fairweather found his host and hostesses and Philip Winter very comfortable in the study, with a large fire and pipes and drinks. From what Philip had told them the Carters were not unprepared for Captain Fairweather's news, but they managed to receive it as a complete surprise and with far more outward manifestations of joy than the Birketts had shown. When Kate went to bed the two soldiers fell into army talk, of which Everard took advantage to finish the House reports. At a quarter to twelve he had signed the last and when he had put them into their envelopes he got up and stretched himself.

"I *am* sorry, Everard," said Philip, conscience-stricken. "I had forgotten you were alive."

"But I am," said Everard, sitting down in a large chair by the fire. "It was pleasantly like old days to hear you talking, Philip."

"I don't know," said Philip, whose conscience appeared to be rearing its head in more directions than one, "why you didn't kick me out of the House, Everard. I haven't a great opinion of myself now, but when I think what a frightful, blethering, Communist nuisance I was, with every antenna, if that word has a singular, out to find offence and take it, I feel I ought to be condemned to live in the London School of Economics for the rest of my life."

"You weren't too bad," said Everard. "Do you remember when you accused Swan of looking at you through his spectacles?"

"That boy had a devilish and subtle mind," said Philip. "I still believe that he forced his mother to buy those spectacles so that he could look at me through them. Where is he?"

"Cambridge," said Everard, "my old college. He gets called up next month."

"I think, sir," said Captain Fairweather, "it's almost rottener for schoolmasters than anyone. I mean all these youngsters getting called up."

"That's nice of you, Geoff," said Everard. "It takes the heart out of one sometimes. But it isn't one's own body that is going to be blown up or drowned, and one has no right to such damned sensibility about things. It doesn't help. One can't help envying Swan and all the others. If only there were something to *do*. Anything but schoolmastering; keeping safe."

Philip, in all his experience of Everard had never heard him speak with such impatience and realised, with the sensitiveness that had formerly made him such a nuisance to himself and his colleagues, how much Everard, and thousands of men of his age, in his position, might be suffering; but found nothing to say.

Captain Fairweather with the patience that the good professional fighter has for the civilian said:

"It's rotten for you, sir. That's where fellows that aren't brainy like John and me are so lucky. I expect you brood a lot. I've noticed that pretty well everyone wants to be doing something different. If you don't mind my saying so, sir, I think it's a jolly good job. I mean looking after all these kids. Lots of our fellows have got brothers or nephews or cousins here and they're all glad to think of the kids having a good time. That's thanks to you and old Pa Birky and the rest, sir. I admit we get most of the fun, but that's our job. And we don't have all your troubles with rationing and evacuees. I can tell you one sometimes feels a bit ashamed with nothing to worry about and all you people sweating away teaching and running the games and the exams. It's really a frightfully decent show, sir."

He was then afraid that he had talked too much, shook hands violently and went off to bed, where he fell asleep at once and to Kate's intense pleasure did not come down to breakfast till ten o'clock.

Everard and Philip alone looked at each other.

"That's a good boy," said Philip. "Geraldine's in luck. He sees straight, which is more than the brainy ones as he calls them can always do. I suppose I'm a bit of a giddy harumfrodite, myself; soldier and schoolmaster too. You know, Everard, you're an extraordinarily good fellow yourself, though severely handicapped by brains."

"To think that I should live to hear my Junior Housemaster talk like that to me," said Everard. "Signs of the times. You go up and I'll put out the lights."

13

BRIEF WINTER INTERLUDE

•

Two days after Christmas it began to snow in Barsetshire. By the end of the next week the whole county was one vast skating rink on which men, women, horses, motors, lorries and bicycles slipped and slithered and swore. The Hosiers' Boys, who had never seen a country winter before, went about with grateful hearts for benefits conferred. The river rose and flooded the cricket ground a foot deep, so that the Hosiers' Boys had the supreme bliss of rowing on it on a Friday and skating on it on a Saturday. Mr. Birkett had holes punched in an old boiler and turned it into a brazier which the Hosiers' Boys kept supplied with wood from Thumble Coppice. The skaters, who came in dozens from the neighbourhood, warmed their hands and feet at its glow and gratefully drank hot soup which Mrs. Birkett and Mrs. Morland brought down in fish kettles and heated. Mrs. Phelps suddenly showed herself a first-class skater and for once justifying her trousers and lumber jacket performed the most dazzling evolutions with Everard Carter. Kate brought Bobbie down in his perambulator, and as he slept the whole time he was considered to have enjoyed himself very much and shown great intelligence. All the evacuees slid in one corner, threw snowballs at each other with uncertain aim, got wet through twice a day, were smacked, dried and put to bed by their foster mothers and returned next day as full of zeal as ever. Manners, the nicest of the

Hosiers' Boys, made with the assistance of Edward the odd man a wooden sledge, upon which he gave rides to the children below school age.

At Evarard Carter's House the bathroom cistern froze and a pipe burst, reminding Matron of the time that Hackett left the hot tap running and nearly flooded the lower dormitory. The Birketts' supply of coal and coke was held up by the state of the roads and for three days there was no central heating, which made Mr. Birkett go to London and spend two nights at his club, where he had some incredibly dull conversations with the older members who were all waiting to pounce on any fresh face and tell it their valueless views on things in general.

Adelina and Maria Cottage spent all their evenings together at Maria partly to save fuel and partly because Mrs. Bissell could not go out at night as Mrs. Dingle couldn't stay and keep an eye on little Edna with the roads in that state.

At the Barchester Hospital such a crop of road accidents came in that the German measlers were despised by the nurses, nearly all of whom had chilblains, and Geraldine was so cheered by compound fractures that she almost forgot the mortification she had received at young Mr. Gissing's hands and wrote long letters to Captain Fairweather about the horribleness of Matron who had put the most attractively maimed patients into D Ward.

The water main in the Close burst and the Bishop's cellar was flooded, which had last occurred in 1936, and gave intense joy to nearly all the inferior clergy, Mr. Miller at Pomfret Madrigal going so far as to refer to it, in conversation with Mrs. Brandon, as a crowning mercy. Ribald rumour had it that the Bishop's second best gaiters had been washed onto the front door steps of Canon Thorne, a peaceful elderly bachelor with High Church leanings, whom the Bishop had accused of being a Mariolater and having no soul, but it was universally recognised that this was too good to be true.

In the middle of all this Noel Merton came down for a night to the Deanery and rang up Lydia Keith, which was just as well, for next day two miles of telephone wires came down, and Sir Edmund Pridham said any fool would have known they could never stand the strain between Grumper's End and Tidcombe Halt and wrote a long letter to the *Barchester Chronicle* which they printed with a number of cuts that made nonsense of it.

"I'd love to see you, Noel, but I'm most frightfully busy," said Lydia's voice on the telephone. "Wait a minute. I've got to go and see about some pig food and there's a Red Cross thing here and it's the day I do the Communal Kitchen—look here, could you possibly come here directly after lunch, about two o'clock? I could fit you in then. If you want a bath, our hot water's all right."

Noel thanked her and said the Deanery water was luckily all right so far and he would come at two o'clock unless the chains fell off his car, or the road at Tidcombe Halt was flooded. When Lydia had rung off he felt for a moment unreasonably depressed. It was not like Lydia to say she would try to fit him in. Then he gave himself a mental shake and reminded himself that Lydia was a very busy person and that so far she had done very much more useful work than he had. He returned to the library and was writing some letters when the Dean's secretary came in.

"Oh, good morning," said Mr. Needham, with a well-simulated start of surprise. "I hope I'm not disturbing you."

"Not a bit," said Noel. "If anyone is doing any disturbing, I am, writing my letters here."

"I expect you are frightfully busy," said Mr. Needham.

One is not a distinguished barrister for nothing and

Noel's ear at once detected the voice of someone who wanted to talk, probably about himself. So he licked up an envelope, put his fountain pen in his pocket, and said he had just finished.

"Come and keep me company," said Noel. "How is everyone? I got here late last night and came down disgracefully late to breakfast and I've hardly had a word with Mrs. Crawley."

Mr. Needham said the Dean was very well and very busy; *very* busy and *very* well, he added, with an earnestness which he hoped might cover the idiocy of his reply.

"And how is Octavia?" asked Noel Merton. "Still at the Hospital?"

Mr. Needham's ingenuous face assumed a reverent expression.

"Octavia is quite magnificent," he said. "She simply lives for the Hospital. Even when she is at home she talks about nothing else. It makes me feel so useless."

"Oh, come, come," said Noel. "Think how much the Dean needs your help."

"Anyone could do a secretary job," said Mr. Needham dejectedly. "I'm frightfully fit and strong and it seems such waste to be writing letters when all my football friends are doing their bit. There are heaps of people with flat feet or something who could do my job; or even women. I mean it's a great privilege to be working for the Dean, but it's pretty awful, especially when I think of Octavia."

"I suppose you won't believe me," said Noel, "but I often feel exactly like that myself."

Mr. Needham stared.

"But you're a soldier, I mean an officer," he said.

"As a matter of fact I'm a secretary like you," said Noel. "Secretary in uniform. I have hopes of being blown to bits or rotting in an enemy dungeon some day, but for the moment I chiefly fill up forms and do odd jobs of interviewing people. And if it is any comfort to you, when I look at Lydia Keith and see how much she is doing, I think it's pretty awful myself."

Mr. Needham almost gaped. That Mr. Merton, that ex-man-of-the-world, now practically a Death's Head Hussar, or at least a Secret Agent of high degree, should feel as out of things as a Dean's secretary, was extremely upsetting to all his ideas. And yet comforting.

"The fact is," said Noel, partly to reassure Mr. Needham, partly following his own thoughts, "everyone wants to be doing something different since the war began; except the people who are actually in the thick of it. I don't suppose either of us are particularly afraid of the idea of danger or discomfort, but we feel we are wasting our time. As a matter of fact I don't believe we are. Lydia and Octavia make one feel rather ashamed," said Noel, basely pandering to Mr. Needham by throwing in Octavia of whom he had no very great opinion though quite in a friendly way, "but they have had the luck to find their jobs made to their hand, and the great self-control to stick to them. I know Lydia is pining to nurse, but her mother needs her and so does the estate, and all the local things. Octavia always wanted to nurse, didn't she?"

This slight denigration of Octavia could not pass without a protest.

"She loves her work, especially head wounds," said Mr. Needham, "but she did once tell me when we were talking about things that she thought it would be splendid to train as a medical missionary," said Mr. Needham.

Noel nearly said he would be sorry for the savages, but restraining himself said it was a very fine ambition.

Mr. Needham said a missionary's life was of course in many ways the highest calling one could imagine, but of course if one could possibly be a Chaplain at the Front— He stopped, diffident at having betrayed a secret, mumbled something about meeting a train and went away, leaving Noel to finish his letters with a divided mind.

After an odious drive along the by-roads, which a fall of snow the day before and a fresh attack of freezing had made into one long pitfall, Noel got to Northbridge Manor, where he found Lydia angrily strewing sand on the front door steps.

"Hullo," said Lydia. "Our idiot kitchen maid washed the steps with hot water this morning to melt the ice and father nearly broke his leg when he went out to get the car. Come round on to the terrace, and help me to carry some things indoors. I'll have to take those two bay-trees in tubs into the hall, or we'll lose them. I did put straw round them, but it won't be enough."

Noel accompanied her to the terrace, where though the air was cold there was shelter from the wind, and a pale sunlight gave a faint illusion of warmth. He and Lydia were able to lift the two trees and carry them through the garden door into the hall, where they looked very well, though lumpy.

"I'll take the straw off afterwards," said Lydia, surveying their trussed shapes. "Come outside for a moment. I feel so stuffy after that Communal Kitchen."

"Was it rabbit stew?" asked Noel, falling into step with her on the stone flags, where the frozen snow had been partly scraped away.

"Shin of beef and dumplings, and tapioca pudding," said Lydia, "and we had to bring all the water in pails because the pump froze. I'm *pleased* to see you, Noel."

"So am I," said Noel; which Lydia quite understood.

Lydia then put Noel through a searching examination about his physical welfare and the general state of things at the Deanery. It did not pass unnoticed by Noel that she never asked about his work. He was able to report that he felt disgustingly well and the food in the mess was good. He then gave her a fairly faithful narration of his conversation with Mr. Needham.

"He and Octavia don't seem to get down to it," said Lydia, with a touch of her old intolerance for any methods but the most direct and bludgeoning. "I must speak to Tommy. He's really a bit too stupid for Octavia but she is pretty stupid too. I think they ought to get engaged and then Tommy ought to be a Military Chaplain and they could get married after the war. Octavia won't want to stop being a nurse, but if Matron gets any more horrible she might go to France and then if Tommy were there she might see him sometimes."

Having thus disposed of her young friends she stopped and they took another turn.

"You don't think I ought to be nursing, do you, Noel?" she asked with what for Lydia was almost diffidence.

"No," said Noel. "You are a good girl; a *very* good girl. And you are doing everything you ought to do."

Lydia returned on him a look of such gratitude that he was abashed to receive so much for so little. They continued to pace the terrace in silence, very comfortably.

"I wish Mother would get better," said Lydia, with such a forlorn note that Noel's heart was wrenched.

"So do I," he said. "And if you need me you will let me know, won't you? I could probably manage to get over at any time if you needed a bit of comforting."

"I'd like it more than anything in the world," said Lydia, "but I wouldn't ever, ever ask you, however much I wanted it. Thank you most awfully though."

She slipped her hand into Noel's as they walked. He, surprised and touched by her mute appeal, so unlike the Lydia he knew, gave her hand the slightest pressure and then let it lie in his, anxious not to presume in any way upon her confidence. If a kind but ferocious hawk had suddenly perched on his hand in a friendly way he would not have been more surprised. Glancing at her profile as she walked beside him in the pale afternoon sunshine he noticed a faint shadow under her cheek bones that again strangely wrung his heart. It occurred to him that ever since he had known her Lydia had been shouldering other people's burdens, sometimes it is true in a very rambunctious and almost interfering way, but always with the best of intentions; and of late in a quieter, more self-effacing way, she had taken responsibility more and more upon her, till her father, her mother, the house, the little estate and much of the local war work seemed to depend very largely upon her. Noel thought of his own life, among men of his own sort, doing work that was more interesting than he was allowed to say, full of food for his mind, with no particular troubles except such as the world in general had to share. There was his Lydia, doing work beyond her years, often alone, tied by an ailing mother, the long evenings spent with parents whose life and interests, much as they loved her and she them, were far away from hers. It seemed to him that his Lydia needed a friend. Not needed perhaps, for she seemed to be unconscious that anything was wanting; but a friend she ought to have, someone older than herself who could give her help and support, someone not so much older that he could not see things as she saw them with her younger eyes. What Lydia needed, in fact, he decided, was someone rather like himself, very fond of her, loving her for her very faults, her brusqueness, her occasional overbearing ways; loving her too for her courage, her newly-learnt patience, her capable ways and above all for the rare moments when she let herself bend a little under her burdens. Such a moment was upon her now and Noel cherished it. Deep peace lay on the downs, the water meadows and the Manor. A white unfamiliar landscape, quiet as midnight, untouched by the world's trouble.

"It is all very solitaire et glacé," said Lydia, half to herself.

"If we are spectres évoquer-ing le passé," said Noel, "it is a very nice past. What fun we have had here. Do you remember the picnic on Parsley Island and how dreadful Rose Birkett was?"

"She was ghastly," said Lydia, withdrawing her hand from Noel's as if the spell were broken, but so kind a withdrawal that Noel felt it almost as a caress. "And the day Tony and Eric and I cleaned out the pond and Rose threw her engagement ring at Philip."

"And you had on that dreadful short frock with no sleeves and all your arms and legs were the colour of a beetroot," said Noel.

"And then Philip dropped the ring into the pool below the pond. I wonder if it is there still. Rose got engaged about twelve times before she married John. If I got engaged, I'd *get* engaged," said Lydia with a flash of her old arrogance.

"I think you would," said Noel. "And mind, you promised to mention it to me when you do, so that I can see if he is good enough."

"Of course I'll tell you," said Lydia. "But I don't think I will at present, because unless it was someone like you I wouldn't like them enough."

Then Noel knew that it was not as a friend that he wanted Lydia to need him. The blow to his heart made it impossible for him to speak for a moment. Divided between a wish to tell Lydia that she was the core of his life and a fear of disturbing her peace, wrenched suddenly by the violence of his own feelings, his self-possession lay shattered. For the first time in his life he was entirely at a loss. They had come to the end of the terrace.

"Lydia," he said, as they turned. And on that his foot slipped on the frozen snow and he would have fallen if Lydia had not supported him with her powerful grasp.

"Hold up!" said Lydia reprovingly. "You ought to

have nails in your shoes for this weather like me," and she turned up the sole of one of her heavy country brogues to show him serried rows of nails.

The moment had fled. Lydia said she was frightfully sorry but she must go to a meeting in the village and would walk, as it was so slippery to bicycle. Noel offered to drop her there on his way back to Barchester.

"It's Mrs. Knowles's, that stone house with the blue door," said Lydia as they slithered down the village street. "Thanks awfully, Noel. Give Octavia my love."

"Take care of yourself," said Noel, for banalities seemed the only thing to say. "I'm more than likely to be at the Deanery when I get any leave and I'll always let you know."

Lydia crushed his hand to a jelly and strode up Mrs. Knowles's garden path to the front door, her heart very heavy. The unwonted load lay upon her all that day and for many days and she found herself entirely unable to account for it.

14

DINNER AT THE DEANERY

•

The long winter of everyone's discontent like a very unpleasant snake dragged its slow length along. Pipes continued to freeze, burst and thaw with wearisome regularity. Southbridge School and the Hosiers' Boys went back to work. Men in their early twenties were summoned away and men a little older registered. More than half the evacuated children were taken back to London whence they wrote long letters to their country hostesses expressing a determination to come back and live with them for ever as soon as they were old enough. Those children who remained became stouter of body and redder of face every day, and with wearisome regularity had to return to the clinic to have their heads cleaned. Party feeling raged high over this question, the London teachers saying that their children were infected by the cottagers; the local committees asserting that the cottage children were free from any infection until the London children brought it back from town on their visits to their parents. Mrs. and Miss Phelps, taking no notice of either side, cleaned all heads with violent impartiality. The Admiral had the intense pleasure of welcoming Bill and Tubby again as his guests when they returned from a cheerful violation of Norway's highly un-neutral waters, with their rescued fellow-seamen; and when Mrs. Birkett heard that Bill had the ocarina with him on that glorious occasion she felt that she had in no small measure contributed to the victory and the rescue and became quite bloated with pride.

Two outstanding events are to be mentioned in that long depressing season before early Summer Time came in again.

The first was the end of the Gissings, preceded by a crop of rumours which were a perfect godsend to the county. Many people who ought to have known better announced as gospel truth the following perfectly unfounded reports:

(*a*) That Mr. Gissing was in the Tower. Origin unknown and firmly believed by everyone until the birth of

(*b*) that Mr. Gissing was under arrest in the film studios with an armed guard at the door and only allowed to eat boiled eggs into which it is practically impossible to smuggle notes, files, prussic acid, or bombs. Origin: Mrs. Dingle, who cleaned at the studios once a week and saw some sandwiches going in and a sham soldier waiting to go on the set for a faked propaganda film, who playfully presented a dummy bayonet at her.

(*c*) that Mrs. Gissing was under observation by the Secret Service for Luring Officers to tell her Things (unspecified). Origin: Mrs. Phelps who had been to town for a day's shopping, for once in a coat and skirt, and was taken to lunch at the Café Royal by one of her many naval friends, where she had seen Mrs. Gissing, more dripping with foxes and pearls than ever, drinking Pernod with two dark men who looked like soldiers in civilian dress. The Admiral had rounded upon his wife, reminding her that soldiers did not go the Café Royal in mufti and she ought to know better. But Mrs. Phelps, who hated Mrs. Gissing without reserve for her self alone, refused to be checked.

(*d*) that all the Gissings had been shot. Origin: Mr. Brown of the Red Lion, who after young Mr. Gissing had been throwing his weight about more than usual in the Red Lion, said he wished they were all put up against a wall. This rumour gained immense credence among all the patrons of the Red Lion, whose faith was untouched by the fact that all the Gissings were seen in the village on the following day. But as Eileen said, patting her new bubble curls into place with her well-manicured hand, it was easy to dress up like some people and it stood to reason the Government would do things on the quiet; which convinced all but the most hardened unbelievers.

(*e*) that young Mr. Gissing had been caught red-handed spying on the railway and was to be deported. Origin: the station-master at Tidcombe Halt, who had found young Mr. Gissing travelling to Barchester with a very suspicious tin case which might have been a bomb if it hadn't been film negatives. Young Mr. Gissing had refused to open it and produced his identity card, upon which the station-master had said he didn't hold with them things and they didn't prove nothing and hauled young Mr. Gissing out of his first-class smoking carriage and locked him into the porters' room while he rang up the police, to whom young Mr. Gissing had been so rude, obstructing him in the execution of his duty and threatening actions at law, that his father had had to go and make a quite grovelling explanation and apology.

After two months of such delightful hopes and fears it was a distinct disappointment to everyone that the Gissing family all went to America and were not even torpedoed on the way over. When Geraldine heard that they were going she was afraid that she might mind, but to her great relief she found that she didn't, which made her write several very long dull letters to Captain Fairweather about a trepanning case and a dislocated pelvis. Captain Fairweather rightly interpreted these letters as a proof of love and confidence and carried on with his military duties.

The second event, perhaps of less general interest, but deeply exciting to our immediate circle at Southbridge, was the publication of Miss Hampton's new novel, *Temptation at St. Anthony's,* which was chosen as the Anti-Sex Immorality Society Book of the Month in U.S.A., and the *Daily Dustbin* First Pick for April in England, besides having in a more intellectual daily a slashing review which sent its sales up by thousands.

Miss Hampton had wished to dedicate her book to Mr. and Mrs. Bissell, from whom, she said, she had learnt many interesting facts hitherto unknown to her, especially from Mrs. Bissell, whose studies in the psychology of educational establishments were as profound as her mind was innocent. But the Bissells, though immensely flattered by the idea, felt that such notoriety might be prejudicial to them in their profession, in which, they said, one must always consider the weaker members, so Miss Hampton dedicated it to All Brave Spirits who have been my Friends. The Bissells, whose social education had advanced by leaps and bounds during a winter's association with Adelina Cottage, burst into a small sherry party to celebrate the event, particularly inviting Mrs. Morland as a literary light.

"It is always," said Mrs. Morland, shaking hands warmly with Miss Hampton, "so difficult when you want to congratulate someone, because you are never sure if they want to be congratulated, but I can't tell you how pleased I am about *Temptation at St. Anthony's*. I haven't exactly read it, but I'm just as pleased as if I had and of course I shall."

"I wouldn't if I were you," said Miss Hampton. "Strong meat. Not for people with your sensitive outlook."

This surprised Mrs. Morland very much, for though she knew that she was no good at being coarse, she had never thought of herself as sensitive, having been for many years far too busy to consider such things.

"No, no," continued Miss Hampton. "You and I needn't read each other's books. We write for Our Public, not for our friends. Mercenaries, you and I. Must say though we work for our pay."

"Well, that is a great relief," said Mrs. Morland, picking up her gloves which she had dropped, "because I never expect people—I mean real people—to read my books, and I must say I have never read any of yours, though I'm sure they're frightfully good. It is funny about one's friends. Sometimes one likes the book and not the friend and sometimes the friend and not the book; and sometimes both, or neither. You know George Knox, don't you, who lives near me at High Rising? I am very fond of him and I admire his books though one would never guess they were the same person. But with Mrs. Rivers I feel exactly the opposite, not that she is a friend, because I only met her once, years ago, at a lunch party. I don't mean that I admire her and am fond of her books, which would be the exact opposite; but I find them both very unsympathetic. Then there is Mrs. Barton whose books about Borgias and things are entrancing, but somehow we've never quite hit it off. And I do really like you so much, but I know I wouldn't like your books, so that is perfect."

"You're a pretty good sort yourself," said Miss Hampton, giving her tie a jerk. "You had some kind of Book of the Month once, hadn't you?"

"I couldn't really help it," said Mrs. Morland apologetically, "and it pleased my publisher frightfully. I call it my Child of Shame."

At this simple piece of wit Miss Hampton laughed uproariously and said she wished she had thought of that.

"I'll give it you," said Mrs. Morland. "I haven't used it much."

Mrs. Phelps, who had been listening with deep interest, said she simply couldn't understand how people could write books, but she was always telling Irons he ought to write his life, as he had been pretty well everywhere. She had, she said, found a splendid title for him: Irons in the Fire, because his friends called him Irons and the Fire part would mean partly that he had been under fire and partly that he had a lot of irons in the fire in every sense of the word.

Mrs. Morland and Miss Hampton, who had a pretty good idea of what the book would be like, looked at each other with eyes of despair and said in a jumble of simultaneous speech that it would be perfectly splendid. The Admiral, pleased though modest, said he was only a rough sailor and all his diaries were lost in that fire at the Pantechnicon while he was at Simonstown, but he would like to try his hand at it.

"You ought to collaborate with Bent, Admiral," said Miss Hampton. "Tell him your idea, Bent."

"You know I make a special study of Vice, Admiral," said Miss Bent.

Miss Phelps said father was a Rear-Admiral.

"Tut, tut," said Miss Bent, to the great admiration of her audience, who had never known those words used outside a printed book before. "Vice. Unnatural Vice. Now, Admiral, I would like to pick your brains about the lower deck."

This reasonable and scientific request frightened the Admiral so much that only the intervention of Mrs. Bissell kept him from summoning his wife and daughter and going home at once.

"Pardon me, Miss Bent," said Mrs. Bissell, "but you have the stick by quite the wrong end as the saying is. It would be quite useless to ask Admiral Phelps, because his protective or escapist complex would not allow him to open his eyes to social evil. You would do much better to read the chapter on the Libido-Involuntary in *A Concept of Neo-Phallic Thought* by Spurge-Mackworth. He used to lecture at the Training College and is a lucid and courageous thinker."

"It's very good of you," said Miss Bent, who was sincerely fond of Mrs. Bissell, "but you know my motto: One Crowded Hour of Glorious Vice. The Admiral could tell me more in ten minutes than your friend could in ten books."

But the Admiral could bear it no longer and took his wife and daughter away to meet some young naval friends who were arriving by the 6.40.

"It's a pity," said Miss Bent, sadly. "When I think of the side lights you and Mr. Bissell have given us on school psychology—"

"But you must remember, Miss Bent," said Mr. Bissell, "that Mrs. Bissell has made a study of psychology. Of course she can't write fiction like you ladies, though I often say to her, You never know till you've tried, but her knowledge of the subject is very thorough. I assure you the County Libery simply cannot keep pace with the books she asks for. In February alone she had out seventeen books, didn't you, Mother?"

"Mr. Bissell has omitted to state," said Mrs. Bissell, looking affectionately at her husband, "that two of them were for Mrs. Dingle. Her husband is apt to be troublesome, and I thought she might get some help."

"What kind of psychology did you get for her?" asked Mrs. Morland with much interest.

"Oh, not psychology," said Mrs. Bissell pityingly. "That would be quite useless without previous training. I got her a book on curing alcoholism without the patient's knowledge and another one on elementary ju-jitsu. She is a well-developed woman in intelligence and physique and I gather their home life has been quite a different thing."

Mrs. Morland then said good-bye, leaving Miss Hampton and Miss Bent to make a night of it with the Bissells, which they did till nearly half-past eight, when Miss Bent said they ought to go down to the Red Lion and see who was there, so she and Miss Hampton departed, with Mannerheim in tow.

As April came on, life altered a little. Oxford came down and Mrs. Morland left the Birketts for her own house at High Rising. By an amicable arrangement her publisher's wife Sibyl Coates had transferred herself and her nurse and children to her grandmother at Bournemouth for the Easter Vacation, so that Mrs. Morland would have her youngest son Tony at home with her. Mrs. Morland's new book of short stories came out and all the reviewers said "Another vintage Morland," or "Mrs. Morland can be relied upon to give her readers exactly what they expect, and in her new book has given them generous measure, pressed down and overflowing," or "A laugh and a thrill on every page." Mrs. Morland, who never read press notices, was pleased to get her advance on royalties and felt that Tony's education and the pocket money of her other boys were safe for the present. Her books made no great noise, but her publisher Adrian Coates rejoiced in their steady sale and had the great pleasure of finding out, through underground channels, that a loudly boomed novel called *My Burning Flesh,* translated from the Mixo-Lydian by a young woman on the staff of the *Daily Dustbin,* and described by his friends and rival publishers, Johns and Fairfield, as a stark and gripping piece of realism, had only sold half as many copies as Mrs. Morland's.

Various people in Southbridge, and indeed all over England, were embarrassed by parcels of food from friends or relations in Canada, Australia, the United States, Kenya and other more or less English-speaking countries. While deeply grateful for the kindness that prompted the dispatch of such parcels to a starvation-haunted England, they were much annoyed by the excessive duty they had to pay, and in several cases wrote to *The Times,* whose *défaitiste* attitude towards the Crossword had by now alienated many of its staunchest supporters.

Miss Hampton and Miss Bent had the first serious difference of opinion in a companionship which had lasted for some twenty years. The cause of this rift was the invasion of two small and defenceless northern kingdoms, which were thus automatically added to their list of gallant little nations. Not that they differed by a hairsbreadth in their hatred and condemnation of the invaders, but the question of moral support from Mannerheim drove them into separate camps. On the chief premise, namely that there was nobody one had ever heard of in Norway or Denmark except Hans Andersen, they were united, but Miss Bent, less impetuous than Miss Hampton, insisted that Norway's claims should be further examined, and to that end took the temporary Mannerheim round to the Bissells one Saturday morning, followed by the protesting Miss Hampton.

Mr. and Mrs. Bissell, always delighted by an intellectual discussion, were quickly put in possession of the facts and brought their minds to bear on the question.

"I quite see what you mean about Norway," said Mr. Bissell. "One might of course mention Nansen."

"No!" said Miss Bent, quite violently. "Look at the trouble the League of Nations has got us into. Besides, Nansen is *no* name for a dog."

With such conviction did she speak that all her hearers felt that if they called a dog Nansen she would hate it.

"Of course there is Longfellow," said Mrs. Bissell.

"Long Tooth, you mean," said Miss Bent.

"No; Longfellow," said Mrs. Bissell, placidly. "His beautiful rendering of that fine old saga about King Olaf. I learned many a canto of it by heart when I was a girl, and I used to teach it to the girls in the Fourth Standard.

"Einar then the arrow taking from the loosened string,
Answered: That is Norway breaking 'neath thy hand, O King"!

This quotation was felt by her audience to be vaguely and uncomfortably too near the present state of things and a depressed silence fell, broken by Mr. Bissell, who said:

"Hayken."

"Harken, Daddy," said Mrs. Bissell.

"Hawkon, I think," said Miss Hampton.

Miss Bent said she knew one pronounced it Marterlinck, but that was perhaps different.

"Call him Haakon if you like, Bent," said Miss Hampton, going rather white and sounding suspiciously as if she were going to cry. "You know I only want to please you."

At this sudden collapse of Miss Hampton, whom her friends had always taken for the strong and gentlemanly spirit of the pair, the Bissells stood amazed. Mr. Bissell wished he were safely in the Masters' Common Room, but Mrs. Bissell, a psychologist first and foremost, quickly recovered her poise and looked on with kind detachment at this interesting practical demonstration of all she had learnt in theory, and suggested a nice cup of tea. Miss Hampton and Miss Bent suddenly knew, as Aurora Freemantle had once discovered, that a nice cup of tea was the one thing in the world worth while, and though the Red Lion had been gaping for them for the last half-hour, they were glad to accept Mrs. Bissell's offer. Miss Hampton blew her nose violently, Miss Bent said "Sorry" in a gruff voice, and after a great deal more discussion, on the most amicable terms, it was decided that pending further political moves Mannerheim should be called Andersen, Mrs. Bissell pointing out with her usual excellent common-sense that he would probably not hear the difference between the two names and so answer to his new name more readily.

The ladies then left, happy and reconciled. As they walked down Maria's little front path a car drove past.

"There's Lydia Keith," said Miss Hampton. "Nice girl. She looks thin lately. Wonder if anything's wrong."

"Miss Keith is a very peculiar and I might say almost abnormal type," said Mrs. Bissell.

"How?" said Miss Bent, hoping that Lydia might afford her some side lights on Vice.

"She is perfectly normal," said Mrs. Bissell. "Good-bye, Miss Bent. Good-bye, Miss Hampton. Good-bye, Andersen, old fellow."

Now that the days were longer, or as the Dean said, the hours of daylight were perhaps a more correct expression, Mrs. Crawley decided to give a dinner party, nominally in honour of a retired Colonial Bishop who was going to do locum work in Little Misfit whose vicar, Mr. Tompion, had managed to get abroad as a Chaplain with the Barsetshires, but really because she felt that she would die unless she for once got into proper evening dress and knew that many of her friends shared her feelings. It was to be a slap-up party of eighteen, with all the leaves but one put into the dining-room table, which when fully extended could take twenty-four, but Mrs. Crawley made a concession to the troubled times by inviting people who were either staying in Barchester or could come in the same car and save petrol. Under the first heading were the retired Bishop, who was staying at the Deanery till the Vicarage at Little Misfit was ready, Noel Merton who was again down for a night's leave and Miss Pettinger who of course lived near the High School in a charming Georgian house which was far too good for her. Under the second were Mrs. Brandon, Delia Brandon, and the Millers from Pomfret Madrigal who were coming with Sir Edmund Pridham in his car, and the Archdeacon from Plumstead and his daughter who would pick up the Birketts on their way. Mr. and Mrs. Keith had been asked, but Mrs. Keith was not well enough to come, so Mrs. Crawley had asked Lydia instead, knowing that Noel would be pleased to see her.

The party from Pomfret Madrigal were the first to arrive. Mrs. Brandon with a charming and quite illusory air of fragility wafted herself into the drawing-room in a chiffon cloud of every soft colour of sweet pea, followed by Mrs. Miller in a dark blue dress with a dark blue velvet jacket and Delia in green.

The Colonial Bishop was introduced to Mrs. Brandon and being unmarried at once felt thankful that Little Misfit and Pomfret Madrigal were only three miles apart. True, petrol was rationed, but he was a confirmed bicyclist, having covered on that exhausting machine many hundred miles of his sub-Equatorial diocese where he was known to his flock as Mbanga Ngango, or roughly in English Roly-poly Witch Doctor.

"I am delighted to hear that you are coming to Little Misfit," said Mrs. Brandon. "Mr. Tompion is quite delighted and so is his wife, but of course as he is an Army Chaplain he is not there."

The Colonial Bishop, by now almost demented with admiration, said No, of course, one could quite see that.

"And his wife, who is very nice indeed," Mrs. Brandon continued, looking pensively at her left hand on which shone the diamond ring, legacy of her husband's rich aunt, Miss Brandon, "has gone back to Leamington for the duration to her parents who are a very charming retired Colonel and his wife called Parkinson. I wished she could have stayed on at the Vicarage because she is splendid with children owing to having none of her own and was such a help with my nursery, but with you coming I suppose she couldn't."

The Colonial Bishop longed to explain to Mrs. Brandon that though a joint household of Mrs. Tompion and himself might have presented difficulties Mrs. Tompion would have been scrupulously respected by him; but finding this not easy to put into words, he asked if Mrs. Brandon had a large family.

"Only two," said Mrs. Brandon, with an exquisitely melancholy inflection as of a Niobe to whom Apollo had spared the last of her brood.

"But luckily in the nursery," said the Colonial Bishop, glad that his new friend was not likely to suffer through her children.

"Well, not often," said Mrs. Brandon. "Delia really likes children very much, but of course as she is mostly at the Hospital she has to go to bed a good deal when she is at home, and Francis is at work all day and the children are in bed when he gets back, but he will have to register next month and then he will feel much better."

At this point Mrs. Birkett most luckily intervened and took away the Colonial Bishop, who would otherwise have gone mad, to introduce him to the Archdeacon, who was burning for a new audience to whom he could repeat himself about the difficulties of the West Barsetshire pack in war-time.

Noel Merton now claimed Mrs. Brandon, who said it was a long time since she had seen him, implying by her voice and look the epithet "deceiver."

Noel said with proper gallantry, Not half so long as it was since he had seen Mrs. Brandon, and they both laughed, for they were excellent friends and voyaged about the Pays du Tendre in great comfort, with return tickets.

"Listen, Lavinia," said Noel, serious for a moment.

"Mrs. Crawley has put me between Mrs. Birkett and Miss Pettinger. I love the one and have every intention of hating the other, but what I really want is to have a talk to you. Will you league with me after dinner?"

"Of course I will," said Mrs. Brandon. "This dress fluffles out very nicely and if I sit on the little green settee, there won't be room for anyone unless I choose to make it."

And then the party from Plumstead and Southbridge School came in, the Archdeacon's daughter apologising for their being late, but she had been working the tractor at Starveacre till the last moment and was so stiff she could hardly get her breeches off.

The Keiths and Lydia followed hard upon, and then the whole party had to wait for Miss Pettinger. Lydia, Octavia and Delia said loudly that the Pettinger had done it on purpose, and it was just like her horribleness. Mr. Needham came in and said someone had rung up to say that Miss Pettinger had been delayed, but was just starting and hoped they wouldn't wait.

Dinner was therefore put back ten minutes, at the end of which time Miss Pettinger was announced. Her gracious entry was marked by a black lace dress, a white rabbit-skin coatee, and a very large white, shiny handbag.

"I must really apologise for keeping everyone waiting," said Miss Pettinger, "but my secretary had mislaid my gas-mask. How are you, Mrs. Crawley? And the Dean? And Lydia and Delia and Octavia? It is nice to see so many old High School Girls."

Mrs. Crawley introduced such of the party as were not known to Miss Pettinger, who had just had a very tight new permanent wave (for she believed in setting a standard of personal care to her girls), which made her hair, as Delia said to Lydia, look as false as her teeth.

"You may wonder where I put my gas-mask," said Miss Pettinger, while the parlourmaid vainly tried to announce dinner. "I carry it in my evening bag at night and I had asked my secretary to transfer it for me, but she had forgotten and so it could not at first be found, till I looked on my writing-table and there it was. So I put it into my bag, took my torch and braved the terrors of the black-out and here I am."

Octavia said, rather too loudly, that it was bright moonshine to-night and received an admonishing look from her mother.

"Never take my gas-mask out to dinner," said Sir Edmund, who had had more than one tussle with Miss Pettinger on committees and had no fear of her, nor indeed any opinion. "Can't eat with a mask on. Bad manners, too."

"There's only one person that can, Pridham," said the Archdeacon, who hated Miss Pettinger because she used the word blood-sports and in a deprecatory sense, "and that's a fox."

Mrs. Birkett herded her guests downstairs, hoping that Miss Pettinger had not heard the Archdeacon, as indeed she had not, for she was already explaining to the Dean, who took her down, how useful it was to have a white, shiny bag for one's gas-mask in the black-out, and how hers also held her torch, her identity card, and her name and address on a visiting card contained in a talc-fronted case, besides, she added laughingly, her make-up and other feminine trifles.

"Much as I like sitting next to you," said Noel, who was between Miss Pettinger and Mrs. Birkett, to this latter lady, "I am looking forward with rapture to the moment when half the heads will turn to the left and half to the right, instead of half to the right and half to the left as at present. I am longing to hear my neighbour's views on make-up. Tell me, how is the School?"

Mrs. Birkett needed little pressing to give Noel an account of the activities of Southbridge School and the Hosiers' Boys during the current term and as he knew a good many of the characters concerned, he was properly interested.

"Talking of the Bissells, Miss Hampton was there not long ago," said Mrs. Birkett, "and she saw Lydia Keith as she was coming away and thought she looked thin. I haven't seen her till to-night for some time and I think so too. I think she worries about her mother, poor child."

It is one thing to think your nicest friend is thin yourself, but quite another to have a third person say so, and Noel almost disliked kind Mrs. Birkett for taking so much interest in Lydia. He would have liked to look at Lydia again and satisfy himself about her, but unfortunately she was on the same side of the table, next but one to Mrs. Birkett, and heavily involved with Mr. Miller on the question of a Communal Kitchen, which Pomfret Madrigal had not yet instituted. So he had to content himself, which indeed he found it easy to do, with Mrs. Birkett's agreeable company, until such time as the heads should turn.

Beyond Lydia, Mr. Needham and Delia were prattling away very harmlessly, and beyond Delia the Archdeacon discussed with Mrs. Crawley on his right the opening of the new building at Hiram's Hospital, a charitable institution that was one of the prides of Barchester. The reparations and additions to Hiram's Hospital had been carried out by Mr. Barton, an architect who did much of the cathedral work and about whose wife's books we have heard Mrs. Morland's opinion. The ceremony of opening them was to be performed by the Earl of Pomfret, the Lord Lieutenant of the county.

"I was talking to Foster at the Red Cross Committee today," said the Archdeacon, alluding to Lord Pomfret's cousin and heir who had for some years been taking an active part in county work. "He tells me that Pomfret is not at all well. He has never really been the same since Lady Pomfret died. What a beautiful woman she used to be. I remember her when I was a boy, driving in a victoria and pair under the archway of the Close to a garden party at the Palace."

Mrs. Crawley, who was fond of Lord Pomfret in spite of his sometimes terrifying manner, expressed her sorrow at this news.

"There's no doubt Foster will do well," said the Archdeacon, "but Pomfret would be very much missed. He stands for a great deal that we need at the present moment."

"Sally will do very well too," said Mrs. Crawley, for Mr. Foster's wife, who had been Sally Wicklow, was a great friend and ally of hers.

"They are a good lot, the Wicklows," said the Archdeacon. "You know her brother, Roddy, Pomfret's agent?"

Mrs. Crawley said she did and was very fond of little Mrs. Roddy Wicklow, daughter of Mr. Barton, the architect.

"That all brings me round to what I wanted to tell you," said the Archdeacon. "I don't know if you remember Mrs. Roddy's brother, Guy Barton. He and my girl have known each other for a long time and the engagement will be announced in a few days, but I wanted you and the Dean to know before it is public. He left his father's office last September and is in the R.A.F. and they want to get married before he is sent abroad, which might be fairly soon."

Mrs. Crawley expressed sincere pleasure, but her thoughts were more with Lord Pomfret than with the young couple. She and her husband had known him for a good many years and his passing would mean the passing of an old order, far too much of which was already engulfed. Mrs. Crawley did her best to be broadminded about social changes and managed to have faith that the next generation would make the world a little better, but all her broadmindedness could not make her think that it would be so happy for the people of her own age who had seen the golden Edwardian prime. Whatever happened it would mean eating other people's mental bread and treading strange stairs, and Mrs. Crawley sometimes felt that she would like to shut herself up in the Deanery, stop her ears, and there decay gently in a corner, living in a dream of the past. Pomfret Towers had for many years been a friendly house to her and her husband. When Lord Pomfret died the new Earl and his wife would bring to their duties the same admirable devotion that old Lord Pomfret had always shown and would if possible bring up their children in the same spirit. But with death duties and war taxes the estate would be grievously crippled. The Towers would probably be shut, or the new owners would live in part of one wing, economizing; a small runabout instead of the three large cars and the chauffeurs; vegetables, fruit and flowers sold instead of being used in the house or given away on the estate, shooting let to a syndicate, horses put down, nasturtiums sown in the Italian garden whose bedding-out had been the head gardener's joy. The tenants, she knew, would be the last to suffer, as the new Lord Pomfret and his wife would roof a cottage or mend a gate before they would give themselves a new bathroom; and that was as it should be. But when those days came Mrs. Crawley knew that she and her contemporaries would find themselves in a world where their chief use would be to oil the wheels where they could and to die in decent time so that the young might inherit a world whose most enchanting pleasures they had not known and would not miss.

Mrs. Crawley looked down the long table at the end of which she was sitting with the Archdeacon. Who among her guests were to inherit this new world? Lydia, Delia, Octavia, the Archdeacon's daughter; Mr. Needham. Noel Merton perhaps, though his life and thought lay more with the older generation. Four nice, ordinary girls and a young man of no very particular ability. That they would all behave well in any given circumstances Mrs. Crawley did not doubt, but what standard of life were they going to keep? Then she blamed herself for harsh judgment of a generation that had not yet been tried. She remembered that Delia and Octavia were diligent at the Hospital and never tried to change their hours for the sake of a treat, that the Archdeacon's daughter was training land girls with efficient zeal, that Lydia Keith, who she thought looked more subdued than was her wont, was managing the little estate and both her parents, besides her many other activities, that Mr. Needham was a painstaking secretary though his spirit longed for more active work. "Good, good children," she said to herself.

And marriage. Would those girls care to marry? How many would lose a lover, a friend that might have been a lover? If Octavia would only show the faintest interest in men, thought her mother almost angrily, for she herself had married young and had all her large family by the time she was thirty-five, partly owing to the twins, and metaphorically speaking had the decks cleared for action by the time she was forty and full of energy. Were Octavia, Delia, Lydia to go on being nice useful girls for ever? She almost champed with rage at the thought.

And all this went through her mind while the Archdeacon was talking about Hiram's Hospital and repeating his anxieties about Lord Pomfret's health, so that he got a very long innings, by which means the Colonial Bishop, whose name does not matter and who indeed only comes into this book as an excuse for a dinner party, was able to immolate himself thoroughly at Mrs. Brandon's shrine, who like an exquisite and tender Juggernaut was rolling over him, talking delightful nonsense all the time. While she thus carried out her mission, Mr. Birkett on her right was able to get from the Archdeacon's daughter some excellent advice about putting in winter greens, to which end he had just had a new piece of ground dug up. This professional talk threw Sir Edmund and Octavia together; not that Octavia minded, for one audience was to her as good as another and she had an abdominal on her mind that she required to get off it. But Sir Edmund, who liked girls to be pretty and ready to flirt, and wanted to talk to the Archdeacon's daughter about the vixen at Tolson's corner, did not enjoy himself at all until, Octavia stopping to take breath, he told her about the wound in his leg that he got at the Battle of the Marne and found for once a thoroughly sympathetic listener.

Beyond Octavia, Mr. Keith talked quietly to Mrs. Miller about some new books and the fate of Brandon Abbey, which had been left by old Miss Brandon as a kind of Home of Rest for veterans of her brother's regiment.

But owing to trustees and things, Mrs. Miller said, it had not yet been properly organized, for a great deal of alteration and new plumbing had to be done and there was a good deal of red tape with various Ministries. Now, however, the Government had taken it over, plumbing and all, as a military hospital, so it was just as well, and she was sure old Miss Brandon would have been pleased. Looking across the table at Lydia, she said she was so glad to see Miss Keith again, and how delightful she looked, but a little tired. She could not admire the girls enough and the way they tackled everything.

Mr. Keith also looked at Lydia and wondered if seeing his daughter every day made him not realize how much thinner she had grown. But as she was almost perfect in his eyes, he decided that Mrs. Miller was not only wrong, but slightly interfering, and became rather reserved, which Mrs. Miller did not notice in the least though she found him so heavy in hand that she was relieved when the Dean, who was sitting beside her at the opposite end from Mrs. Crawley and the Archdeacon, took advantage of a moment's pause in Miss Pettinger's monologue to ask her advice about a giant assemblage of Mothers' Unions which was to be held in the Cathedral in the following month. At this Mrs. Miller said, Ha-ha! inside herself, for daughter of a vicarage and wife of a vicarage, Mothers' Unions were in her blood and she knew she could organize for ten thousand women if necessary without the slightest difficulty.

"Our chief stumbling block," said the Dean, "in the Cathedral Service, will be the gas-masks. They have all been told to bring them, but I know, I *know* that they won't, and I have had, however reluctantly, to rule that no mother will be allowed into the Cathedral without showing her mask."

"I know what I would do," said Mrs. Miller quietly, "though it would be quite wrong. I would collect as many cardboard containers as possible and have them at the various points of assembly. Then each mother who has not brought her mask could first be spoken to severely about her negligence and then given an empty box to carry. My dear father would, I fear, have condemned this as mere expediency, but there are moments when expediency becomes a necessity, and this seems to me the moment."

The Dean thanked her warmly and said he would privately make this suggestion to those responsible for convening the various branches.

Mrs. Miller said that gas-masks in the Cathedral, though showing a sense of public duty, would be entirely useless. Last time she went to Evensong, she said, her mind wandered, as one's mind is, alas, too apt to do, and she could not help reflecting that if a single bomb fell anywhere in the neighbourhood, the rose window, the monument to Lord Pomfret's grandfather, Vice-

Admiral Thorne's Trafalgar monument with Neptune and a mourning Britannia, besides the draped statue of the Honourable Augustus de Courcy, the last representative of old Barum before it was disfranchised as a Rotten Borough, would at once have fallen in glass splinters and masses of masonry on her head, not to speak of the whole of the roof of the North Transept where it was being repaired.

"I know, I know," said the Dean. "We should of course try to get everyone out as quickly as possible. But I must confess, though I could not say this to everyone, that I always hope I may be in the Cathedral if there is an air-raid, just to observe some of our clergy and elder choristers leaving the building as they are officially commanded to do, with all reverent speed. I feel that the speed would, in so many cases, get the upper hand. But I oughtn't to talk like this."

Mrs. Miller, however, being of the inner circle, took the remark in very good part and they laughed so much in a quiet way that Mr. Keith, grappling with Octavia, felt very depressed and wished he could share the fun. Sir Edmund, having exhausted the story of his wound, from which he still suffered though he never complained, was thus enabled to turn with relief to the Archdeacon's daughter and from her got the most valuable support about the vixen, who had been much harassed by the ploughing of a field that she regarded as her own and had practically implored Sir Edmund's protection.

Mr. Birkett, having done his duty by winter greens, had a very pleasant chat with Mrs. Brandon, as indeed everyone always did.

"I do want you and your wife to know," said Mrs. Brandon, "before it is in *The Times,* that Delia is going to marry our nice cousin, Hilary Grant. When I say cousin, he is really no relation at all, only a connection which makes it all right though in any case they wouldn't be first cousins which is, I believe, where the bad blood comes in."

Mr. Birkett said he was delighted and he knew his wife would be, and asked if Hilary was in the Army, as nearly all the young men he knew now were.

"Well, not *exactly*," said Mrs. Brandon, "because his eyes are not good enough, but he speaks Italian very well and has been taken on for a temporary job in a Government office which I am not supposed to mention though everyone knows about it and exactly where it is. I know it is wicked," said Mrs. Brandon plaintively, "but I cannot help being glad that Hilary won't be killed at once. Of course if there is a bomb or anything he will do his best, but it is so *very* nice to feel that Delia won't be a widow for the present. If he is sent abroad she will go back to the Hospital unless of course she is going to have a baby which I do hope she will, or Nurse will never forgive me, and then she would come home."

Mr. Birkett, disentangling Mrs. Brandon's various emotions, said a suitable word for each, adding that he saw nothing wrong in being glad that one's daughter was not likely to be a widow at once.

"You know," he said, "that Geraldine is engaged to Geoff Fairweather of the Barsetshires, whose brother married Rose. They are a very undemonstrative couple but they have known each other for years and we are very happy about it. And Rose is to have a baby in August."

Mrs. Brandon was enchanted and they plunged together into an orgy of grandmothering and grandfathering that lasted them till dessert.

The Colonial Bishop had meanwhile been taken over by Mrs. Crawley and cautiously sounded as to his views about the Bishop of Barchester. With great disloyalty to a colleague he said he already saw eye to eye with the Dean, so he and his hostess got on very well.

Delia being now claimed by the Archdeacon, Lydia

found herself at liberty to deal with Mr. Needham, tucked up her wristbands and came into the ring, asking her neighbour how he had been getting on. Mr. Needham said quite well thank you and how charming Miss Brandon, whom he hadn't met before, was.

"Oh, Delia," said Lydia. "She's awfully nice, but I shouldn't have thought you'd have noticed it. I thought it was her mother you were gone on. Most people are."

"Of course I do admire Mrs. Brandon frightfully," said Mr. Needham, casting a sheep's eye across the table to where Mrs. Brandon was enjoying herself with Mr. Birkett. "But there is something so very nice about Miss Brandon. She is so very pretty."

"That's why she's engaged," said Lydia, determined that Mr. Needham should not be distracted from the one suitable object. "She told me before dinner."

"Oh," said Mr. Needham, a little dashed.

"I should have thought you might have noticed her ring," said Lydia severely, "considering which finger it's on. How's Octavia? I mean is Matron being horrible? I didn't have time to ask before dinner."

"I think Matron is being very unfair," said Mr. Needham chivalrously. "She has put the worst abdominal in D Ward and Octavia was just going in for abdominals, because she says she has enough head wounds and wants more general experience. Octavia was marvellous about it. I wish I thought about my work as much as she does. But then she's doing real work and I'm—"

"That's enough, Tommy," said Lydia. "I told you before that you were doing jolly good. I think Octavia looks ripping to-night."

She looked firmly across at Octavia, who was certainly not looking any less uninteresting than usual and finding Mr. Keith curiously unsympathetic to her account of a patient who had had a heart attack.

"She makes me think of some heroine," said Mr.

Needham, "and I feel so ashamed of myself. I know I couldn't be a hero, but—"

"Oh, shut *up*, Tommy," said Lydia, exasperated. "I'd hit you on the back if it weren't a dinner party. What about you being a military chaplain? Then if you got wounded Octavia could nurse you."

Mr. Needham's eyes gleamed.

"And now tell me about the Choir School football team," said Lydia, feeling that she had done enough for Mr. Needham's love affairs.

He needed no encouragement to tell her all she didn't want to know and she was able to listen in a kind of dream, her thoughts in the past, on a cold winter's day, walking on the terrace at Northbridge Manor.

All this time Mr. Miller had been comparing notes with Mrs. Birkett about evacuees and Mrs. Birkett had secretly come to the conclusion, as she always did, that Mr. Miller was that nicest of things, a really good person who was wholly unconscious of being good, and felt that only a devil would have disliked most of the Southbridge evacuees as much as she did, so that it was quite a comfort to her when Mr. Miller confessed that he had harboured un-Christian thoughts against the worst of their boys who had drowned six chickens and kicked the hen and broken her leg.

"What did you do, Mr. Miller?" Mrs. Birkett asked.

"The old Adam rose in me and I beat him," said Mr. Miller. "Not even after reflection, I fear, but in anger."

"Then I am certain that you did him a great deal of good," said Mrs. Birkett firmly, "and probably saved him from the gallows later."

"That is what my dear wife said," said Mr. Miller, casting an adoring look at Mrs. Miller who was in the middle of the Mothers' Union with the Dean, "and indeed, indeed I hope that it may be so, though I fear the gallows are still gaping for that boy. He has been trying to dig to Australia among the lettuces, thus causing considerable loss of good food. But my wife is the greatest comfort in these trials and her influence over the boys is astounding."

By now Noel was well in possession of Miss Pettinger, but much to his annoyance the game of Pettinger-baiting which he had promised himself had lost its savour. It was not that Miss Pettinger had lost hers, for her horribleness was more pronounced than ever, but instead of being amused Noel found her simply boring. Dinner seemed to him quite interminable. After what felt like hours of the Pettinger's voice he suddenly heard the words, "Lydia Keith" and came to attention with a jerk.

"Lydia Keith and Delia Brandon and the dear Dean's Octavia and so many more of our Old Barcastrianas are doing excellent work," Miss Pettinger was saying, "worthy of the very best traditions of Barchester High School. I was very much gratified to have a letter this morning from Miss Wixett, our first head mistress and still among us at Lyme Regis I am glad to say, bidding us all God-speed in our work. I read her letter aloud to My Girls after prayers."

"How like you," said Noel admiringly. "I am sure it is largely due to your influence that Octavia and the others are doing such good work."

This appalling lie was, as Noel fully realised, merely a bait to Miss Pettinger to go on talking about Lydia, though for some reason Noel found it impossible to mention her name at the moment and had to include her among others.

"I do my best to carry on the wonderful traditions of our old school," said Miss Pettinger bridling, "and I think I can say that no girl passes the School Certificate from Barchester High School without being in some way moulded or even changed for the good."

"I am sure Octavia was," said Noel generously.

"Dear Octavia is just the type that we wish to turn

out," said Miss Pettinger, looking with an almost human look at her ex-pupil's dull but self-satisfied face.

"I know I would feel exactly the same about her," said Noel in the pleasant certainty that Miss Pettinger would not understand.

"As for dear Lydia," said Miss Pettinger, "she is a warm-hearted girl, but I could wish she had had the Honour of the School more at heart. She never seemed to realise the importance of attending to every rule in the School's Code of Honour. I remember that in her last summer term I had to give her four Red Marks and one Black Mark for repeatedly hanging her shoe bag on the wrong peg in the Senior Cloakroom. Now her elder sister Kate was quite different; so conscientious. And her sister-in-law, Mrs. Robert Keith, who was Edith Fairweather, was a wonderful influence among the girls, so good at hockey and cricket and keenly interested in *The Barcastriana,* our School Magazine. It is a pity that Lydia has not kept up with us more. She has only come to one Old Girls' Reunion since she left. She does not look to me so fit as I like to see our Old Girls. I wish she would take up nursing, or land work, or some healthy form of war activity, but one cannot well interfere."

"No, indeed," said Noel, who, having gained his wish and heard Miss Pettinger speak of Lydia, would now have liked to strangle her.

But at this moment Mrs. Crawley collected her ladies' eyes and rose.

The conversation of women is on the whole so much more interesting than that of gentlemen that we will leave the Dean and his guests to discuss local and world affairs and waft ourselves up to the drawing-room. Here Mrs. Brandon, true to her promise, seated herself on the little green settee, but did not fluffle out her dress, because she wanted to talk to Mrs. Crawley.

"Come and sit with me," she said to her hostess. "I want to tell you about Delia before it is in *The Times.*

She is going to marry our nice cousin Hilary Grant. I am telling everyone, so really *The Times* will almost be a war extravagance, but one cannot quite get engaged without it."

Mrs. Crawley expressed warm congratulations and was glad to hear that Hilary would not at present be in danger.

"We are *all* in danger," said Mrs. Brandon stoutly, not wishing anyone to think that Delia would be too comfortable. Mrs. Crawley said it was in a way a comfort.

"No, I really can't agree with you," said Mrs. Brandon with one of her devastating attacks of truthfulness. "It would be much nicer if we weren't, only one doesn't quite know where to draw the line. If all the children and everyone under about thirty was safe it would be much more comfortable and it wouldn't matter so much about us, except for all the ones that are being *really* useful like your husband and Sir Edmund and the Birketts and practically everybody one knows. But what is really annoying, because though it may not be dangerous it is very worrying for her friends, or at least the people that know her, is Hilary's mother."

"What has happened to her?" asked Mrs. Crawley.

"Nothing," said Mrs. Brandon, "which is just what I complain of, because she *will* not leave Calabria where she lodges with a very short, stout chemist and his wife who is often a bandit in a small way, at least he is, called Marco Aurelio, and is writing a book about Calabrian folk-lore which she knows far too intimately. And I am so afraid Hilary will feel he ought to go out and bring her home, which she certainly would not do and would be a very great trial to everyone when she got here owing to having no settled home. She spent a few weeks at the Cow and Sickle in the village when she was last in England and owing to her trying to teach Mrs. Spindler to cook macaroni in the Calabrian way with goat's cheese, which of course one luckily cannot get, Mrs. Spindler has hated me ever since, though all I did was to go and call on Mrs. Grant once or twice."

"I think I met her at Lady Norton's," said Mrs. Crawley. "All homespun and sensible shoes."

"And hung with distressed jewellery," said Mrs. Brandon. "And do tell me about all your family."

This Mrs. Crawley was not averse to doing and when duty compelled her to move on to Miss Pettinger, who was being held at bay valiantly by Mrs. Miller who made her promise to lend the School Hall for a summer meeting of G.F.S. branches before she could think of an excuse, Mrs. Brandon fluffled her dress and sat all over the little green settee looking like a delicious double sweet-pea, so that the Archdeacon's daughter, who wanted to tell her about her engagement to Guy Barton, had to bring up a little stool.

"I am very fond of Guy," said the Archdeacon's daughter, clasping her competent, workman's hands round her knees. "He used to be a bit of an ass, but we've always got on well and the R.A.F. will do him all the good in the world. I don't think we'll get married yet, because I've got all the Land Girls to organise for West Barsetshire. Either after the war, or when he is invalided out, if he crashes."

Mrs. Brandon, not quite sure how much of this detachment was real, how much a mask, said she didn't know Mr. Barton, but she had heard how very nice he was.

"A bit too nice if you ask me," said the Archdeacon's daughter dispassionately. "He didn't behave frightfully well to Phoebe Rivers when he was engaged to her, but he won't do that again."

"Wasn't she a cousin of Lord Pomfret's; a good-looking girl, very smart?" said Mrs. Brandon.

"Jolly good-looking," said the Archdeacon's daughter.

"She married Humberton, Lord Platfield's eldest son, down in Shropshire. I was a bridesmaid and Lord Humberton can't stand Phoebe's mother, so that's all right. It was a nasty slap in the eye for Guy and I had to take him in hand."

And now the men came in and Noel advanced upon Mrs. Brandon, who suddenly shrank to half her former size and smiled to him to sit down beside her.

"Need I say how exquisite you are looking?" said Noel.

"Of course you need," said Mrs. Brandon. "It is only women who trouble to tell other women that they look nice, so coming from a man it has great value. But this dress is a rag."

"You are not only the most charming, but the most untruthful woman I know," said Noel, so that they both laughed.

"And now," said Mrs. Brandon, who would undoubtedly have tapped him with her fan if she had had one, "what is it you want to say? And pray be quick, for I see the Dean's eye on me."

"It's difficult to be quick," said Noel, "because you see I've never fallen in love before, and I am a little shamefaced about it."

Mrs. Brandon's enchanting face assumed the expression of a child who sees a very large ice-pudding.

"Do you mean you want to tell me about it?" she said.

"I do, Lavinia," said Noel. "And nobody else."

"Is it Lydia?" said Mrs. Brandon, pretending as she spoke to assure the fastening of one of her diamond earrings, so that her face was half concealed from the room by her arm.

"How did you know?" said Noel, utterly taken aback.

"Because I've seen it coming ever since the Vicarage fête at Pomfret Madrigal two years ago," said Mrs. Brandon placidly. 'And I must say I have been an extremely good warming-pan for your attentions, though to call it chandelier as the French do is much more elegant and I hope you are grateful."

"Devil!" said Noel, looking so affectionately at Mrs. Brandon that Lydia Keith, who happened to be looking that way, couldn't help noticing it and almost wishing she were Mrs. Brandon.

In a less sophisticated age, Mrs. Brandon would automatically have said: "Oh, you naughty man," but though she was quite capable of such an anachronism she merely smiled one of her most bewitching smiles and asked if she could help.

"I don't know," said Noel. "You see I never knew it till all that cold weather we had. And now I can't help reflecting that I am a great deal older than she is and might lose a perfect friend by trying to gain a wife. Do you think she would consider my application?"

"Of all the nincompoops!" said Mrs. Brandon, which made Noel, who although considerably her junior had always felt like her comtemporary, suddenly realise that she looked upon him as a young man, not belonging to the real world of grown-up people.

"You think I could, then?" he said.

"How long are you on leave?" said Mrs. Brandon.

Noel said he had to go back to town by the night train in about an hour.

"Well, you *might* manage it to-night, though it would be difficult," said Mrs. Brandon. "If you can't, you must do it the very next time you get leave."

"Thank you, Lavinia. You are an angel," said Noel.

"And if you don't, you need never come to Stories again," said Mrs. Brandon. "Oh! Dr. Crawley, I *did* so want to talk to you. What do you think the Bishop's wife said at Lady Norton's the other day?"

Noel took this *congé* and the Dean, saying that whatever that woman said would be in keeping with the Palace traditions, sat down beside her to gossip. Noel looked towards Lydia, but she was conversing so earnestly with Mr. Needham in a corner that he suddenly felt old and fell into talk with the Colonial Bishop.

It was not altogether of Lydia's own will that she was talking again to Mr. Needham, but that young gentleman had waylaid her, to explain to her all over again his efforts to be a military chaplain.

"I believe I could get to France now," said Mr. Needham, "because two or three of the people who deal with that are old Internationals but I can't decide if it is my duty or if I am only being selfish. After all I am a priest."

"A clergyman, you mean," said Lydia severely. "Priest sounds like a monk. Look here, Tommy, have you read the Thirty-Nine Articles?"

"Do you mean the Thirty-Nine Steps?" said Mr. Needham, who could not believe his ears.

A year or two earlier Lydia would have said: "Of course not, you great fool," but that arrogant Lydia was far away, and Miss Lydia Keith said to Mr. Needham that she meant Articles and supposed he was a Christian.

Thus challenged, Mr. Needham said rather huffily that he saw no point in such a question.

"I'm only trying to help you," said Lydia patiently. "I've been reading it myself and I must say I think it's a frightfully good bit of work; I mean, there's room for everyone in it. And it says that it is lawful for Christian men to wear weapons and serve in the wars, so there you are. And if you want a Magistrate to command you, I know Sir Edmund would, or Mr. Keith. They're both J.P.'s."

At this jumbled and earnest piece of special pleading, the scales fell from Mr. Needham's eyes and to his intense joy and relief he suddenly saw the paths of duty and desire for once coinciding. With real gratitude and humility he thanked Lydia.

"That's all right, Tommy," said Lydia, "only don't ask anyone's advice again. You just go ahead."

"Do you think I ought to tell Octavia?" said Mr. Needham.

"Of course," said Lydia. "And I'd tell her at once if I were you."

"If I had anything to offer," said Mr. Needham, "do you think she would wait for me till I came back? Or perhaps it wouldn't be fair to ask her."

"Don't be an ass," said Lydia, with a flash of her old impatience. "Take her for a walk when she comes off duty to-morrow and tell her everything."

Then Sir Edmund, who was very fond of Lydia, came limping upon her and she exerted herself to be the kind of girl Sir Edmund liked and gave him an amusing evening. The party broke up early and by half-past ten the guests had said good-bye to Mrs. Crawley and assembled in the hall for their last glimpse of light before plunging into the black-out. Lydia, waiting for her father to get his coat and hat on, found Mr. Needham at her elbow.

"I asked Octavia if she would have a walk with me tomorrow," he said in a voice of subdued excitement, "and she was going to an extra lecture on peritonitis, but she is going to cut it for me. You are an *angel*, Lydia," he said vehemently.

"Write to me at once, won't you?" said Lydia. "I can't tell you how happy I am."

And she slipped her arm through Mr. Needham's and gave it a friendly and encouraging squeeze.

"Sorry, Noel," she said, as she bumped her elbow against Mr. Merton, who had been jammed between Sir Edmund and the Archdeacon and so had very unwillingly heard Mr. Needham call Lydia an angel and

Lydia beg Mr. Needham to write, besides seeing her take that young gentleman's arm. He was used to his Lydia's ebullient ways but he found himself hating Mr. Needham in a most unseemly way for being so much younger than himself.

"Good-bye, Noel," said Mrs. Brandon, all furred and cloaked (for these phrases come naturally to one's mind when speaking of her). "Don't forget."

"You may command me in anything," said Noel. "Bless you," and he lifted her hand to his lips for she was one of the few women he knew who could take such homage with grace.

Owing to the squash Lydia could not disentangle her arm from Mr. Needham's in time not to see what she saw, hear what she heard.

"Good-bye, Lydia," said Noel. "Shall I see you when I get my next leave?"

"Of course," said Lydia, wondering, as they shook hands.

Their eyes met, asking questions that this was no time, no place to answer. Lydia drove home with her father and Noel caught the night train to London, each thinking, just like people in novels, that the other's heart was not so warm, not so near, each determined to die sooner than infringe by a hair's breadth the freedom of the other.

15

STORY WITHOUT AN END

•

The loveliest spring that England could remember had emerged from the long hard winter and went flashing by in luxuriant riot into early summer, at cinema speed. And with the quick and profuse blossoming of almond, wild cherry, hawthorn red white and pink, buttercups, lilac, laburnum; with the onward rush of the trees from a mist of tender green to a heavy and sullen leafage, the rush of events came thundering down from the Arctic Circle across the Low Countries, marshalled by the Powers of Darkness.

The Earl of Pomfret died quietly in the small hours of the morning, early in May. I do not think he had any fears or regrets. His heir, whom he had at first mistrusted and gradually come to value, would carry on, under changed conditions, work for which he knew he would soon have been unfit, and had already two sons. His heir's wife he liked and respected, for she had the best hands in the county and good common sense. They were both by his bed when his eyes failed to see the sunlight flooding his room. He held a hand of each and spoke the name of his dead wife and the son who had been killed a lifetime ago in a frontier skirmish. The eighth Earl of Pomfret looked down on the seventh Earl and took up his burden.

Old Lord Pomfret was buried quietly in the parish church-yard. There was a Memorial Service at St. Margaret's, Westminster, for the outer world. Then there was a Memorial Service in Barchester Cathedral, attended by the whole county, high and low; the last time that many of those in the great congregation were to see each other.

Lydia Keith and her father were among those present. Lydia had half hoped that she might see Noel Merton in the Deanery pew, but when he was not there, she knew that her thoughts had been self-delusion. She went home by train alone, for her father was to stay on in Barchester for a committee and dine with his son Robert to discuss some business of the firm. Mrs. Keith had not been so well and depended more and more on Lydia, who handled her mother with firm and unaltering kindness. Lydia and her father knew that Mrs. Keith's heart was less satisfactory each month, and they both felt a chill shadow of private grief among the shadow of general sadness and apprehension, and both bore the shadow with courage and worked all the harder.

But the shadow was not to touch Mr. Keith. When he left Robert's home that evening he walked down to the Country Club where he had left his car in the morning. In the uncertain light he stepped into the road in front of a stationary car, was hit by a lorry and taken unconscious to the Barchester Hospital. He had only done what thousands of people do every day, and paid the penalty. The lorry driver was in no way to blame, rather to be pitied for the sense of guilt that Mr. Keith's carelessness must have caused him. Lydia was fetched by her brother Robert early next morning. As Mrs. Keith was used to her husband and daughter being out and about before she came down, she felt no alarm. Mr. Keith lingered, always unconscious, for two days and then died without recognising Robert or Lydia.

It had been necessary to tell Mrs. Keith that her husband was injured and this Robert and Lydia had managed with such kindness that she was not made ill, as they had feared. When she had to be told that her husband was dead she was more stunned than unhappy. Luckily Nurse Chiffinch, an excellent nurse who had been with old Lord Pomfret and was known to Mrs. Morland, could be secured, and was installed to look after Mrs. Keith for the present.

Lydia, who had prepared herself for her mother's possible death, was shaken to the core by this turn of fate, but held valiantly to her post. Robert's wife offered to come and stay with her, as did her own sister Kate, but with many thanks Lydia said she could manage it better alone. Robert took over all business matters for her. Northbridge Manor was left to him. As he and his wife had no wish to live there at present it was agreed that part of the house should be shut up and Mrs. Keith go on living there for the present under Nurse Chiffinch's care, while Lydia would do her capable best with the estate and all Mr. Keith's local activities.

To Lydia's intense joy her brother Colin was able to get twenty-four hours' leave on the day when Mr. Keith was buried. He was well and fit and absorbed in his soldier's life and for a moment Lydia's burden was lifted. Of his future movements he gave Lydia no information, for he had none. Lydia asked if he had heard of Noel, but he had dropped out of touch with many old friends, Noel among them. There could be no Grand Opening of the boating season this year, so they took the punt up to Parsley Island and laughed at remembering the picnic there when Rose Birkett had taken Noel's and Everard's coats to shelter her pink dress from the thunderstorm and Philip had been so unpleasant and Communist about flowers in churches.

Colin had to go back the same evening. Lydia sat with her mother till Nurse Chiffinch announced that her patient ought to be thinking of Bedfordshire now, which she did with a brightness that only Mrs. Keith's apathy and Lydia's restrained grief kept them from resenting, though she was so good and kind and conscientious that they were really grateful to her. Lydia sat up till late answering letters of condolence for her mother and went to bed so tired that being young she was able to go to sleep at once.

Next day, in the full loveliness of spring, the world was told of the betrayal of a little army, sent in answer to a stricken country's cry for help. Every heart was stunned by the thought of what might come, every heart was steeled to bear the very worst, and darkness covered the sun. England held her breath and was silent, waiting, while the author of the betrayal slipped into black oblivion, beyond human blame, beyond human compassion.

Lydia, wisely considering activity the best remedy for most ills, after seeing her mother and Nurse Chiffinch had a few words with Palmer about the silver. It had been arranged that most of it was to go to the bank for the present, a step which Palmer chose to take as a direct personal insult. Lydia accepted Palmer's notice with complete equanimity and even relief, and after putting on an overall began to turn out things in the drawing-room, for it had been decided to shut it up and use the small study or library. For a couple of hours she rolled up rugs, took the washing covers off chairs and sofas, dust-sheeted much of the furniture, wrapped china in tissue paper and put it in a hamper to be stored in the garage. Then she turned her attention to the books. Some she proposed to put in the study, the rest she began to pack in empty cases supplied by the gardener. As always happens when one begins to finger books she opened first one and then another, read snatches, rebuked herself and went on with her work. And all the time sunshine was flooding the room and the scent of wistaria came piercingly on the light breeze through the open french window.

Presently she found an old volume of Grimm's *Household Tales* which had belonged to Mrs. Keith's childhood and had been read aloud to all the young Keiths in turn. Turning its rather battered pages, many of them loose with age and hard use, she fell completely into its charm and was reading earnestly, perched on the uncomfortable edge of a packing case, when a shadow fell on the book. She looked up and saw Noel Merton who had come in by the french window. Lydia laid down her book, got up, and went straight to Noel's arms. Noel, hardly able to believe that his proud Lydia could lay her head so on his shoulder in peace, held her very lightly and said nothing. Then, sensitive to a faint withdrawal on her part, he let her go.

"Lydia; I didn't know," he said, speaking as if nothing had happened between them. "I hadn't seen a paper for days, or only the cheap rags, and I never knew about your father. I ran into Roddy Wicklow in town last night and he told me."

"It was pretty bad for Mother," said Lydia. "But Robert and Edith and Everard and Kate have been angels and we have a splendid nurse. And Colin did get down for the funeral and we went on the river. I am *pleased* to see you, Noel."

Noel asked a few questions about the future of Northbridge Manor and satisfied himself that Lydia and her mother were being well looked after. Then he did not quite know what to say. His Lydia looked well though her eyes were shadowed, but he missed her uncaring arrogance and wondered with a pang if he had bad news for her. But it had better be told.

"I came down to the Deanery to-day," he said, not adding that he had come solely to see Lydia and give any help he could, "and found Crawley and Mrs. Crawley transported with joy, though a duller thing to be joyful about have I never seen. Had you heard about Octavia?"

"She isn't engaged to Tommy, is she?" said Lydia, suddenly alive with pleasure and interest.

Noel nodded, with such a revulsion of relief that he could not speak.

"I don't want to boast," said Lydia, "but I practically did it. I gave Tommy a most *awful* talking to that night at the Deanery and he promised he'd take Octavia for a walk next day when she came off duty. Good old Tommy. When are they to be married?"

"That part is even duller, if possible," said Noel. "Needham has just heard that he can go abroad, and he and Octavia have decided that it is their duty not to get married, though for no reason at all as far as I can see except that it makes them both feel heroic and Daisy-Chain-ish. I think the Crawleys would have liked to see Octavia married; in fact I know they would because Mrs. Crawley told me so, but of course they can't thrust their child into matrimony if she and her bridegroom don't want it. However, Octavia proposes to go abroad with the Red Cross and her eyes are glistening at the thought of meeting Needham in a hospital one mass of head wounds and abdominals."

And at this they both laughed in a very un-serious way till Lydia suddenly stopped.

"Gosh!" she said. "If I loved anyone I'd marry them at once."

Then to Noel's intense surprise her face went bright pink and she looked at him as if imploring forgiveness.

"You couldn't think of me in that light, I suppose," said Noel. "Because if you did I would be more than willing. Much more."

For the first time since he had known his Lydia her gaze dropped before his.

"I thought perhaps I wasn't grown-up enough for you," she said in a small, desolate voice. "I mean Mrs. Brandon and people are the sort I thought you really liked."

"Listen to me, my girl," said Noel; "and let me tell you that I thought perhaps I was too old for you. I am ashamed to say that I thought you might like Needham."

"Tommy?" said Lydia, lifting her eyes in wonder at Noel's stupidity.

And upon that she gave such a very credible imitation of a small fit of hysterics that Noel had to hold her until her voice and body were steady again; which did not take long, for she had herself well in hand.

"I've always thought you were the nicest girl I knew," said Noel. "And when you said in that voice that you would marry anyone you loved at once, I couldn't bear it any longer."

"Of course I will," said Lydia. "I'll have to go on living here and looking after Mother and the place of course, but then you'll probably be busy and you can always come here when you get leave. We couldn't get married to-day, could we?"

"I'm afraid not," said Noel. "But I think we could manage it to-morrow if you like. And as for leave, I think I'll be sent abroad at any moment."

"That's all right," said the old Lydia. "I mean, I expect you'll be much happier abroad. We'd better tell Robert and Kate. Oh, and Colin."

Without wasting any more time over sentiment Lydia rang up her sister Kate who was enchanted, and very untruthfully said she had always known it. Kate said she would get Robert and his wife to dinner and Lydia must bring Noel. A telegram was sent to Colin who answered with the longest and most expensive Golden Telegram ever sent of love, approval and regrets that he couldn't get away. Kate had undertaken to tell the Birketts and a few old friends. Then Palmer grudgingly came in to ask if Mr. Merton was staying for lunch.

"It's Captain Merton," said Lydia. "Yes, he is. And we are going to be married to-morrow, so you'd better tell Cook and everyone. Come on, Noel."

Mrs. Keith was staying in bed till the afternoon, so

they only had Nurse Chiffinch for lunch. That excellent creature was delighted by the news and eagerly entered into the discussion as to when they should tell Mrs. Keith. It was finally decided that Lydia, who as she pointed out was twenty-one, should say nothing to her Mother till the marriage had taken place. Noel wondered if it was rather deceitful, but Nurse Chiffinch said so firmly that her patient would only worry if she heard of the engagement that she got her way.

Noel then had to go back to Barchester.

"I'll come and fetch you this evening," he said from the inside of the car, "and take you to Kate's. I do like your Chiffinch."

"She's an awfully good sort," said Lydia, "and an angel with Mother, even if she is a bit nurse-ish. I know she will count on her fingers from the moment we are married and take offence if I don't engage her almost at once."

"I hadn't really considered that question yet," said Noel, wondering if he were blushing, and thankful for the years of comradeship with Lydia that made her unabashed frankness so easy a thing.

"Babies, you mean," said Lydia, with all her old severity. "Well, I really hadn't much either," she added frankly. "I should think I'm more a wife than a mother, but you never know. Anyway, we'll not bother and see what happens."

Noel found nothing to say. He pressed Lydia's capable hand that lay on the door of the car and was answered by such a look of mute adoration as seriously disturbed his driving.

At the Carter's house the millennium appeared to have set in, in spite of every discouragement. Noel, who had spent the afternoon over various matters of business, some at his father's office (a solicitor as it may be remembered in Barchester), some with other authorities, was able to report that he and Lydia would be married to-morrow and the Dean insisted on performing the ceremony himself and Mr. Needham was to be allowed to help. With Robert he had a short talk which showed Robert that his young sister's material interests would be well cared for.

Kate, who was joyfully in her element of kind fussing, then said that she knew the sight of Bobbie would do Mrs. Keith more good than anything and that she proposed to bring him and his nurse over to Northbridge on the following day and stay there as long as Noel could get leave, so that he and Lydia would be free to go where they liked.

Mrs. Brandon then rang up to say that she had to go to London for a few days to get some clothes for Delia and would be deeply offended if Noel and Lydia didn't use Stories for their honeymoon.

"You are an angel," Lavinia," said Noel, who had taken over the call.

"Of course I am," said Mrs. Brandon. "That is all an old woman like myself is fit for."

"I refuse to make any comment on that remark," said Noel.

"Nincompoop. Bless you a thousand times," said Mrs. Brandon and rang off.

Then Mr. and Mrs. Birkett came over full of congratulations. Mr. Birkett was preoccupied with the School measles which were wavering between German and plain, but extremely cordial. Mrs. Birkett not unnaturally felt that the engagement was a peg on which to hang conversation about Geraldine, who was to be married at the end of May all being well and had been allowed to assist at a blood transfusion; but she was warm in her congratulations.

"Is there any news of Philip?" said Noel.

"None, since he went abroad," said Everard.

But for the moment the shadow of the little army fighting its way stubbornly back from treachery to the friendly sea was not allowed to intrude.

When Noel and Lydia left, Everard caught Noel for a moment.

"Have you any idea of what your movements are likely to be?" he asked. "I'm not being Fifth Columnist, but we'd like to know what Lydia can count on."

"It is three days' leave," said Noel.

"That means," said Everard, "that you have to go back the day after to-morrow. We'll take care of Lydia."

Noel left Lydia at the door of Northbridge Manor.

"Noel," she said out of the darkness, "I suppose you will have to go abroad fairly soon."

"The day after to-morrow," said Noel.

"That's all right," said Lydia, and vanished into the house.

Kate was as good as her word and not only brought Bobbie over, but managed so to insinuate into her mother's mind the horrible idea of Lydia's being an old maid that Mrs. Keith said she had always been afraid when Lydia did so badly in her exams that she would never get married, and what a pity it was that Noel Merton, who was so very nice, wasn't a little younger as he might have taken an interest in Lydia. With this to work on Kate managed to break the news that Lydia and Noel, properly married by the Dean, would be back to lunch, and by this time Mrs. Keith was so sure that she had foreseen and arranged the whole thing herself that her greatest anxiety was having mislaid a very hideous set of garnets belonging to her grandmother that she wanted Lydia to have. By dint of Kate and Nurse Chiffinch's united efforts in looking in all the places where Mrs. Keith was sure the garnets were, they were at last discovered in the one place where she knew that they weren't, and she was able to welcome the married couple and was reported by Nurse Chiffinch to be standing it splendidly.

"I must say," said Lydia, as she and Noel, after an astoundingly good dinner, sat under the Spanish chestnut in the garden at Stories, "that being married feels much the same."

"Only nicer," said Noel. "You are much the nicest girl I ever met in my life, Lydia. In fact, perfect."

"It is all so nice and comfortable," said Lydia, "because I know you so well. I mean it must be rather a bore to marry someone you don't know. They mightn't be as nice as you think. Where shall we live, do you think, when you come back? I mean when you really come back for ever."

"We'll have to consider it," said Noel.

"Will you ring up or send me a telegram as soon as you get back to England?" said Lydia. "I should be so glad to know."

Noel said he would.

"Of course it might be a telegram to say you were dead," said Lydia, facing facts with her usual firmness. "But I'd go on loving you just the same."

On the next day Noel went. Lydia came back to Northbridge Manor and took up her old way of life. Kind Kate stayed on for a time and kept Mrs. Keith from asking Lydia more than once a day if there was any news from Noel. Full spring merged into early summer with incredible riot of blossom and leaf, while the sea before Dunkirk was covered with a thousand ships. Philip Winter returned to the Carter's house, looking aged by many years, and spent most of his time sleeping. On a hot afternoon he bicycled over to Northbridge Manor to see Kate and Lydia.

Kate was sitting on the terrace by her mother who was better that day. Bobbie was on the grass, being headed off from the flower beds by his Nurse. Lydia, in a garden apron, was weeding at the other end of the terrace, for the warm days and a reduced garden staff had made weeds spring up everywhere and it was not easy to pull them up from the sun-hardened earth. Philip sat and talked with Mrs. Keith and Kate for a little and admired Bobbie's peculiar manner of speech, unintelligible to all, but considered a masterpiece of elocution by those best qualified to judge.

"Everard sent you his love, Kate," said Philip, "and he has some good news. Mr. Bissell told him that Mr. Hopkins has been rounded up as a Fifth Columnist and interned."

Kate, who simply had to be kind to someone, said it would be very horrid for the people Mr. Hopkins was interned with, which is perhaps the most unkind thing we have ever known her say.

Presently Palmer, who had withdrawn her notice after the gentle Kate had spoken words of fire to her, and been allowed to stay on, came out into the garden, carrying a salver.

"It's a telegram for Miss Lydia, madam," she said.

Kate and Philip exchanged glances.

"Please remember to say Mrs. Merton, Palmer," said Kate in her best housemaster's wife's voice.

Palmer meekly said she was sorry she was sure.

"I'll take it to her," said Philip as carelessly as he could, while Kate headed her mother's thoughts towards the enormity of Palmer calling Lydia "Miss Lydia."

Philip walked along the terrace to where Lydia was weeding.

"It's a wire for you, Lydia," he said.

Lydia looked up and her face was white, but she got to her feet and took off her gardening gloves.

"Shall I open it?" said Philip, his heart beating furiously with his anxiety.

"No, thank you," said Lydia. "I think I ought to open my own telegrams. And whatever it was I'd love Noel just the same."